The Birth

Mall Rats

HARRY DUFFIN

CUMULUS PUBLISHING LIMITED

CW00687863

Published in 2012 by Cumulus Publishing Limited

Copyright © 2012 Cloud 9 (The Tribe) Ltd

First published November 2012.

ISBN: 978-0-473-23149-1

Visit The Tribe's website at **www.tribeworld.com**

Contact addresses for companies within the Cloud 9 Screen Entertainment group can be found at www.entercloud9.com

Dedicated to the fabulous young cast of The Tribe,
the brilliant writers of the series,
and to Raymond Thompson for his wonderful, original
concept and inspiring support,
with many thanks and great admiration.

PROLOGUE

Where the virus came from no-one knew. From dark deepest space, germ warfare, or some nation's scientific experiment gone horribly wrong? Only an intensive enquiry could answer that. But there was no-one left to hold such an enquiry. No adults anyway.

And the children left behind were too busy surviving to worry about what had plunged them from a sophisticated hi-tech world into a primitive hell of anarchy, confusion, danger and fear.

With no adults to guide, rule or protect them, the children of the world were on their own. Their task: to build a New World in their own image...Whatever that image may be...

HARRY DUFFIN

ONE

Bray gazed down at the devastated city lying ten stories beneath his feet. He ran his fingers through his long brown hair, distractedly, hardly able to believe his eyes. How could a thing so small, invisible to the naked eye, have destroyed a world many trillion times its own size? He didn't have the answer to that, the riddle of the virus, but the facts lay all around him, unavoidable, unbelievable.

Vivid flames licking from the shells of a dozen blazing buildings sent acrid, blue-black smoke pouring unchecked into the cloudless sky, blotting out the morning sun. The remnants of the once proud city – gutted tower blocks, burnt out vehicles, paper, plastic, glass and concrete debris, abandoned looted goods, and the occasional rotting, rat-eaten, fly-infested corpse, were scattered in the streets and alleyways below. The whole city resembled a scene from an apocalyptic virtual wargame, or a vast art installation created by a crazed, psychopathic genius. Maybe it had been? Maybe someone was responsible for this chaos? But that question was for the future. If there was one. The crucial question now was how to survive?

He was a tall, leanly muscular youth who wore his mix of plainsman and eco-warrior clothes with ease. A green feather hanging from the long plait of hair to one side of his face echoed the Native American Indian whose traditions and lifestyle he deeply respected. A tradition so alien to the mayhem stretching away as far as he could see. The handsome face reflected deep despair as his eyes roamed the wasteland that had once been his city. The place where he was born, raised and happily went to school and where, if he was careless, he could soon die a brutal, early death. He shook his head to banish that morbid thought. He couldn't let that happen. He had to survive. He'd promised her.

As he watched a lone ragged figure sprinted across the littered avenue far below him, weaving through the debris, looking over his shoulder in blind terror. Then he heard it, the piercing 'whoop-whoop-whoop' of a police car siren approaching. Despite himself he smiled at the irony. There was no law and order here. Not anymore. It was time to go. Foolish or not, he'd made her a promise.

TWO

Amber skated nimbly around the blackened carcass of a school bus which lay on its side at the top of the alley. It was essential to keep to the warren of alleyways to avoid being spotted. There was no telling what murderous eyes were roaming the city looking for easy prey. Her diminutive companion, Dal, scurried after her, a little out of breath.

'Not so fast, Amber,' he called to his pretty companion who, though they were the same age, was at least a head taller. 'My legs aren't as long as yours.'

'We have to get clear of the city before nightfall, Dal. It's too dangerous to hang around.'

They had been traveling for over an hour from their homes in the once-cosy suburbs to the East. They were heading towards the lush countryside to the West of the stricken city but, despite their roller blades, progress was slow. Every corner held potential danger; the spectre of a lone maniacal killer, or a violent gang of feral youths looking for 'fun'.

In the distance came the wail of a police siren, a familiar sound that once gave reassurance, but now bred instant dread.

Dal glanced at Amber. 'What are the Locos doing in this sector?'

Amber shrugged. 'Sunday afternoon drive?' Despite the irony her expression beneath the war-paint was grim. Like many of the kids left in the city, she had taken to wearing the paint as a form of protection. It was a sign that was meant to say 'Danger, keep away.' But if anything the black shadowed eyes, the flame red cheeks, and diagonal slash of green across the

5

forehead, emphasized the young girl's beauty and vulnerability. Still it gave her reassurance. And in this world you grasped at any straw you could find.

'Is it Sunday?'

'Who knows?'

Dal looked at his friend. From the day he set eyes on her, Amber had always been beautiful to him. First as a fresh-faced, high-spirited school girl, and now with her painted face, knee-length black leather coat, roller blades and her long dark hair tied in tight blonde knots around her head, she was his Amazonian street-fighter. He worshipped her, but knew she was far beyond his reach; her little Asian friend who she had protected from his first days at school.

Listening to the approaching siren he dreaded to think of Amber falling into the hands of the Locos and their terrifying leader, Zoot. There were rumours, stories that woke him in the dead of night in a cold sweat. True or not, he didn't want to hang around to find out.

'Let's go, Amber!'

But she wasn't listening. Her eyes were staring from the alley into the avenue beyond. Standing in the middle of the deserted, debris-strewn road, transfixed by the now almost deafening 'whoop-whoop' of the siren, was a small girl, clutching a teddy-bear to her chest.

'They're going to get her!' Amber gasped.

Before he could stop her, Amber shot from the alley in the wide open space of the avenue.

'Amber!'

Dal's scream was lost in the wailing siren as the police car with its fearsome occupants swooped around the corner.

THREE

The four teenagers waited nervously in a burnt out railway wagon on the fringe of the vast deserted rail yard. The leader, Lex, a hard-faced, leather-jacketed youth, with long black hair and war paint like a Sioux warrior, hung from the edge of the carriage scanning the yard impatiently.

'Where is he?' asked Zandra anxiously. She was a pretty girl, looking conspicuously out of place in this bleak environment, dressed in a riot of coloured furs and feathers, her bright blue and red hair held in place by flowered hairgrips. 'Maybe you got it wrong? Are you sure this is the meeting place?'

'Quiet! I'm thinking.' Lex snapped.

'Yes, Zandra, let the man think,' Glen sneered. 'If he can't think he can't come up with all those brilliant plans!'

Glen was cursing himself for letting Lex talk them into this crazy meeting. They had been doing alright on their own, scavenging the lawless city. He, Lex and Ryan were a formidable fighting force. Urban warfare guerillas. They had been successfully intimidating the city's waifs and strays for food and evading the bigger gangs, since the adult world collapsed. Joining one of the dominant tribes was a gamble. The tribes were all volatile, given to outbursts of unprovoked violence against strangers, or even their own kind. He should have stood up to Lex. But that would have meant taking him on, and Lex was a mean street-fighter. Lex was mean, period. He didn't like or trust him.

'I don't like it here,' whined Zandra. 'Out in the open. Anything could happen.'

'Shut up, the both of you! Zoot'll keep his word.' Lex insisted.

'Where is he then, the legendary leader of the Locos?' Glen taunted.

'You heard the siren!'

'Siren?' scoffed Glen. 'That could have been anyone! The Demon Dogs, the Roosters. Any of the gangs. This sector's a war zone!

'The whole city's a war zone, in case you hadn't noticed!' Lex growled. Despite his show of confidence a worm of concern was gnawing inside. Had his message got to Zoot? Was this a set-up? The Locos were the most feared of the city tribes, violent and unpredictable. They were the top dogs and Lex wanted to be there. At the top where he belonged. There was no future in their little group going it alone any longer. Sooner or later their luck would run out. But was Glen right? Had he led his little band of followers into a trap?

FOUR

Her blades screaming over the tarmac, Amber snatched the little girl into her arms and swept them both behind a smoking garbage skip as the Loco's swooped around the corner.

From the alley Dal stared wide-eyed, his heart thumping in his ears. He'd heard of the Locos, of course. Who hadn't? But nothing had prepared him for the eerie vision gliding down the street towards his hiding place, its piercing siren shattering the silence of the ruined city.

It was a blue and white police car, a riot vehicle, its bank of blue lights flashing above the metal-grilled opaque windshield. 'Locos' in blood-red spray paint obliterated 'Police'. Clinging to the rear roll-bars and blading alongside, like a pack of jackals savaging a wounded animal, were bizarrely clad creatures from a space-war fantasy; helmets, grills, welders' masks, medieval body-armoured, bristling with weapons. Above them protruding defiantly from the sunroof, like gargoyles at the gates of hell, were Zoot and his feared lieutenant, Ebony.

Amber felt the little girl beside her preparing to scream. She clamped her hand roughly over the girl's mouth and held her own breath as the cavalcade roared by.

When the monstrous procession had turned the corner Amber took her hand away. 'Sorry,' she said gently. 'Did I hurt you?'

The little girl shook her head shyly, then started back as Dal shot across the road to them.

'It's alright, he's a friend,' Amber reassured her.

Dal was breathless. 'Amber! Did you see that? Did you see them?'

'Hard to miss, Dal.'

'Crazy!'

'Pretty normal these days. Have to say I was a bit disappointed.'

He stared at her wide-eyed. 'You're kidding me?'

Amber smiled, a grim smile. 'Yes, Dal, they were scary. Very scary.'

FIVE

The steel-grey van with smoked black windows crested the hill of the exclusive estate, its loudspeaker blaring the message being repeated all over the city. 'Code One, civil priority. Isolation now in effect. To avoid the risk of contamination stay indoors and await further instructions.'

As the van rolled by with its grim message, Trudy stood in the lounge with her anxious parents, watching the grave television announcer take up the theme. 'Authorities are appealing for calm throughout the evacuation process. All children under the age of eighteen should report to their local sector for transportation.'

Trudy grasped her mother's hand. 'I don't want to go! I don't want to leave you!'

'It's too late for us, Trudy,' her father said sadly. 'You have to accept that.'

'No!'

'You have to save yourself. For your mother's sake.' He cradled his daughter's head in his arms, his voice breaking. 'And mine.'

'No! No! she screamed.

Before Trudy's frightened eyes her parent's faces began to dissolve, transforming their features into hideous, ghostly images that swirled around like her echoing screams.

She sat bolt upright with a start, her body cold with fear. She was lying fully-clothed in the make-shift bed. They had both decided it was safer to sleep in the lounge so they wouldn't be trapped upstairs if the roaming gangs arrived and would stand more chance of escaping. She turned fearfully as the front door opened and a figure entered.

'Oh, Bray!'

Bray threw down his rucksack and went to her. 'What is it?'

'I had the dream again,' she sobbed. 'The nightmare. They were here. Mom, Dad, in the house. Like it was yesterday. I didn't want to go. I didn't want to leave them. But there was nothing I could do.'

Bray put his hand to her chin tenderly and turned her face towards him. 'Trudy, there was nothing anybody could do.'

She leant her head against his shoulder, burying her face in the warmth of his jerkin. 'Bray, I'm so frightened.'

He put a reassuring arm around her. 'Trudy, we have to go.'

She looked up sharply. 'What?'

'The gangs are getting closer. I saw the Roosters. They could be here any time. We're not safe here.'

She looked at him through tearful eyes. 'We're not safe anywhere.'

SIX

The little girl was trembling, still clutching her teddy bear tightly to her chest. The siren faded into the distance, leaving the avenue eerily silent once more. Amber crouched down beside the girl. 'It's alright,' she said soothingly. 'We're not going to hurt you. What's your name?'

The girl looked at her warily.

'I'm Amber and this is Dal. We're friends. Do you have anyone?' Amber coaxed. 'Family? Brothers and sisters?'

The girl's suspicious eyes stared back. She clutched her teddy more tightly. Mute.

'She doesn't understand,' Dal said, a little impatiently. 'Let's just go.'

'Dal! She needs help!'

'We all need help! That's the way things are.'

Amber stared at her friend, torn. The world had been turned upside for them all. What seemed the right thing to do only a short while ago was now uncertain. The rules had changed. They had been making good progress across the city. This was a complication they didn't need.

'I'm sorry, Amber, but we agreed we were going to leave the city before nightfall. You said it. How are we going to do that with this thing tagging along?'

She knew Dal was right. On their blades they had a chance of outrunning any danger they met and reaching the relative safety of the surrounding countryside. And surely it would be easier to survive out there, where the gangs didn't bother to go? She sighed heavily, and looked at Dal with sad eyes. Turning back to the little girl, who was still staring uncertainly at her, Amber smiled and stroked the teddy bear's head, 'I bet I know his name. 'Teddy', right?'

The girl nodded and half smiled.

Amber grinned. 'What about you?

'Cloe.'

'What are you doing out here, Cloe?'

'Playing.'

'Can we play?'

The girl was gaining confidence. 'If you like. Patsy and Paul are hogging the swings, but you can play on the slide if you like.'

Dal looked at Amber grimly. The little waif had clearly lost it. That wasn't surprising. Who knows what horrors she'd seen since she'd lost the protection of the adult world? It was tragic, but...He saw the expression on Amber's face and his heart sank.

'I'm sorry, Dal. You'll have to go without me.

Dal grimaced.

'I'm sorry. I can't leave her, Dal.'

It was Dal's turn to heave a deep sigh. He shrugged. 'That's okay. We've come this far together.'

SEVEN

The siren was getting closer. In the burnt shell of the rail carriage the tension in the little group was tangible.

'They're coming,' said Glen. His voice sounded hoarse.

Lex grinned. 'What's the matter, Glen? Not getting scared, are you?'

'I wanna know what you agreed with Zoot?'

'What do you mean?' Zandra's voice was high and sounded more frightened now. Since they'd got together she had been torn between the two youths. Lex was all alpha-man, tough, aggressive, assertive. He was moody and dangerous, and something in her responded to that despite herself. Glen had the same lean, tough build as his rival, but there was a gentler, more humourous, side to him that was appealing. For the moment she was playing both off against each other. But she knew that sometime she would have to make her choice. And then all hell would break loose. That's if the Locos didn't finish them off first. She was shaking inside.

Glen turned to her. 'Don't be thick, Zandra! Do you really think we're gonna be able to join the Locos just like that? I'll tell you what's gonna happen. Old Lex here, he'll be okay, you can bet on that. But the rest of us might not be so lucky!'

Lex snarled. 'Anyone who doesn't like it can get out. Now!'

'And how far would I get before you ratted on me to the Locos, you cheating scum!'

Lex leapt at Glen and the two youths grappled ferociously inside the carriage. Zandra turned frantically to the big youth who was sitting alone, head buried deep inside his hood. 'Ryan, stop them!'

Ryan glanced up, but didn't move. It was all too confusing. He didn't know who or what to believe. Better to just do nothing.

The siren was deafening now. Lex turned his head. 'They're here!' He shoved Glen aside and strode to the end of the carriage as the police car and its bizarre entourage entered the rail yard.

Zandra stared horrified. Since the virus she had tried very hard to blot out the many weird and scary sights they had come across as they roamed the city. If you pretended not to notice, she told herself, they couldn't hurt you. But there was no avoiding the ghastly spectacle of Zoot and the Locos. The shaking inside now wracked the whole of her body. What had Lex let them in for?

EIGHT

Cloe led the way along the garbage strewn alleys of Sector Ten, with Amber and Dal following behind. Dal was still trying to convince his friend. 'Look, all I want to do is find a little place of my own that I can call 'home'. A little piece of land where I can grew my own food, not scratching for leftovers like an animal.'

'It's a nice dream.'

'It's more than a dream. Look around you, Amber.' He gesticulated to the looted, graffitied buildings surrounding them. 'There's no future here. The tribes have got the city. Let them live on tinned food!'

Amber stopped and turned to him. 'And what happens when the tinned food runs out? You think they're gonna leave you alone in your country estate..? I dunno, Dal. I know we agreed but, now, somehow it just feels like running away. I know we can't stop the tribes taking over. I just hate to see them getting away with it.'

Dal pulled a disappointed face. The two friends had debated long and hard before they set off on the perilous trek across the city. As the feral tribes closed in on their once quiet, genteel suburb they knew they had to make a decision. The rocky mountains to the East afforded plenty of hiding places, but they would soon starve among the barren rocky landscape. The countryside West of the city was their only hope, Dal insisted. They would be able to find food there, growing wild, until they were able to reach a safe haven to grow their own. Now Amber seemed to be changing her mind.

'This is where I grew up, Dal. It's my city. You might be able to walk away, but now I've seen it...all this,' she gestured at the desolate scene, 'I can't just walk away. It's not that simple...' She stopped, looking around. 'Wait! Oh, no! We've lost Close already!'

'No, we haven't,' Dal pointed.

Amber looked in the direction of his pointing finger and stared. Among the grey, gaunt deserted buildings, nestled like colourful quartz inside a giant, bare rock-face, was a small childrens' playground; remnant of a city crèche for working mothers, now long dead.

Inside the playground Cloe was scrambling eagerly up the ladder to the top of a tiny slide. Another girl, about Cloe's age, was playing with a large golden Labrador, while seated on a swing alongside a small boy was a teenage girl with glowing copper hair, chatting to the boy as if they didn't have a care in the world.

Amber blinked in disbelief and looked at Dal. He shrugged and shook his head. It was like a dream. As weird as a scene from 'Alice in Wonderland'.

NINE

Zandra stared in horror at the police car, its large red flag, adorned with a skull and cross-bones, fluttering in the breeze. A dozen menacing youths with battledress and weapons straight out of a space-war DVD flanked the car. She had never felt so scared in all her young life. Her voice was shaking as she spoke. 'I thought you said he'd be alone?'

'Welcoming party?' Glen quipped, trying to hide his own fear.

Zandra was too frightened to get the irony. 'Don't look very welcoming to me.'

Lex looked grim. 'I'll do the talking.'

'Suits me,' Glen said.

Lex jumped down from the carriage and heaved a large canvas hold-all onto his shoulder. He hesitated as Zoot leapt athletically from the sunroof and strode down the car bonnet to the ground.

'Not getting scared, are you, Lex?' Glen taunted.

With more bravado than he was feeling Lex strode to meet the infamous Loco leader. The big youth, Ryan, jumped to the ground, clasping another bag, and joined his friend.

The three youths stopped a handshake apart. But Lex sensed Zoot wasn't the hand-shaking kind. In fact, he was the strangest, most intimidating creature he'd ever seen, outside of an X-rated movie. Taller than Lex, his lean, muscular body was clothed in a tight-fitting biker's red leather suit. Beneath his black military jacket, festooned with goth-like paraphernalia, he wore an incongruously clean white shirt and black tie. On his head was perched a black, gold-rimmed military peaked cap topped with Nazi tank-commander goggles. His gaunt face was scrawled with vivid blood-red whorls, like ancient celtic battle-scars. But it was the eyes that made Lex's blood run cold. Staring from pools of black war-paint, pupils shrunk to pinpricks, were the ice blue eyes of a killer.

'Zoot! Lex said with a lightness he wasn't feeling. 'Thought you weren't coming.'

The killer's eyes bored into his skull.

Lex gabbled on, feeling the ground slipping beneath his feet. 'Yeah, well, guess time-keeping's not your thing, eh?'

The evil eyes didn't flicker.

Lex attempted a grin. 'Me neither. Time's dead. That's the old way. We make the rules now, right?'

The voice was flat, ominous. 'What's in the bag?'

Lex dropped the canvas bag to the ground. 'Glad you asked, friend. Glad you asked.' He opened the top revealing an assortment of electronic gadgets. 'Walkie talkies, batteries, CD players, you name it.'

Zoot looked unimpressed. 'Food?'

'We've only got enough for –'

'Hand it over.'

A Loco stepped forward, hand outstretched. Lex shifted uneasily. Ryan was looking at him for a lead. Lex nodded. Reluctantly, Ryan held out a plastic bag, which was snatched away. Watching from the carriage, Glen glanced at the terrified Zandra. They couldn't hear what was being said, but things didn't look to be going well.

'Why do you want to be a Locust?' Zoot asked.

Lex slipped into his prepared speech. 'Hey, you guys are the best outfit around. You're the top man, Zoot. You really cut it.'

Zoot waited, expressionless. The eyes of the Locos were all fixed on Lex. He was floundering now. He'd expected a more positive reaction to his flattery. He stumbled on. 'You're... really...'

The voice was insistent now, impatient. 'What? Really what?'

At that moment Lex wished he'd listened more at school. He wracked his brain for the biggest, most impressive word he could remember. 'You're...scandalous.'

For an instant Zoot was taken back. 'We're what?' Then he threw back his head and let out a huge roar of laughter. The rest of the Locos joined in, baying like a pack of hyenas. The sound echoed through the rail yard. But there was no humour in it. It was deadly laughter.

'Run!' Lex yelled, slamming his shoulder bag into Zoot's face. Taken by surprise the Locos were slow to react. In one movement Ryan swept up the canvas bag and hurled it fiercely at the Locos, the contents flying in all directions. Glen was already pulling Zandra along the carriage to the other end. Lex and Ryan joined them, racing for a tall wooden fence surrounding the yard. Leaping onto a stack of crates by the fence Ryan yanked Zandra up, roughly tumbled her over the other side and followed. Lex jumped onto the top crate, straddled the top of the fence, and kicked away the crate.

'Lex!' cried Glen, stranded. 'What are you doing!'

'Just another of my brilliant plans! Lex yelled, pulling himself over the fence. 'Good luck, friend!'

Lex leapt to the ground and set off after Ryan and Zandra. Hearing the Locos descending on Glen with loud cries on the other side of the fence, Zandra turned back. 'Glen! she cried.

Lex grabbed her arm and pulled her away. 'They've got him! There's nothing we can do! Zandra, we have to save ourselves. Glen would have wanted us to!'

He pulled the wailing girl away, with the sound of Glen's pained cries ringing in their ears.

TEN

The copper-haired girl on the swing looked sad and resigned. Amber would understand why when she heard her story later. She'd had a rough time trying to care for the three kids she'd found wandering the streets, avoiding the tribes and trying to find enough food to keep them alive, day after day. It had been a long, tough journey. Tough even for a seasoned drifter let alone an innocent young girl and she was at the end of her rope. 'What tribe are you with?' she asked, her voice flat and empty.

'We're not with any,' Amber replied. 'I'm Amber. This is Dal.'

'Salene,' the girl said in response.

'Did you know Cloe was wandering the streets?'

'I can't keep my eyes on them all the time,' Salene said defensively. 'She doesn't understand. She wanders off looking for adults.'

'It's dangerous. The Locos nearly got her.'

'What difference does it make?'

Amber looked at her in surprise.

Salene went on, her voice drained, close to tears, 'I can't go on any longer. I was going to give us up...then I found this place. I thought they could have a play, one more time, before...'

Before. The word spoke volumes. Amber looked around at the three young children playing happily on the slide and with the dog. What would happen when they were caught, she wondered? From what she'd seen and heard all the tribes seemed as lawless and brutal as each other. A dark evil had descended on the world; mankind at its most desperate, ruthless and savage. If they fell into the hands of the tribes would they live or die, be enslaved, or tortured till they cried out begging to die? She screwed up her face and tried to rid her mind of the images. No matter what it took, she couldn't let that happen.

ooo

Lex led the little group picking their way through the debris-strewn street. Zandra stumbled after him in her designer shoes, more suitable for a catwalk than a war-torn city. Ryan was bringing up the rear, glancing behind him from time to time. The street behind them was deserted. The Locos had seemingly given up the chase. Probably satisfied with the capture of the betrayed, abandoned Glen.

'Did you see that guy!' Lex fumed. 'What was his problem? These tribe leaders, they get too much power! I'll show him! I'll get even with him. That's a promise!'

He took Zandra's arm. 'Come on, Zan, keep up.'

Zandra pulled her arm away. 'Don't touch me!'

'What's your problem..?' He registered the tears smearing Zandra's carefully applied makeup. 'For the last time, Zan, I'm sorry about Glen. It couldn't be helped...'

Zandra sniffed loudly.

'You had a thing about him, is that it?'

'No!'

'Then stop your sniveling! He wanted to be a Locust. He got his wish...Do you know what I think? I think he sacrificed himself. Deliberately. To save us. Can't bear to think about it.'

Zandra stopped, flooded with tears. As Lex went back to her she dissolved into his arms, physically and emotionally exhausted. 'Oh, Lex!'

Lex held her, secretly elated. He'd got rid of his rival. It was only a matter of time now. When the time and place was right.

Well, in a world like this you had to take what pleasures you could, didn't you? And no questions asked. He looked at Ryan standing watching their embrace.

'What are you looking at?' Lex growled.

'Lex. Listen!' Ryan said.

They were all suddenly silent, looking about, listening intently. From nearby came the sound of little children playing.

ELEVEN

A blood red dusk was falling across the city. From the distance, beneath the children's laughter, the sound of a brutal skirmish reached the playground. In earlier times it would have been the cries of a football crowd cheering on their champions. Now, Amber thought, who knows?

Dal looked at her and read her thoughts. 'I'll go scout around, Amber. Find somewhere safe for the night,'

'Thanks, Dal. I'll share the food out,' she said, taking a plastic bag from her rucksack.

'You'd better, friend.'

They all looked up at the menacing voice.

'You'd better,' Lex said, striding into the little playground.

Amber sprang up to confront the tough-looking youth. There was a girl and another boy with him. At least it wasn't the Locos.

'See, I own this sector,' Lex went on. 'And you're trespassing. But I tell you what. I'm feeling generous. Just give me the bag and I'll say no more about it.'

He looked around at the children who were still playing. 'And don't think of running. You might get away, but they won't.' He approached Cloe, who snatched up her teddy bear as if to protect herself against the threatening youth. Lex leaned down and thrust his face into Cloe's. 'Boo!'

Cloe jumped back, alarmed, dropping the teddy on the ground.

Amber knew that they were no match for the youth and the bigger one standing behind him. But in this world you didn't just roll over and play dead. Or you would be.

'Who are you?' she asked, as boldly as she could make herself sound. 'I don't recognize your tribe.'

'Don't tell me you've never heard of us?' Lex's bluff was interrupted by Ryan grabbing his arm.

'Lex!'

'What!' Lex snapped.

Ryan pointed, panicked. 'Loco's!'

Around the fence and at the gated entrance to the playground the ominous figures of the Locos had suddenly appeared, with Zoot at their head.

'Get them!' Zoot cried.

With the instinct of a hardened street-fighter, Lex slammed a swing into the face of the first Loco into the playground. Then, shoving Amber, Salene and Dal between them and the advancing Locos, he scrambled Zandra away with Ryan close behind. The confusion of the melee was enough to give them a head start. They tore along an alley, with Zandra whimpering in fear.

'This way!' Lex yelled, racing into a gloomy railway arch scattered with debris. As they rounded a corner, their footsteps echoing in the tunnel, the sunset streamed brilliantly in at the other end. Lex pulled up abruptly. Out of the dazzling light a line of tall figures appeared, menacing silhouettes against the setting sun.

'Demon Dogs!' he cried.

They turned back just as the Locos rounded the corner. There was no escape. They were trapped.

'Lex!' screamed Zandra, terrified.

Grabbing Zandra roughly by the arm, Lex hurled them both behind a row of garbage bins and crouched down. Ryan tumbled in on top of them, out of breath. They watched helplessly as the two tribes stopped and confronted each other. Lex could feel Zandra trembling with fear in his arms. He held her close, almost as scared as she was.

The Locos and the Demon Dogs faced each other in two battle lines. The Locos with the blackness of the tunnel behind them, the Dogs bathed from behind in bright crimson light. Lex, Zandra and Ryan held their breath.

Then, with a demonic cry Zoot launched forward towards the line of enemy, the Locos baying at his heels. The Demon Dogs responded with war-cries and raced forward to clash with the advancing Locos. Lex and the others watched transfixed. It was like a scene from a medieval battle, or a virtual wargame, but this was for real. Weapons crunching into bodies, arms and legs flailing, screams and cries of pain and fury.

'Let's get out of here! Lex yelled above the din of the fight.

TWELVE

Bray and Trudy trudged wearily towards the fierce red orb of the setting sun. It hadn't been easy to persuade Trudy to leave her elegant suburban home, the place where she had been born and which held all her fondest memories. She felt safe there, the home she had instinctively returned to after the failed evacuation of the children. After all the adults had died. But Bray knew it was essential for them to leave.

On his way back from scouting the city, he had seen the infamous Roosters searching house by house in the neighbouring suburb, looking for loot and survivors hiding in fear. 'Ours will be next,' he had told her. Finally, with many tears, she had relented and allowed him to lead her away from her past and into her future.

The journey to the city was not a long one, but they had been traveling for most of the day. Taking the direct route along the main road was out of the question. Apart from the Roosters, other small gangs of feral youths were scouring the suburbs for food and excitement. Bray and Trudy had to hide from them all along the way, sometimes for an hour or two at a time, until the gangs moved on.

During those long waits in hiding, Bray had to constantly reassure the panicking Trudy that they would be okay. By nature a highly-strung young girl, who had been cosseted from birth by her doting parents, she was totally unfitted for the dangerous and unpredictable world she now found herself in. It had been a tiring journey for them both, physically and mentally. For Bray, trying to keep Trudy from going to pieces was like clinging to an icy cliff-face by his fingertips.

Charting a path that took them from one hiding spot to another Bray got them within the city limits as night was falling. Their first priority now was to find a safe place to spend the night. Though, exhausted as he was, sleep was probably out of the question.

THIRTEEN

The car park was in the central, commercial part of the city, an area of multi-national banks, insurance firms and trading companies. Surrounded by soaring towers of offices that held no real interest for looting gangs Sector 10, as it had become known, was not controlled or occupied by any of the warring tribes.

In normal times the car park had been full with top of the range vehicles, symbols of their owner's wealth, status and importance. Now they were all gone, along with their owners. In their place was just a bleak and empty wind tunnel, littered with whatever city debris the wind had blown its way.

'Must have been a car park,' Dal said, as he and Amber led Salene, the young children and the dog inside. In the confusion at the playground the Locos had been so focused on catching Lex they had ignored Amber and the rest, and they had been able to walk out, unscathed and very relieved.

'Yeah, I remember it,' said Amber. 'There was a shopping mall attached to it. Very classy stuff.'

'That'll be all gone then,' Dal replied.

'But the mall might still be there, yeah?'

'Worth a try. It's too late to start looking for anything else.'

They exited the car park through a metal door and found themselves in a long L-shaped corridor. As they turned the corner they saw double doors at the end.

'I hope it's safe,' said Salene, close to tears. The burden of looking after the young children had taken her almost to breaking point and she knew any other nasty shock would be too much for her. She was so thankful to have been found by Amber and Dal, who seemed to be natural leaders. She was happy now to let someone else take control and tell her what to do.

'Come on,' Amber said decisively. 'Let's check it out.'

She led the way down the corridor and pushed open the double doors, tentatively.

'Wow!' she said in awe.

They rest followed her inside and gazed up at the atrium of the mall which stretched high above them. As Dal had predicted, the mall had been looted but the structure was still intact. No pyromaniac had, as yet, burnt it to the ground, and the fixtures still retained their stamp of quality and elegance, despite the graffiti. An ornate sweeping staircase rose to the upper levels which were bordered by gilded wrought iron balcony rails. Towering above them in the centre of the ground floor was a gigantic bronze statue of a bird about to take flight. It was lit, incongruously, by a myriad tiny bulbs floating high above its head; quartz lights with a life of their own, independent of the now defunct electricity supply.

The mall looked quiet and deserted.

'Seems to be empty,' Dal said. 'I'll go and have a look.'

'Dal,' warned Amber. 'Be careful.'

He grinned. 'No worries.'

As he set foot on the staircase, out of sight on the floor above him, a hand poised over a lever waiting.

FOURTEEN

With the light beginning to fade, Lex and Zandra waited in the bleak and windy car park, tired and on edge. The day which, for Lex, had begun with a cautious optimism had dissolved into a nightmarish hell.

Miraculously, they had escaped the Locos for a second time that day, but the experience had left them all with frayed and jangled nerves. Experienced street-fighter that he was, Lex had never seen such a brutal battle as the one between the Locos and the Demon Dogs that had given them time to escape. He was impressed and the adrenalin was still pumping wildly around his body.

Zandra had been horrified and was almost hysterical, thinking of what could have happened if they had been caught. What could still happen if they couldn't find a safe haven for the night. 'Where is he?' she wailed. 'He's been gone ages!'

Ryan had ventured into the gloom of the car park to check it out. As the seconds ticked by Zandra grew more and more afraid. 'Maybe they've got him, Lex! Maybe we should go! Maybe they were waiting in there!'

'Shut it, Zan. Ryan can take care of himself.'

They waited, ears alert for any sound, eyes roaming the desolate wasteland that had once been the financial hub of the city. Of half the civilized world.

Suddenly Zandra gave a startled gasp. From out of the dark recesses of the car park footsteps were approaching.

'Sshh!' Lex hissed.

A large figure loomed out of the darkness. Zandra cried out. 'Ryan! Thank God!'

'Anything?' Lex was impatient.

Ryan shook his head, glum. 'Nothing.'

Lex grimaced. 'We'd better get back to Sector 12 while there's still light.'

Running from the Locos had taken them away from the part of the city they called 'home'. A sector where they knew all the best hiding places for the times when the tribes came 'visiting'.

Leading the way out, Lex stumbled over an object on the ground. He swore, then bent to pick it up. As he looked at the object in his hand a malevolent grin spread over his face. It was a teddy bear.

FIFTEEN

The little group was huddled anxiously beneath the statue of the bird. It was a phoenix, Amber realized. Symbol of new life rising from the ashes. She hoped that was an omen. This tiny group of waifs and strays needed all the good luck that was on offer.

She was weary and a little confused. It seemed a very long time since she and Dal had set off on their journey that morning. By now they had expected to be camping out in the countryside, under the stars. She looked up at the glowing lights floating in the air above the bird, and smiled. Not quite what they'd had in mind.

While they were waiting for Dal to come back from checking out the mall, Amber had learnt more about the others. Patsy and Paul were eight year old twins. The dog, Bob, was their family pet. Salene had found them and Cloe wandering the central park of the city shortly after the virus claimed its last adult victim, and had been looking after them ever since. Amber was impressed. It must have been very hard keeping such innocents safe in the violent world into which they had all been plunged.

They looked up expectantly as Dal came back down the sweeping staircase.

'Did you have any luck?' Amber asked.

Dal shook his head. 'No. There's a lot of stuff left, but not food.'

'Well...' Amber leant down, opened her rucksack and took out two cans of beans.

Dal shrugged. 'We don't have much.'

'We weren't expecting a party,' Amber said wryly. 'Oh, Dal, this is Pasty and Paul. Paul seems a little shy.'

'He's not shy. He's deaf and dumb,' Patsy said.

'Oh. Do you lip read, Paul?' Amber asked.

Paul signed a reply. 'He said he prefers to sign,' Patsy explained.

'Okay. I guess we'll all have to learn then,' Amber said smiling.

Paul signed again, his hands moving urgently.

Amber frowned, 'What does that mean?'

Dal looked in the direction that Paul was staring. 'It means we're in trouble!'

Their eyes followed Dal's frightened gaze.

Lex strode arrogantly into the mall with Zandra and Ryan behind. He glared at the little startled group, a malicious smile distorting his face. 'Now where was I before I was so rudely interrupted?'

SIXTEEN

Under the black night sky, in the vast rail-yards that Zoot had chosen for their headquarters, the Locos were licking their wounds after the battle, by the light of a dozen fires.

In the privacy of their first class rail carriage, Ebony was bathing Zoot's bruised face with a cool, damp cloth. She would have much preferred a hotel to live in. Despite the looting and the fires, there were plenty still left standing. But Zoot was adamant. Hotels were vulnerable to siege or arson. They could be trapped inside if rival gangs united against them. Which was likely. For the Locos were the most hated tribe in the city. With good reason.

Their leader, Zoot, was the best street-fighter Ebony had ever seen. And in her short, tough life she had seen a lot. In the beginning there had been many rivals for Zoot's affections, but she had beaten them all. Either by brute force or deceit, attributes she had learnt the hard way growing up. Watching her battle and deceive to gain his favour, Zoot had recognized a soul-mate in the diminutive hellcat, with the piercing eyes staring out of the black band of makeup that was her trademark. He had chosen her to be his lieutenant and, eventually, his lover.

It had taken her longer than she expected to win her way into his bed. Zoot was a private being, wary and distrustful of everyone. Added to his native intelligence and natural cunning, this aloofness served him well. He was not easily fooled. But she had fooled him. Her own desperate need for control and power, to never be vulnerable again, had finally found a way to win him over.

Her sexual expertise had delighted him. Almost shocked him, coming from a more reserved environment than the cesspit she had been brought up in. Complete now, they were a powerful duo. On a mission to conquer their world.

SEVENTEEN

In the mall, Amber's tiny group stared at Lex transfixed and afraid. One moment they had felt safe from the violent world outside. Now it was glaring them in the face.

'Oh, yes. Food!' he said menacingly. 'You were going to give me your food.'

As he moved forward a loud metallic rattling echoed around the mall. Everyone looked up. Barred metal grills shot down from the ceiling blocking the mall entrance, leaving Lex's group on the outside.

Lex grasped the bars and rattled them, surprised and angry. 'How the hell did you do that!' he snarled. 'We'll find another way in. You're not getting away that easy!'

He spun round to leave and the whirring, rattling sound rang through the mall again. The grills dropped down on the outside, trapping Lex and his group inside a barred cage. He strode back to the inner grill and glared at Amber.

Amber allowed herself a smile. She didn't know what the hell was going on, but for the moment luck was with them at last. 'Looks like you're the ones not getting away.'

'Open it up! Lex demanded. 'Open it up or you'll regret it!'

The little ones stared at Amber, believing that somehow she had worked a miracle.

'I'm gonna count to ten,' Lex said. 'One! Two! Three! –

'Four! Five!' They all looked around as a strange new voice took up the count, the sound ringing in the air. On the count of 'ten' they saw a small youth with wild flaming red hair and short trousers standing in the gloom at the top of the stairs.

On his forehead he wore a strange contraption that was half spectacles half microscope. Amber's immediate thought was of an absent-minded professor crossed with a techno-nerd.

The weird youth stepped casually down the stairs. 'So what happens now?' he called to Lex. 'I think you'll find that was a fairly empty threat. You didn't quite think it through, did you? Not to worry.'

Amber and the others stared at their 'saviour' lost for words. At the end of a long and traumatic day this apparition was almost too much to take in.

'Hi,' he said to Amber. 'I'm Jack. And I think you've got something to say to me?'

Amber was puzzled. 'Like what?'

The boy grinned. 'Well, in my day it was 'Thanks'. But I guess times are changing.'

EIGHTEEN

Night had fallen by the time Bray and Trudy found the disused railway tunnel in the heart of the city. It was a short tunnel blocked at one end by a brick wall, used for housing engines which were not in use. Bray had checked that it was empty and decided it was as safe a place as any to spend the night. No tribes ventured out in the darkness. It was too dangerous and unnecessary. Daytime was the best time for 'fun'.

He shook out the camping blanket from his shoulder bag and wrapped it around her. 'Here,' he said gently.

Physically and emotionally drained, Trudy hugged it to her and began to cry softly. Bray sat down beside her and put an arm around her shoulders. She leant into his chest, whimpering. He stroked her hair and began to rock her soothingly, like he would a small child.

After a while he felt her body relax against him. Her crying ceased and was replaced by a gentle, fitful snoring. Bray gazed out at the night. An orange-tinged half moon was rising above the roofs of the city. A dead calm had fallen in the streets, broken only by the occasional cry of a cat, or a desperate child. He couldn't tell which.

It was so peaceful. A gentle night breeze blew softly. Stars twinkled in the ink-black sky. The earth slept. Nature hadn't changed. It was hard to believe they were living in hell.

He rested his head against the cool tunnel wall and wished he could be far away. Far away alone. He could survive, he'd no doubt of that. He knew the woods, the fields and the mountains. He was a city boy with the soul of a native. He envied the aboriginals with their instinctive communion with nature. There was nothing natural about the way he was living now.

Trudy stirred in his arms, still asleep. A heavy weight pressed on his heart. She was his responsibility now. He had promised to take care of her, and he would. He would, despite his longing to be far away, alone.

NINETEEN

Jack was enjoying his sense of power. 'These gates can only be opened with a special winch,' he told Amber. He turned to Lex, who was peering furiously and frustrated through the gilded bars of the grill. 'I'll open the far one when you guys have had a chance to cool off. Let you back on the streets.'

'No!' pleaded Zandra. 'I don't want to go out there!'

Jack turned and smiled at Amber. 'Come on, I'll show you around.'

He led the way up the stairs with the air of a lord showing off his stately home. Amber and the rest followed, relieved and even slightly amused at their host's proprietorial manner. For the moment they were safe. They were allowed to smile.

Downstairs Lex rattled the bars of the grill impotently. 'Hey!' he yelled. 'Where're you going!' He kicked the grill savagely. The bars didn't yield. They could have kept out an elephant.

As they reached the first landing Amber asked, 'Why are you doing this?'

'Doing what?'

'Helping us. We could be Demon Dogs for all you know.'

It was Jack's turn to smile. He looked around at the others. 'You guys?'

Amber grinned. 'Well, maybe not. All the same you didn't have to let us in here.'

Lex's angry cries echoed up to them and around the mall. 'Hey! Are you listening! I'm warning you!'

'Got a bit of a temper your friend,' Jack said.

'He's no friend of ours,' Dal said.

'I've been living out of a crate of tinned beans for the last few weeks,' Jack went on, 'and even that's running low.'

'We haven't got much food either,' Amber replied.

'But you could help me to find some. That's the least you could do after I helped you out with your little problem down there.'

'Thanks for your help,' Dal said, 'but we have to move on. First thing in the morning, right, Amber?

Jack shrugged. 'Suit yourself, but you won't find a better place to crash than this.'

He stopped at the top of the stairs and waved his arms about him. They looked around them in the semi-darkness. Through the large glass roof of the atrium the moon and starlight gave the mall a soft glow. Everywhere there were empty shops, some half looted, some almost untouched. It was as if the looters had been disturbed and had fled, never to come back. It felt safe.

'I'm tired,' moaned Cloe.

'Me too,' said Patsy.

Salene looked at Amber. 'What are we going to do?'

'I've got a blanket,' Amber replied. 'The kids can have that. The rest of us will just have to make do.'

Jack grinned. 'Sounds cool, but I can go one better.'

He led them up a short flight of stairs to the next landing and waved an arm again, like a magician presenting his favourite illusion.

Amber stopped and stared disbelievingly. 'No. It can't be.'

The kids were already racing into the furniture store where the beds waited invitingly. The others hurried inside, echoing Amber's delighted disbelief.

'Real duvets!' gasped Salene.

'And pillows!' shouted Dal. 'They've got pillows!'

Patsy, Paul and Cloe were leaping excitedly from bed to bed, screaming with joy.

'Cool it, kids!' Amber called. 'Don't break the beds!'

Lex's empty threats echoed up to them from the floor below. 'Hey! Open these gates! I'm warning you! You're gonna regret this!'

Amber turned to Jack. 'What are we going to do about those three?'

Jack shrugged. 'Forget it. That's what you do with animals. Lock 'em in a cage. Don't worry, they're not going anywhere tonight.'

TWENTY

An eerie silence had fallen over the darkened city. In the rail tunnel Bray slept fitfully, with Trudy snoring in his arms. At the rail yard perimeter Locos kept watch, guarding Zoot and Ebony, entwined together asleep in the comfort of their first class carriage. Bathed in soft moonlight the world seemed at peace.

In the mall Lex fumed silently, gripping the bars of their 'cage'. He'd given in to Zandra's pleading to stop shouting. 'You'll bring the Locos!' she wailed.

Worn out and fretful, Zandra had crashed on a large sofa, a remnant the looters had left behind in the entrance. She knew her makeup was smudged and she could do with a good wash, but at this moment she didn't care. Inside the cage she was safe for another night. It was all she could ask, for now.

'This place ain't so bad, Lex.' Ryan said, aware of his friends simmering anger. 'We've slept in worse places.'

'Shut it!' Lex snapped. He slumped onto the sofa, shoving Zandra aside sulkily.

Ryan lay down on the floor, tucking the teddy bear under his head for a pillow.

Zandra cuddled up to Lex, whimpering. 'Shut it! he snapped. 'You'll bring the Locos!'

In the furniture store Amber was tucking the children into their new beds, comfortable for the first time since they could remember. Patsy snuggled under her fresh-smelling duvet. Next to her Cloe was crying.

'What's the matter?' Amber asked kindly.

'She can't find her teddy.'

'I want my teddy! I want to go home!' Cloe cried.

Amber sat beside her and stroked her cheek. 'I know. I know. It's alright. This is your home, for now.'

Warm and cosy in her bed Salene stared at the ceiling in the semi-darkness, lost in her thoughts. For tonight she was safe, and for that she was grateful. But what new horrors would tomorrow bring?

TWENTY ONE

Bray was awake before dawn. He hadn't really slept and his limbs were stiff from lying on the hard tunnel floor. He got up quietly so as not to wake Trudy, still sleeping soundly wrapped in the blanket. He stretched and stood at the tunnel entrance watching the early light touch the tops of the tower blocks and gradually creep into the city.

The fires had mostly burnt themselves out, mercifully without creating a firestorm that could have killed off the remaining survivors. Maybe it would have been better if it had, he thought. What future did any of them have?

Since the last of the adults, and the remains of authority, had died the city had descended into lawlessness, and he couldn't see any way of turning that back. In time one dominant tribe would emerge. That was the way it worked. The Locos? The Demon Dogs? It didn't matter which. There were no rules anymore. Whoever clawed their way to the top could do whatever they pleased with the rest. And Bray knew enough history to know the depths human beings could sink to if left unchecked.

Was there a solution? Suicide was cowardly; just running away. And he'd never been one for ducking a problem. But this one was too big for him to handle. So it came down to the simple question of survival. It was every kid for themselves.

Sounds began. Cries too distant to know whether of anguish or joy. He doubted it was the latter. Trudy stirred and opened her eyes. She blinked and rubbed a hand over her face, disorientated.

'Bray?'

He turned and saw her face crumple as the surroundings and the situation hit her.

'Oh, Bray!' she sobbed.

With an inner sigh, he knelt beside her. There were no words of comfort he could think of. 'The last of the food is in the bag. You should eat.'

'What about you?' she asked through her tears.

'I need to look for more. And find us a safe place.'

She grasped his sleeve fearfully, her nails digging into his arm. 'Don't leave me, Bray!'

'Trudy, I have to go. We can't stay here. I have to find you a safe place and I can travel faster on my own.'

Trudy broke into sobs again. Bray fought down his fatigue and his irritation. 'I'm sorry. There's some crates and stuff at the end of the tunnel you can hide behind. You'll be safe there. Nobody will want to come in here in the daytime.'

'How long will you be?'

'As long as it takes, Trudy.' There was no point in lying to her.

She puts her hand to her mouth, trying to stifle her tears, which she knew were not helping him.

'Come on,' he said gently. 'I'll help you build a safe hideout.'

TWENTY TWO

Despite the comfort of her bed in the mall, Amber had hardly slept either. There was too much to think about. To decide. Yesterday it had seemed so simple. Escape to the relative safety of the countryside and start a new life. Probably nomadic as there would always be the threat of the tribes, no matter where they were. But for centuries generations of people had lived that kind of life and survived, so why couldn't they?

Today was different, and lying in the comfort of her bed wouldn't get anything done. She flung off the duvet and got up. Salene and the kids were sleeping soundly, exhausted from their ordeal. They had been sleeping rough since it all started, while, until yesterday, she and Dal had been living safe in their suburb, sleeping in their own beds, until the looters ran out of places to ransack in the city and started moving outwards.

She walked out to the landing barefoot and down the stairs to the first floor. Leaning on the balcony rail she looked down at the three intruders laying in their cage a floor below.

Ryan's snores were echoing through the cavernous mall. Lex, wide awake and still fuming, hit him hard on the shoulder. 'Shut it! I'm trying to think!'

Zandra woke and sat up. 'Oh,' she groaned. 'I feel terrible!'

'You look terrible,' Lex quipped.

Grabbing a compact from her bag, Zandra opened it and inspected herself in the tiny mirror. Her blue and red hair stood out in all directions, makeup smeared her face. 'It's not my fault!' she snapped. 'You're the one that got us into this mess! How are we going to get out?'

'That's what I'm trying to figure out, if you'll stop whining!'

Amber called down from the balcony. 'You were saying, when you get out?'

Lex leapt up and went to the bars. 'You'll see! You can't keep us in here forever!'

'Is that a fact?'

'You're gonna wish you'd never done this! Only by then it'll be too late for wishing!'

'It's easy to make threats from behind bars.'

'It's not a threat,' Lex snarled. 'It's a promise!'

Amber straightened up and walked away. Lex smashed his fist on the bars, impotently. 'I'm warning you!'

She found Jack in the electrical shop where he slept among piles of electronic bits and pieces that she hadn't a clue about. He was fiddling with the dials of a short wave radio, frustrated.

'Jack,' she said. 'The animals are awake. We need to decide what to do.'

TWENTY THREE

Yesterday's battle with the Demon Dogs had been a stalemate. Along with a few broken bones, cuts and bruises, the Locos captured just two prisoners, who would be kept as slaves, until they could be indoctrinated into the tribe proper.

The Locos numbers were growing. Waifs and strays were rounded up daily by raiding parties and put to work with prisoners captured from the other tribes. But along with the growing army came the problem of control. Apart from the fear of severe and cruel punishment for disloyalty, Zoot's main method was oratory. Words. For centuries people had been swayed and kept obedient by the spoken word. The Locos were no different.

Zoot was a product of his time, a techno-freak, a fanatical and feared wargamer on the world-wide web. But he had also heard about Hitler's Nazis rallies, of Churchill's radio broadcasts that gave the British nation courage in their 'darkest hour'. He guessed that many famous rulers in the distant past had also been gifted speakers. There were no written records for great leaders like Attila the Hun, or Genghis Khan, but Zoot was certain they had been able to work magic with words too. Someone had once said 'The pen is mightier than the sword' and there was truth in that. Words had proved more powerful than bullets many times in the history of the world. And he could use them too.

He stood on top of his railway carriage, the morning sun bathing him in a golden glow. Ebony stood two paces to the side. Her job was to respond to his oratory. To encourage the others by her example.

Zoot raised his hands. The gathered Locos fell silent. 'Brothers! Sisters! LOCOS!' he yelled.

Ebony began the chant. 'Locos! Locos! Locos!

Zoot let the chant run on, then cut them off with a gesture. They were hanging on his every word. 'The adults are Dead!

Ebony started a cheer, which Zoot cut short.

'History is Dead! The corrupt ways of the adults are Dead! The ways that destroyed the world are Dead!'

He let the cheer that Ebony initiated die a natural death, and then went on. 'But our world has just begun! The world of the Locos! The world of the future! Our world! No past! No adults. No rules!'

A cheer was growing again without Ebony's help. Zoot raised his arms above his head in a crossed-wrist salute and yelled at the top of his powerful voice. 'POWER AND CHAOS!!!'

The echoing cry of the Locos was heard for miles around.

TWENTY FOUR

Amber, Jack and Dal were leaning on the balcony rail looking down on Lex standing at the bars. As the elders of the little group it seemed that it was up to them to make the decisions for them all.

'For the last time, let us out of here!' Lex stormed.

'Well it could be the last time,' said Jack calmly, 'if we left you in there to starve.'

A snarl curled up Lex's mouth, 'You couldn't hurt anyone if your life depended on it, you nerd!'

'Lex!' rebuked Zandra. She came to the bars, looking up at them plaintively. 'He doesn't mean it really!'

Amber, Jack and Dal looked at each other, shrugged and walked away.

'Now look what you've done!' wailed Zandra. She flung herself on the sofa, in a sulk.

Lex saw Ryan looking at him perplexed. 'What are you looking at, moron!'

Out of sight and hearing the trio stopped. Dal looked at Amber. 'So what are we going to do about them?'

'The first question is, what are we going to do about us?'

Jack frowned. 'What?'

Amber went on. 'Well they can't get in, but can we get out?'

'There's another way out, through the old sewers,' Jack said. 'Come on, Amber, just let's go.'

Amber took a deep breath. 'Dal, we need somewhere to stay. I think it should be here.'

Dal's brow furrowed. 'But I thought we were headed out to the country? That was the plan.'

'Yeah, well plans change. You and me, maybe we could make it. But what about the others? How are we gonna get all the little ones out without running into the Locos, or one of the other tribes?'

Dal was growing more and more unhappy. 'But why do we have to look after them?'

Amber looked at him as if surprised by the question. 'Because they'd never survive without us, would they?'

Dal sighed and looked down at his feet. He was losing the argument and it irked him. Everything he and Amber had talked about, decided on, was fading away.

Amber sensed her friend's disappointment. 'Dal, this is the safest place for all of us, for now. If we stick together.'

'You mean like start our own tribe?'

Amber shrugged. 'Maybe.'

'But what do we do about them?' Dal nodded in the direction of the cage.

'Easy,' Jack said, 'I just pull up the outside gate. Let 'em take their chances out in the street,'

Amber nodded. 'We can't trust them.'

'But can we trust them outside? What if they go to the Locos and bring them here?'

Amber was silent. Dal had put his finger on the real dilemma.

'So,' Jack began, 'do we let 'em in, or kick 'em out, boss?'

The word 'boss' stopped Amber in her tracks. Without realizing it, she had chosen to take the initiative. The rest were all looking to her now, and it scared her.

TWENTY FIVE

He skateboarded along the deserted streets of the city, his eyes constantly on the lookout for danger. When the virus struck and was raging through the country like wildfire, the authorities had divided the city into administrative sectors with numbers for easy identification and control. Each sector was cordoned off from the next to try and contain the outbreak, but the virus had no respect for physical barriers, or adult systems of containment. It marched on through the city, through the country, through the world, like a tidal wave of death.

After the adults were all dead and gone, the numbering system had stuck and the various tribes had made individual sectors their own. He had a pretty good idea which tribe controlled which sector, and he knew that none of them were safe for strangers.

Bray had learned to skateboard when he was six, but he never dreamt he would be using it as his fastest mode of transport as a teenager. With the tribes controlling what fuel supplies that were left, cars or motorbikes were out of the question. That was a pity because he had a shelf full of medals for trail-biking back home. All worthless in this world. You couldn't eat medals.

There were plenty of bicycles lying around, but they were a liability in the city. You couldn't just pick them up and run if you had to get away from the roaming gangs. But a sturdy skateboard in the right hands was a formidable weapon. So his skateboard was his transport and his defence.

In the first few weeks after the city's collapse into chaos the tribes had looted all of the normal food supplies, but food wasn't such a problem. As the world he knew was disintegrating, Bray had the sense to stock up on lightweight energy foods, anything easily portable and nutritious. And, having been hooked on native societies and their survival skills since he learnt to read, he knew what wild plants to eat and how to extract and filter water from natural vegetation. Food may be a problem for the future. But for the moment a safe place to stay was top priority.

But in this world, where was safe?

TWENTY SIX

In the mall everyone was up and very hungry. They were seated where Amber had gathered them in the large first-floor café, which had been the hub of the mall in its heyday, providing trendy breakfasts and lunches for the busy shoppers and city workers. On the walls photos and posters of colourful, appetizing dishes mocked them. Salene gazed at them longingly. She couldn't remember when she and the kids had last eaten a proper meal.

Amber and Dal put their rucksacks on a table and emptied them of the few cans of food and water bottles they had been able to carry from home. It was a meager supply for so many mouths.

'If we're going to stick together we all have to share what we have,' Amber announced.

Patsy produced a handful of wrapped sweets and gave them to Amber. 'Thanks, Patsy...Jack?'

Jack shifted uneasily. 'I haven't got much.'

'Much is better than nothing. Show us.'

It was clear that Jack was reluctant, but he walked into the kitchen at the rear of the café, with the rest following behind. Opening a cupboard on the wall he revealed a dozen or so cans of food and bottles of mineral water.

Dal's eyes lit up. 'Ketchup! You've got ketchup!'

Jack forced a smile. At first he'd been happy to share his 'home' for the company, now he didn't look so sure.

'Great!' Amber said. She took a tin out of the cupboard and showed it to the others. 'So who's for baked beans, tinned meat and ketchup?'

'And we don't have to have it cold!' Jack said lifting a camping stove from under the sink.

Dal beamed. 'Hot food and ketchup! This man's a genius!'

Jack grinned modestly. Amber smiled along with the rest. When had she last had something to smile about? Maybe it was an omen?

TWENTY SEVEN

There were not many times in life when Lex didn't have an answer, but this situation was one of them. As an alpha male, bullying came naturally to him, verbally and physically. Growing up as a tough kid from a rough neighbourhood he'd always been able to get his own way, in the playground and the street. He'd grown used to it.

Now he was stuck in a cage, helpless. And, what made it worse, he was being taunted by a girl and a nerd. It was humiliating and Lex didn't do humiliation. He was determined to get his own back. But how? He had to get out of the cage first, and the bars that imprisoned him and his two friends were meant to keep out hordes of rampant shoppers at sales time. The three of them stood no chance of breaking them down.

Ryan, who was sitting morosely on the floor, suddenly sniffed and looked up. 'Food! I can smell food!' He got up and went to the bars, eagerly.

Sure enough, Amber was approaching carrying a plate of steaming food. She stopped before the bars and confronted them, feigning a confidence she didn't fully feel. 'Now, you have a choice. We've been talking and we think the best thing to do is to open the outside gate and let you out into the street.'

'No, please! Don't!' Zandra cried. She looked at Lex, who was glaring sullenly at Amber. 'Lex! Say something!'

For a moment Lex remained staring at his tormentor. Finally he spoke. 'What choice?'

'Ah, it can listen.'

The others were coming nervously down the stairs, anxious to hear what was going to happen.

Lex looked at them, taking them all in for the first time. There were none who would be a problem for him and Ryan. 'Are you in charge of these kids?'

'Maybe, for now.'

'So, this choice?' Lex snapped.

'You can take your chances out there with the Locos, or you can join with us. But on our terms. We all share what we have, we work together and maybe we stay safe. Maybe.'

Jack looked at her anxiously. 'Amber, how do we know we can trust them? The Locos might have sent them.'

'If that were true we'd be happy to go back outside, wouldn't we?' Zandra said scornfully. 'You're not very smart for a nerd.'

'Yeh, well, smart enough to trap you, zero,' Jack retorted.

Lex couldn't contain his anger. 'And you'll wish you'd never done that!'

'Sounds like you've made your choice,' Amber said decisively. 'Open the outside gate, Jack.'

Zandra was panicking. 'No, wait! I wanna stay!'

Lex turned on her. 'Zandra, shut it! I make the decisions here!'

Paul suddenly became agitated, waving his hands at his sister. 'Paul said 'shut up'. All of you. He heard something!'

For a moment they were all alert, listening, hardly breathing.

Dal looked puzzled. 'How could he? He's deaf.'

'He feels things,' Patsy explained. 'Vibrations. Through the floor.'

Salene turned round, startled. 'What was that?'

They could all hear it now. Muffled footsteps. They turned in the direction of the sound.

'It's coming from the sewers,' Jack said.

Amber looked at him. 'Can anyone get in there?'

'Could do. I haven't had time to secure it yet.'

'Could be the Locos,' Lex taunted. 'Still don't want to let us in?

TWENTY EIGHT

The sun had risen high in the sky. It was a bright warm midday, with a light breeze rustling the leaves on the city trees. But instead of streets full of happy shoppers, they lay empty, unswept and dangerous. In the old days Trudy had liked to come into town with her mother shopping for clothes, shoes and nicknacks. Back at home her closets and drawers were stuffed with things she had hardly ever worn. Now she would never get the chance. She had not been able to carry them on her trek into the city with Bray.

Trudy had been waiting fearfully all morning, hidden from sight in the grimy rail tunnel, jumping in fright at every noise. The minutes had seemed like hours. The hours like days. Her fear had distorted time.

She had tried to pass the time sleeping, but the sounds of the city were now everywhere, making her fearful that at any moment she could be discovered. Distant sirens, cries, screams punctuated long stretches of eerie silence. For the anxious young girl, the silence felt just as threatening as she waited for the next sound. The sound that could mean it was all over for her.

She had tried to block her mind from imagining what she might happen to her. But no matter how hard she tried the thoughts kept coming back. Over and over. Horrific, unbearable images she didn't even want to put into words. If only Bray would come back! She would be safe then. He would hold her and the images in her brain would stop. But another thought was lurking there too. A thought that wouldn't go away.

Bray would never abandon her, she knew that. From the very beginning he had promised to look after her and he'd been as true as his word. But the city was dangerous and deadly. Anything could happen at any time, even to someone as intelligent and resourceful as Bray. She prayed that he would return to her safely and soon. For she knew she could never survive without him. But, despite herself, the thought returned. What if he didn't come back?

TWENTY NINE

Alone, Amber and Dal stood listening intently at the heavy metal door leading to the sewers. Amber had told Jack to take the others up to the café and wait. There was no knowing who or what was lurking behind the door. The noise of footsteps had stopped, but they needed to find out what was going on underneath their new 'home'. They were both carrying heavy cricket bats that Jack had fetched from the half-looted sports store. Amber put her hand on the handle of the door.

'Are you sure this is a good idea, Amber?'

'No. But we're going in anyway.'

Cautiously she opened the door. It was pitch black inside.

'Can't see a thing,' she said.

'Good job I brought my torch then.'

Warily Dal led the way inside, the light from the torch picking out the dank, slimy walls of the sewer tunnel. On the slippery floor rats scurried away from the light, leaping with tiny splashes into the black, smelly water trickling along the central gulley.

They inched their way carefully along the narrow path that ran alongside the gulley. At the end of the tunnel the main path branched into several other tunnels. Dal shone his torch down them all. 'We could get lost down here.'

'Lost only matters when you've got a home, Dal.'

'Thanks for reminding me.'

'Sshh!'

They both stopped and listened, holding their breath. Above the sound of the trickling water and the squeaking of the rats, there were the footsteps again.

'Down there,' Amber whispered, pointing along the main path. She took the torch from Dal and motioned him to follow. Wincing at every little noise she made, she crept slowly down the long narrow tunnel. At the far end the tunnel turned ninety degrees. Amber peered warily round the corner.

ooo

Upstairs, from behind the bars of the grill, Lex watched Jack shepherding the others up the stairs to the café.

'What if they don't come back, nerd?' Lex called. 'The Locos could be on their way in right now!'

Patsy was hanging back, watching Lex, afraid. 'Come on, Patsy!' said Jack, trying to block out Lex's words.

But Lex's voice echoed around the mall. 'I saw the Locos catch somebody once! Just like you, Jack! They tied him to a tree and then they –'

'Stop it! Stop it!' Salene shouted back from the top of the stairs. 'You're frightening the little ones!'

'They should be frightened! And so should you!' Lex was enjoying himself now, working on all their fears. 'The Locos love pretty girls like you!'

'Shut up! Shut up!' Salene put her hands over her ears. Patsy screamed, setting the dog, Bob, barking furiously. The noise was deafening in the empty space.

'Open up!' Lex called again. 'Let us in! We can help you!'

Salene looked anxiously at Jack. 'What are we going to do, Jack?'

Lex pressed on relentlessly. 'You've got no choice, nerd! You gonna take on the Locos by yourself?'

Jack was wavering uncertainly. 'I don't trust you!'

'Trust! We're talking about survival here! It's your only chance! Open up before they get in here!'

Salene's voice was desperate now. 'Do it, Jack!'

Jack hesitated, looking between Salene and Lex. He started towards the manual unit that controlled the winch for the grills, just as Amber and Dal appeared downstairs. 'What's all the noise?' she called. 'What's going on?'

Jack stopped, guiltily. 'Er...We thought you weren't coming back!'

Lex was wearing his 'honest' face. 'We offered to help.'

'I bet!' Amber snapped.

Jack moved away from the winch. 'Did you find anything?'

Amber looked up the stairs where the rest were standing looking lost. 'Salene take the kids to the café. It's okay, really.' Amber waited until Salene and the children had gone, then turned to Jack. 'There was someone down there. We heard footsteps.'

'We need to make it secure down there, Jack,' Dal said.

Lex seized his chance. 'It's too late!' he crowed. 'They're here. Inside! You heard them. Now are you gonna let us in? Before you all get killed?'

THIRTY

The idea had come to Zoot after his speech to the Locos that morning. He needed an event. Something symbolic that the Locos could all join in with. Symbolic events, he knew, were very powerful for bringing people together and creating loyalty. Football games, vast political rallies, tacky television game shows, all worked in the same way.

He sensed that the fight with the Demon Dogs had been unsettling for some of the Locos. It was unplanned. Accidental. Chaotic. Chaos was at the very heart of his rebellion but, paradoxically, he wanted to control it. Controlled chaos was his goal. His control, other's chaos. For control was power. Power and chaos!

He needed to reinforce his message about history. History being dead. He wanted to rid the Locos minds of any of the old ideas that might contaminate his new vision of the world. Ebony gave him the clue, when they had made love after his address to the Locos.

She was stretched out on her back, naked, lying across his chest. Her tiny, brown body was beautifully formed and toned like an Olympic athlete. He played idly with her firm young breasts.

'A great speech,' she said. 'You should write them down.'

'What? Write what down?'

'Your speeches.'

Zoot frowned. 'Why?'

'As a record. For history.'

'History is dead.'

'Yeah, but –'

He squeezed hard with both hands.

'Ow! That hurts!' she squealed, trying to scamble up out of his arms. He held her to him in a vice grip.

'Have I taught you nothing?' he rasped into her ear. 'History is dead. The future doesn't exist. There is only the here and the now.'

She stopped struggling. It was futile. She went on, a little sulkily. 'Yeah. But everybody else, you know, all those leader guys, they all had their speeches and stuff written down, in books. So years later, hundreds of years maybe, people could read what they said.'

He pushed Ebony aside roughly and sat up. The event complete in his mind. 'Yes, they did, didn't they?'

THIRTY ONE

Her Dad used to have an expression, 'Between the devil and the deep blue sea.' Today it was 'Between a rock and a hard place.' Same difference. She was there.

If she let Lex inside the mall he could easily take revenge for being caged up. Amber didn't approve of violence, but she wasn't afraid of a fight. When all else failed she'd had to resort to fists once or twice at school, but she knew she was no match for Lex. None of them were. But if the Locos were in the sewers, she would need Lex and his big friend, Ryan, to stand any chance against them. It was her first big decision as leader. If she got it wrong, she wouldn't get a second chance.

Lex sensed Amber's indecision and pressed home his advantage. 'Did you hear that, Ryan? Must be a whole pack of them down there!'

Amber hadn't heard anything. But her head was buzzing with confusion. She approached the grill. 'Do you accept our terms?'

Lex smiled smugly. 'For now, yes.'

'For now wasn't the deal. You're heading for the streets! Jack!'

Jack started back up the stairs towards the winch.

Lex held up his hands. 'Okay! Okay! You win..! Now let us in.'

Amber nodded to Jack. He shrugged uncertainly but continued up the stairs.

Dal was uneasy. 'Amber!' he warned.

Jack reached the winch and told hold of the handle.

Watching from the cage Lex didn't want to lose the moment. 'Get on with it you wimp!'

Slowly Jack turned the winch handle. The grill rose with a well-oiled whirr. Triumphant, Lex ducked under the bars before they reached the top, and strode up to Amber, pushing his face close to hers.

She could smell his earthy male scent and feel the power emanating from his toned body. She was shaking inside, but kept her voice steady. 'You accepted our terms.'

'Did I? Maybe I lied.' He snatched the cricket bat that Amber was still holding. She flinched away, fearing an attack. He glared at her. 'You and me, we're not finished yet!' He turned and strode towards the sewer entrance. 'Ryan, come on!'

Zandra called after him, miffed. 'And me! You're just gonna leave me here?'

'Stop your whining!' Lex called back over his shoulder. 'You wanted to get out. You're out! Do something useful. Fix your makeup!'

Ryan approached Amber, sheepishly, holding out Cloe's teddy. 'I wanted to give it back.'

Amber smiled at him warmly. This guy was a million miles away from Lex. 'Thanks. She missed it.' She held out the torch. 'You'll need this.'

Dal held out his cricket bat. 'And this.'

Ryan took it with a shy smile and followed after Lex.

Amber looked at Dal, shook her head and breathed a sigh of relief. First round to her, on points. But she sensed the fight with Lex wasn't over yet.

THIRTY TWO

Holding the torch, Lex led the way cautiously along the sewer path. At the end of the first tunnel he held his hand up. Ryan stopped behind him, straining to see in the dim light.

'Listen.' Lex whispered. Footsteps echoed down the tunnel. 'Come on!'

They hurried on and reached the corner just in time to see a pair of boots disappearing up the short ladder that led to the sewer entrance.

'Got him!'

Rushing to the ladder Lex leapt up. His boot slipped on the slimy metal rung and he tumbled back against Ryan. Cursing, he scrambled back up the ladder with Ryan close behind.

They hauled themselves out of the sewer manhole into bright sunlight and blinked. It took a moment for their eyes to adjust. And then they saw the figure racing away.

'After him!' Lex ordered.

The youth had a head start, and was fast. He turned back, saw the two youths pursuing him, and quickened his pace, racing away across patch of spare land that had been flattened to make way for yet another towering office block, planned before the virus made all such plans redundant. Sprinting two at a time up the steps of a rail bridge the figure ran across the metal bridge spanning the branch line and down the other side.

'He's heading for the rail yards!' Ryan called. 'That's the Locos sector!'

'Maybe he is a Loco!' Lex gasped, already out of breath. Fighting was his thing, not running. 'We've got to get him before he reports back!'

'We're gonna lose him!' Ryan shouted.

He was right. By the time they reached the first burnt out carriage, on the fringe of the railyard, there was no sign of their quarry. 'He's in here somewhere,' Lex panted. 'Come on.'

'Careful, Lex!' Ryan warned. 'The Locos might be around!'

Lex looked about him. There was no sign of life. He motioned Ryan on. They crept deeper into the yard, past the abandoned rolling stock, crouching down to search beneath each wagon. Out of their sight the figure doubled back the way he came.

They were in the middle of the yard, looking about them, when they heard it, and their hearts nearly stopped.

Whoop! Whoop! Whoop!

Peering round the corner of a carriage they saw it. Zoot was approaching in his customized police car, surrounded by hordes of Locos. Lex looked at Ryan. They were trapped.

THIRTY THREE

Amber had gone up to the café, trying not to show her concern to the others that Lex and Ryan had been gone such a long time. It didn't look good, but she had to stay in control. 'Salene, get the kids somewhere safe. Hide them. And don't come out whatever happens.'

Salene had a worried look on her pretty young face. 'Okay.'

Zandra was hovering at the entrance to the café, uncertainly. With disheveled hair and makeup smudged over her cheeks she knew she looked a mess, but that was the least of her worries at the moment. She felt like an interloper. She was Lex's girl and he hadn't made any friends in the mall. 'What about me?' she asked timidly.

Amber had forgotten she was there. 'You help her. Zandra, isn't it?'

The young girl smiled, gratefully. 'Yeah.'

Satisfied, Amber started back down the stairs where Dal and Jack were waiting anxiously by the sewer door. They had replaced the cricket bats with any weapon they could find, chair legs, metal rods, anything that would do some damage if the Locos broke in.

Amber looked at the two slight boys gazing at the door, gripping their weapons tightly. Inwardly she sighed. They were brave, but they were no match for Locos. She picked up a heavy chair leg and joined them. Her heart was pounding, her mouth felt dry.

ooo

They had been waiting for what seemed like hours but it might only have been minutes. Over the past terrible weeks, they had all learned that fear had a way of distorting time.

Jack was the first to voice their anxiety. 'They've been gone a long time, haven't they?'

'You should have secured the entrance, Jack. You've been here long enough. What were you thinking?'

'Hey, cut it out, Dal! I was busy doing other things!'

'Stop arguing, you two!' Amber snapped. 'And listen!'

For a moment there was silence, then they all heard it. The footsteps again.

'Do you think it's them? Lex and Ryan?' Jack asked.

He had brought another torch from his workkshop. Amber took it from him. 'Only one way to find out.'

Flicking on the torch, she raised the chair leg and led the way inside the sewer with Dal and Jack following close behind. They moved cautiously along the tunnel. The footsteps were coming towards them now. They stopped in alarm as a tall figure rounded the corner. Amber shone the torch at the intruder. Caught in the light, the handsome face smiled.

'It's alright,' he said. 'Put down your weapons. I'm a friend.'

THIRTY FOUR

In the rail yard, the Locos were gathered around the police car, which had arrived towing a large open trailer piled high with books. Hidden behind a carriage, unable to escape without being seen, Lex and Ryan watched the Locos with puzzled expressions.

Lex looked at Ryan in disbelief. 'Zoot's setting up a library?'

His question was soon answered. Zoot stepped from the back of the police car onto the trailer, standing on top of the books. Bending down he picked up a book at random and read the title out loud derisorily. 'Alice in Wonderland!'

He tossed the book onto the ground behind the trailer, and leaned over to pick up another. 'The Great Gatsby!' Zoot called out. That book was tossed after the first one. He continued picking up books reading the titles and tossing them casually onto a growing pile on the ground.

'The Complete Works of Shakespeare! Origin of Species by Charles Darwin! The Odyssey! Harry Potter!'

He stopped and looked down at the jumbled pile of books on the ground. Then he turned to the waiting Locos and raised his arms skywards. 'No more school! No more teachers! No more books! Burn the books!'

Standing beside the trailer Ebony led the chant. 'Burn the books! Burn the books! Burn the books!'

As the chant was taken up by the Locos, one youth poured liquid from a can onto the piled books. A flaming torch was handed up to Zoot. 'Power and Chaos!' he yelled. 'Burn the books!'

He tossed the blazing torch onto the pile which burst into flames with a roar. The chant went on as the Locos emptied the trailer, throwing its contents onto the flaming pile.

'Burn the books! Burn the books! Burn the books!'

Zoot stood, arms raised in the Power and Chaos salute, roaring at the top of his voice like a wild animal.

Ryan looked at Lex, grimly. A shiver ran down his spine.

THIRTY FIVE

Dusk was settling on the city like a shroud over a corpse. The sounds that had been drifting on the air throughout the day were beginning to peter out as the light drained from the sky. Night was not a time to be out and about on the streets. The night-time city centre revelers had long since gone, along with the bars, clubs and discos that had once provided their entertainment.

Trudy had been too young to join in the bustle of the city's nightlife. Some of her friends had been allowed to, or had sneaked out when their parents weren't around, but she had never had the nerve to do anything as daring as that. Her parents had kept her close at home, conscious of the dangers that cities could pose for young, innocent girls like their precious daughter. Now she would never have the chance, and that thought made her cry.

She had been waiting all day for Bray to return, starting with fear at every sound. The deserted tunnel magnified each noise from outside, and she had been on the edge of screaming for hours. Finally, worn out with fear and anxiety, she had cried herself to sleep in her little snug hideout. When she awoke, stiff and cold from the chilly evening air, it was dark. And there was still no sign of Bray.

The tears began again softly, her body trembling with grief. If Bray wasn't back by now, she knew that he would never return. Something terrible had happened to him. He was either captured by one of the tribes, or dead. She couldn't bear to think about it.

She was on her own now. Of that she was certain. She had been hoping, praying, all day for his return, but now all hope had gone. She didn't know what to do. If she tried to return home, where she had always felt so safe, she may run into the Roosters, who Bray had said were combing the suburbs looking for loot and easy prey. The countryside to the West may be the safest place, but she doubted she had the courage to run the gauntlet of the tribes to try and reach its sanctuary.

Perhaps it was better to do nothing? The world outside the tunnel was too dangerous. Terrible things could happen to her out there. Things she couldn't even bear to frame into words in her head. She was safe here. She would stay and try to sleep. Sleep was best. She would stay here sleeping, until the end.

THIRTY SIX

'Do it again, Bray! Do it again!' Patsy squealed with delight.

They were all seated around the big table in the café, lit by candlelight. Bray smiled and put the two coins in the palm of each hand again.

'Okay. Now you see it.' He slapped his hands face down on the table. 'And now you don't'. He lifted his hands. The coins had vanished. Reaching up he produced a coin from behind Patsy's ear. She giggled. The others around the table smiled. Bray handed one coin to Patsy and the other to Paul. 'There you go. Don't spend them all at once.'

Amber looked across the table at Bray. He had startled her in the sewer tunnel, but he had more than made up for that since. In the light of the candles her eyes were glowing. She never believed she could ever feel this way, and certainly not in this new world of daily terror. Sure, she'd had crushes on boys before. But this was way different.

Bray reached behind Cloe's ear and produced another coin out of thin air. He handed it to Cloe, and took a little bow as everyone around the table clapped.

'I thought I told you to put a guard on the sewer!' Lex was striding up the stairs with Ryan close behind. Frustrated at having to wait for the burning of the books ceremony to end and the Locos to disperse before they could make their escape, Lex was tired, hungry and in a very bad mood. At the top the stairs he noticed Bray, and recognized him immediately.

'Who's this?'

Patsy jumped up excitedly, 'It's Bray! He does tricks!'

Lex walked around the table and eyeballed Bray with a mean and menacing look. 'Well, I don't like tricks, Bray.'

'Stop it, Lex! He just wants shelter.'

'Can't he speak for himself, Amber? Well, Bray, are you dumb?'

Bray leaned back coolly. 'I don't shout my mouth off. You call that dumb?'

Lex addressed the others round the table. 'This guy has been hanging around spying on us! That's his trick..! Ask him why he's been spying on us!'

'I told them,' Bray said calmly. 'I had to be sure it was safe.'

'Safe for what? So you and your tribe can muscle in!'

'I don't have a tribe.'

'Unlucky for you, 'cos we have!' Lex said fiercely.

'Lex, that's enough!'

'I haven't even started, Amber!'

Amber stood up. 'We told you when we let you out, our terms!'

Lex looked around and waved his arms in frustration. 'So this guy just turns up, spies on us and we welcome him with open arms! What if he's checking it out for the Locos?'

'I'm not.'

'Sez who!'

Salene turned on Lex. 'Bray does. And we believe him!'

'You can't be too sure though,' Dal said.

'He hasn't threatened us or tried to steal from us, Dal. Unlike some people,' Amber looked meaningfully at Lex.

'Look,' Bray went on. 'I don't want anything from you. Just shelter for the night. You might have noticed it's dangerous outside.'

'Which is why we shouldn't be taking in strays!'

'Does that mean you and your friends are leaving too, Lex?' Amber looked around at the others. 'We're all strays now.'

Lex folded his arms. 'Well, I say he goes!'

Unconsciously, Amber folded hers in response. 'Well, you're in a minority of one. We've already decided.'

'You're all fools!' Lex snarled and stormed away. He turned back at the top of the stairs. 'You'd better hope he doesn't strangle you all in your beds!'

THIRTY SEVEN

Fires were burning brightly around the perimeter of the rail yard, sending sparks dancing into the night sky. In the centre of the yard another larger fire was smoldering. Books took a long time to burn.

Zoot was walking around the acrid smoking pile, absorbed, prodding it to life with a pick-axe handle. He didn't want one page, one word, to survive. Ebony was seated on the edge of a carriage watching silently. As with royalty, you waited for Zoot to speak first.

He tossed the handle aside, came over to Ebony and placed both his palms on her warm, shapely thighs. He felt hot, not just from the fire. When things went well Zoot became aroused. She mentally prepared herself for a long night.

He looked deep into her eyes. 'It went well.'

'Very well.'

His next words shocked her. 'Can I trust you, Ebony?'

'Of course, Lord Zoot!'

'Forget the flattery. Can I trust you?'

'Why do you think you can't?'

'You're devious. Sly. Not like me. I say what I think.'

'That's your privilege.'

'Pretend you're the leader. Tell me what you think. Do you disapprove? Destroying the world's history? Its heritage. Seeing it, all that scholarship, that creativity, go up in flames? Tell me.'

Ebony shrugged. 'What's the point? You'll only think I'm saying what you want to hear.'

Zoot threw back his head and laughed. His coarse laughter rang out across the yard and into the city beyond. He picked her up roughly in his arms and strode off towards their carriage.

The books smoldered on into the night.

THIRTY EIGHT

Amber was awake well before the dawn. She lay staring at the dark ceiling, restless and disturbed by her feelings. She was being crazy, she knew. In this world there wasn't room for sentiment, for caring too much about someone else. Life was too precarious. Too unpredictable. You could get hurt. She didn't want to get hurt anymore.

The grief over her parents was still raw. She knew, despite her inner strength, it had left her vulnerable. Open to a friendly gesture. A handsome smiling face. A coin from behind the ear. She smiled at the memory. He seemed such a strong young man, but yet so gentle and caring. The kids had loved him, for giving them back their sense of fun. For a brief moment he had taken them out of the harsh world that had become their everyday existence. For existence was all it was. It was not living.

Maybe...Maybe if life was so precarious, so bleak, it made sense to make the most of it? To take what pleasure you could, when and wherever? To give what pleasure you had to give before it was too late? Before the opportunity had passed. Gone forever.

Her heart was thumping in her chest. Despite the cool night air, her whole body felt hot. She felt her cheeks, her brow. They were moist with perspiration. Silently she rose from her bed. She had chosen a room of her own away from Salene, the kids and the dog. She was so glad of that now.

She tiptoed out onto the landing, holding her breath. He had gone to bed in the store across the way, dragging a mattress from the furniture store, with her help. Their eyes had met as they made his bed together. Had she imagined what she saw in that moment? She knew she was vulnerable. Slightly crazy. But she didn't care. No one could blame her. In this world no one had a right to blame anymore. Much worse things were happening all around. And this was a good thing, wasn't it? Something positive, life affirming. Maybe a new beginning? Like the phoenix promised.

She paused at the entrance to the store and hugged herself for a moment, trying to stop the trembling. She didn't want to appear foolish and childish to him. The store had been a travel agent's and pictures of romantic places still hung on the walls. A Tuscan terrace at sunset, a Venetian gondola for two, Paris by moonlight. It was a perfect setting. She stepped inside. His mattress lay underneath a large photograph of a tropical beach. And it was empty.

ooo

Jack went straight to the food cupboard and opened the doors. 'There's some stuff missing!'

The rest were all up now, milling around, sleepy but agitated.

Amber looked into the cupboard, shaking. 'It's my food! He took my food!'

'It was all our food, Amber, remember?'

'That's not helping, Dal!' she snapped.

Lex was standing aloof in the café, arms folded, leaning against the wall. 'I told you! You're weak, all of you! Pathetic! You could have been murdered in your beds! And it would have served you right!'

'Just shut it, Lex!' Amber said furiously. 'You were supposed to be on guard, Jack!'

'No point taking it out on, Jack,' Dal said. 'We were wrong to believe him, that's all.'

'I didn't! Remember?' Lex said smugly. They had all played straight into his hands. He rounded on Amber. 'You were supposed to be in charge! Not anymore! You put us all in danger. Well I'm in charge now. No more of your do-gooding! Your saving stray dogs! Got us a long way, didn't it, Amber? Getting your knickers in a twist about lover boy!'

Amber rushed round the café at Lex in a rage, fists raised. Lex backed behind Ryan, mock-scared. 'Oh, Ryan, help me! She's going to tear me apart!'

Feeling completely foolish and humiliated, Amber suddenly dropped her fists and sank onto a chair, head down, holding back her tears.

Lex was reveling in the new situation. He wanted to rub it in, hard. 'I don't know how you lot have lasted this long. You've all had more luck than you deserve! My bet is Mr Wonderful will be back, only this time he'll come mob-handed!' He looked around at the others standing silent and subdued. 'Now, if you want me to protect you, you do as I say.'

They all looked at Amber, but she remained head down, silent, holding her fists to her mouth to stop the sobs.

THIRTY NINE

The acrid smell of burnt paper filled the air of the rail yard. Seated in his carriage at breakfast, Zoot breathed in deeply. 'Smell all that knowledge, Ebony! Didn't I tell you books stink?'

Ebony smiled indulgently and unwrapped the newspaper from around a large red apple.

Zoot raised an eyebrow. 'What's that?'

'An apple. They keep for ages if you store them right.'

'I meant, what would you want to eat an apple for?'

'They're good for you, Zoot.'

Zoot make a sound like a horse snorting. 'Good for you! Good for you!' he repeated mockingly. 'You're a Locust! Locos only eat stuff that is bad for you! All that crap, that junk food the food companies sold to the poor sods who didn't know any better! That garbage stuffed with additives and chemicals that made people fat and ill! That's Loco food!'

Ebony had heard this argument many times before. It was Zoot's idea of irony to embrace the throwaway junk culture that had wrecked so many people's health in the old world. It was like a challenge to him. 'Come on, do your worst, you blood-sucking vultures! You can't kill me!' he would say as he devoured another piece of junk that had no nutritional value whatever. Ebony wondered how he managed to keep so fit and healthy. She put it down to his manic will to survive and succeed.

A Loco had been hovering near the open door for some time. Zoot noticed him at last. 'Come in, Spike!'

Spike entered. He was a tall, unpleasant looking youth, with a long face and terrible acne. He could do with a few apples, Ebony thought.

'Well?'

'That thing you wanted, Lord Zoot?'

'Yeah?'

'It's ready, sir.'

Zoot's eyes lit up. 'It works?

'It's taken a while, Lord Zoot, but yeh, it works.'

'And nobody knows about it?'

'We haven't told anyone, Lord Zoot. No one knows anything.'

Zoot nodded his approval and waved Spike away. When they were alone again he smiled, an evil smile. 'So the Demon Dogs think they're top dogs, do they? Think they're going to take over the city? Well, we're going to show them who's really the boss. Power and Chaos.'

'Power and Chaos,' Ebony repeated.

FORTY

Later that morning Salene entered Amber's room. She had knocked but got no reply. Amber was lying on her bed, face turned firmly to the wall.

'Amber?' Salene said apologetically, sensing that Amber was hurting about being made a fool of by the stranger, Bray. She had been fooled too. He had seemed so genuine, so...Well, that didn't matter, now, she thought sadly. He was gone.

Amber shifted slightly, but didn't turn around.

'Amber, Lex is throwing his weight around...He's just sitting in the café telling people to get his breakfast, and ordering people about.'

There was still no response.

'Amber-'

'What do you expect me to do about it!' Amber snapped aggressively, still not turning to face her.

'I'm sorry, but he's scaring people.'

'He's a scary person, Salene!'

'You're not scared of him...We'll all help you...If you stand up to him...'

'I don't care, Salene! I don't care! Just leave me alone!'

Salene turned as a new sound rang out in the mall. It was the sound of the metal door of the sewer clanging open. Patsy screamed from the café. 'The Locos!'

Salene let out a gasp, scared. Amber leapt up and rushed past her towards the café.

Lex was already standing defiantly at the top of the staircase holding a cricket bat in both hands, with Ryan by his side. The rest were all gathering behind.

'Let 'em come!' Lex snarled.

They all watched in the semi-gloom, listening to the sound of footsteps approaching the stairs. Amber's eyes widened as Bray came into view, supporting a young teenage girl who was white as a sheet and looked very frail. Bray mounted the stairs and stopped, looking at the group gathered at the top. 'Everybody, this is Trudy.'

Trudy slumped down on a step, clearly exhausted. Her coat fell open revealing her swollen belly.

Patsy pointed. 'I know what that is! That's a baby!'

Bray nodded. 'That's right, Patsy. Trudy's having a baby and we need a safe place to stay.'

The group at the top, all holding makeshift weapons, looked at each other in surprise, waiting for someone to take the lead.

'Trudy needs somewhere to have the baby,' Bray continued. 'This is the safest place I've found.'

Lex took a pace down the stairs. 'No!'

Bray stared at him. 'And you speak for the whole group, do you?'

Before Lex could reply, Salene spoke up. 'No. Of course she can stay! She can stay, can't she, Amber?'

'I said 'no'!' Lex insisted.

Amber took a moment to find her voice. This was such a shock. Maybe more disappointing to her than Bray just going away. 'Does she want to stay?'

Despite, or maybe because of, her long, lonely ordeal waiting for Bray, Trudy had gained a new strength. A belligerence not usual in her. 'I've got a name!'

'Sorry. Do you want to stay, Trudy?'

Trudy bit her lip, suddenly close to tears again. 'Yes..Please.'

ooo

They found Trudy a seat in the café. There was no doubting how weak and fragile she was. Patsy had wanted to stay and listen, but Salene had sent the kids off to play, sensing the situation between Lex and Bray could get ugly. They had seen enough violence in their young lives already. The rest of the group stood or sat around. This was a new situation, and no one knew quite how to proceed.

Amber was very conscious of her acute embarrassment at seeing Bray again. She remembered standing at the door of his room, only hours before, about to give herself to him. Just the thought made the skin around her neck flush pink. Now he had appeared with his pregnant girlfriend. She didn't know whether she was pleased to see him again, or crushed that her little fantasy had faded away as quickly as the night. She tried to cover her discomfort by being businesslike.

'Did anyone see you come in?'

Bray looked at her and shook his head. 'No one sees me if I don't want them to.'

Lex was leaning back, arms tightly folded. 'The answer's still "no"!'

Jack spoke up. 'Hang on a minute! Don't I get a say? This is my place after all.'

Lex fixed him with a stare. 'Not anymore, nerd!'

Jack looked away, intimidated. Lex was the school bully he had always lived in fear of. Jack got up and mooched sulkily out of the café.

Salene looked at Lex. 'You can't just chuck her out like that!'

'Why not?'

'She's going to have a baby, Lex!'

Lex turned to Zandra. 'Who rattled your cage!'

'I just thought –'

'That's a novelty!'

Zandra stood up abruptly, and swept out, calling out after her, 'Ryan! Come with me!'

Ryan got up meekly and followed her out.

Lex looked at the remaining group. 'Are you all thick or something? We need people who are useful! I am, she's not!'

Bray bristled. 'You're very good at shooting your mouth off. What else do you do that makes you so special?'

'Want me to show you?'

'Try me.'

The air in the mall was thick with testosterone.

'Go ahead, guys!' Amber said angrily. 'Have a fight. Make a lot of noise. Get the Locos in here and let's all get caught!'

Salene turned to Trudy. 'You look half-starved. Come with me. I'll fix you something.'

Lex held up his hand. 'Hold on! We haven't said they can stay yet!'

Amber snapped. 'It's just a meal, Lex! Go on, Salene.'

Salene looked at Bray with a shy smile. 'Don't worry, I'll look after her.'

Bray smiled in return. 'Thanks.'

As Salene helped Trudy into the kitchen, Lex looked at them all with a hard expression. 'A meal! Then we get this thing settled!'

FORTY ONE

Dal had wandered out of the café unnoticed. Girls and babies weren't his thing. He had nothing against Trudy. In fact, despite her condition, she looked quite pretty. But he was sure the others would sort it out, one way or the other, and let him know what happened. If he'd had his way, he and Amber would be far away by now, making a new life in the countryside. It still irked him. The mall was no substitute.

The sound of static was coming from Jack's electrical store. Intrigued, he popped inside. Jack was crouched over a short wave radio set, with large headphones over his ears. After a moment he gave a huge sigh, took off the cans and said to himself. 'Maybe if I took it outside? On the roof.'

'Wouldn't make any difference.' Dal said.

Jack spun round, not having heard Dal come in.

'What?'

The radio's fine,' Dal went on. 'It's everything else that's wrong.'

'Very scientific!' Jack snapped, a little annoyed that someone had wandered into his den uninvited.

'There's no one out there, Jack. That's why you can't hear anything.'

'Don't be stupid! This radio can pick up signals from the whole world!'

Dal spread his hands in the air. 'That's what I mean. Remember the last few days? The virus was everywhere. Nowhere was safe. It spread too fast.'

Jack shuffled the headphones around on his desk, unconvinced.

'Think about it, Jack. There's no television. No internet. If there were any adults out there they'd be doing what you're doing, using the radio.'

Jack pulled a face. 'They can't all have gone! Not all of them.'

'Jack, we're on our own. There's no one out there.'

'There must be! I can't be the only one to get a radio to work!'

'And even if you do make contact, will you like what you find?'

Jack looked at him, puzzled. 'What do you mean?'

'That signal is an advert for where we are. All I've seen out there are madmen and crazies, but that doesn't mean they're stupid. If they pick up that signal they'll follow it straight here.'

With an exasperated grunt, Jack turned off the radio and stood up.

'Where're you going?'

'To get some peace,' Jack snapped. 'I wish I'd never let you guys in here!'

FORTY TWO

Salene was busy preparing a hot meal for Trudy, who was seated nearby at the kitchen table, looking tired and miserable. She felt so sorry for the young girl. What must it be like being pregnant, having a baby, with so much craziness all around? But she did have her boyfriend, Bray, Salene thought. That must be a big compensation.

From the moment she set eyes on him, Salene's pulse had been racing. She'd read about 'love at first sight', and even heard other girls at school say it had happened to them, but she'd put it down to silly girlish romantic talk. Girls were programmed that way she guessed, but Salene had always felt she was more of the mothering kind. Practical and caring. Until she saw Bray.

She turned the hot dogs over in the frying pan. The beans were already warming on the other ring.

'So when's the baby due?'

Trudy's reply was flat, drained of life. 'I don't know. Soon I think.' She has been ecstatic, almost disbelieving, when Bray had returned to her in the tunnel just before dawn, but that emotion had gone now. To be replaced by a fear of what was to come. Something she couldn't avoid. She was scared again.

'What do you want, a girl or a boy?' Salene asked brightly.

'A boy. Definitely a boy.'

Salene turned and smiled at her. 'Like his dad.'

Trudy looked away and was silent.

'He seems really nice. He's very good-looking, isn't he?' Salene had meant to keep her feelings a secret, but they were bubbling out despite herself.

'Yeah.'

'He's really taking care of you. That's lovely to see. Not many guys like that.' Shut up, Salene, she told herself! The poor girl's got enough problems without you trying to steal the father of her baby!

'Have you been here long?'

Salene could see Trudy was clearly reluctant to talk about Bray. Maybe she'd sensed her interest already? Girls had a natural instinct about that.

'Only a couple of days. Except Jack. He was here when we got here.' She smiled again. 'Thinks he owns the place.'

She put the plate on the table in front of Trudy, who looked at it with disgust. 'I'm sorry, I can't eat that!'

'Why not? It's good food.'

'I'm a vegetarian. I don't eat meat.'

Salene couldn't keep the mockery out of her voice. 'You don't believe in making it easy for yourself, do you? I eat anything I can get.'

Trudy burst into tears. Salene put her arm around her trembling shoulders. 'I'm sorry. I didn't mean –'

'I'm so scared!' Trudy sobbed. I don't know what to do! I've never had a baby before!'

'Don't worry. I'll help you. We all will.'

Trudy went on through her sobs. 'I thought I might find a doctor somewhere! Or a nurse or someone! But there's no one! Just kids!'

Salene stroked her shoulders. 'It'll be alright. Babies have been getting born for a long time now.'

Trudy looked at Salene, her eyes full of tears. 'Not in this world they haven't.'

FORTY THREE

One of the Demon Dogs the Locos had taken prisoner from the skirmish in the rail tunnel was too badly injured to be questioned. He would be left to fend for himself. Live or die, it was up to him. That was the Locos motto. Survival of the fittest.

The other one was tied to the central pole in the interrogation carriage. A tall, well built youth. Once a proud Demon Dog, now a young teenager with fear in his eyes. And with good reason.

In the old adult world torture had been commonplace in some countries, and even the more civilized societies often turned a blind eye if it suited their interests. But in this new world there was no hypocrisy about torture. There were no humane organisations protesting. There were no barriers. No rules. The only limits were the boundaries of the interrogator's imagination. And Zoot had a lot of imagination.

The inner core of the Locos, the squad leaders, were obliged to attend. Most of them did so willingly, but Ebony secretly hated these 'interrogation' sessions. They made her sick to her stomach. She wasn't against physical violence. She reveled in the hand to hand combat of the street fight. There was something almost erotic in the contact between body and body. But inflicting pain on a helpless victim wasn't her bag.

'It's for the greater good,' Zoot had tried to tell her. 'If your baby was kidnapped, and in danger, wouldn't you do all you could to save it?'

She didn't have any babies. Didn't want any. She could see Zoot's argument, but it didn't stop her stomach turning.

'Again!' commanded Zoot. The victim screamed out in agony again. His long, terrible cry carried for miles over the city.

There was a commotion as one of the watching Locos projectile-vomited over his companions.

'Get him out!' Zoot roared.

As the culprit was heaved unceremoniously out of the carriage, Zoot approached the helpless boy, hanging limply from the pole. He put his mouth close to the victim's ear and whispered. After a moment he put his ear to the boy's mouth, avoiding the drool dripping from the victim's chin. He listened. The boy's lips moved.

Zoot straightened up and smiled to Ebony. 'Deal with him.'

FORTY FOUR

Salene had taken Trudy for a nap. Lex had protested at first, but the poor girl was exhausted and even he could see there was no way he could kick her out if she couldn't walk. He waited impatiently with Amber and Bray in the café. Lex was glaring malevolently at Bray, biding his time.

Amber thoughts and feelings were still jumbled, but she needed to be practical. She looked at Bray who, despite his cool demeanor, she thought must be on edge. 'Are you sure Trudy wouldn't be better off somewhere else?' she asked kindly.

Lex grinned. 'I'll drink to that.'

'If there'd been a better place I'd have found it. The whole city is controlled by the tribes.'

She pressed on. 'Well, some of them are well organized. They have their own food stores, medical supplies. Wouldn't they be a better bet?'

'Sure they would. Right on, Amber!'

'Shut it, Lex!' Amber snapped.

Bray sighed wearily. 'There's a war for control going on. No one can be trusted. And a war zone's no place for a baby. I thought you lot looked different.'

'And that's why you've been watching us?

'Yeah. It's safer here. Everywhere else is just crazy. Locos and Demon Dogs. They'd use us for target practice.'

Lex stood up abruptly and stared at Bray. 'Well, look harder!' He walked arrogantly from the café, his boots ringing on the floor.

Bray looked across at Amber. She turned away, feeling her cheeks burning again.

'We're trying to make something work here,' she explained.

'We'?' he queried. 'Seems to me you're on your own.'

'It's not easy.'

'I can see that...' His voice was soft and kind. 'Maybe I could help?'

Amber turned to him, struggling to keep both her anger and disappointment in check. 'You? With a baby to look after? You're going to be a dad soon...Hadn't you better go and see how Trudy is?'

Bray looked as if he was about to say something, then changed his mind. He got up, sadly, and walked out.

Amber put a hand to her mouth, holding in her feelings.

FORTY FIVE

Looking behind him furtively, Jack slipped into the storeroom that had once been used by the mall cleaning staff. It was tucked away at the rear of the mall, a bare, unwelcoming little room that no one would want to spend any time in. Perfect.

He was still irritated by Dal's negativity about the radio, and the sudden unwelcome complication with Trudy and the baby. This was his place and he felt like he had been invaded. Taking a small key from his pocket, he unlocked a large metal cabinet which stretched from floor to ceiling. He opened the double doors and sighed with happiness, gazing at his treasure.

'Now, which?' he muttered to himself. 'Which do I deserve today? Peaches! That's it. Peaches!'

Picking a can off a shelf, he pulled the ring and popped the can open. He took a spoon from his pocket and began to eagerly devour the sweet fruit, not caring that the syrup was running down his chin. That was part of the fun. No one telling him to 'eat nicely'.

'I'm not having it,' he grumbled with his mouth full. 'This is my place. They stick by my rules, or they're out!'

Outside the door he heard a squeal. It was that silly little girl Patsy. That was another unwelcome problem. Kids!

'Stop it! Stop it!' Patsy squealed. Suddenly the door burst open and she rushed inside with Paul chasing her wearing a monster mask.

Patsy stopped, staring in surprise. Jack was standing rigid, spoon in one hand, the open can in the other. But that was not what Patsy was staring at. Her eyes were fixed on the cupboard behind Jack, which had every shelf crammed with food. Cans, packets, chocolate bars, water bottles and sweets! Sweets!

Paul pulled off his mask and signed excitedly to his sister.

Jack was frantically trying to think of an explanation. He stalled for time. 'Er, what's he saying?'

But Patsy wasn't listening. 'It's fantastic! All that food! Here all the time! We can have a party! Come on, Paul!'

'Where are you going?' Jack gasped.

'To tell Salene and Amber!'

'Hey, hey! No! This is mine!'

Patsy was puzzled. 'Yours?'

'Yeh. Mine.'

'But we're supposed to share. Amber said.'

'Well, Amber is welcome to share her stuff if she likes,' Jack said determinedly, 'but this stuff is mine, get it?'

Both twins were looking at him accusingly.

Jack pleaded. 'Look! I could last months on this! If I had to share it, it wouldn't last five minutes!'

Paul was signing again.

'What's he saying now?'

'L – E – X,' Patsy explained. 'Lex.'

'NO!' Jack was panicked. 'I don't want him in here!' Wearing a cheesy smile, he adopted a wheedling tone. 'You're not going to tell the others about this, are you? They don't need to know. This could be our little secret, couldn't it?'

Paul held out his hand. Patsy did the same. Jack grimaced. If only he had locked the door! He held out the opened can. 'Peaches?'

The twins stared, stony-faced, hands out.

Jack picked up another tin. 'Macaroni cheese?' There was no response. He looked to where their eyes were glued and sighed. 'Sweets.'

They nodded happily.

FORTY SIX

Amber was seated in the café, alone with her thoughts. Since early morning her emotions had been on a roller coaster ride. Everything had happened so quickly. Bray arriving like someone out of a dream, her instant passion for him, her crushing disappointment at his disappearance, and the equal disappointment at finding he had a girlfriend, who was about to have his baby.

She heard footsteps and looked up. It was Lex. The last person she wanted to see.

He sat down and put his feet up on the table. 'Where's lover boy?'

Amber gave him a surly look. 'Checking on Trudy.'

He sucked on his teeth, 'Pity he's already spoken for, isn't it?'

'What d'you mean?' she said guiltily.

'You fancy the pants off him, don't you?'

'Don't be a moron!'

'That's why you're so keen on him staying.'

Amber looked away. She wondered it if was that obvious? If Lex had seen it surely all the others had? Maybe he'd just made a lucky guess. Trying to stir up trouble as usual. She decided to go on the attack.

'Lex, this isn't about whether they go or stay! It's about how we make decisions. I'm not letting you bully or blackmail us just to get your own way. While I'm around this is going to be a democracy.'

'And what you say goes, does it? Some democracy!'

Amber stood up abruptly. She wanted to be anywhere Lex wasn't. He got up as well and blocked her way out of the café.

'I want to leave, Lex.'

Lex put on a misunderstood smile. 'I'm not attacking you, Amber. I think you and me could work together.' He put his hand on her arm. 'Matter of fact I think you and me could get on really well, if you know what I mean?'

She shoved his hand away. 'Back off, Lex!'

Lex shrugged. 'Your loss...I'm just trying to defend what we've got, Amber. You don't know anything about them. They turn up out of nowhere and you roll out the red carpet.'

'No decision's been made yet,'

His mood changed. His face became mean. 'You fancy him! And that's destroying your judgement!'

Amber had had enough. 'Let's get the others! This needs sorting! Right now!'

FORTY SEVEN

The warehouse in the railyard was closely guarded. Zoot had seen to that. All the guards, on a twenty-four hour watch, had been sworn to secrecy on pain of death. Even Ebony had been kept in the dark about its secret. And that annoyed her.

She had become aware that something was going on inside the warehouse a few weeks ago, but Zoot had said nothing, and ignored any hint of a question she had tried him with. She was intrigued and irritated, but she kept her mouth shut. She was Zoot's favourite, for the moment. But Zoot was erratic, unpredictable, his moods changing like the wind. She had learned to play him, up to a point, but she knew you never challenged his actions or his judgement.

It was only a short walk to the warehouse, but Zoot never walked anywhere. Leaders had to be above mere mortals. Wherever they went, they rode.

Zoot hadn't told her, yet, what secret the tortured prisoner had finally revealed to him. Whatever it was, she was convinced it was somehow linked to whatever the warehouse was concealing. But Ebony was relaxed. She was his lieutenant and he relied on her for her iron discipline and skill for organisation. She knew he would show her in his own good time. And the time was now.

During the short ride to the warehouse Zoot had been silent, with an air of eager anticipation about him. The driver stopped the police car beside the large double doors, and they got out.

Two guards were waiting by the doors. Zoot flicked his hand, the signal for the doors to be opened. As the guards slid the heavy metal doors back, the light flooded deep inside. Ebony gasped.

It was beautiful. Beautiful and deadly.

FORTY EIGHT

They had chosen the large space of the furniture store for the meeting. It was gloomier than the café, but more comfortable, having large roomy sofas and chairs that had somehow escaped the vandals. Zandra had been redesigning it with Ryan's help as their communal space, and she was very proud of her efforts. She may become an interior designer when the world got back to normal, she thought. That, or a beautician. Whichever, she had a flair.

She swept her arm grandly round the room as the others filed in. She and Ryan were seated on the largest sofa, reclining on a bed of scatter cushions. 'Welcome to our humble abode! Make yourselves at home. We've given the servants the night off, or it would have been cocktails in the conservatory.'

'Right, are we all here?'

'Cloe's missing, Amber. We haven't seen her all morning.'

'Okay, Pasty. We'll have to go on without her.' Cloe apparently had a habit of wandering off on her own and no doubt would wander back when she felt like it.

Ryan jumped up. 'I know what's missing!'

Amber called after him as he dashed out. 'Ryan! We're going to vote!'

'Forget about him!'

'He gets a vote, Lex!'

'He agrees with me,' said Lex smugly.

Bray appeared at the entrance of the store with Trudy on his arm. She was looking a little refreshed after her nap.

Lex pointed at them. 'They're not going to get a vote!'

Amber sighed. It was going to be a tough meeting. 'They're entitled to be here, Lex. It's their life we're voting on.'

'They don't get a vote!'

The argument was interrupted by Ryan, who hurried in carrying a large object which he placed in the middle of the coffee table opposite his sofa. He sat down again with a satisfied grin.

'There! That's better!'

Zandra looked at him witheringly. 'Ryan, it's a cardboard television!'

'Yeah, well, all the real ones were smashed up.'

Jack shook his head. 'Ryan, there's no electricity. The real ones wouldn't work anyway.'

'I know. I know. I'm not stupid,' Ryan said a little defensively. 'I just feel better with it there, that's all.'

'Can we get on now?'

Ryan settled back on the cushions. 'Sure, sure, go ahead, Amber!'

Amber waited until Bray had settled Trudy in an armchair and sat beside her on the arm, protectively, then she began. 'This is the problem. Not enough to eat. The more mouths there are, the more we have to feed. And if we let Trudy stay that's two more.'

'Three. Don't forget the brat!'

Trudy glared at Lex, who screwed up his face at her.

'There's still some cans in the café,' Salene was clearly on Bray and Trudy's side.

'And Paul and I have some sweets!' Jack shot Patsy a warning glance. She grinned back at him mockingly.

'Great! That should just about do us for a morning snack. Look, if we don't eat, we die!' Lex was glad Amber had started with the problem of food, not some wet stuff about responsibility and caring for each other.

'There's still food out there,' Dal said.

Lex gave him a sarcastic look. 'Yeah, there's plenty put there. But you can't just pop down to the supermarket and pop it in your shopping trolley, cretin!'

Dal pulled a face and looked down, intimidated.

'And it's not just about food,' Lex was warming to the argument. 'There's the baby. All that crying. You can never stop 'em! That'd put us all in danger!'

'Rubbish, you know nothing about babies!'

Lex gave Salene a hard look. 'Yeah? Well, don't come crying to me when the Locos come after you!'

Amber sensed the meeting was going to get out of hand. 'We know all the arguments. They're simple. We need to vote. We'll do it by a show of hands. One person one vote.'

Lex looked at her. 'What? The kids get to vote too!'

'They live here, Lex.'

'And the dog? Does it get a vote as well?'

Bray glared at Lex. 'They're letting you vote.'

'Wait a minute.' Lex pointed at Bray and Trudy. 'They don't get a vote!'

'Agreed,'

'Why not?' Bray looked at Amber, surprised.

'You and Trudy aren't part of the tribe yet,' she replied unhappily.

'And you might be a bit biased.' Lex added.

Bray flared at him. 'And you aren't?'

'So!' Amber wanted to cut it short before there was any violence. 'All those in favour of Trudy and Bray staying?'

Salene, Patsy and Paul shot up their hands. Slowly Zandra raised hers.

'Zandra, what are you doing? Put your hand down!'

'No, Lex, I won't! This is a democracy. I've got rights! And I like babies!'

'Dal?' Salene pleaded. 'You must be on our side!'

Dal looked apologetic. 'Sorry. I just think it's too risky. The more there are of us, the more chance of getting caught.'

'Okay, four' Amber said. 'All those against?'

Lex shot up his hand, closely followed by Ryan, Jack and Dal.

Zandra was disgusted. 'Wouldn't you know it? All the guys!'

'That's four all,' Jack said.

'Wait a minute.' Salene looked at Amber. 'Amber, you haven't voted.'

'I know.' Amber stared down at the floor. The rest waited expectantly. Finally she looked up and raised her hand. 'I'm... against.'

FORTY NINE

While Paul was chasing Patsy through the mall, Cloe had opened the metal door to the sewers to hide. She didn't want to play monsters anymore. Monsters were scary and she had been frightened enough already. Boys were silly. Noisy and rough.

But it was dark and scary too inside the sewer tunnel. She was about to go back into the mall when she heard a noise. She listened intently. The noise came again, echoing down the tunnel. It must be coming from outside. Cloe smiled. She knew what it was.

She rushed back inside the mall, straight to Jack's room. A torch was lying on the bench. Snatching it up, she ran back to the sewer door, breathlessly, and went inside. The torch lit up the slimy brick walls. She heard the trickling sound of water and the scurry of tiny feet running from the light. They must be rats. She wasn't scared of rats, they were just little animals. Animals weren't mean and nasty like people could be.

The sound came along the tunnel again. Carefully she picked her way along the narrow pathway. The tunnel turned at the end and in the distance she could see a faint light shining down onto a metal ladder leading to the outside.

She hurried to the ladder. The rungs were very far apart for her little legs, but she hauled herself up to the top, panting with the effort. The round lid of the sewer above her head was very heavy. She braced her feet on the ladder, put her back against the lid and pushed with all her might. The heavy metal manhole cover shifted slightly. Taking a deep breath she pushed again. The cover moved enough for her to squeeze her way out into the fresh air.

She stood up and looked around, blinking at the unaccustomed brightness of the daylight. And there it was, not far away. She smiled and called. 'Come here! Come here!

Startled by the sudden sound the little black and white calf loped away.

'No! Don't go!' Cloe cried. 'Don't go! I won't hurt you!' But the calf ran on. She took off after it excitedly. Heading towards the deadly city streets.

FIFTY

For a moment, after Amber cast her vote, there was a stunned silence in the room. Then Salene and Zandra both spoke at once.

'Amber!' Salene cried.

'I don't believe it!'

A broad grin spread over Lex's face. 'Neither do I.'

Bray and Trudy were both staring at Amber in shocked disbelief. Her face grew hot. As the leader she knew she had to justify her choice. But why had she voted for them to go? Was it common sense? A logical practical decision for the good of the tribe? Or was it just pure jealousy? Of not being able to stand the thought of living in the same space as Bray with his baby? Of seeing Trudy with him every day? In that moment she didn't know. She stumbled on, uncomfortably.

'Look, we're talking about a baby here. Not a dolly, Zandra! We're just a bunch of kids! Babies need looking after! They need feeding. We don't even know if we can feed ourselves..!' She tried to look at Bray, but couldn't. 'There must be somewhere else, Bray. Somewhere better...I'm sorry, Trudy.'

Trudy was staring at the floor, crestfallen.

Bray stood up, directing his anger straight at Amber. 'Keep your sympathy! And you know what you can do with your democracy!' He turned to face the others. 'What sort of people would turn away a pregnant girl? What kind of world are you planning? One with no babies in it..? Well, you won't last long, will you? You people make me sick! You're no better than the Locos! At least they don't pretend to be anything!'

112

He leant down and took Trudy's arm, gently. 'Come on, Trudy.'

The rest watched in embarassed silence as Bray helped Trudy out of the room. She looked frail and helpless, but she was bravely holding back her tears. She was not going to let them see her cry.

At the door Bray turned back, his face distorted with fury. 'And you can keep your food! I hope it chokes you!'

As the couple left Lex dropped onto the sofa, adjusted a cushion behind his head, and settled back with a smug look. No one else in the room could look anyone in the eye. They listened as Bray and Trudy's footsteps descended the staircase. Time seemed to stop. With the exception of Lex, they all wanted it to hurry up, to move on. For this awful moment to pass, so they could get on with their lives and let their mutual shame fade away.

Amber was about to call out. To say she had changed her mind. That she had made a bad mistake. But the words stuck in her throat.

Then a cry split the silence, echoing to the very top of the mall, making the hairs stand up on the back of their necks. A prolonged cry of pain. 'Aaahhh!'

Amber was the first out of the room, followed by Salene and Dal. Halfway down the stairs Trudy had collapsed, clasping her stomach in agony.

'Bray!' she gasped. 'It's coming! The baby's coming!'

FIFTY ONE

Cloe was distressed. She looked about her, lost. The calf had vanished among the deserted alleys of the city and she was suddenly aware that she shouldn't be out there on her own. While she was running after the calf she had lost all sense of danger. But now, all alone, she was suddenly very frightened. She knew she should try to find her way back to the mall, but she didn't want to leave the poor animal outside all alone. It was dangerous. There were bad gangs roaming the city. If they found it, they would kill it and eat it. It was only a baby. She had to find it before they did.

She became aware of strange sounds at a distance. She couldn't tell what they were, or from what direction they were coming, but they sounded harsh and threatening. Despite the warm sunlight falling on her shoulders, she felt cold.

'Oh, please! Please come back!' Her plaintive cry was lost among the tall brooding buildings. 'I won't hurt you! I want to help you! I want to help you find your mummy!'

Hearing a noise she spun around. The calf was standing at the top of an alley, looking at her with sad brown eyes. It was tiny. Hardly a few days old, it seemed.

Moving very slowly, taking tiny steps, she moved towards it, calling softly. 'That's a good girl. I won't hurt you. I promise. I want to help.'

The calf stood still watching her uncertainly. She was getting closer, but at any moment it might break away and run. A thin rope hung around its neck. If she could just reach it.

She knelt down and stretched out her hand. 'Come on. Please!'

The calf took a step towards her. She tried to contain her excitement. 'That's it. Come here, that's a good girl.' Very slowly the calf made its way towards her. It stopped just out of reach. If she lunged for the rope and missed she knew she would never get the chance again. The calf would be gone forever. She waited, holding her breath.

Suddenly the calf looked up, startled. She had been so absorbed trying to catch it, that she had forgotten about the strange, menacing sound she had heard at a distance. But now it was upon her. Deafening and terrifying. The ground began to shake beneath her feet.

She leaped forward, snatched the rope, and hung on grimly as the calf bolted away. As the calf dragged her around the corner, she glanced back and caught a glimpse of it. The monster rumbling into the street.

FIFTY TWO

They were all standing at the top of the stairs looking down at Trudy moaning in pain and fear. 'It's coming, Bray!' she cried tearfully. 'The baby's coming!'

Lex arrived behind them, scowling. 'What's going on now!'

Salene turned to him. 'Trudy's going into labour! The baby's coming!'

'It's a trick!' Lex snapped.

As Bray helped Trudy stand and walked her slowly back up the staircase, Lex stepped forward. 'Where do you think you're going?'

Bray looked at him grimly. 'Trudy's not leaving! Not now!'

'We voted you out! I'm not having this!'

'You've no choice!' Both youths were eyeball to eyeball.

Salene looked at Amber, pleadingly. 'Amber, we can't throw her out now!'

'Suppose it's true, Lex?'

'Butt out, Zandra! I don't buy it!'

Trudy was clinging onto the rail, groaning in agony. Salene went to her. 'Trudy! Are you sure?'

'Listen to them!' Lex snarled. 'It's a put up job! They're in it together!'

Bray suddenly lunged forward and grabbed Lex by the throat. Lex grabbed Bray's arms and they grappled fiercely on the stairs. Amber lunged in between them. 'Stop it! Both of you! Fighting won't solve anything!'

Trudy moaned again and cried out. 'My water's have broken!'

Salen looked down at the stairs. They were wet. 'It's coming, alright!'

Amber took hold of Trudy's arm. 'Help me, Salene.'

'You're letting them back in!'

'We're not throwing her out now, Lex!' Amber replied fiercely. As she helped Trudy back up the stairs, she felt a flood of relief wash over her. She had wanted to change her vote, but hadn't had the courage. A leader had to be decisive. Confident. To give the rest reassurance. It would have looked weak if she had changed her mind so quickly...Now she'd been thrown a lifeline. She hoped she could make better use of it from now on.

FIFTY THREE

Somehow, through the maze of alleys and unfamiliar streets, Cloe had found her way back to the mall. Maybe it was the calf, returning by instinct to the only patch of grass in the area, which had once been packed with city workers having lunch in the sunshine. Cloe stroked the calf as it munched contentedly.

'That's it. Eat up, Bluebell. Good girl.' She had named the calf after a cow she had read about in a storybook. She liked that story, which her dad used to read to her at bedtime. She wished she still had the book.

She knew she had been gone a long time and wondered if the others were worried about her? They probably were, and perhaps had sent out a search party to look for her? She should get back before they found her and her new pet.

'Come on, Bluebell. You can't stay here. It's too dangerous. I know a place you can stay. I can't take you into the mall. Lex might want to eat you. But don't worry, I'll look after you until we can find your mummy.'

Gently she coaxed the calf away from the grass towards the deserted car park adjacent to the mall. There was nothing there for anyone. No one would find it there.

As she tied it up to a railing out of sight from the street, she remembered the monster and shuddered. She would have to warn the others.

FIFTY FOUR

While Lex sat fuming alone in the café, convinced it was all a trick, the others had gone with Trudy, who had been taken to an empty store where a bed was being been made up for her. When it was finished Trudy sat down on the bed gratefully. Bray sat beside her, with the others looking on.

Amber felt that before the situation overwhelmed them, it was time to take control. 'Alright, everybody. Show's over. Everybody out! Make yourself useful. We need towels and hot water.'

The others trooped out leaving Amber with Salene and Zandra.

'You too, Bray.'

'No, Amber!' There was panic in Trudy's voice. 'Don't go, Bray!

He patted her hand. 'Don't worry, Trudy. I'm here.'

Amber and the other two girls exchanged glances.

'Does anyone know anything about delivering babies? Salene?'

'Not really, Amber.'

'Zandra?'

'Me? You're joking!'

Trudy lay back on the bed. Bray held her hand reassuringly. 'How long have you been having the contractions, Trudy?'

'Feels like hours.'

Bray looked up at the girls. 'We may not have very long. We should get ready.'

Amber dared to look at him for the first time since she had voted them out. He looked calm and assured, in control. Despite everything, the whole messy situation, she was glad he was still here. 'What do we do?'

He seemed unruffled. 'We're gonna need scissors and rubber bands to tie the cord. Tissues, and soap.'

Amber frowned, questioning. 'You mean...You?'

Bray looked at her evenly. 'Any objections?'

'But...Have you...?'

Bray smiled. 'I'm not a gyneacologist, if that's what you mean.'

She shrugged. 'You heard the man,' she said decisively. 'Who's got soap?'

'Zandra, you've got lots.'

'That's my special soap, Salene!'

Amber sighed. 'Zandra, go get the soap!'

With an exasperated gasp, Zandra flounced out. Amber looked at Bray again. He grinned. She smiled back, shyly, still acutely embarrassed at having voted to throw them out. It was going to be tough if they were now going to stay, but she guessed she was just going to have to live with it.

FIFTY FIVE

The cathedral had stood for over seven hundred years. Its elegant medieval spire had once dominated the landscape around, but it had long since been dwarfed and engulfed by the towering office blocks surrounding it.

Through the centuries it had welcomed many congregations, but it had never seen such a gathering as was crowded into its nave that afternoon. A crowd of youngsters, ranging from eight to eighteen, dressed in the bizarre eclectic costumes of their chosen tribes, were excitedly chatting amongst themselves. They had come from all over city at the request of the Demon Dogs.

The meeting was unprecedented. Its location kept a secret until the very last minute. The only tribe conspicuous by their absence were the Locos. The Locos had not been invited. For the purpose of the meeting was to bring them down.

The crowd gradually fell silent as the leader of the Demon Dogs, Silver Demon, stood up in front of the altar and raised his hands. A shaft of sunlight shone through the magnificent East window, the rays from its stain-glass transforming his silver-painted face and uniform into a myriad of muted colours. Not having Zoot's gift as an orator, he got straight to the point.

'Fellow tribes! Welcome! You all know me. You all know why we are here today! Zoot and his Locos are getting too big for their boots!'

Enthusiastic cheers greeted his statement. They all knew that Zoot had ambitions to take over the city. All of them had suffered Loco raids on their food and supplies stores. Their fellow tribesmen had been taken prisoner by marauding snatch gangs wearing the distinctive Loco emblem. They were all agreed that it was time to call a halt to Zoot's megalomania.

Silver Demon stood, hands raised. Then, as the nave fell quiet they all heard it. A deep rumbling that began to shake the ground beneath their feet. Shouts of alarm echoed through the vast space. An earthquake?

The rumbling grew louder. Panic began to spread among the crowded nave as the building around them began to tremble. Silver Demon spun around, just in time to see the stain-glass window shatter into a thousand pieces as the East wall of the cathedral exploded inwards sending stone, plaster and slabs of masonry flying amongst the scattering tribes. The noise increased ten-fold as, through the newly-made hole, there came a huge tank, rearing up over the rubble, crushing Silver Demon beneath its tracks.

Far from being camouflaged, the tank was garishly painted bright red, and covered in Loco graffiti. Fearsome eyes were painted either side of the gun turret, and below the evil-looking spout was a Jaws-style gaping mouth full of menacing teeth.

FIFTY SIX

Trudy's cries of pain echoed through the mall. Ryan, Jack, and the kids were sat at the top of the stairs, not wanting to wait in the café where Lex was sitting, snapping at anyone who came near.

'Two to one it's a girl,' said Ryan. 'Come on, that's good odds.'

'What do we use for money?' Jack asked.

Amber appeared from Trudy's room busily. 'Ryan, did you get those rubber bands?'

'Couldn't find any, Amber.'

'Well, find some string or something. Don't just sit there. Improvise.'

Ryan frowned at the unfamiliar word, but he got up to go and 'improvise' nonetheless.

Dal arrived holding a bowl. 'Got the hot water, Amber.'

'Thanks, Dal,' she said gratefully. 'Take it inside. Patsy, Paul, see if you can find some rags, sheets, anything as long as its clean…Where have you been, Cloe?'

Cloe was coming quietly up the stairs. 'Nowhere', she said guiltily.

'Ask a silly question,' Jack said.

As Dal came out of the room again Amber handed him a scrap of paper. 'Dal, can you find these? It's stuff for the baby.'

Dal read the list. 'I might have to go outside.'

Amber looked at him. "Is that okay?'

Dal shrugged. 'I guess.'

Amber put a hand on his arm. 'Well, be careful.'

Dal smiled and headed off. Amber watched him go, concerned. Trudy's scream rang out again. She hurried back inside.

In the café, sitting all alone, Lex waited impatiently, brooding, biding his time.

FIFTY SEVEN

There was pandemonium in the shattered cathedral. Screams and cries echoed around the towering stone columns and out into the bright sunlit air, as the gathered children tried to escape the death and destruction inside.

Crunching over the rubble in the centre of the nave the bizarrely painted tank spat flame. The huge West window, famed throughout the world for its unique beauty, exploded in a fountain of tiny coloured fragments which rained down like jewels on the kids racing away outside.

As the tank burst out from the front of the old cathedral, the West wall collapsed behind it, raining hellish stone gargoyles down onto the mayhem below. Terrified kids ran in all directions, to be met by Locos emerging from hideouts, led by Ebony, wielding clubs and improvised weapons.

The battle was short-lived. In deep shock, reeling in confusion, the bulk of the tribes raced away as quickly as they could. After the surprise of the attack there was no stomach for a fight.

The tank came to a halt in the square at the front of the ruined cathedral. The top hatch opened and Zoot emerged triumphantly. Standing on top of the tank he raised his arms in salute. 'Power and Chaos!' The Locos echoed the salute and his cry.

Out of the corner of her eye Ebony caught a swift movement. She yelled out a warning. 'Zoot!'

A lone Demon Dog, appearing from out of nowhere, leapt onto the tank holding a Molotov cocktail. Zoot wheeled round to confront him, but the lone attacker hurled the flaming bottle into the open hatch. The inside of the tank exploded in a vivid flash of orange flame which hurled Zoot and the Demon Dog into the air and smashing onto the ground.

Ebony raced to Zoot. He lay twisted and still.

FIFTY EIGHT

Bored with sitting alone in the café, Lex was kicking a ball against the wall on the ground floor. He was angry. Trudy was still crying and moaning upstairs. So it wasn't a trick. It was for real, but that didn't make him any less annoyed.

He didn't want another male in the mall. Not one like Bray who wasn't frightened of bullies. He'd met them at school. The big, goody-two-shoes kid that you couldn't boss around and who you didn't want to take on in case you got beat. Once you got beat your reputation was zero.

He lashed the ball angrily at the statue of the big stupid bird. It rebounded straight at Zandra who was coming down the stairs.

'Hey!'

'Sorry, Zan!'

'You should watch what you're doing!'

Lex grinned. 'I'd rather watch you...Come to keep me company?'

'I've come for an aspirin. I know you had some. Have you got any left?'

'You don't need an aspirin. I'll give you a neck rub. That always works. Relieves the tension.'

Zandra sighed exasperated. The subject was always the same with Lex. 'It's for Trudy.'

Again the lascivious grin. 'What'll you give me for it?'

'Lex!'

Lex threw up his arms. 'I'm getting desperate, Zan! Even Ryan's starting to look sexy!'

It was Zandra's turn to grin. 'I'd go for him if I were you.'

Lex put on his hurt little boy expression. It generally worked. 'What's wrong? Don't you fancy me anymore?'

'That's beside the point, Lex,' she replied enigmatically. 'I know guys like you. After they get what they want, they split.'

'Not me, Zan. I've fancied you forever. I didn't say before 'cos I thought you were hot for Glen, but...'

'I know where I've been, Lex. I can't say the same for you.'

Lex spread his arms again. 'I'm clean. Clean as a whistle. You better grab me, babe, before one of the others do.' He reached in his pocket and tossed an aspirin packet to her. 'See? I'm all heart.'

'Whatever. Thanks.'

Lex watched admiringly as Zandra ran back upstairs. Trudy's scream echoed through the air again. His admiring gaze turned to an ugly scowl.

FIFTY NINE

Zoot lay on his bed in the rail carriage as Ebony pressed a damp cloth to his forehead. They had ferried him in the police car from the scene of devastation at the cathedral and he had only recovered consciousness a few minutes ago.

'You had me worried. I thought you were toast.'

His eyes moved to look at her. His neck hurt too much to move. 'Would that have upset you?'

Ebony stood back and looked at him in surprise. 'Of course! What d'you mean? Of course I was worried about you!'

Zoot's smile was half-ironic. 'Would have left the way open for you though, wouldn't it?'

Ebony laughed. 'Me? I don't want to be leader, Zoot! I couldn't do what you do. No way.'

She wet the cloth again and pressed it to his brow. He took hold of her wrist and stared deep into her eyes. She stared back. Looking away would have looked guilty. Like she had something to hide.

He held the moment. She could feel the tension rising in his body. He smiled. 'Fear is erotic, isn't it?'

'I'm not afraid.' She slid her hand down his body, surprised at his powers of recovery, and his sensual appetite. Maybe his sense of power was an aphrodiasiac to himself?

There was a sound at the door. Someone coughed. Ebony took her hand away and they both looked up. Spike was there, looking unhappy. The bearer of bad news.

Zoot pushed Ebony away. 'Well?'

Spike shrugged. 'I'm sorry, Lord Zoot. It's had it. Totalled. The whole inside's a mess. Couldn't repair it even if we had the parts.'

A dark look of anger flashed over Zoot's face. Snatching up the bowl Ebony was using he hurled it at the doorway. Spike ducked as the bowl shattered against the metal frame.

'They're going to pay!' Zoot yelled. 'They're going to pay!'

Ebony looked away. Keeping her thoughts to herself.

SIXTY

Trudy was exhausted and tearful. She had been in labour for what seemed like hours, and at that moment she didn't care whether she lived or died. Anything to stop the agony. 'It's no good!' she cried to Bray, who was sitting beside her, holding her hand.

Bray wiped the sweat from her brow. 'You're doing fine, Trudy. Take a break and relax.' He smiled at her, hiding the deep concern he was feeling inside. He wasn't certain how much more Trudy could take. He hadn't realised before what an ordeal giving birth was. No wonder they called it 'labour'.

Amber and Salene were watching out of earshot. Neither had ever been at a labour before. They had seen baby's born on the television, but never had witnessed the real thing close at hand. It was both awe-inspiring and terrifying. The two girls were privately wondering if they ever wanted to go through such hell.

Salene looked at Amber, concerned. 'You don't think there's anything wrong, do you?'

Amber didn't know, but there was no point in meeting trouble before it arrived. 'She's just exhausted, that's all.'

Patsy and Paul rushed into the room carrying some colourful material, which Patsy handed to Amber brightly. 'You could tear this up!'

Amber held it. It was a designer dress. 'You little devils! That's Zandra's! Is this all you could find?'

Patsy grinned and nodded, patting Bob the dog.

Bray looked up and frowned. 'Get that dog out of here!'

'Sorry,' Patsy and Paul fled.

'Where are the scissors?' Bray asked. 'They need to be sterilized.'

'I'll get right onto it,' said Amber. 'How's she doing..?'

Bray looked at her blankly. It was a needless question. Things didn't look good but they would all just have to wait. Wait and hope.

SIXTY ONE

It was a hopeless task. Every pharmacy and baby shop in the sector had been stripped bare. Dal could understand the drugs being looted, but who would take stuff for a baby? But, then again, the virus had spared babies as well as older kids, and someone had to look after them, didn't they?

Dal daren't venture too far. The adjacent sectors of the city were more crowded than Sector 10 and they were too lawless and dangerous to risk roaming around looking for nappies. He decided he had better head back to the mall with the bad news.

As he turned the corner and saw them. A pack of Locos blading along the street towards him. Dal had heard about the snatch parties. Small fast groups that fastened onto one poor stray and pursued them til they caught them and took them back to their tribe as slaves.

At that moment one of them spotted him and pointed. 'Get him!'

Spinning round on his skates Dal took off with the Locos speeding after him, baying like a pack of wolves.

He didn't really know the area. He only knew his way back to the mall. But he didn't want to head there and take the Locos straight back to his friends. If he was going to get caught, he wanted it to be as far away from the mall as possible.

The Locos were gaining on him. They were taller and faster. He knew he hadn't a prayer of outrunning them. Hiding was his only chance. He looked around for an escape and sped down a narrow alley, praying that it wasn't a dead end.

The alley opened onto a large, smoke-filled courtyard with several short alleys leading off. For a second he was out of sight of his pursuers. Which alley to chose?

At the rear of the courtyard stood a large metal industrial container, brimming with smoking rubbish which was filling the yard with a thin blue haze. The container's sides were taller than he was and he cursed himself for being so small. It was too tall for him to climb into, but it was his only chance. Blading towards it at full speed he timed his leap and launched himself into the air, arms flailing like a long-jumper to try to gain height. His body crashed against the rim of the metal skip, but with a superhuman effort he somehow managed to hurl himself inside, crashing onto the hot debris below. He lay panting and winded. Waiting, trying to hold his breath.

If they looked in the skip he was a goner. He was banking they had seen how small he was and would figure he could never have got inside. It was a big gamble, but it had to work.

He heard the hiss of the blades as the Locos entered the courtyard. The noise stopped for a second and then he heard the command, 'Split up!'

He listened as the blades swished away down the alleys.

SIXTY TWO

'Okay, Trudy? Ready for another go?' Bray was trying to keep his voice calm and reassuring, but inside he was growing more and more concerned.

He'd heard that it was normal for some labours to last for many hours, but this situation was very different. There were no trained doctors or nurses, no gas or air, or any of the other modern medical aids that helped mothers through the experience. Trudy was tired and weak long before the labour started. She hadn't had the pre-natal exercises, or a decent diet that normal mothers-to-be had in the past. And Trudy had endured weeks of stress and anxiety about her own safety. He knew that years ago it was common for women to die in childbirth. Trudy must be a prime candidate.

'I can't,' Trudy pleaded. 'I can't push anymore!'

Bray knew he had to be tough. 'You can, Trudy! You can. Come on now. Just one really big push. Ready?'

Trudy took a deep breath and gathered herself, tears streaming down her cheeks.

'Push!'

With a prolonged agonizing yell of pain Trudy pushed again. The cry went on and on, reverberating through the mall. Jack and Ryan, waiting outside with the little kids, covered their ears in alarm.

'I saw some kittens being born once,' said Cloe. 'It was magic!'

Patsy grimaced. 'Doesn't sound like magic to me!'

Inside the room Zandra put her hand to her mouth. 'I can't bear to watch!' she gasped, and rushed outside.

Amber stared at the amazing sight. 'The head's coming! The head's coming!'

Trudy held out her hand to Amber, her face contorted in pain. Amber grasped her hand firmly and smiled encouragement, though Trudy's grip was almost crushing her fingers. 'Push, Trudy! Push!'

Bray pulled firmly on the bloodied, slippery head and suddenly it was all over. The baby girl slipped out into Bray's waiting hands.

ooo

It had been a long day for everyone. For Bray, for Amber, for all the rest. And it had been the longest day for Trudy. But it was all over now.

She lay exhausted but relaxed in her bed holding the sleeping baby in her arms. Bray was sitting beside her smiling, glad that Trudy would never know how worried he'd been about her.

Amber came in, a little hesitantly. 'Well, Trudy, are you ready for the rabble?'

Trudy looked up at Bray, then smiled and nodded.

Popping her head out the door Amber said, 'Okay, you can come in now. But be quiet.'

The others trooped in, shy and eager, Cloe leading the way. She held out a mobile, made from string and odds and ends she had found lying around. 'It's a mobile. For the baby. They like to look at them.'

Trudy smiled gratefully. 'Thank you, Cloe. That's lovely.'

'I knew it was gonna be a girl,' Ryan said, putting the whistle that he had won from Jack in the bet onto the bed.

Patsy was next, placing a small pile of sweets on the duvet beside the whistle.

'Can I hold her?' Zandra said eagerly. Trudy smiled and let Zandra take the baby out of her arms.

Jack entered carrying baby scales.

'This is my present,' Salene said. 'Thanks, Jack.'

Patsy looked puzzled. 'What do you want scales for?'

'So you can see if it's putting on weight,' Zandra explained importantly.

'What's it going to eat?' asked Cloe.

'Milk for a start,' said Salene.

Patsy was wide-eyed. 'What, breast-feeding?' She signed to Paul and the twins giggled.

Salene went on, 'Then after a few months you wean it onto solid food.'

Ryan grinned. 'I hope it likes beans!'

Dal arrived as they were all laughing.

'Dal!' Amber cried, relieved to see her best friend back safely in the mall.

'What's the joke?' he asked.

'The baby's arrived!' Patsy said excitedly. 'Look!'

'Wonderful!' he said with a broad grin. 'Well done, Trudy.' He held out a large wicker basket. 'I thought this would do for a cot.'

Zandra was dismissive. 'There's plenty of cots in the baby store. The looters didn't want them.'

Dal looked a little put out. 'Yeh, but I thought...'

'It's a very nice thought, Dal,' Trudy said warmly.

'Did you make it, Dal?'

'Yeah, Patsy, I've just finished weaving it.'

'Where did you get it?' Jack asked.

'It was knocking around in a skip,' Dal said casually. He looked at Amber. 'I'm sorry, Amber, I couldn't get the baby things you wanted.'

'Not to worry, Dal,' she smiled. 'We'll manage. At least you're back safe.'

Bray arranged a blanket in the basket. Salene took the baby and placed it inside. They all looked on at the sleeping child with a sense of reverence. It seemed like a very special moment for them all. The first baby born into their new tribe. A real live symbol of hope.

SIXTY THREE

Night was drawing in over the city. The sounds of the day, cries of laughter or despair, had faded away. There was no traffic. Not even the sound of Zoot's police car siren. Most of the fuel was now gone, wasted in an orgy of car chases in the first few weeks after the adult world died. It was predictable. At that time the kids all thought that they would be the next, so they played as hard as they could. Live now, pay later.

Bray slipped silently along the streets, keeping to the shadows. Hardly anyone came out into the city at night, but the moon was bright and he didn't want to take any chances.

Being all alone after the last few intense days of argument and drama in the mall felt blissful. Like floating on calm water. In the still moonlit air it was almost as if the virus had never happened.

After the long and harrowing ordeal helping to delivery the baby, he was tired, but he was very relieved, and happy to be out in the cool night. He breathed deeply. Such a contrast to the claustrophobic stuffy air of the mall. He couldn't quite believe it, but even in this crazy, screwed-up world, he actually did feel happy. He had delivered the baby. And he'd fulfilled his promise as he said he would. He had found a safe place for Trudy and the baby. Suddenly he felt a burden lift from his shoulders. He felt free.

SIXTY FOUR

Lex was tucking into a heaped plate of food, with Zandra sitting beside him talking excitedly.

'It was amazing, Lex. And the baby –'

'I'm not interested!' Lex tried to snap, but it was difficult with his mouth full.

'It's got hair and everything,' Dal said.

'And it's a great weight!' Jack said proudly, having found the scales tucked away in the baby store.

Lex looked at him sarcastically. 'Sounds like it will have a good appetite then.'

Amber stared at Lex's plate. 'Looks like it's not the only one. You've got enough on that plate for a week, Lex.'

Lex stuffed another heaped forkful into his mouth, ignoring her.

'This can't go on. We've got to set up some system of rationing.'

Ryan looked at Amber concerned. 'Rationing?' Food was the only thing that mattered these days. That was a priority. Making sure you had enough.

'Yes, Ryan. We can't afford to waste anything.'

Lex watched Patsy feeding a biscuit to Bob, the dog. 'Well, you can stop feeding that thing for a start. Unless you're fattening him up for later.'

Patsy patted the dog's head. 'It's alright, Bob, he doesn't mean it.'

'Oh yeah?'

Zandra gave him a dig in the shoulder. 'Stop it, Lex!'

'I'm serious! Who comes first? Human or animals? We can't afford to feed animals, unless we're gonna eat them.'

Patsy screamed. 'No! Stop it! You're horrible!'

Amber sighed. 'Can we get back to rationing, please?'

'It makes sense,' Dal said supportively.

'Especially now we've got a mother and baby to feed,' Amber added.

Lex looked up at Amber, fork halfway to his mouth. 'What?'

'Here we go again!' gasped Zandra.

'We voted to throw them out before the brat was born!'

Lex!' Zandra was shocked. 'You can't throw a helpless baby out into the streets!'

Ryan looked uncomfortable. 'We've just given it presents and everything.'

'Like it or not, Lex, the baby's changed everything.'

Lex glared at Amber. 'You've changed your tune.'

'Can you really throw a helpless child onto the street?'

'It's not our responsibility!'

Amber's was incensed, her voice rising. 'It's everybody's responsibility, Lex! Bray's right. What kind of a world are we making if we throw a new born baby and its mother to the wolves out there!'

Lex scowled. 'Bray has to sort it out. It's his problem.'

Jack looked around. 'Where is he, anyway?'

'He's in with Trudy,' Zandra said.

'No, he's not,' Amber replied.

'Where is he then?' Zandra's brow furrowed.

Jack shrugged. 'Haven't seen him for ages.'

'Me neither,' said Dal. 'I've just been round checking everything's secure for the night. I didn't see him.'

Lex's laughter rang around the café. He put down his fork and looked around smiling.

Zandra looked at him. 'What are you laughing at?'

'You just don't see it, do you?'

'What?'

'He's done runner, you thickhead!' Lex crowed. 'He's dumped his girlfriend and his brat with us, and he's split!'

ooo

Amber sent Salene to double-check all the stores on the first two floors, while she and Dal climbed the stairs to the upper floors of the mall. 'Whatever you do, don't say anything to Trudy,' she warned Salene. 'I'm sure he's around somewhere but we don't want to say anything to alarm her.'

Salene nodded solemnly. 'Lex is wrong. Bray wouldn't go off and leave Trudy and his baby. He's not like that.'

'Let's hope so.'

Salene frowned. 'Amber?'

Amber shrugged 'Seems to me Bray pretty much does as he pleases. I haven't figured the guy out yet.'

'If Lex is right, maybe you never will,' Dal added gloomily.

'He's not right, Dal!' Salene was adamant. 'Lex is just trying to stir up trouble!'

'Yeah well standing here arguing won't help,' Amber said. 'Come on, Dal.'

ooo

Sometime ago, before Jack or any of the others had arrived, a fire had been started in the upper section of the mall. Luckily it had burnt itself out before it had spread down to the lower floors. The upper stores had all been damaged and still smelt of smoke. It wasn't likely anyone would choose to sleep there, but they looked everywhere nonetheless.

Salene was standing on the second floor balcony when they returned. 'Anything?' she asked more in hope than expectation.

Amber shook her head wearily. She was tired. She wanted to sleep. But she knew she wouldn't. Since she first met him, Bray had never been far from her mind. Was it only two days ago? It seemed like a lifetime. She'd had to suppress her feelings and disappointment when Trudy arrived pregnant, and mask them as she watched him deliver the baby so calmly and well. But Bray had just added another complication to her life.

Dal provided the vital question. 'Who's gonna tell Trudy?'

SIXTY FIVE

Like in most other cities the bulk of the warehouses were located by the docks. As he approached them in the moonlight they loomed large and grey like cliff faces towering above him. While searching for a safe place for Trudy, Bray had seen the Demon Dogs heading towards them, pulling handcarts and wheelbarrows full of supplies. Their store must be among them somewhere.

He knew the Demon Dogs headquarters was three blocks away in an apartment block, and he hoped they would only have a couple of guards on the warehouse. If so he was pretty sure he could take care of them. A strong and natural athlete, Bray had improved on his basic strengths by learning martial arts. He was glad he'd taken the trouble now.

Trudy had been sleeping soundly when he left. She was completely exhausted and would probably sleep for hours. With any luck he would be back before she even knew he'd been gone. He hoped so. After all she had been through she was pretty ragged emotionally, and he didn't want to add any fuel to that.

He had no problem finding the store among the rest of the warehouses. Someone had conveniently spray-painted the logo 'Demon Dogs!' across the whole side of the building. They must be pretty confident, he thought, advertising it to the rest of the city. But this was their patch. The Demon Dogs' sector. You had to be crazy to trespass there. He smiled to himself. So what did you know? He was crazy.

SIXTY SIX

Jack was sound asleep which was just as well, as he would have been furious if he'd seen Lex passing the time playing a game on his gameboy in the café. Jack had tried to impress on everyone in the mall that batteries were precious. Once they were gone that was it. There was no way of making any more. And playing games with them was criminal.

'I don't believe it!' Zandra said to no one in particular.

Ryan was busy eating a big supper before Amber's rationing started and hadn't heard Zandra. Eating was a serious business.

'Neither do I,' said Lex disgustedly. 'The batteries just died.' He flung the gameboy on the table.

'I mean Bray! I can't believe he just left Trudy and his little baby, just like that!'

'Get real, Zandra! He's been conning us all along. I told you, but did anyone listen? 'Oh Bray, you're so wonderful! So handsome! So clever!"

Zandra looked up as Amber, Salene and Dal walked in. 'Any sign of him?'

Amber shook her head wearily.

'We looked everywhere,' Dal said.

Lex smiled smugly. 'He's gone alright.'

Zandra was incensed. 'The rat!'

Salene sat down at the table dejectedly. 'Poor Trudy!'

'Poor us!' Lex corrected. ' We're the ones stuck with his girlfriend and his brat! Wouldn't mind betting he's gone to fetch the Locos to come and do us over!'

'Lex, if you can't say anything sensible keep your mouth shut.' Amber was angry. Angry at everything at the moment.

'And you're defending him 'cos you fancy him!' Lex scowled.

Zandra perked up. 'Do you, Amber?'

'Of course not! Don't listen to that idiot!'

'Mind you, I wouldn't blame you.'

Lex glared at Zandra. 'What?'

Ryan looked up from his plate. The sound had been going on for a while, but no one seemed to notice. 'What's that noise?'

Salene stood up, preparing to leave. 'It's just the baby crying.'

'What's wrong with it?' Ryan pulled a face. 'Sounds like it's being murdered.'

'It must be hungry.'

'Why isn't Trudy looking after it?' Zandra sounded irritated.

Amber got up and joined Salene. 'Let's go and see.' She led the way out with Salene and Dal following behind.

Lex was glaring at Zandra suspiciously. 'So you fancy Bray as well, do you?'

Zandra smiled coquettishly, 'That'd be telling wouldn't it?' It never harmed to keep Lex off his guard. Like him, she was biding her time, til the right moment came. Of course she was Lex's girl. Or going to be, one day.

SIXTY SEVEN

Bray couldn't believe his luck. The warehouse was unguarded and unlocked. Something strange must be going on with the Demon Dogs, he thought, but whatever it was had played right into his hands.

Once inside he lit his torch. The warehouse was vast. Shelves of goods stacked to the ceiling stretched way back almost out of sight. He hoped he could find what he needed quickly. He was beginning to have a bad feeling about the unguarded, unlocked treasure trove. Like most things in life, if a thing looked too good to be true, it generally was.

He guessed what he was looking for would be at the far end of the warehouse. The Demon Dogs wouldn't have much use for such things. Skateboarding down the long aisle to the end, he began to search quickly, but systematically, row by row, shining his torch up and down the shelves. He could hear his own breathing in the still air. Don't panic, he told himself. Panic will slow you down.

On the third row he found them. Everything he needed in one section. Taking out his knife he slit open the cardboard boxes, and began packing his rucksack, cramming as much as he could inside. He knew it was foolish, but the vast emptiness of the warehouse was beginning to spook him. He didn't want to be making many more trips back here.

The rucksack full, he flipped his skateboard onto the floor and was about to skim down the long aisle when he heard them outside.

The Demon Dogs were arriving, in spades.

SIXTY EIGHT

They had found Trudy lying listlessly in bed, soaked in sweat. Dal had rushed to get his thermometer while Salene took care of the crying baby. 'I'll take her out the way. Give her some of that creamer stuff we use for coffee,' she told Amber.

'I don't think that's a good idea, Salene.'

'Well, what else are we going to give her? Listen to her! She's starving, poor thing!'

Dal arrived with Zandra, who was keen to see what was going on.

'Where's Bray?' Trudy moaned weakly.

Amber mopped Trudy's brow. 'Hush a minute, Trudy. Let Dal take your temperature.'

Zandra watched intrigued as Dal put the thermometer under Trudy's tongue. 'Where did you get that?'

Dal looked up. 'Around. Thought it might be useful.'

Zandra was impressed. 'Just like the real thing. Dal the doctor. I bet you used to watch all the hospital soaps, didn't you..? I miss television. It's so boring now.'

Amber looked at her, eyes wide in surprise. 'Boring? Which planet are you living on, Zandra?'

'What d'you mean?' she asked, with a puzzled expression.

'Well, you could call it scary or tough or dangerous, but 'boring' isn't a word I'd use.'

'I miss it anyway,' Zandra sighed. 'I could tell you all about all the characters in all the soaps.'

'Fascinating.'

Zandra missed Amber's irony. 'Really. Now they're not there anymore. I don't know what they're doing.'

Amber's eyes grew even wider. 'They're not doing anything, Zandra! They're not real!' She shook her head and turned to Dal who was reading the thermometer. 'Well?'

'It's high.'

'So what do we do?'

'Give her some aspirin. Bathe her head with cold water.'

'Did you swallow a medical book, or something?'

Dal looked at Zandra, a sad look clouding his face. 'My dad was a doctor. So was my mom. Satisfied?'

He pocketed the thermometer, got up from the bed and walked out. Zandra stared after him, guiltily. 'I just wish I could cut my tongue out sometimes!'

Trudy moved her head fretfully. 'Bray! Where's Bray?'

Yes, Amber thought angrily. Where are you, Bray? If he didn't come back she sensed that Trudy might never get over it. And they would be left to pick up the pieces.

SIXTY NINE

The Demon Dogs were drunk. They had arrived looking shell-shocked and angry, and were now drinking their store of booze from the warehouse. In all there were about twenty of them. And they were all sprawled across the entrance, or in Bray's case the exit.

Bray had no time to escape before they arrived. Now he was hiding at the far end of the warehouse, deeply concerned. There was no way he could get out without being seen and beaten to a pulp or worse. They were in a bitter and angry mood. Something had happened to their leader, Silver Demon, and the Dogs were drinking to drown their sorrows and in honour of his memory, shouting out threats and curses alternately.

The Dogs were the Locos bitter rivals for control of the city, Bray knew. From what he could gather from the snatches of conversation that drifted to him Zoot had something to do with Silver Demon's death, and the Dogs were out for revenge. There was mention of a hand-picked suicide squad being formed to take Zoot out. Several of the youths volunteered. After they had paid their homage to their dead leader, that would be the time to strike.

As the night wore on, Bray settled down to wait. The Dogs didn't look like they would be moving very soon, so he would have to bide his time until the booze took its effect and all of them were asleep. It could be a long night.

SEVENTY

Dawn was slowly seeping into the mall through the glass roof of the atrium. Far below in her room Trudy lay very still, wringing with sweat, eyes closed, hardly breathing.

Amber and Dal were seated at either side of Trudy's bed. Trudy had been like this for several hours. Dal looked at Amber deeply concerned, 'It's the fever, Amber. I think she's slipping into a coma.'

They had taken it in turns to watch over Trudy during the night. Salene had taken the baby to sleep with her, and Zandra had gone to bed. Amber had promised to wake them if there was any change.

The world was a dangerous place outside, but with no doctors or hospitals to go to, illness was as frightening as anything else. 'What can we do, Dal?'

'We have to get her some antibiotics.'

'But you said yourself, the pharmacies are all looted.'

He hesitated and then said, 'I know a place where there might still be some.'

Amber looked at him closely across the bed. He was clearly wrestling with something in his mind.

'My dad had a surgery in the hospital. He kept some stuff in there.'

'The Locos rule that sector, Dal.'

'I know. But if I set off now, I could get there and back before they wake up.'

'I'll come with you,' she said resolutely.

Dal smiled. 'And leave Lex in charge of the mall? He may have thrown Trudy and the baby out by the time we get back.'

'Take Lex with you then. For protection.'

'No way!' Dal exclaimed. 'I wouldn't trust him not to beat me up himself.'

Amber grimaced and shook her head. 'I don't like it, Dal. It's very dangerous.'

'Not half as dangerous as it is for Trudy if we don't get her some antibiotics. She could die, Amber.'

'I know. It's just...I know.'

'I'd better get going,' Dal said grimly. He'd made the suggestion, but he was remembering his lucky escape the last time he ventured outside. He hoped his luck wouldn't run out this time.

'Dal!' Amber put her hand on his arm. 'Be careful.' She leant down and kissed him fondly on the cheek.

He smiled shyly. It was worth the danger just for that.

SEVENTY ONE

Bray had seriously underestimated the Demon Dogs capacity for alcohol. Maybe it was their anger that kept them awake? Anger at what had happened to their leader. But whatever it was most of them had stayed awake drinking all through the night, sprawled across the exit, his only way of escape. He was fretting now, anxious that Trudy would learn he was missing and go into a panic.

Dawn was breaking as the Demon Dogs began to stand up. The tallest one, who had clearly assumed the role of new leader, gave instructions to two of the youths to stay behind. He led the rest away, amazingly still capable of walking, if pretty unsteadily. Bray guessed they were not about to mount an assassination attempt on Zoot just yet.

To his dismay, the two Dogs left behind slammed the warehouse doors shut as the others were leaving. Skating swiftly down the aisle to the door he heard the sound of a heavy lock and chain being attached to the door outside. He was locked in, with no other way to get out.

But there was no way he could stay there. He had to escape. Waiting until he judged the rest of the Dogs were out of sight and sound, he banged on the door and called loudly. 'Help! Let me out!'

He listened to the two youths shouts of surprise, then climbed high up onto the nearest shelf and hid.

He heard the sound of the chain being pulled away and light flooded inside as the two youths flung open the doors. From his hiding place he saw them step inside looking around, weapons at the ready. They were both as tall as him, with improvised body armour and biker's helmets decorated with the Demon Dogs' insignia. Better to wait til they went further inside, he thought, and he could use his surprise and speed to get away. Taking them both on, protected and tooled up as they were, was a risk.

The two youths stood by the entrance looking around. One shouted, his voice echoing round the vast warehouse. 'Come out! Whoever you are!'

They waited and listened. Bray held his breath, waiting for his moment. Then he saw the second one turn to the other. 'Forget it. They can't get out.'

His companion nodded and they stepped back outside, about to close the doors again. It was now or never. He wouldn't get a second chance. Bray sprang down from his hiding place, breaking his fall by cannoning into the first youth, feet first. The youth went sprawling head over heels, well out of it.

Leaping to his feet, Bray was just in time to duck as the second Dog flailed his weapon viciously at his head. Wrenching his skateboard from his back, Bray swung the heavy wooden board with all his strength. He heard the helmet shatter and saw blood fill the visor.

Flinging the board down on the ground Bray leapt on it and shot away, weaving deftly around the corner of the warehouse, headed towards the street.

He knew he had to get back to the mall as soon as he could, but he had one more errand to run first.

SEVENTY TWO

While she waited anxiously for Dal to return safely to the mall, Amber tried to take her mind off her friend's dangerous mission by organizing her rationing system. She had roped Jack in to help, and was jotting down a list as he went through the food store shelf by shelf.

Jack closed the door of the cupboard. 'And that's the lot, boss.'

Amber looked at the list and frowned. 'Not very much, but if people eat sensibly.'

Jack raised his eyebrows. It was a big 'if'.

'I'll draw up a daily ration,' Amber said.

'Got to try and make it as nutritionally balanced as possible.'

She gave him an ironic look. 'Like I have a lot of choice, Jack.' At home her food had always been fresh. Organic vegetables and meat. Free range eggs. Crusty wholemeal bread. Now it was processed, out of tins and packets. She sighed to herself. Welcome to the post-apocalyptic world.

Lex entered the kitchen breezily, brushed past them and opened the cupboard door. 'Ah, breakfast!'

'Hang on, Lex. I'm just drawing up a ration list.'

'No one decides what I eat, Amber. I'm not a kid.'

Amber put down her list, exasperated. 'Lex, we've been through this! We have to ration the food!'

'And the water,' Jack added. 'Especially the water.'

'What about batteries?' Lex threw a couple of AA's on the table. 'These are dead.'

Jack was defensive. 'There's no more,' he lied.

'I bet.'

'We all get an equal share of food each day,' Amber pressed on. 'It doesn't grow on trees, Lex.'

Ryan had followed Lex into the kitchen and overheard. 'That's not fair. I need more than the little kids. I'm big.'

'I'm sorry, Ryan, but they need as much as you. They're growing.'

'And we can't just let people keep taking water from the tap.'

Ryan looked at Jack, frowning. 'Why not?'

'The water comes from a tank on the roof. There's only so much in there.'

'Can you cut the tap off, Jack?' Amber asked. 'So we can ration it?'

Jack nodded. 'I'll go see what's in the tank. But we'll have to go easy til we can find water somewhere else.'

Lex took hold of Jack's arm as he prepared to leave. 'We'll go with you.'

Jack looked uneasy. 'It's okay, I can manage.'

'Nah, we'll come with you, Jack. Not that we don't trust you. Just don't want you falling in and drowning.' Lex grinned. 'Might contaminate our water, eh, Ryan?'

ooo

The streets were deserted as Dal bladed nervously along them. At that time in the morning the city was deathly quiet, and the only sound he could hear was the swish of his own blades on the tarmac. He wished they could be quieter, but he knew it wasn't likely he'd run into a Loco snatch party so early in the day. That wasn't really what he was nervous about.

He hadn't been to his father's surgery since the virus struck. But he had been there many times before. Dal had planned to become a doctor when he grew up. He wanted to help people, to do some real good in the world, like his parents had.

155

They had been a very close family. Dal was their only child and both his parents doted on him, but without spoiling the young boy. They spent much of their spare time playing with their son, teaching him many things from cricket to calculus. Their family holidays were always great fun, exploring many parts of the world and experiencing the culture and history of the different people and races they met. He was very proud of his parents and adored being with them. He had been a very lucky boy.

He reached the hospital without incident and glided along the familiar corridors to his father's surgery. The door to the room was open. Dal took a deep breath and went inside. The small surgery had been cursorily trashed by looters, but Dal knew where his father had kept his store of drugs secure. He found the catch beneath the desk and opened the secret drawer.

Inside the pills boxes were still intact, untouched. Gratefully he emptied the contents into his rucksack. He glanced at the window. The sun was coming up and he needed to get back.

As he made to leave a ray of sunlight struck a framed photograph still upright on the desk. The glass shone in his eyes. He picked up the photograph and gazed at the three smiling figures frozen in time inside the frame.

He hesitated, then put the frame back down and skated out into the corridor. He didn't need the baggage of a photograph to remember them. He had them in his heart.

SEVENTY THREE

Salene was watching over Trudy, who was still semi-conscious, muttering and twisting her head feverishly. Salene wiped Trudy's brow deeply concerned. She hadn't much experience of illness, but Trudy looked in a very bad way.

'Come on, Trudy! You can make it! You have to, for the baby!'

Amber walked in, yawning. She'd tried to have a nap while Salene took over, but she couldn't sleep. 'How is she?'

'Wringing wet. Rambling. Talking about dying.'

'What a mess! Poor thing.'

'She'll be okay when she gets better.'

Amber looked skeptical. 'How do you figure that?'

There was a wistful note in Salene's reply. 'She's got Bray, hasn't she?'

'Yeah? Well where is he?'

Salene glanced up at Amber, a defensive look on her face. 'I don't know. But I know he'll be back!'

Amber looked at her but Salene didn't meet her eyes. Amber sighed inside. Not another complication! Her voice had a warning tone. 'Salene, he's got a baby, and Trudy, you know.'

'I know!' Salene said defensively. 'I just wish he were here, that's all.'

'Maybe it'll be better if he doesn't come back.'

'Don't say that!'

Amber softened. She shouldn't have said that. She'd let her guard down and her jealousy about Bray and Trudy show. 'Do you want me to take over?'

'No. I'll be fine. I'll wait here for Bray.'

That's what worries me, Amber thought.

ooo

The water tank was on the flat roof of the mall, ten stories above the city. It was a large sealed tank with a ladder leading up to a small inspection hatch on the top. At the bottom of the tank there was a tap and a thick white plastic tube which ran from the tank into the mall.

Jack was at the top of the ladder using a long pole to gauge the depth of the water in the tank. Lex and Ryan were standing at the foot of the ladder, enjoying being out in the fresh air and sunshine. 'Could set up a little patio up here, Ryan. Couple of deckchairs, barbecue, a few beers.'

'We haven't got any meat or booze, Lex.'

'Always got to spoil it, haven't you?' He called up to Jack. 'How you doing?'

'Down quite a bit since I last checked.'

Lex pulled a face. 'It's that Trudy, using it for the baby.' He shielded his eyes against the sun as he looked up. 'How much do we get, Jack?'

Jack began to climb back down the ladder. 'Well, you divide the volume by the amount of –'

Lex put a strong hand on Jack's calf, stopping him halfway down. 'You're not listening, Jack. How much do we get?'

Jack frowned. 'Let go! I'm explaining.'

'Let me explain, brains. Me and Ryan get double.'

'Double? Why?'

'Because I say so. Don't I, Ryan?'

'Yeah, Lex.'

Lex handed Jack a plastic bucket. 'Starting now!'

SEVENTY FOUR

Zoot was feeling much better and planning his revenge. The Demon Dogs had destroyed his prize weapon. His beautiful tank which had been liberated from the city's military museum and so painstakingly brought back to life.

When civilization was falling apart, one of the last orders the city authorities gave was for the destruction of all weapons. Or at least to make them unusable. It had been clear for some time that only children would be left alive and some far-sighted, caring official had realized what carnage would follow if kids were left the arsenal of weaponry that the adult world had stockpiled. Well, maybe you didn't have to be that far-sighted. Virtual war games had been an obsession with the young.

Under Zoot's instruction, Spike and his team had lovingly restored the ancient tank, which didn't require sophisticated computers to function. It would give the Locos the edge over all the other tribes. With that weapon at his disposal the city would be Zoot's in no time at all. Now it was gone. A useless piece of junk like all the rest.

He had assembled his council of war, Ebony, Spike and two other 'generals' to outline his next plan. 'Chaos' was his slogan, but Zoot knew that you didn't gain 'Power' without planning.

'The Dogs have lost their leader. You can bet there's gonna be a hiatus for a while.'

'A what, Lord Zoot?'

Zoot looked at Spike witheringly. 'A pause. A gap.'

Spike looked at him uncomprehendingly.

'They're gonna take time to regroup. To find a new leader.'

Spike nodded a little shamefaced.

'So we hit 'em while they're still disorganized.'

There was a knock on the carriage door. A Loco was standing outside holding an envelope. Zoot motioned him inside.

'Yeh?'

The youth held out the envelope. 'I found this, Lord Zoot. Some guy came up on a skateboard and chucked it into the yard. It's for you.'

'Some 'guy'?

'Yes, Lord Zoot.'

'What did he look like?'

'I didn't get a proper look. He was there and gone in a flash. Tall kid. Long brown hair.'

Zoot took the envelope and walked away from the group. He opened it and read the brief note inside. Then, taking a lighter from his pocket, he held the note by one corner and set light to it, holding it until it was a blackened, twisted scrap. He let it fall.

Ebony watched the charred paper fall to the ground, intrigued.

SEVENTY FIVE

Salene was still waiting by Trudy's bedside. She told herself it was from her concern about the unconscious girl, but in reality she was longing for Bray to arrive. She had told Amber that he would be back, and she knew it. She had only known him for a couple of days, but she felt the two of them had a special bond. Trudy may have his baby, but Salene had sensed that all was not right between her and Bray.

Trudy moaned. As Salene wiped her brow again, she heard a noise behind her. Turning, she saw Bray standing in the doorway. She leapt up, straight into his arms.

'Bray! Bray, you're back!'

Feeling his surprise at her sudden, fierce embrace she moved away, embarassed. 'I'm sorry. Only we didn't know what had happened to you! We were really worried!'

'What's wrong with Trudy?' Bray asked, going over to the bed.

'We don't know. She's very ill, Bray.'

Bray felt Trudy's forehead. 'She's ice cold.'

'She keeps going from fever to icy. Been like that all night.'

'I didn't know...' he began guiltily. 'I've been getting some stuff for the baby.'

He began to unpack the rucksack, taking out disposable nappies, cream and tins of baby formula.

Salene watched him, thrilled that he was back, delighted she had been proved right. 'I knew you hadn't left.'

Bray looked up at her, puzzled. 'Left?'

'Well, some of the others thought...' She was suddenly uncomfortable.

'That I'd run out on Trudy?'

'I knew you hadn't! You're not like that.'

She gazed at him, adoringly. He held her gaze for a moment then looked away as Amber entered the room.

Her voice was ice. 'Where've you been!'

Salene rushed to his defence. 'He's found some things for the baby! Look!'

Amber glanced at the things dismissively.

'Did you get the antibiotics, Amber?' Salene asked, trying to break the sudden tension in the room.

'No,' Amber snapped. 'Dal's gone to his father's surgery in Sector 15.'

Bray looked at her, shocked. 'Sector 15! Why didn't you stop him! That's suicide!'

Amber flared at him, with fiery eyes. 'Well where were you, Bray! She's your responsibility!'

'What's all the shouting about?' Dal was standing in the doorway.

Amber rushed and threw her arms around him. 'Dal! You're back!'

Dal grinned.

ooo

Dal had managed to get the unconscious Trudy to swallow the antibiotics and now all they could do was wait. Amber had taken over keeping watch over her, while Salene took a break, having been with Trudy for hours.

She entered the café where some of the others were were having a meal.

Lex was hunched moodily over a bowl of cereal, not happy that Bray had returned to the mall. 'Cereal with no milk! It's revolting! Like eating bird food!

'My apologies, your Lordship.' Dal was in a buoyant mood. He'd become something of a hero by getting the antibiotics and was enjoying the feeling. 'I didn't have time to look for fresh dairy produce while I was out getting Trudy's drugs.'

Salene looked around. 'Has anyone seen Bray?'

'No, and we don't want to,' Lex snarled.

'I can't find him anywhere.'

'How's Trudy?' Zandra was feeling guilty at not having taken her turn at Trudy's bedside, but she didn't do sick people. They made her feel 'yuck'.

'Delirious. Coming out with all strange stuff. She's soaked through the bedding. It's dripping wet.'

'Do you mind!' Lex slammed down his spoon. 'It's hard enough keeping this muck down as it is!'

Salene looked concerned. 'I've looked everywhere for him. I don't understand it. He's only just got back.'

Lex suddenly perked up. 'He's gone again! Gone for good this time, I bet. Run off and left us to deal with his mess!'

'Don't be so mean! If he's gone outside I'm sure he has a good reason!'

Lex sneered. 'And the reason you're defending him is 'cos you fancy him rotten!'

Salene felt her cheeks flush. 'I do not! I just think it's unfair to judge someone without having all the facts.'

Ryan was looking philosophical. 'If my girlfriend was sick, I'd stay with her.'

'That'd make her more sick!'

Ryan gave Lex a hard look, but didn't respond.

'A girl likes a man who's caring and considerate, Lex.'

'That a fact, Zandra?'

'It is actually.'

'Let's face it,' Lex said feeling much more cheerful. 'Bray couldn't hack it. He came back, saw his tart was dying and didn't have the guts to stick around!'

SEVENTY SIX

Sneaking out of the mall Cloe had taken the calf a drink of water mixed with coffee creamer. It was the nearest thing she had to milk. The calf lapped the drink up, but Cloe was very worried about whether it could survive without its mother.

The others hadn't believed her when she told them about the monster she had seen. They'd actually laughed at her, which made her feel stupid and then angry. But she could talk to the calf. Bluebell didn't laugh at her.

She knew it needed grass, so she untied it and was leading it out of the car park when she saw Bray skateboarding away from the mall. He hadn't seen her. Cloe was puzzled. He'd only just got back and Trudy was very ill. Why was he going away again so soon?

'Come on, Bluebell. Let's go see.'

Bray was travelling faster than she could, but she could see which direction he was headed. She broke into a run with the calf loping alongside.

Shortly she found herself in a broken down area of the city. A place of old warehouses and disused buildings that had been that way long before the virus struck. But Bray was nowhere in sight. She had lost him.

As she turned back towards the direction of the mall, she heard voices. In the still air of the deserted city voices traveled a long way. She crept towards a corner, peered round and immediately jumped back in shock. Not believing what she thought she'd seen, she peered around the corner again.

It was true. Bray was standing at the rear of an abandoned burnt out lorry, talking animatedly to another youth. Cloe had seen the other boy before, the day she had been rescued by Amber. He had been standing up in the police car that sped past where she and Amber were hiding. It was Zoot.

SEVENTY SEVEN

In the mall word had quickly got round that Bray had disappeared again. There was a general air of surprise and incredulity. What was he up to this time? Lex was crowing in the café, and Amber had gone back to her room frustrated and angry.

Salene was surprised that Bray had left so soon, considering how ill Trudy was, but she was convinced that he had a good reason. She knew he would come back and, when he did, she wanted him to see that she was looking after his baby. She wanted to show him how much she cared.

She had left Dal watching over Trudy and gone to seek out the others help. Jack was fiddling with his radio when she entered the electrical shop, his den. He looked up shiftily at Salene.

'Jack? Am I disturbing you?'

Jack grunted, non-committal.

'You do that every day, don't you?'

Jack nodded and continued turning the dials on the machine. 'You never know when you're going to strike it lucky.'

'You really think there's someone out there? Some adults?'

Jack was adamant. 'There has to be! The virus can't have killed them all!'

'I suppose it's like being stranded on a desert island. Putting a message in a bottle and sending it out to sea?'

'Yeah.' He was impatiently humouring her. 'Something like that.'

She came to the point. 'I wanna give the baby a bath. She's starting to smell.'

Jack looked up at her, frowning. 'What are you telling me for?'

'Because it's gonna take more than one water ration. And as we're sort of a group and share everything, I thought I'd better ask people first.'

He stared at her indignantly. 'You're not using my ration for that!'

'She needs to be clean, Jack!'

'And I need not to die of thirst!'

'Don't be so dramatic!'

'I'm not! I'm being pragmatic! You go ahead. Ask the others. Maybe they'll be dumb enough to give you some of theirs!'

Salene sighed and went out. Jack uncovered the opened can of peaches he'd concealed on his desk and carried on eating, moodily. With Lex stealing the water supply they'd soon have none left anyway. And then the real problems would start. Before the virus he'd read that the next world war would be fought over water. Bathing babies could start it!

SEVENTY EIGHT

Cloe was very confused. What was Bray doing to talking to a bad man like Zoot? They seemed to be having a friendly conversation not an argument. At one point they both even laughed.

She knew she should get back and tell the others. They might be in danger. But would they believe her? They hadn't believed her about the monster. At that moment Zoot gave Bray a friendly punch on the shoulder and trotted away.

Bluebell, bored standing beside her, mooed. Bray looked up at the noise. Cloe ducked back round the corner. Had he seen her? Her heart began to race as she heard him call.

'Cloe?'

She turned and ran, dragging Bluebell behind. Hearing the sound of Bray's skateboard behind her, she turned into a small side street. But she knew it was hopeless. There was no way her little legs could outrun Bray.

Along the street the door to an empty building stood gaping open. She rushed inside, frantically looking for a place to hide. Seeing an old cupboard under some burnt out stairs, she pulled open the door and crawled inside. There was just enough room for Bluebell to squeeze in beside her. She closed the door behind them and waited in fear.

She heard Bray's footsteps echoing in the deserted building. Holding her breath, she put her hand over Bluebell's mouth, praying it wouldn't give them away. Moments later the cupboard door opened. Bray leant down and smiled. 'Hello, Cloe? Who's your friend?'

SEVENTY NINE

Lex stepped onto the roof carrying a large red bucket. Ryan was following behind wearing a puzzled expression. Striding over to the water tank, Lex handed Ryan the bucket.

'There you go, Ryan.'

'Lex, I don't get why we're doing this. Is it because of what Salene said? About the baby smelling?'

'Got it in one, my friend. Which must be a record for you.'

Ryan ignored the insult. 'But you don't even like babies!'

Lex smiled smugly. 'It's politics, Ryan. I know that's a big word, but trust me. It don't do any harm to be popular. If I can make myself look like a hero for Zandra, I will.'

'For Zandra? I thought it was for Salene?'

'You heard what Zandra said, Ryan, in the café. She likes her men to be caring and sensitive. Well, that's me.'

Lex's logic was eluding Ryan. 'So why are we up here again?'

'To get the water for the baby's bath. Out of the tank.' Lex looked at Ryan, exasperated. Sometimes talking to Ryan was like pulling teeth.

'The tank? But that's everybody's water, Lex.'

'So? Who's gonna know the difference? Water doesn't have anybody's name on it.'

Ryan's face lit up. 'Oh! So you're going to tell Zandra that you're giving the baby your ration?'

'Careful, Ryan, you're gonna strain yourself. All that thinking. And you're gonna back me up, aren't you? Tell everybody I'm like a camel.'

'A camel, Lex?'

'They can go for days without water.' Lex nodded at the bucket. 'So go on, Ryan, make me a hero!'

EIGHTY

Bray had told Cloe not to be scared, but she was. Very scared and confused. He helped her and the calf out of the cupboard and then stroked the calf's head gently, smiling at Cloe all the time.

'Does she have a name?' His voice was calm and sounded kind, but she felt it was a trick.

'Bluebell,' she replied reluctantly.

'Bluebell. That's a cool name. Cool name for a cool calf.'

She began to panic. 'I wanna go! Let me go!'

His smile never wavered. 'Don't be scared, Cloe. I'm not going to hurt you. I'm your friend, remember?' He held out his hand to her. 'Come on, let's get back to the mall. It's not safe here.'

She didn't take his hand. She was very bewildered. 'What were you doing with that Zoot? He's a bad man!'

Bray's smile faded. He suddenly looked very serious. 'Well, now, Cloe, that's a secret. Our secret.'

Taking hold of the string around the calf's neck he began to lead it out of the building. Cloe followed fretting.

'But he's bad! If he's your friend I should tell Amber!'

Bray stopped at the doorway and looked at her. 'Believe me, Cloe, he's not a friend.'

'But you were talking and laughing!'

Bray leaned down close to her. 'Listen, Cloe, if you keep my secret I won't say anything to the others about Bluebell. If they find her, you know what they'll want to do with her?'

Cloe shook her head, doubtfully.

'They'll want to eat her. They'll want to kill her and cook her and eat her.'

Cloe screamed. 'No!'

Bray shrugged. 'It's your choice. If you don't say anything about Zoot, I won't tell anyone about Bluebell...Have we got a deal?'

Cloe hesitated, uncertain. She felt it was wrong, she knew she should tell the others, but she didn't want Bluebell to die.

'Our secret?' Bray asked.

Cloe nodded.

EIGHTY ONE

Paul was chasing Patsy around the bird statue with Bob jumping and barking loudly around them. Patsy was screaming at the top of her voice, the sound echoing around the empty mall.

Amber came out of Trudy's room and shouted down to them. 'Can you two go and play quietly somewhere? I'm looking after Trudy and the noise is driving me nuts!'

'Sorry, Amber. Come on, Bob.' Patsy led Paul and the dog away.

Amber went back into Trudy's room and sat down by the bed again. Dal had given Trudy another dose of antibiotics, but she didn't seem any better.

'Come on, Trudy,' Amber said softly. 'You can beat this. Think of all you have to live for. Like your baby. You don't want to miss out watching her grow up. And there's Bray...So much to live for.' Her expression grew sad, thinking about her own life. What did she have to live for? Generally, she tried not to give it any thought. It was better that way. 'Where are you, Bray?' she said aloud. 'Where are you when she needs you?'

She looked up expectantly at a sound by the door. It was Zandra. 'How's Trudy?'

'No better.'

Zandra sighed heavily. 'I can't make Bray out. I mean does he love her or not? I mean, where is he..? I thought he was so nice at first, didn't you?'

Amber hoped she sounded casual. 'I didn't give it a thought.'

'You're a quiet one, aren't you? I mean you say a lot, but you hide stuff.'

Amber looked at her, puzzled. 'Like what?'

'Like, was Lex right about you fancying him?'

'Me? Fancy Lex?'

Zandra tutted. 'No! Bray! You know what I mean.'

'Zandra! He's Trudy's boyfriend for god's sake!'

'Wouldn't stop me.'

Amber felt Zandra's eyes studying her closely. She abruptly changed the subject. 'Have you seen Cloe? She's not with Patsy and Paul.'

Zandra shook her head. 'Haven't seen her all day,'

Amber gasped, exasperated. 'Great! Here we are trying to get something together and nobody's ever here! I mean, they just keep going off, disappearing! What's the point of that?'

Zandra smiled. 'So you do fancy him then.'

ooo

Lex and Ryan were rummaging through the piles of electrical junk that Jack had accumulated in his workshop. Every surface, shelf, even the bed and floor was littered with stuff they didn't even know the names of.

In the final days before the world he'd known had collapsed, Jack had ransacked every store he could find for batteries, wire, anything vaguely electrical he thought he might be able to use in the new world they were all being plunged into.

Since it had been discovered and harnessed way back in the eighteenth century, electricity had changed the world. The power it generated had made the world go round, until now. Always a science geek, Jack was fascinated by the power of Nature, and electricity fascinated him most of all. His workshop was a shrine to Nature's powerful, invisible force.

Ryan picked up an object and turned it round in his hand. 'What do they look like?'

'Batteries, Ryan! They look like batteries! I know Jack's got some hidden somewhere.'

'How do you know?'

'Because he said he hadn't got any more and he's a lying little geek!'

Lex sat down on the bed and immediately sprang up. Pulling back the blanket he revealed a small pile of batteries. He was triumphant. 'Ah! What did I tell you?' Snatching up two batteries he inserted them into the gameboy he took from his jacket pocket. He turned on the machine. 'Now where was I?'

As Lex settled himself back on the bed and began to play a violent urban war game, Ryan, bored, began to fiddle with the knobs on the short wave radio.

'What are you doing? Leave that alone!' Jack had entered, horrified that someone had invaded his special place and was messing with his precious radio.

Ryan jumped back. 'Sorry. I was being careful.'

'Well, never touch it again!'

'Lay off him. It's only a useless piece of junk.'

Jack glared at Lex. 'Junk! This radio could be our only lifeline to the outside world!'

'What are you expecting to pick up?' Lex sneered. 'The news? 'Good evening here is the news. Today was crap like yesterday!''

'And who gave you permission to use my batteries for that moronic game?'

'It's not just a game. It's training. Sharpening my fighting skills. My reflexes.'

'It still doesn't give you the right to waste our vital energy resources!' Jack said indignantly.

Lex switched off the game and stood up. 'I was getting bored with it anyway.'

'Where are you going? Give me my batteries!'

Lex walked out ignoring him.

'I'll tell about the water!' Jack gasped out, and immediately regretted it.

Lex turned back, his face suddenly ugly. Seizing Jack's wrist he twisted his arm up the boy's back, viciously. 'Don't even think about it, nerd. You don't have any teachers to protect you now!' He twisted Jack's arm again.

Jack squealed. 'Ow! That hurts!'

Lex grinned malevolently. 'Welcome to the real world!'

EIGHTY TWO

As Bray and Cloe entered the mall from the sewers, he stopped and bent down to her.

'Now remember.'

'No Zoot, no Bluebell,' Cloe said unhappily.

He smiled. 'Good girl.'

Emerging from her room on the first balcony, Amber saw them and called angrily. 'Where have you been!'

Bray continued calmly up the stairs with Cloe. 'All over the city, looking for medical supplies.'

Her tone was still accusative. 'Did you get anything?'

He shook his head. 'Everywhere's stripped bare. I found Cloe wandering the streets and brought her back.'

Amber stood in front of him as he reached the top of the stairs. 'I'm curious, Bray. Where exactly have you been?'

Bray smiled. 'I told you.'

'Why should I believe you..? You say you've been all over the city, but somehow you manage to come back completely empty-handed.'

His smile faded away. 'It was all gone,'

'Everything? Every plaster, every tube of toothpaste? Every toothpick?' she added sarcastically.

'I was only looking for what Trudy needed.' She was beginning to needle him now. 'There wasn't time for anything else.'

Amber's tone was becoming more and more aggressive. 'Not even a split second to pick up something we might need? Something useful?'

Drawn by the raised voices Zandra came out of the café with the baby in her arms.

'Give him a break, Amber,' Zandra said. 'He was trying to help Trudy.'

'So was Dal!'

'And I'm very grateful to him.' Bray said sincerely.

'Only him?' Amber's pent up feelings were boiling over. 'You come in here seeking our help, our shelter, stuffing down our food, but you don't seem to think you owe us anything in return! What is it with you, Bray? The comings and goings! The air of mystery! Is it all a pose or is it for real? Come on, Bray! What's the big secret?'

Bray glared at her, his eyes meeting her's angrily. 'None of your business!'

He stormed off towards Trudy's room.

Lex had come out of the café and heard the exchange. He watched Bray go. 'Well, we'd better make it our business, hadn't we?'

EIGHTY THREE

Ebony was watching Zoot closely. Since the incident with the note he had been strangely quiet and thoughtful, not at all his usual energetic, charismatic self. She was very curious. What had the note said? And who was the mysterious youth who had sent it? She knew who the description fitted, but it seemed unlikely it was him. She hadn't seen him since...Best not to think about those days. It still hurt.

Zoot had not said anything about the note to her. Not even when she tried to get around to the subject in bed. 'Must have been very important? Or very trivial?'

He smiled and pinched her arm, hard. She pulled away. 'Ow! What was that for?'

'You know why.'

She did. The deal was to ask no questions and to obey all demands without question. What Zoot said was law. And he was above the law. He didn't have to answer questions, or for his actions. It irked her. She hoped that in time he would mellow, become more open to her and easier to live with. But for the moment she was better off than most. She had food in her belly, a safe roof over her head, and a position of status in her tribe. What more could anyone ask for in this new world order?

But she knew that could change in a moment. Zoot could be fickle and impulsive. And he had total control over his world. He could have anything he wanted. Any partner he wanted. There was no guarantee she would always be flavor of the month. So she kept her mouth shut, and her eyes wide open.

EIGHTY FOUR

'Who do think she looks like, Bray or Trudy?' Zandra was walking about in the café holding the baby proprietorially. Trudy was still not responding to the antibiotics, and Zandra and Salene were taking it in turns to be 'mother'.

Lex looked up from his plate. 'Pity the kid if it's Bray.'

'Babies don't look like anyone if you ask me,' said Ryan. 'They just look like...babies.'

In the kitchen Salene put down her dishcloth by the sink, which was groaning with unwashed pots and pans. 'That's it!' she called. 'I'm on strike! My turn for nanny duty!'

She came out of the kitchen and walked towards Zandra holding out her arms.

Zandra turned away. 'No way! I've just got her off. You might wake her.'

'Babies sleep through anything. Come on, Zandra, give her to me.'

She reached for the baby again. Zandra spun away. 'You had her earlier! It's my turn.'

Ryan looked concerned. 'Careful. It's not a toy to pass around.'

'Well said, Ryan! Zandra, give Salene the baby. Be a good girl,' Lex added patronizingly.

Zandra sat beside Ryan, putting herself between him and Salene. 'She only wants it so I'll have to do the washing up!'

Ryan pulled a face and looked down at the baby. 'Urh! What's that smell?'

Zandra leapt up, holding the baby at arm's length. 'Uhh!' she cried. 'I'm all wet!'

Lex and Ryan burst into raucous laughter.

Zandra was panicking. She held the baby out to Salene. 'Here! You want her, you can have her!'

'Couldn't possibly, Zandra,' Salene replied haughtily. 'I might wake her!'

Salene walked out of the café, leaving Zandra holding the baby, as Lex and Ryan howled with laughter.

ooo

Bray was sitting beside Trudy musing about his meeting with Zoot. It was unfortunate that Cloe had seen them. He hoped the little girl could keep their secret. He was unpopular enough without adding that to the equation.

He heard Trudy stir and turned to her. Her eyes were open. She blinked, disorientated.

'Bray?'

A flood of relief washed over him. 'Trudy! You're back!'

She looked puzzled. 'Where did I go?'

'To a very far away place. We were all scared you might not come back.'

She tried to sit up. He helped her, putting the pillow behind her back. 'You're talking in riddles, Bray. What happened to me?'

'You've been very ill. With a fever.'

Trudy looked surprised. 'And you thought I might die?'

He nodded gravely.

'How long have you been here?'

'All the time,' he lied. He couldn't tell her the truth just yet.

She smiled gratefully. 'Thank you for taking such good care of me.'

'All I did was hold your hand.'

Trudy reached out, took his hand in hers tenderly, and looked into his eyes. 'Don't let go, Bray.'

He smiled, a little awkwardly, and looked away. Now wasn't the time. She was too fragile. He'd have to wait. But he couldn't wait long.

EIGHTY FIVE

Salene was standing in front of the locked food store in the kitchen, defiantly confronting Lex, Ryan and Zandra. She folded her arms, clutching the keys to her protectively.

'I'm sorry, Lex. No washed dishes. No food!'

Lex scoffed. 'Stop fooling around, Salene. Give us the keys!'

'We've all got to do our share!' she said doggedly. 'You can't just leave it to a few of the girls!'

'Come on, Sal!' Lex pretended to plead. 'I'm a growing boy!'

'No. How else can I convince you this is a job we all have to do?'

Lex shrugged. 'What's the problem? You take a plate, you clean it, you eat!'

Salene pointed at the pile of dirty dishes piled in the sink and on the work surfaces. 'Leaving all that humongous dirty pile to fester, attracting rats! We've got a baby here now. We've got to keep the place clean for its sake!'

Ryan looked at her pleadingly. 'Can we talk about it another time, Salene? I'm starving!'

'Then you'll just ignore the problem til the next time!'

Salene felt she was fighting a losing battle, all on her own. Now Trudy was recovering Bray was with her all the time, and Amber was going around like a bear with a sore head. Who was going to support her?

Lex was getting angry. 'Haven't you got the message? We're not into washing dishes!'

Salene was afraid of Lex's anger, but she bravely stood her ground. 'We've got to do them all the same! We can't go on like this!'

'Right.' Lex looked grim. 'I've had enough! Give me the keys!'

'No!' Salene cried.

Lex took a step towards Salene.

'Lex!' Zandra stepped in front of him. 'Let me handle this.' She suddenly raised both hands and began to tickle Salene around the waist. Salene squirmed.

'Stop it! Stop it!'

Trying to catch Zandra's hands, Salene dropped the bunch of keys. Lex swooped to snatch them up.

'Nice one, Zandra!' he said, holding the keys aloft.

Salene cried out in frustration. 'Why won't anyone ever listen to me?' Bursting into tears, she rushed from the café.

ooo

Bray was changing the baby with Trudy watching from her bed. She hadn't shown very much interest in her little daughter since she had recovered from the fever, but Bray put that down to her still needing to rest. She had been very ill.

'So, on the mend?' Lex was standing in the doorway. He smiled. 'Door was open so I thought I'd pop in, see how you are.'

They both looked at him suspiciously. He went on, still smiling cheesily. 'Did she have a good bath?' He nodded at the baby.

Trudy looked at him, puzzled. 'Pardon?'

'Didn't Salene tell you? I gave up my water ration for the little mite.'

'No...Oh, thanks.'

'Don't mention it.'

Bray was staring at him coldly. 'What do you want, Lex?'

Lex shrugged. 'Like I said, just wanted to check how our invalid was.'

'I'm feeling a lot better. Thanks.'

'Good.'

'I'm glad you're pleased.' Bray was still not buying into the sharing caring Lex image.

Lex caught his tone. He held out his hands in an open, honest gesture. 'Look, I wouldn't chuck a mother and new baby on the streets. What do you take me for?'

'Fine. As long as we've got that straight.' Bray couldn't wait to get rid of him. 'Was there anything else you wanted?'

'It was just a friendly visit. I'll leave you two lovebirds to snog in peace.' He left them with another cheesy smile.

Trudy shuddered. 'I don't trust him an inch. He gives me the creeps!'

Bray seized his opportunity. He wanted to move things on for all their sakes. 'Speaking of your favourite people.'

Trudy looked at him warily. 'Do we have to?'

'He wants to see you.'

She looked surprised. 'You've seen him?'

Bray nodded. 'Yesterday.'

Trudy frowned. 'You said you were with me all the time?'

'I'm sorry, I lied. I didn't think it was a good time...Well?'

'No way, I can't, Bray.' There was a scared look in her eyes.

'That's what I told him you'd say.'

She was relieved. 'Good.'

Bray pressed on. 'So he asked me to ask you again.'

'The answer's still the same.'

Bray held the baby in his arms, rocking it gently. 'Can you at least think about, Trudy?'

Trudy sighed moodily. Just when she was feeling better and content with Bray and the baby, a dark cloud had crossed over her life again. 'Alright. But I'm not saying I'll change my mind.'

EIGHTY SIX

Amber was concerned by her outburst at Bray. People had stared in surprise at her venom. Though to be fair to herself, she felt she had a right. As the leader she needed to know what was going on, and Bray had been acting very strangely, coming and going as he pleased, without any explanation. But she had allowed her personal feelings about him and Trudy to show. She had shown a weakness which she couldn't allow.

She knew she had to get control of her feelings and start acting like a leader again. Doing practical things would take her mind off Bray and Trudy. And there were many practical things to do. They were only just beginning to get to grips with their new life.

Dal and Jack were together pouring over a book on electrical systems when she entered Jack's workshop.

'Ah. I'm glad I've caught you both.'

'What can we do for you, Amber?' asked Jack.

'I've been thinking about the sewers. Bray and Cloe just wandering in and out. It's not safe. I mean, if they can come and go as they please, what's to stop the Locos getting in?'

'Exactly.' Dal said.

'So I wondered if you two brainy guys could come up with some sort of security system?'

Jack grinned. 'Like an alarm system, you mean?'

'Yeh, right. We need to be able to get in and out, but we also need to know if someone else gets in.'

Jack held up the book. 'You mean like this?'

Amber peered at the book. It was open at a page showing a wiring diagram which meant nothing to her.

Dal smiled. 'We're onto it, boss.'

It was Amber's turn to smile. 'Great. I knew I could rely on you.'

ooo

Bray had taken the baby to the canteen for a feed, leaving Trudy to rest. He had told her about his hair-raising encounter with the Demon Dogs in the warehouse when he was getting the nappies and baby formula. She had been scared for him, but very grateful that they now had proper food for the baby. She couldn't bear the idea of breast-feeding, even if she could produce enough milk.

She was reading an old magazine, looking at the latest women's fashions before the virus struck. Designers would be astonished now at the clothes the kids were wearing. The girls, raiding boutiques and fashion stores, had a field day. Today's fashion motto was 'the more bizarre the better'. Zandra was case in point, with her lime green tank top, her fake zebra skin hot pants and matching boots.

Trudy looked up as someone entered the room. She went cold. It was Lex. This time he wasn't smiling. He leant casually against the door frame. 'So, what are your plans?' he asked.

'How d'you mean?'

'Now you don't need all of us running after you. What are you gonna do?'

Trudy put the magazine down. 'I still don't understand. Same as the rest of you.'

Lex shook his head, came into the room and sat on the bed. 'I don't think so.'

Trudy instinctively moved away, disturbed by his presence and his tone. 'Do you know something I don't?'

'Yeh. You're not welcome.'

'You've changed your tune!'

Lex sneered. 'Oh, that. Just sweet-talk for the boyfriend. I want you out. You and the brat.'

Trudy was worried. She wished Bray would hurry up and come back. 'When exactly?'

'Soon as you're well enough to get up.'

Trying to bluff it out, sounding tough, she flared at him. 'Are you sure you don't want me to go now! When I can barely crawl out of bed!'

'I wouldn't be so mean.'

Tears were welling up, despite herself. 'What have I done to you, Lex?'

'Nothing personal, girl. We voted you out and now you're leaving.'

'Bray invited me to stay!'

'And who's he to do that? Some of us don't want him either.'

'Do I have a choice?'

Lex stood up and leaned over her. Trudy shrank back. 'Yeh, you can go tomorrow or the next day.'

'Gee thanks!'

'Don't mention it.' He leant closer menacingly. 'Specially to lover boy. You wouldn't want to see his pretty face get all messed up, would you?'

Trudy was cowering down in the bed. Lex looked up at a sound and stepped back.

Bray entered frowning. 'What's going on?'

'Talk of the devil. We were just missing you, weren't we, Trudy?'

Bray stood by the open door. 'Would you like to leave now, Lex?'

'Pleasure.'

On his way out he smashed his shoulder into Bray's. Bray was about to react, but Trudy called out.

'Bray! No!'

Bray relaxed and went over to her. 'Has he been hassling you?'

She tried to shrug it off. 'Nothing I can't handle.'

189

'Because if he has -'

She took hold of his hand. 'I said it's nothing. Really...But I've had a chance to think.'

'And?'

'I'll see him.'

Bray was relieved. 'Good.'

'Only inside the mall. I'm not setting foot outside. Tell him those are my terms, take it or leave it.'

EIGHTY SEVEN

The days were getting shorter, but Amber didn't know what date it was. It would have been easy to keep track with a calendar, but there didn't seem much point. In fact it was probably better not to. The world that they had all known had ended, and to be reminded of special days, birthdays, Christmas, New Year, would only be upsetting. Bringing back memories of happier times, with people they loved who they would never see again.

As leader Amber decided she should make a tour of the mall each night, while people were settling down to sleep. It rounded off the day. Chalking off another day that they had survived. Would it always be like this, she wondered? Would there ever come a time when they could sleep easily in their beds, feeling safe and secure from the outside world? To wake up and be able to go outside, to feel the sunshine, to run in the fields, to swim in the sea. To feel normal again. That seemed a long way away.

Salene was already tucked up in bed with her face to the wall when Amber entered the room that Salene shared with the little ones. Though there were more than enough stores for everyone to have a separate sleeping space, Salene had chosen to sleep alongside Patsy, Cloe and Paul. They would still wake in the night with nightmares, fearful and upset about everything that had happened to them in their short lives and Salene wanted to be close by to comfort them.

The little ones were still quietly playing a space board game by candlelight.

'We had this game on DVD, didn't we, Paul?' Patsy said. 'We had a nice house. I miss it.'

'I miss my mom and my dad.' Cloe began to cry.

'Hey,' said Amber. 'What's up, chicken?'

'She misses her mom and dad.' Patsy began to look tearful. 'Me too. Why did they have to die, Amber?'

Amber sighed. 'I'm afraid I don't know, sweetheart. I wish I did...Anyway it's way past your bedtime. Come on, bed, all of you.'

She watched as they all tucked themselves in bed, kissed them all 'goodnight' and then continued her rounds through the darkened mall.

Bray waited until Amber had passed and then slipped quietly away into the sewers.

EIGHTY EIGHT

He knew that Ebony had been watching him like a hawk. But there was no way he could explain the situation to her. She would have felt threatened and vulnerable, and who knows how that would have made her react? Ebony was a hellcat, a fireball waiting to explode. He didn't want to light the fuse until he had everything under control.

He looked down at her, his beautiful, dangerous leiutenant. She was snoring, sound asleep. The powder he had slipped into her drink had worked fast. He hoped he hadn't overdone it. She would probably wake with a headache, but that was nothing to the headache he was going to present her with in the morning. It would take some explaining, but he was sure he could square the circle and keep everyone happy. He was leader of the Locos. He could do as he pleased. And if Ebony didn't like it, well, it would be a pity. But she would have to go.

ooo

There was no moon that night, but there was starlight and his eyes had become accustomed to the darkness. He saw Bray waiting at the pre-arranged rendezvous and together they made their way through the silent night as the city slept uneasily.

They crossed swiftly in the shadows to the commercial sector, where Bray climbed down a camouflaged manhole at the rear of a large shopping mall. As Bray switched on a torch to show him the ladder, he followed, his boots ringing on the metal rungs.

At the bottom of the ladder inside the sewers he had a moment of doubt. 'So where's Trudy..? If this is a trap!'

'It's not a trap!' Bray said genuinely, trying to reassure him. 'I'll go and get her. You wait here.'

He watched Bray disappear into the blackness of the sewers leaving him in the dark. He followed quietly behind keeping the light of the torch in sight.

Bray slipped through a door at the end of the tunnel and closed the door behind him. It was suddenly black as pitch. Creeping along the narrow path at the side of the tunnel, using his hands to feel his way along the slimy wall, he reached the heavy metal door and carefully prised it open.

Warily Zoot entered the silent mall.

EIGHTY NINE

Though the rest of the mall slept, there was no way Trudy could sleep. She lay propped up in bed with the sleeping baby in her arms, waiting anxiously. After what seemed an eternity, she heard quiet footsteps and Bray came into the room. He put a finger to his lips and motioned to her. She followed him out, suddenly fearful. But it was too late to change her mind now.

Zoot was waiting for them at the bottom of the staircase.

'I told you to wait in the sewers!' Bray hissed.

'No way. I don't like nasty surprises.'

Bray smiled grimly. 'Well, here's a nice one. Say 'hello' to your daughter.'

For a long moment Zoot stared at Trudy with the baby in her arms. 'How do I know it's mine?'

'You're the only one. I've never been with anyone else.'

Bray looked at him. 'She's your daughter. You know she is.'

Zoot recovered from his surprise quickly. 'So that's why you brought me here?'

'She's your responsibility.' Bray said.

'You took her, you keep her,' Zoot said sulkily.

'I didn't take her,' Bray insisted. 'She ran away from you and the Locos because she was scared. I found her, and looked after her, that's all.'

Zoot was thinking fast. He looked at Trudy in the dim light. She looked paler and thinner than he remembered, but in some ways that made her seem more attractive. 'That right, babe? You gonna come back with me, then?' He had always wanted Trudy. She was his weakness. And now with a baby...

195

Great leaders should always leave a dynasty, someone to carry on the name.

Trudy was silent, holding the baby close to her.

'You and the kid will be safer with me and the Locos than with a bunch of losers.'

'We're not losers, Zoot,' Bray said firmly. 'We're survivors.'

'Get real, man! You've seen it out there! The only people who are going to survive are the strong. Like me and my warriors.'

ooo

Up above them Patsy shook Lex awake. 'What's going on?' he snapped.

'Paul heard somebody in the mall!'

'He's a deffo!' Lex said gruffly. 'Go back to bed.'

'He hears things! Vibrations!'

Bob the dog suddenly began to bark. An insistent warning bark. Lex jumped out of bed and shook the sleeping Ryan.

'Ryan! Grab a weapon!'

ooo

Zoot was getting impatient. That dog was going to wake the whole place. He didn't want to hang around. 'You're my woman, Trude! Let's go! Come on!'

'I can't!'

'That's my kid! Come on!'

'You want her, you stay here with me!' Trudy cried.

Their voices were raised now and he could hear that others in the mall were awake. 'I can't do that!'

'Yes, you can!' Bray took hold of Zoot's arm.

Zoot shook him off. 'Get lost, man! Power and Chaos! That's the only way!'

Bray was desperate now. There were alarmed voices above them. He didn't have much time. 'Don't you think there's been enough death and destruction? We've gotta start putting things back together again!'

'Why?'

Bray took the baby from Trudy and put in Zoot's arms. 'For her! That's why!'

'What a pretty picture!' Lex appeared on the stairs brandishing a baseball bat. Ryan was close behind. Seeing Zoot was alone, Lex shouted to Ryan. 'Ryan, watch the sewers!'

Ryan leapt over the balcony rail and rushed to the sewer door, to guard against any Locos coming in. With Zoot's escape now cut off, Lex advanced down the stairs towards him, weapon raised.

'He's on his own, Lex!' Bray shouted. 'He's unarmed!'

Lex kept coming, grimly. 'Well, you don't look so tough now, do you? The Great Zoot! We've got a score to settle!'

Bray met him at the bottom of the stairs, barring his way. 'Listen to me!'

Lex tried to barge past him to get at Zoot. Bray grabbed his arm and held him back.

'Trudy!' Zoot yelled. Thrusting the baby into her arms, he leapt up over the banister and up the stairs looking for another way out.

'After him!' Lex shouted to Ryan. He fought Bray off and ran back up the stairs, as Amber and the rest appeared on the balcony, dazed from sleep and panicked.

'What's going on!' Amber cried.

'It's the Locos!' Ryan shouted.

The kids began to scream. The dog joined in, barking frantically. Lex shouted above the mayhem. 'It's alright! There's only one of them!'

Salene was frantic, looking about. 'Where is he?'

'He's hiding. He can't get out. Leave him to me and Ryan!'

Bray ran back up the stairs. 'Hold it! Hold it! You don't understand!'

'I understand alright,' snapped Lex. 'He's the traitor! Grab him, Ryan!'

Before Bray could react, Ryan pinned his arms from behind.

'Traitor!' Lex slammed the bat into Bray's stomach. Bray doubled up with a loud cry of pain. Lex raised the bat to crash it on Bray's unprotected head.

Amber screamed. 'No!'

'Leave him!' Zoot had suddenly appeared on the balcony. 'If you wanna fight, fight me!'

Lex turned to face him, weapon raised. As Zoot rushed ferociously at him, Lex sidestepped deftly at the last moment. Zoot was running too hard to stop. Tumbling headfirst over the balcony rail, he crashed to the floor below with a cry and lay still.

NINETY

She awoke with a thumping headache, which was most unusual for her. She took three aspirin and lay with her eyes closed waiting for them to take effect. She tried to concentrate through the throbbing pain in her head. It was early. And Zoot was missing. He was not an early riser so something was definitely wrong.

It had to be something to do with the note, she was sure of that. The note that Zoot had burnt. He had been secretive and mute about its contents, but she had caught him in odd moments looking unusually thoughtful and preoccupied. She hated to be out of the loop. Information was the way you stayed ahead of the game. Knowledge was power. Without it there was only chaos.

After ten minutes the pain had receded to a dull ache and she got up. She threw on a richly embroidered kimono, slipped on her high-wedged sandals, and went outside. She wandered the whole of the rail yard looking, but not wanting to alert anyone else. If Zoot was missing she needed time to think. She managed to question the Locos who had been guarding the perimeter last night without giving anything away, she hoped. No one had seen Zoot leave. But she knew he was no longer there.

In the centre of the railyard, Spike was taking some new recruits through a martial arts drill. Normally she would have joined in. She got a thrill from the bodily contact. Enjoyed showing off her own fighting skills which were second only to Zoot and perhaps Spike. She had never fought Spike in earnest.

She hoped she would never have to. If she had to fight Spike, that would mean that Zoot was no longer around. And this morning, he wasn't.

NINETY ONE

Zoot was dead. His neck broken by the fall. They had all gathered around the body in shocked silence, as Bray checked for signs of life. There were none. He stood up, looking pale, and went to Trudy who was sobbing uncontrollably. He took her in his arms, gazing down at the body grimly.

Lex was triumphant. 'I showed him! Nobody messes with Lex!'

'Shut it!' Amber snapped, in no mood for Lex's gleeful boasting. No matter who it was, death was not a cause for celebration. She asked Salene to take the little ones away to the café. When they had gone she turned to Bray. 'I think you have some explaining to do.'

'He wasn't going to hurt anybody,' Bray said sadly.

Lex was not convinced. 'Yeah? What was he doing here then?'

'He came to see me,' Trudy said. 'And his baby.'

They all looked at Trudy, amazed.

'His baby?' Amber repeated. 'But we all thought Bray was...' She couldn't finish. The news was such a shock.

'Bray found me after I ran away from the Locos,' Trudy explained. 'He looked after me, that's all.'

Not convinced that Zoot had come alone, Lex took Ryan and Jack to check the sewers. While they were gone Amber fetched a large white sheet and covered Zoot's body. She looked up at Bray questioningly. He was still standing gazing down at the shrouded figure, transfixed. He looked at her, but was clearly in no mood for explanations.

Bray led the sobbing Trudy up the stairs to the café. Amber followed, confused. They waited in sombre silence, until Lex and the other two came back and reported they had found nothing.

'Bray was telling the truth, for once,' Lex sneered.

Amber turned to Bray. 'We need to decide what to do with the body. It can't stay here.'

Bray looked distraught and withdrawn. He nodded. 'I know,' he said quietly.

'No problem!' said Lex. 'Just dump it in the street with the rest of the garbage!'

'No!' Trudy cried out.

Bray looked up, suddenly animated. His voice was fierce. 'You're not going to dump it anywhere! We're going to give him a proper burial, Lex!' Bray glared at Lex. And if looks could kill, Lex would have dropped dead on the spot.

Lex shifted uneasily under Bray's murderous gaze. 'Do what you like with it. I don't care,' said Lex moodily.

'You should,' Trudy glared at Lex. 'You killed him!'

'I didn't kill him! It was an accident! I saved all your lives and this is the thanks I get!' Lex strode out in a sulk.

Amber looked at Bray. There was something very strange going on that she didn't know. 'All the graveyards are full, Bray.' Amber said.

Bray finally spoke. 'I was thinking of something else. Something he would have wanted.'

Amber looked at him curiously. How well had Bray known Zoot, and for how long?

NINETY TWO

Death had become commonplace in their world. At the end so many were dying that communal graves were dug in the parks and on the outskirts of the city. Huge diggers with gaping mouths gouged up flower beds and football pitches, and wagons piled high with corpses filled in the cavernous holes.

The ritual of the funeral had been abandoned in the last days of the old world. But, with the exception of Lex, and Ryan who agreed with everything Lex said, everyone else in the mall felt that this was somehow special. They had all witnessed the death of Zoot, and it seemed only right to mark it properly. As it used to be.

The funeral party took their lead from Bray and Trudy. Gone were the wild mix of coloured clothes and tribal face paint. In their place were somber blacks and hats made of crows and raven's feathers, heralds of death.

While Zandra and Salene stayed behind to look after the baby and the little ones, Bray led Trudy, Amber, Jack and Dal out through the sewers with Zoot's body wrapped in the white sheet. Outside they placed the body in an abandoned shopping trolley and set off towards the sea. That way was safer, as the tribes were concentrated in the city, but that wasn't the reason Bray had chosen it.

After half an hour they reached the coast. Bray scoured the empty beach with his eyes. Where once many boats had bobbed at anchor close to shore, or lain beached on the shingle, there was not one in sight. All had been taken by the last adults trying to escape the virus, or by kids who had sailed away fleeing the violence in the city. They searched the dunes beyond the beach and found, almost covered by the sand, an old rowing boat so decrepit that no one had dared to take to sea in it.

'This'll do fine,' Bray said.

Bray dragged the boat to the shoreline, while the others searched the beach for driftwood, anything that would burn. Dal found a can of outboard motor fuel in a run-down fishing hut and came running along the beach waving it excitedly.

'No outboard though, I'm afraid,' he told Bray.

'No problem, the tide is going out.'

On Bray's instructions they piled the boat with driftwood which Dal then poured the remains of the petrol can over. Bray lifted the wrapped body, tenderly laid it on top of the driftwood, then knelt down beside the boat. Uncovering Zoot's face, he took a leather studded necklace from around the dead boy's neck, as tears began to run down his cheeks.

'Goodnight, Martin. 'Have a safe journey to the other side. Everybody will be there waiting for you.'

Standing close by, Amber, Jack and Dal exchanged puzzled looks.

Bray covered the face with the sheet again and stood up. Striking a match he applied the flame to the wood. Then, as the flames caught hold and began to lick around the corpse, Bray waded into the water and pushed the boat out to sea. They watched as the tide took the blazing boat out across the gentle waves.

'Just like a Viking burial,' Jack said. 'They did it for their warrior chiefs.'

Trudy stood watching the boat, her eyes filled with tears.

Amber was standing beside Bray. 'Martin?'

Bray nodded gravely. 'Yes. That was his real name...He was my brother. My kid brother.'

Like Zoot's departing spirit a large white seagull crested the waves and soared into the sky, its lonely cry echoing to the horizon.

NINETY THREE

Ebony was deeply worried. Zoot had disappeared during the night and at midday he was still not back. It wasn't possible that he had been kidnapped from inside the rail yard. There were too many guards around. He must have left, voluntarily, but it was possible that he could now be being held against his will. But by whom?

There had been rumours of Demon Dogs suicide squads. Retaliation for the attack on the cathedral meeting. But Zoot had left of his own free will, for his own reasons, and it was beyond coincidence that he had stumbled into one of those. Especially at night, when no one ventured out. So where was he?

There was no way she could keep his disappearance a secret from the rest of the Locos. With their leader missing, she would have to assume command and hope that the Locos would accept her leadership without question. She knew there were people like Spike waiting for a chance to seize control, and just because Zoot had picked her as his deputy didn't mean the Locos would go along with that now he was not around. She had to act fast and decisively. Gathering all the tribe together, she stood on the bonnet of the police car and addressed them.

'Zoot is missing!'

Mutterings started in the crowd which she stopped with a wave of her hand.

'We will search the whole city 'til we find him! Leave no stone unturned! Take prisoners from the tribes and bring them back here for questioning! Find Zoot!'

She raised her arms in the familiar crossed wrist battle sign. 'Power and Chaos!'

The assembled Locos repeated the mantra. 'Power and Chaos!'

Ebony jumped down into the front seat of the car and gave the order. The car sped off, siren screaming.

NINETY FOUR

The day had been a long one. The mall was silent, swathed in darkness. There was no moon or stars that night. To Bray, standing alone on the stairs, it felt that was how it should be.

Leaning on the balcony rail at the place where Zoot had fallen to his death, he turned his brother's leather necklace round and round between his fingers. The necklace he had bought Martin years ago when his little brother was going through his 'hippy' phase.

He was remembering the times before the virus. The happy times, when the future had seemed so bright. Two intelligent young boys with their whole lives ahead of them. Now one was dead, and the other? What future was there for him?

Hearing footsteps behind him, he put the necklace in his pocket but didn't turn around.

'Bray?'

'Salene? What are you doing up?'

'I couldn't sleep.' She had been aware of his gloomy mood all day. Since he had come back from the funeral. She didn't want to intrude, but she wanted to be near him in his strange sadness. Now that the truth about the baby's father was out in the open, she saw no reason to hold back about her feelings for him. 'Do you mind if I join you?'

Bray shook his head, still staring at the spot on the floor below.

'Amber told me about Zoot. I know he was evil and everything –'

Bray cut across her. 'He was my brother, Salene.'

Salene was taken aback. Amber had told her about the Viking style burial, but she hadn't mentioned that.

'Your brother?'

'My kid brother, Martin.'

'But how? How did he..?'

'Become Zoot?' Bray heaved a huge sigh. 'Martin was the baby of the family. My parents loved him to pieces. Took him everywhere. Always playing, laughing together. The three of them were inseparable...And then, when the virus struck, and they died...' He didn't go on.

'He changed?'

'He was so angry. So bitter. You wouldn't believe this but Martin actually was a very gentle boy. I had to protect him when he first started school. Some kids used to bully him...' He looked up at her, his face full of sadness. 'I didn't protect him last night, did I?'

'Bray, it wasn't your fault.'

His tone was bitter now. 'I brought him here. He'd still be alive if I hadn't.'

'But you wanted him and Trudy to be together again. For him to look after his baby. It wasn't your fault, Bray. You were trying to help.'

'Maybe people should just leave things as they are and not get involved.'

'I'm sorry, Bray. So sorry.' She put her hand up and gently touched his shoulder. 'You're cold. I'll go and make you a hot drink, okay?'

'Thanks.'

She stroked his shoulder fondly and left. As she went back up the stairs her heart was beating fast. He hadn't opened his heart to Trudy. He'd opened up to her. Maybe this was her time. The moment.

NINETY FIVE

At midnight Ebony was restlessly tossing and turning in her empty bed. All day the Locos search parties had turned the city upside down looking for Zoot, without success. They had snatched dozens of prisoners and interrogated them all, with the same result. No one knew anything. Except by now all the city's tribes knew the legendary leader of the Locos was missing. And that was a problem.

Would they try to take advantage of the situation, feeling that the Locos had been weakened by his loss? And was he lost, or had he voluntarily gone into hiding, for some reason known only to himself? Too many questions, too few answers.

But she knew the biggest question she had to find the answer to right now. Who was going to take control of the Locos in Zoot's absence? Who was going to become the new leader, temporary or not?

That morning the Locos had obeyed her instructions to find Zoot without question. To search for him was the logical thing to do. But now it was clear he was nowhere to be found, would they keep obeying her? And what should be her next move?

She knew that Spike was a potential rival. She thought he was stupid, but he was tall and powerful and commanded respect among most of the Locos. How should she proceed in the hours, the days ahead? When would Spike's challenge to her leadership come? For she knew it would come, any day, at any moment.

She got up. There was no point in trying to sleep. She had to prepare a plan of action to survive.

NINETY SIX

The whole mall was woken by Salene's screams. Trudy was first into the café. She rushed in and stopped dead, staring at the sight of Salene cradled in Bray's arms.

'What's going on, Bray!' she demanded.

'Rats!' Salene gasped. 'All over the café!'

Bray disentangled himself from Salene's embrace as the others filed bleary-eyed into the café.

'Salene was getting a hot drink,' Bray explained. 'They were on the tables eating off the plates.'

Lex yawned and scratched his chest. 'Is that all? I thought someone had been murdered or something.'

'Rats aren't a joke, Lex!' Amber snapped. 'They spread disease. Maybe even the virus for all we know.'

Patsy's eye widened in fear. 'Have they got the virus?'

Amber bit her tongue. 'No, Patsy. I didn't mean that.' The last thing she wanted was to scare the little ones.

'But they can be dangerous,' said Dal. 'They attack you if they're cornered.'

'Or bring in their Loco friends to kill you in your beds.' Lex was glaring at Bray.

Bray made a move towards Lex, his fists clenched. Salene clutched his arm. 'No, Bray!' She looked at the rest defiantly, protecting her man. 'Zoot was his brother.'

Ryan's eyes widened in amazement, 'His brother?'

'Oh,' Zandra said. 'It all makes sense now.'

The information didn't deter Lex. 'What difference does it make? He's still a traitor! We should kick him and his tart out!'

Bray moved away from Salene and confronted Lex face to face. 'You killed her baby's father! She's not going anywhere!'

The sound of the baby's loud cries were echoing round the mall.

'Shut that brat up!' Lex snarled, storming out of the café.

Amber looked around at them all. 'Alright everybody. I think we've all had enough for tonight. But as soon as we get up, we clean up this pigsty!'

Everyone trooped wearily from the room. Salene remained, gazing longingly after Bray. She saw Trudy glaring at her as she crossed the balcony to her room. With a determined look, Salene followed after her.

ooo

Bray entered the room and picked the crying baby out of the cot. Trudy was right behind him.

'Do you want her?'

'No. You have her!' Trudy sounded miffed. She flounced onto the bed and lay back. Bray groaned inwardly, sensing she was in one of her moods.

Salene entered the room boldly. 'Can I help?'

'No!' Trudy snapped. 'Get out!'

'I think she needs feeding, Salene. Do you mind?'

Trudy looked daggers at Bray for not backing her.

Salene smiled. 'Course not.' She held out her arms to take the baby. 'Come on little no-name. Let's get you sorted.' She flashed Bray a big smile and left.

'Cheeky cow!' gasped Trudy when Salene had gone.

'Trudy!'

'Little no-name! What did she mean by that!'

Bray shrugged. 'It's the truth. You haven't given her a name yet.'

Trudy remained stubbornly indignant. 'What business is it of hers?'

Bray tried to be conciliatory. He sat on the bed, adopting a calm tone. 'Look, Trudy, I know you're upset. But don't take it out on Salene. She's only trying to help.'

'Huh! I know what she's trying to do! What were you doing out there with her anyway?'

'I wasn't with her. I was on my own, thinking about Martin.'

'He wasn't Martin anymore, he was Zoot!'

Bray looked at her, frowning. 'I thought you liked him?'

'I did...once.'

Bray's tone turned icy. 'Well, if you'd changed your mind, why did you let me bring him in here?'

Trudy looked a little guilty. 'I wanted to see...what I felt.' She sat up, gazing into his eyes. 'Don't you know, Bray? Can't you see?'

Bray looked away. He was irritated now and didn't want to hear what she was going to say next. 'Trudy –'

'I love you!'

He gave a little groan. 'Oh, Trudy.'

'No! It's true, Bray!' She put her hand on his shoulder, rushing on, anxious to let him know her feelings. Things she had kept bottled up for so long. 'I want us to be together! To bring up the baby! That's why I haven't given her a name. I want us to chose, together!'

Bray felt suddenly very weary. 'Trudy, so much has happened to all of us. We're all hurting, confused...I don't know how I feel. All I know is Martin's dead...' He stood up. 'I need time. Give me time, Trudy. Please!'

He walked out. Trudy fell back on the bed miserable and confused, the image of Salene wrapped in Bray's arms burning into her brain.

NINETY SEVEN

Zandra picked up her duvet and padded silently onto the balcony. She saw Salene at the top of the stairs with the baby in her arms, feeding it with a bottle. Unaware of her, lost in her own world, Salene was talking to the baby.

'Come on, drink up, you want to be a big strong girl for your Uncle Bray, don't you?'

Zandra smiled to herself and made her way to Lex and Ryan's room. Ryan lay on his back, snoring. He could sleep pegged out on a clothesline. Lex was sitting up in bed staring into space moodily. He looked up as Zandra put her duvet down on the floor in a corner of the room.

'Zan, what's up? Can't sleep?'

'It's those rats! I'm sure one of them's got into my place!'

Lex smiled, mock sympathetically. 'Ah, really?' He patted the bed beside him. 'Well, come and lie down with me, babe. I'll protect you.'

'No thanks. I can do without your kind of protection.' She settled down into her duvet.

'I have got protection as a matter of fact.'

Zandra made a disgusted noise. 'Typical. That's all you think about!'

'Wouldn't want any girl of mine to wind up like that poor cow, Trudy, would I? Bringing up a brat in this world. No way, I'm a caring sensitive kind of guy.'

Her tone was sarcastic. 'Yeah?'

'I gave Salene my water ration to bath the baby, didn't I?'

'Wouldn't have had an ulterior motive, I suppose?'

Lex sounded hurt. 'Zan, what do I have to do?'

She turned over in her duvet to sleep. 'I'll let you know.'

Lex settled back on his pillow. 'You do that, babe. I can wait,' he said with a generous tone he wasn't really feeling. Zandra was a strange girl. He was sure she fancied him. She was always hanging around. But she was also hanging back. He'd try the generous bit for a while to see if it won her over, but it went against the grain. Generosity wasn't his strong point. Waiting wasn't either.

NINETY EIGHT

Ebony had finally dozed, but she was up well before the sun rose. Like all the other tribes, the Locos slept late. In the pre-virus days they would have had their parents nagging them to get up for school or college. Now they could do as they pleased. Zoot had never challenged that.

But Ebony sensed she had to move quickly before they absorbed the fact that their leader was now missing for a second day. Move, before they even considered who should be their new leader. She was Zoot's chosen deputy, but she was a girl. In this new macho world that counted against her.

'Power and Chaos' was the Locos battle cry. The Locos chanted it like they echoed football chants in the past. She knew that 'Power and Chaos' was a smokescreen. Zoot was a cunning, highly intelligent youth who knew that organization was the key. But 'Power and Organization' didn't have the same charismatic ring.

She had prepared a battle plan. Drawn up a map of the city with the sectors controlled by each tribe marked in different colours. It was on a white board so the colours could be altered to reflect the changing fortunes of the tribes. The Locos controlled the largest part of the city. But the Demon Dogs were snapping at their heels.

The first light of day was streaking the night sky as she gathered all the squad leaders in the carriage HQ. They stood before her blinking, bleary-eyed, Spike among them.

'I make no apologies for the early call,' she began determinedly. 'We have a big problem. The tribes all know our great leader Zoot is missing. They will think that makes us weak. The Demon Dogs want our sector and before the day is out they will attack. They think without Zoot we will be easy meat. We have to show them different. Attack is the best form of defence. We attack while they sleep. We attack at dawn… Power and Chaos!'

NINETY NINE

Across the city another girl was rallying her troops. Amber banged the metal saucepan with the wooden spoon like a gong. The sound was deafening throughout the mall. She put down the saucepan and waited with a determined look in her eyes.

One by one the others dragged themselves out of their rooms and gathered in the café where Amber was waiting. The noise had set the baby crying.

'Well, that was great,' Lex grumbled. 'Waking up the brat!'

'She'll survive. But we won't unless we get our act together. There's no point in surviving the virus only to die of food poisoning.' With her spoon Amber pointed at a chart stuck on the wall. 'So I've drawn up this.'

Zandra rubbed the sleep from her eyes. 'What is it?'

'It's a work rota. I've divided all the chores amongst us, so we all do everything.'

Ryan peered at his name on the chart. 'Sweeping floors?'

'Only in the mall,' Amber clarified. 'Everyone's responsible for their own living spaces.'

Jack screwed up his face. 'Cleaning windows? Washing up?'

'Where's Bray?' Lex was looking around.

Amber pointed to the chart. 'There. With Dal. Food foraging. We need to get some fresh fruit and vegetables. We can't live on this processed muck for ever.'

Lex folded him arms, smugly. 'I meant where is he? He isn't here, is he?'

They all looked around. Bray wasn't with them.

'Oh, no,' Zandra exclaimed. 'Not again!'

Dal raised his eyebrows. 'Typical!'

'It's alright, Dal, I'll come with you.'

Dal winced at Lex's offer.

'Good.' Amber looked around. 'Any questions?'

Patsy piped up eagerly. 'When do we start, Amber?'

'Now, while we can still see through the dirt! Read the rota and get on with your jobs.'

Amber watched as they gathered unhappily around the rota, chattering and grumbling among themselves. So Bray was missing again? He was impossible. A constant irritant.

The news that Bray was not the father had surprised and shocked her. Like all the rest she had been convinced the baby was his. Salene had clearly taken the news as a green light, and Amber was convinced there was going to be trouble between Salene and Trudy anytime soon. Trouble they could well do without if they wanted to have a future as a tribe.

Bray seemed to bring nothing but trouble. First Trudy and the baby, and now Zoot. Part of her wished he would take Trudy and the baby and find somewhere else to live. Find someone else to annoy. The other part, well, she would keep that part well under wraps.

ONE HUNDRED

It was early but the city was unusually noisy. At that time in the morning people were generally still asleep. In a harsh, bleak world it was hard to remain positive. There was little reason, or incentive, to get up early. Why bother when every day was the same? Where to get food? How to survive the tribes?

Bray was still grieving for his kid brother, Martin. He blamed himself for his death, but he thought bitterly of Trudy. If she no longer loved his brother she should have said. He couldn't understand why she had agreed to meet Zoot in the mall. If only she had been honest he would still be alive. But that was history. Going over it again wouldn't bring Martin back.

He was keen to know who had taken command now the Locos were leaderless. In this lawless, unpredictable world it paid to stay one step ahead. Knowledge was power. And what you didn't know could kill you.

He had left the mall before the others had risen. It was always safer to move around the city early in the day. But today was different. He saw a pall of black smoke rising in the distance. Something was happening over in the sector ruled by the Demon Dogs. Cautiously Bray skateboarded in the direction of the sounds and smoke. He moved like an animal, eyes and ears alert for danger.

Then he heard it. The familiar siren sound. He took cover behind a makeshift barricade, a relic of some past tribal battle. Down the street a cavalcade was approaching. The police car surrounded by a rollerblading war party of Locos.

Standing proudly in the front of the car, like a visiting dignitary, was a figure he recognized immediately. There was no mistaking the arrogant attitude, the ruthless, triumphant look in the cat-like eyes. Bray was dismayed. Zoot had been succeeded by Ebony.

He knew her. Knew her too well. There was history between them. Bad history.

ONE HUNDRED AND ONE

For the first time ever most people in the mall were busy. Amber's rota seemed to be working, with the exception of Trudy who lay brooding in her bed, which wasn't surprising as Bray was missing again, and Salene kept throwing herself at him whenever he was around.

Zandra met Salene on the balcony pushing the baby in a pram. 'You've got a cushy job, haven't you?'

'The baby was bored,' Salene replied. 'She was whingeing. They like movement.'

Zandra looked inside the pram. 'Pretty thing. Hello! My name's Zandra..! Has she got one yet?'

'No.'

'What's Trudy thinking of? We can't keep calling it 'it'!'

'To be honest, I don't think she's interested. Some people don't deserve babies.'

'Well, I don't suppose she planned it, did she?' Zandra said. 'Not with that Zoot anyway.'

'I think she'd rather it was Bray's.'

Zandra agreed. 'Mmm. Do you think he'll stick around? With her?'

Salene shrugged. 'Who knows? She seems to be doing alright so far. Lying around all day playing the tragedy queen.'

'I bet that's post-natal depression. I read all about that. I'll go cheer her up.'

ooo

Downstairs on the ground floor Ryan was listlessly sweeping with a broom, bored. He'd rather be outside foraging for food with Lex, but Amber's rota didn't say that and, unlike Lex, Ryan generally obeyed the rules.

The twins, Patsy and Paul walked by with the dog on a lead. Ryan frowned. 'What are you two doing? Why aren't you working?'

Patsy did all the talking for the pair. Paul only signed to her. 'We are. We're exercising Bob.'

'Call that working?' Ryan sounded miffed.

'Yes. And after Amber said we can go and play.'

'Play? What at?'

Patsy shrugged. 'Dunno. Do you know any good games?'

An idea suddenly dawned in Ryan's mind. It seemed like a very good idea. 'Have you ever played poker?'

'You mean cards? Like 'Snap'?'

Ryan grinned. 'Sort of.'

ONE HUNDRED AND TWO

Lex and Dal had wandered to what had once been the commercial heart of the city, only half a mile from the mall. The pristine avenues, once full of bustling city folk, were now deserted, strewn with litter, garbage and abandoned trash.

Lex kicked a can along the road. 'Look at this place! It's a disgrace! Have to write to the council about it,' he joked.

Dal was fretting. 'We're not going to find anything we want here, Lex. We should have headed for the woods. There's no fresh food here.'

'Relax! What's your problem? We've plenty of time. Did you bring it?'

'Yeah.' Dal looked unhappy.

'Let's see it then.'

Reluctantly Dal took a catcher's mitt and a baseball from his rucksack. Lex grabbed the ball from Dal's hand.

'Get over there!' he instructed. 'Catcher.'

'Lex, we're supposed to be looking for food!'

Casually Lex tossed the ball up in the air and caught it. 'Dal, look around. What do you see?'

Dal looked round at the empty streets. 'What d'you mean?'

'See any Demon Dogs? Any Locos?'

Dal shook his head. 'No.'

'So, let's have some fun!'

He hurled the ball. Dal ducked.

'Strike One! Lex cried. 'Well, go fetch the ball, dummy!'

Dal sighed and hurried after the ball. He hated to let Amber down, but he was scared. Lex was a vicious bully. No point in surviving the Locos only to get beaten up by one of your own.

ONE HUNDRED AND THREE

There was a pile of matches in the centre of the table. Their own piles lay in front of them. By far the larger pile belonged to Patsy and Paul. They were enjoying this new game called Poker. Poker was easy.

Ryan contemplated the cards in his hand and sighed. He looked worried. Paul signed urgently to Patsy.

'We'll see you,' she said confidently.

Reluctantly Ryan lay down his cards. With a huge grin Paul raked the matches over to their pile.

'We've won again!' Patsy crowed delighted.

Ryan nodded gloomily. 'Yeah. You've picked this up quick, haven't you?'

Paul signed to her.

'Another game?' Patsy asked.

Ryan pretended to hesitate, then said, 'Okay. Tell you what. Shall we make it more interesting?'

Patsy looked puzzled. 'How?'

'Let's play for something real.'

Patsy looked at Paul. He signed to her again. 'Okay,' she said brightly.

Ryan scratched his chin, as if pretending to think. 'Now what could we play for?'

ooo

Salene was seated in the café contentedly feeding the baby with a bottle as Amber hurried in carrying a broom, wearing a stern look on her face. 'Where is everyone?'

Salene looked up. 'Who?'

'Well, Ryan for a start.' She held up the broom. 'This is his broom, but no Ryan! And where's Cloe? She's supposed to be cleaning.'

'I dunno.'

'And Zandra? Where is she?'

Salene knew the answer to that one. 'She's gone to cheer Trudy up.'

Amber let out an exasperated sigh. 'She's supposed to be washing up!'

Salene watched as Amber stormed out, then went back to gazing happily at the baby.

ooo

Patsy and Paul were looking glum. Their hand lay face up on the table before them. Ryan laid down his cards chirpily and grinned. His hand beat theirs once again. He consulted a piece of paper.

'So that's sweeping today, washing up tomorrow, cleaning doors and windows the next day and sweeping again the day after...Do you want another hand?'

The twins shook their heads unhappily.

'Okay. Back to work then,' Ryan said briskly. 'I'll finish walking the dog for you.'

ONE HUNDRED AND FOUR

Trudy was lying on the bed listlessly reading an old magazine for the third time. She sighed and threw it down, looking strained and anxious. Salene came into the room breezily wheeling the pram.

'Here we are. She's been a little angel!'

Trudy looked at her sulkily. 'I thought you'd run off with her.'

'Would you care if I did?' Salene retaliated. 'If you didn't want the baby why did you..? With Zoot of all people!'

'You don't know anything about him!'

'I know he was a vicious thug!'

'He wasn't always!'

Salene looked at her, curious. 'How long did you know him?'

'None of your business,' Trudy snapped.

'You must have known Bray then, if Zoot was his brother.'

At the word 'Bray' Trudy glared. 'So?'

'I was just wondering –'

'Well you can stop wondering and you can keep your hands off him as well!' Her expression changed abruptly as Bray walked in the door. 'Oh, Bray! Where have you been? I've been so worried!'

Bray looked at both girls. He'd heard the raised voices but didn't want to get involved. 'Been trying to find out what the Locos are up to, now they've no leader.'

'Did you see them?' Salene asked.

Bray nodded, but said nothing else.

Trudy adopted her pathetic voice. 'I wish you wouldn't go out, Bray. I panic every time you do!' She turned to Salene, dismissively. 'Thanks, Salene, we'll look after the baby now. We're going to choose a name for her.'

Salene glanced sadly at Bray, then went out downcast.

Bray sat on the bed. 'What's been going on?'

'Oh, she's just stirring as usual.'

'What about?

'I don't want to talk about it...' Her expression changed. She smiled brightly and gushed. 'What shall we call her? Have you thought of any names? Are there any you really like?'

Bray's face clouded over. 'Trudy, my brother died yesterday! The father of your child! Don't you care? Haven't you got any feelings at all?'

She looked at him desperately. 'I do! I told you! I love you! I always have!'

'You mean...even when you were with Martin?'

'Of course.'

Bray's eyes narrowed. 'So you went with my brother out of what? Spite? Jealousy?'

Trudy looked genuinely confused. 'I don't know! I thought I liked him. He was nice at first. I'm sorry he's dead, really I am!' She put her arms around him, trying to hold him close. 'Oh Bray, I'll be very good to you! We'll be so good together, the three of us! We can look after Martin's baby together! That's what we'll call her, shall we? Martina, after him?'

Bray pulled away and stood up, his face grim. 'How about Zootina?'

As he began to leave, Trudy called out to him, distraught. 'Bray! I'm sorry! I'm sorry for getting you to bring him here!'

He stopped in the doorway, and sighed heavily. 'Yeah well, it's done now.'

'What if the Locos ever find out what happened to him?'

'I wouldn't give much for our chances, Trudy. Looks like they've chosen Ebony as their new leader.'

The blood drained from Trudy's face. 'What?'

Bray looked grim. 'Just pray she never finds out about the baby.'

ONE HUNDRED AND FIVE

Amber felt like crying. She'd had enough. She had started the day with high hopes, in a positive mood, and that in itself was pretty hard to achieve these days. But she had been determined to set an example. Sitting up most of the night drawing up the rota, she'd felt that at last she was getting a grip on the mall. Creating a system to bring back some order into everyone's lives was a start. But they had just ignored it.

Bray had gone walkabout, as usual, Ryan had duped Patsy and Paul into doing his chores, Zandra had completely ignored hers on the pretence of caring for Trudy, Jack had spent the day fiddling with his stupid radio, and Dal and Lex had returned empty-handed claiming to have being chased by the Locos. Which would have been plausible except for the sweaty baseball mitt which fell out of Dal's rucksack.

It was either tears or retaliation. And Amber didn't do tears. They were no use in this world.

All the culprits were sitting around in the café, at tables piled with unwashed pots. Dal was reading from the rota.

'It says here in black and white, 'Cooking, Amber and Salene. Five thirty.'

Lex looked at his watch. 'Well, where are they?'

Amber walked in, a determined look on her face. 'Here!'

'Where's Salene?' Zandra asked.

'I've given her the night off.'

'So where's the grub?'

'Sorry, Lex? Did you speak?'

'You're supposed to be making us a meal. It says so on that.' Jack pointed to the rota on the wall.

'Oh, really?' Amber went to the rota and read out loud. 'Ryan sweeping, Zandra washing up, Jack cleaning windows... Shall I go on?'

Dal frowned. 'You mean –'

'If you don't do your chores, why should I do mine? No chores, no food.'

'Who sez?' Lex leaned back, arms crossed. 'Who appointed you leader?'

'Well, someone's got to take charge of this chaos!'

Zandra sided with Lex aggressively. 'We don't need bossing about! We had all that with the adults! We can do what we like now!'

Amber suddenly felt weary. 'Is that what you really think, Zandra?'

'Yeah!' Zandra went on. 'Who are you to tell us what to do!'

'Fine. Do as you like.' Amber threw the keys to the food store on a table. 'Eat yourselves stupid! Live like pigs! I've had enough!'

Lex picked up the keys as Amber strode out.

'Right, spam and beans!' He held the keys out to Zandra. 'Zan?'

Zandra gave him a withering look. 'In your dreams!'

ONE HUNDRED AND SIX

By contrast to Amber, Ebony was feeling very pleased. Her day had gone well. She had taken control of the Locos decisively, not giving any of her potential rivals chance to draw breath. Even Spike had gone along with her plan without a murmur. But she didn't know how long that would last.

The dawn raid on the Demon Dogs warehouse had gone perfectly. The few dozing guards had been taken completely by surprise. The Locos had taken what goods they wanted, then set fire to the rest, before the other Demon Dogs in their headquarters several blocks away knew what was happening.

The Demon Dogs would retaliate, she knew that. But she would be ready. After the attack at the cathedral the Dogs had been playing catch up. They were the Locos main rivals and once they had been subdued, she could set about taking control of the city in a more organized, sensible way.

Ebony was a street fighter. That was how she had been brought up. But ultimately violence wasn't the way to true power. She knew enough history to know that ultimately all violent regimes failed. People always rose up against them eventually. Violence bred violence. She wasn't going to fall into that trap. But for the moment it was a necessary evil, and she had to admit that combat gave her a thrill. She hoped she could keep that urge under control.

She had let the Locos celebrate. They were crowded noisily round their fires, eating and drinking some of the spoils of the morning's raid, under the stars. But she couldn't join them. She was the leader and leaders had to stay aloof. For the first time since joining the Locos she felt alone. But loneliness came with the territory. She missed Zoot badly, but this was her opportunity, and she wasn't going to let it slip.

ONE HUNDRED AND SEVEN

The mall was waking up in its usual leisurely fashion. Voices began to echo around the balcony, the start of another day when everyone would do just as they pleased with no thought for tomorrow. For tomorrow never comes.

In her immaculately tidy room Zandra was making up her bed as Lex strolled in.

'Hey, Zan! Is that cosy?'

'What's it to you?'

He leant against the doorpost. 'Just thought I could tuck you in one night.'

Zandra regarded him with one of her classic, affronted young lady stares. 'Get lost, Lex!'

'I've been thinking. You keep a nice place. We should settle down now. Have a place of our own.' He stretched out on the newly made bed.

'Since when have you been interested in a place of our own? The only reason you'd want one is so you could have someone to clean up after you. Oh, and a bit of the other, of course!'

Lex grinned. 'Say no more! I'll tell Ryan to leave.'

'I'm not going anywhere near your place!' She flung a duster at him. 'You can clean it up yourself!'

'Babe, that's woman's work! Great warriors don't do housework.'

'Great warriors don't spend all day sitting around on their asses doing nothing!'

Bray walked in looking grim. He thrust Amber's rota in Lex's face. On the back of the paper the felt-tipped words read, 'Wantid. Disent mutha.'

'Is this your idea of a joke?'

'I think you'll find the rota was Amber's idea, Bray.'

'You know what I'm talking about!'

Lex looked at him coolly. 'I don't actually.'

Bray scrunched up the paper and threw it at Lex. 'Wanted Decent mother!'

Lex shrugged. 'I didn't write it.'

'No, I don't suppose you know how!'

Lex jumped up, stung. 'What's the matter? Can't you take a little joke? Missing mummy too much, are we?'

Bray grabbed Lex by the collar. Lex pulled away and the two youths fell onto the bed, struggling.

'Don't mess up my bed!' Zandra screamed.

Lex rolled away and leapt up, fists raised. Bray scrambled to his feet as Amber hurried in. She grabbed Bray by the arms.

'Bray!'

'I should have killed you along with your brother!' Lex snarled.

'Why don't you try!'

Zandra stepped between Lex and Bray. 'Don't you dare mess up this room!'

Lex kicked the crumpled rota away. 'Seems no one's paying any attention to that anyway!'

'You got any better ideas!' Amber said fiercely.

'Some discipline for starters!' Lex said. 'And a strong leader to enforce it!'

Amber gave him a sarcastic look. 'Got anyone in mind?'

'There's only one man round here fit for the job,' Lex said arrogantly.

Amber looked at Bray to respond. He looked, disinterested. She turned back to Lex. 'Shouldn't we get a choice? It's only fair.'

'Alright, we'll fight for it. That good enough for you?'

Bray thrust his face into Lex's. 'Go play your mind games with someone else, Lex! I'm not interested!'

Turning abruptly away, he walked out of the room.

Amber caught up with Bray on the balcony, heading for Trudy's room.

'I'm not gonna spend my life running after you!'

Bray stopped and turned to her. 'Don't then!'

'You just gonna walk away from this?'

'From what? Lex's little mind games?'

'Call them what you like, Bray, we have to play them to win them!'

'I'm not trying to win anything! If Lex wants to be leader that's fine. It's no problem for me.' Bray turned away again.

Amber spat her words at him. 'Go on then! Just walk away like always! Give up on us!'

Bray stopped and walked back to her. 'Us? Who are you talking about, Amber? What 'us'? There is no 'us'!'

'There is!' Amber retaliated. 'You just don't like to see it! Gets in the way of thinking about yourself, doesn't it! You don't even care about the baby!'

That stung him. 'Don't give me that!'

'Well, it sure doesn't look like it! What sort of future does she get?'

'A good one. That's why I brought her here.'

'And now she's here that's your job done, is it? And if Lex becomes leader you're happy with that? You're happy to leave her future in his hands!'

'Not especially, no.'

'So do something about it, then!' She was exasperated, desperate to make him see. To react.

He surprised her by suddenly taking both her hands in his. A tingle ran through her body at the touch. He looked into her eyes.

'No, Amber, just stop and think for a minute. Who would be good for you all?'

She held his gaze, seeing her reflection in his eyes. There was a catch in her throat. 'You could be!'

His voice was gentle now, all trace of anger gone. 'Amber, do I have to spell it out for you? It should be you! You're what they need. You're a natural leader. Have an election. A fair vote. You against Lex…Let them decide.'

He gazed at her a moment longer then let go of her hands, turned and walked away. She watched him go, her emotions stirred and confused.

ONE HUNDRED AND EIGHT

In the morning Spike was still drunk. Most of the others had gone to bed to sleep it off, but he had carried on drinking. He had a grudge and an agenda. And he needed a little courage to see it through.

As usual, Ebony had risen early. Her routine was always the same, a punishing martial arts drill before breakfast. Zoot had liked to watch her. Lying in bed he would admire her diminutive, but superbly toned, body performing the movements of the ancient Oriental art. She had liked him watching. She was a proud warrior. And it turned him on. There was no one to watch now, but as the new leader she needed to keep up her regime even more.

This morning she became aware she was being watched by a different pair of eyes. Spike was standing in the doorway of the empty carriage which was her gym and training space. She picked up a towel and wiped the sweat from her neck and shoulders.

Spike leant against the doorframe and clapped his hands. 'Very good. Very nice.'

She eyed him steadily. 'You want anything, Spike?'

He grinned lasciviously and eyed her up and down. 'Quite a few things, actually.'

'In your dreams!'

He shoved himself from the doorframe and came to tower over her. She could smell the stale beer fumes on his breath as he leered at her. 'If you're not nice to me, I could become your worst nightmare.'

Ebony sized him up. He was much taller and heavier than she, and he was an accomplished street fighter. But he was drunk. That gave her an edge. Exactly how drunk she didn't know. But she guessed she was about to find out.

'The Locos need a man to lead them. Not a little girl. We don't want to be a laughing stock.'

'You challenging my leadership, Spike?'

He grinned. It wasn't a friendly grin. 'You bet I am.'

He made a clumsy grab at her throat. Ebony spun away, grabbed his arm and hip-threw him to the floor. As he tried to scramble up she slammed her foot as hard as she could between his legs. Spike's eyes bulged and his mouth opened in a prolonged silent scream. With both hands clutching himself he rolled over in extreme agony.

'Now get out!' Her voice was ice. 'Before you make me angry.'

Groaning in pain Spike crawled to the doorway and fell out. She heard him retching on the ground outside. Round one to her. But she had made a bitter enemy. If she tried to throw him out, she knew maybe half of the Locos would leave with him. She would have to keep Spike in the tribe, and watch him very carefully. What was the Chinese expression Zoot was so fond of? 'Keep your friends close, but your enemies closer.'

ONE HUNDRED AND NINE

Amber had thought long and hard about Bray and his challenge to her. Because that was what it felt like. She could tell by his expression as he stood holding her hands that Bray clearly believed in her. That was a surprise in itself and very flattering. But did she believe enough in herself to take on Lex? She decided she had to try.

Her decision made, she went straight to Lex's room and told him that Bray wasn't interested in standing against him, and that a democratic election was the best route to go. Him against her. Lex shrugged and surprisingly accepted the idea without a murmur, which made Amber a little uneasy.

ooo

News of the upcoming election was met with different reactions in the mall. Elections were a thing they all knew about from school, elections for student president, year leader and so on were commonplace. But this one was different. This was to decide how your life was going to be run, day by day, twenty-four seven.

The choice couldn't have been any more of a contrast. Between Lex the intolerant playground bully and Amber the sympathetic head girl. It seemed an easy decision, but just like elections in the old adult days, in this new world things were never quite that simple.

'So everyone's gotta have secret vote, right?' Dal said.

'What's wrong with just sticking your hand in the air?' said Jack.

Dal looked at Jack quizzically. 'You're gonna stick your hand up in public and vote against Lex?'

Jack nodded. 'Ah, yeah, good point.'

'And we're gonna vote for Amber, right?' Dal was excited about the election and the almost certain outcome. 'It's a no-brainer.'

'Yeah. But without Lex getting to know.' Jack added emphatically.

'Simple. Piece of paper each. Into a kind of voting booth. X marks the spot.'

Jack raised a finger. 'Or how about everyone just writes a name on a piece of paper?

'Write whose name on a piece of paper?' Lex had entered without them noticing.

'The candidates. For tonight's vote,' Jack explained a little nervously.

'Why can't everyone just stick their hands up?'

Jack looked at Dal for help.

'It's not democratic,' Dal said.

'What?'

'Everyone will know who you voted for then.'

Lex shrugged. 'What's wrong with that?'

This time Dal looked at Jack.

'Well..er...'

'Whatever,' Lex pressed on. 'Writing's a bad idea. Ryan can't write. And you don't want to make him embarrassed, do you? Make him angry?' Lex clapped his hands together sharply making both Jack and Dal jump. 'Anyway vote for me now and I promise you'll never have to vote again!'

Dal looked puzzled. 'Why not?'

Lex grinned. 'Cos I'll make all the decisions for you!' He swaggered out punching his fist in the air. 'Vote Lex. The vote to end all votes!'

Dal looked at Jack glumly, 'Some democracy!'

ONE HUNDRED AND TEN

Bray had gone out to the beach, to the spot where he had pushed his kid brother, Martin, out to sea on his last journey. It was still hard to grasp that Martin was dead, and that he was mostly responsible. He had sincerely believed that with the help of Trudy and the baby, he may be able to get through to his brother. To turn him away from the destructive path his anger over his dead parents had taken him down.

Gazing out over the silver waves, he twisted the leather necklace he had taken from his dead brother's neck between his fingers, and made a resolution. 'Little no name' as Salene had called the baby, was his responsibility now. And he would try to create a life for her that the real Martin, not Zoot, would have wanted.

ooo

Trudy was seated on the bed staring into space when he got back.

'Hi,' he said pleasantly. 'You heard about the election?'

Trudy grunted in reply.

Bray was concerned. 'You alright?'

'Oh yeah, perfect!' Trudy snapped.

'What's wrong?' He looked around. The cot was empty. 'Where's the baby?'

'Dunno.' That sulky tone again. It drove him crazy.

'Trude!'

'Salene's got her!'

'Good. Without her...' He didn't go on. He knew he'd said too much already.

Trudy looked up at him, accusingly. 'What? Without her, what?'

'Nothing.'

'Just say it, Bray! She's much better than me!'

'Don't be ridiculous, Trudy. It's not a competition.!'

'No? She's the perfect little mother! A perfect little angel, isn't she!'

Bray sat down and sighed inwardly. He tried to keep his voice calm and neutral. 'Trudy, don't take it out on her. Thanks to her your baby's doing okay. She's being looked after until you're feeling better. I think she deserves a little respect, don't you?'

His calming tone had no effect. Trudy's eyes narrowed, her face contorted into an ugly mask. 'Oh, sorry! Am I dissing your precious Salene! Why don't you go and thank her? I'm sure she'd enjoy that! And if she wants the baby she can keep it!'

'You don't mean that!'

Tears were beginning to come now. 'The only reason you're staying is because of it!'

'It's not 'it', Trudy. It's a baby.'

'Oh stop playing Daddy, Bray, and just go!'

'I'm worried about both of you.' He tried to take her hand but she snatched it away.

'You're not worried about me! You care about your niece, that's all! Oh, and Salene!'

He stood up, exasperated, trying to control his anger. 'Listen. They're gonna vote to elect a proper leader. Vote for Amber. At least for the baby's sake. For her future!'

'What future!'

'Just vote for Amber!'

'Oh, of course, it's her you really want, isn't it?'

Perhaps it was hearing the truth that caused him to snap. 'That's enough. Just shut up!'

As he stormed out Trudy yelled after him. 'Why are you wasting your time on me anyway? Go on, run to her!

ooo

'What's Trudy shouting about?' Patsy was seated around the poker table in the storeroom with Ryan and Paul. After their first poker game the twins had become hooked on it, even though Ryan constantly won.

Ryan shrugged. 'She never seems very happy.'

'She should be. She's got a cute little baby.'

Ryan and Paul pulled faces to each other, confirmation of their male bonding about all things 'baby'.

'Raise you one beans,' Ryan put a can in the middle of the table. 'I'm sick of beans.'

In response Paul put a net-bag on the table which rattled. Ryan looked dubious. 'Marbles? Nah, what would I do with them? Sorry, no can do.'

Paul looked at Patsy and showed her his cards, secretively. She looked at him and shrugged.

'If you haven't got any more food to bet, you'll have to fold,' Ryan said.

Paul signed to Patsy, clearly agitated. They had a winning hand at last. She turned to Ryan. 'Hang on a minute. We've got a secret store.'

Ryan's eyes lit up. 'Secret store?'

Patsy was already rushing out, nearly colliding with Lex on his way in.

'Watch it!' he snapped.

'Sorry!' gasped Patsy as she hurried away.

Lex looked at the pile of food and sweets on the table. 'Well, well, this looks exciting.'

'Er, yeah, Lex,' Ryan said distractedly, watching Patsy disappear round the corner. 'Can you keep an eye on these for me?' Handing Lex his cards, he followed after Patsy.

Lex sat in Ryan's vacated seat and examined the cards in his hand. He looked up at Paul. 'What've you got, deafo?'

Intimidated by Lex's stare, Paul showed him his hand. Lex gave a sharp intake of breath. 'Good hand, but not quite as good as these.' He showed Paul Ryan's winning hand. Paul looked dismayed. 'So what we need to do is spice your hand up a bit.' He sorted through the remainder of the pack and brought out three jacks which he showed to Paul. 'Now you want these. But what can you do for me?' He laid the three jacks on the table temptingly. 'How about voting for me tonight?'

ooo

Patsy found Jack in his room fiddling with the short-wave radio, the headset held to one ear. Breathlessly she told him about Paul's great poker hand.

'So?' Jack said, only half listening.

'We need some more food to bet.'

'Forget it.'

'But Paul's got a winning hand!'

'I said forget it.'

Patsy's expression grew stubborn. 'I'll tell.'

Jack slammed the headset down on the bench. 'This has gone too far!'

Dal appeared at the door. 'What's gone too far?'

Jack looked up, startled. 'Nothing.'

Pasty grinned, mischievously. 'Jack's got a secret!'

'Come on!' Jack grabbed Patsy's arm and hustled her away out of the room. Dal watched them go very curious.

ooo

Lex was leaning back in his chair, boots on the table. Paul watched him warily from the opposite side. 'When I'm leader,' Lex was explaining expansively, 'I'll take you to a real casino. How's that? There's one in Sector Two, run by Tribe Circus. It's pretty heavy down there. But, hey, we're talking about Lex here. They've got girls, drinks. It's wild. You ever played roulette?'

Ryan rushed in, holding up a tin can excitedly. 'Lex! Look at this! Creamed rice! I haven't had creamed rice for ages!'

'Where'd you get that, Ryan?'

'It's Jacks! He's got a whole supermarket down there!'

Lex sat up. 'Really?'

Jack and Patsy rushed in after Ryan. On seeing Lex, Jack stopped dead in his tracks, frozen to the spot. Lex stood up, pushed back his chair and walked over to Jack. Grabbing him by the throat he slammed Jack against the wall. 'So what's all this, Jack? Ryan tells me you've got your own private food store. You're gonna be in big trouble when the rest of 'em hear about it.' He looked at the others. 'Now I can probably keep these chumps quiet 'til we decide what to do about it. And, to show your appreciation, you're gonna vote for me tonight, okay?'

Jack nodded wide-eyed. Lex released him and strolled casually back to the table. 'Now we've got a game to finish here. Whose call is it?'

ONE HUNDRED AND ELEVEN

Dal could hardly wait for the evening and the election. He had gone round everyone he could find in the mall to encourage them to vote for Amber. Everyone except Lex's gang, of course. There was no point in talking to Ryan and Zandra, but he reckoned that even without them Amber would win easily.

He was passionate that she was the right person for the role. Every since she befriended him and protected him on his first day at school he had known that she was a born leader. Someone who would fight for fairness and equality for everyone, despite their colour or creed. It was a tough, brutal world they had all inherited, but the only way forward was with people who thought and believed like Amber. They had to create something positive, not destroy everything that was left, like the Locos and the Dogs.

Amber found him pouring over an old book on electrical systems that Zandra had found in the looted antique shop. She had seen a picture of a hairdryer and wanted Dal to adapt hers so it could run off a battery.

He looked up at Amber. She was looking serious. 'You alright?'

She nodded thoughtfully. 'This election, Dal.'

'Yeah?'

'We need to vote for Lex.'

Dal stared at her, stunned. 'Lex?'

'We need him to win.'

He could see she was deadly serious, but his mind was spinning. 'You're kidding me!'

She shook her head. 'No. I think it's for the best. Really.'

Dal flapped his arms confused. 'But he's impossible, Amber! He'll bully everyone!'

'Yeah, I know. But I don't think people will put up with it for very long. It's one thing bullying people, but keeping it up day after day, having to make decisions, even bad ones...I think he'll give it a go and then hate it.'

'Amber, you can win easily tonight!'

She could see he needed more convincing. 'Dal, if I win Lex will never get off my back. That's a role he likes. Being negative, bullying. Taking a pop at people. He'll make my life impossible. But if he wins, when people keep coming to him to make decisions day by day, I bet he'll lose interest pretty quickly.'

Dal shook his head and ran his fingers through his hair. 'That's a big gamble, Amber.'

She put her hand on his shoulder and smiled, 'Trust me, pal.'

'But why not just drop out now? If you want Lex to win?'

'It's better if he thinks he's won fair and square. He won't think I'm trying to trick him.'

Dal shrugged and blew out a breath between pursed lips. 'You're the boss.'

'Great.' She looked at the book, open at a page with an electrical diagram. 'What's that thing?'

'A hairdryer.'

Amber looked skeptical. 'A hairdryer?'

'Sort of.'

She grinned. 'I'm beginning to get worried about you, Dal.'

Not half as worried as he was being asked to vote for Lex, Dal thought. He just hoped Amber's plan didn't blow up in her face.

ONE HUNDRED AND TWELVE

It was just as Ebony predicted. The Demon Dogs were not going to take the raid on their warehouse lying down. Kick a sleeping dog and it will often bite back. She'd banked on that.

With Zoot still missing she needed to keep the Locos occupied. She didn't want to give Spike time to start stirring up dissent about her leadership. She had cowed him physically for the moment, and she knew he would keep that humiliation to himself. But he would be plotting. Looking for a weakness. The aura of being Zoot's chosen deputy wouldn't last forever. A challenge would come eventually. And she would have to prove herself to the rest.

Her scouts had reported the Dogs movements after the warehouse raid. It was clear that they were massing for a revenge attack. Ebony gathered together her commanders and briefed them on the new tactics for the inevitable battle.

Zoot had been an avid, obsessive wargamer before the affects of the virus killed off the internet, along with all other forms of worldwide communication. He'd been a feared and awesome cyberspace hunter-killer, second to none on the web in battles ranging from ancient Rome to mega-galatic conflicts in alien worlds. His obsession with all things warlike led him to become a zealous student of military history and Ebony had learnt a lot from him. She particularly liked the Roman legions technique for close combat and was keen to put it into practice on the city streets.

'We have to meet them head on,' she told the fiercesome-looking youths. 'We know they are going to attack. We can't stop that. But we can choose the place where we fight. That is half of the battle.'

With the Locos battle group assembled, Ebony led them off in the police car, standing up proudly like a warrior queen in her chariot. For the moment the shrill siren was silent.

With their battery driven walkie-talkies the Loco scouts were able to keep Ebony informed of the exact position of the advancing Demon Dogs. A voice crackled from the set in the cab of the car. In the middle of a wide avenue, halfway towards the Dogs headquarters, she held up her hand to halt the column of heavily armed Locos. At a silent signal they began to form a human ring two deep around the police car. The outer ring held police riot shields and short improvised clubs, the inner ring brandished longer weapons as spears.

Ebony took a deep breath, raised her arms crossed at the wrists and yelled at the top of her voice. 'Power and Chaos!' As the Locos took up the chant, the police siren began to wail menacingly. A battle challenge ringing out like the Scottish bagpipes of olden times.

Streaming around the corner, answering the challenge, came the Demon Dogs. Without stopping to assess the new battle formation confronting them, they swarmed towards the car in a disorganized rush of bodies. They were met by a wall of shields and swinging, stabbing weapons.

Used only to chaotic street fighting, where it was every man for himself, the Dogs first charge was brutally halted. They fell back then charged in again blindly. The two rings of weapons swung and stabbed viciously from behind their defensive wall of shields.

The battle was short. As the Dogs' attack faltered against the well-organized defence, the Locos advanced outwards, widening their formation, inflicting severe punishment on the fleeing stragglers.

Ebony stood smiling arrogantly in her police car, arms aloft, triumphant.

ONE HUNDRED AND THIRTEEN

Election fever had gripped the occupants of the mall. There was a feeling that this was a big event and most people had made an effort to dress for the occasion. Notably, Lex and Zandra. She had insisted that he wore an outfit befitting a potential tribe leader and had chosen him a sheer black nylon shirt to show off his honed physique, and tight black toreador pants. The ensemble was topped with a lurid tie with a vivid blood splatter pattern.

Zandra herself had dressed in the multi-coloured finery and feathers that she thought suitable for a first lady. In one sense she could see that Amber would make a good leader. Probably better than Lex with his less than subtle approach to problems. But Zandra was traditional. She had been brought up to see men as leaders and that's the way she felt it ought to be. Besides she was looking forward to lording it over the rest in her new role as Lex's consort.

They gathered in the café around the large communal table, each feeling rather important as part of what could prove to be a life-changing meeting. For a brief moment in time, they forgot about the terrors of the world outside and focused on their tiny world, their home inside the mall.

As the original resident of the mall, Jack had been chosen to host the proceedings, with Dal acting as his deputy. When everyone had arrived Jack stood up and addressed them, clearing his throat self-importantly. 'Ahem. Good evening. We are gathered here this evening to take part –'

'We know what we're here for!' Lex snarled impatiently. 'Just get on with it!'

Jack went on, flustered. 'Okay, so we've got some marbles in this bag. There's white ones and black ones. Amber's chosen white, so Lex is black. We pass the bag round and everybody takes one.'

'Get on with it, nerd!'

Dal took over from Jack, who was clearly unnerved by Lex's interruptions. 'Each voter secretly picks a coloured marble for the person they want to vote for. Then on the signal we all throw the marbles into the box at the same time.' He pointed to the large box in the centre of the table. 'That way no one will know what colour you've picked. Any questions?'

Zandra put her hand up, regally. 'What if it's a tie?'

'What's a tie?' Cloe asked.

Bray looked across at Lex lounging against the wall. 'Ask Lex.'

A few nervous chuckles greeted his joke.

'Okay,' Dal went on. 'Let's start.'

The bag was passed solemnly around the table in silence. Each person peeked inside the bag and made their choice. When they had all chosen Dal held up his hand. 'Ready! Throw!'

The marbles clattered into the box and came to rest. It was close, but there was a result. Seven black marbles against five white.

'Yes!' Lex called out triumphantly.

There was surprised silence for a moment. Then Jack spoke up, sounding perhaps a little relieved. 'Looks like Lex is the winner.'

Lex beamed. 'Anyone who voted for me there's a party at my place!'

'Hey, Lex,' called Ryan. 'Now you're leader, let's dish out the creamed rice!'

The colour drained from Jack's face. Lex scowled. Neither had wanted that little secret getting out.

'Who's got creamed rice?' Salene asked.

Ryan went on, excitedly, oblivious of Lex's scowl. 'Didn't you know? Jack's got loads of it in his food store!'

Dal frowned. 'Oh, yeh? Since when?'

Amber got to her feet. 'What food store is this, Jack?'

Jack shrugged and looked around anxiously as if the walls would provide an answer to the very awkward question.

'He's got a whole load of food he was keeping for himself,' said Ryan. 'Tinned meat, creamed rice, chocolate, everything!'

'Chocolate!' Cloe was wide-eyed.

Zandra was on her feet now, staring accusingly at Jack. 'You greedy little pig! You had all that food and you didn't tell us!'

Amber turned to Lex. 'Did you know about this?'

Lex blustered. 'Of course not! What do you take me for?'

'Well, then,' Amber continued, 'what are you going to do about it?'

Zandra was adamant. 'We should sling him out!'

'Just shut it, Zandra!' Lex snapped. 'I'll decide that!'

'Well we should!' Zandra wasn't going to be silenced. 'Here we are half-starving when we could have had a decent meal. I say we go and get it now!'

Some people began to make a move from the table, but Lex's tone stopped them. 'Oy! Nobody touches it until I say so! I'm the leader. You've all just elected me!'

'Yeh,' said Bray, 'to sort this kind of thing out.'

Ryan chipped in. 'Zandra's right! Sling him out!'

'Let the Locos have him!' Zandra added spitefully.

Jack was panicked by the ugly mood around the table. 'No, Lex! Stop them!'

All eyes were on Lex, the new leader. It was his decision to make. He deliberated for a second then announced, 'We'll have a trial. Then we'll decide what happens to him.'

Jack was shocked, anxious and angry in equal measure. He turned to Lex, 'No! You put me on trial and I'll –'

Lex cut across him, hard. 'You can either have a fair trial or leave now with nothing!' He stared at Jack with cold eyes. 'What's it gonna be?'

Jack's shoulders slumped, defeated.

ONE HUNDRED AND FOURTEEN

The Locos had returned to the rail yards in a buoyant, heady mood. The adrenalin rush created by combat always took quite a while to subside and there was a nervous energy in the air, with lots of joking and macho boasts about the fight. Aided by a ration of booze, a few playful scuffles had broken out to release the last of the excitement racing round in the blood. But, as the last rays of the setting sun turned the tower blocks to the East into a city of gold, the mood changed to inebriated contentment. A job well done. The Locos were top of the heap.

No one was more elated than Ebony. Her tactics had been vindicated. She had taught the Demon Dogs a lesson and they would need time to lick their wounds and regroup. But she had no doubt they would learn from the manner of their defeat. A surprise was only ever a surprise once. She would have to keep one step ahead to stay on top.

Zoot was still missing and there was a lot of talk and speculation in the camp about what had happened to their charismatic leader. Well aware of this, Ebony sent small search parties out every morning, but the result was always to same. No sign or word of Zoot.

Though she would not admit it to anyone else, she was convinced that he was dead. If he had been kidnapped, she reasoned, the Locos would have received some sort of ransom demand by now. Or Zoot would have got a message to her somehow.

She felt a deep pang of regret. Zoot had been a great leader, a tireless lover and a lively, entertaining companion, even though you could never take his loyalty completely for granted. But those feelings were for the old days. That was history and history didn't exist. She was alone now. It was time to plan for life after Zoot. And the first stop was a new H.Q. Something more in keeping with the status of the Locos and Ebony, their warrior queen.

ONE HUNDRED AND FIFTEEN

Bray lay awake for most of the night, surprised and dismayed at the outcome of the election. Lex getting the most votes could only mean one thing. He'd bribed or threatened people to vote for him. Bray was annoyed with himself. He should have seen that coming when he suggested an election to Amber. But he didn't. He hadn't thought it through and he couldn't prove a thing. Now they all had to live with the result. Not a happy prospect.

Amber was preparing breakfast in the kitchen when he came in to get hot water for the baby's morning feed.

'Hi. I'm sorry about the election,' he began.

Amber shrugged. 'You coming to Jack's trial?'

Bray looked uncomfortable. 'I don't think so. Trudy's not feeling too good.'

At that moment the sound of the baby's cry echoed round the vast space of the mall. He shrugged, feeling guilty.

'We could do with you there.' It was a statement not a plea. 'We need someone sensible in case it gets out of control.'

'So that's me, is it? Someone sensible.'

Amber looked at him closely. He felt the intense scrutiny of her eyes. 'Among other things...They're talking about throwing Jack out. We can't do that. He's too valuable. We're going to need techno-nerds like him to help build a new world.'

'You insisted on something being done. Lex wanted to leave it.'

'Yeah, I wonder why?'

'Me too.'

Amber sighed. 'But that wouldn't be right anyway. We can't just let it go...' She looked at him again. This time there was a hint of a plea in her voice. 'I just don't want it getting out of hand.'

The baby's crying was growing loud and insistent. He poured the water into the baby's bottle and replaced the teat.

'I'm sure you can handle it.'

She rounded on him. Her tone was hard now. A challenge. 'Tell me something, Bray! Just when are you gonna decide whether you're a part of us or not?'

With a final furious glare at him she strode out of the café.

ONE HUNDRED AND SIXTEEN

The cage that housed the service lift for the mall was the perfect prison cell. Jack had spent an anxious and uncomfortable night inside with only the rats for company. He was angry and scared in turns. Angry at Lex for not protecting him, and scared at the prospect of being thrown out into the street to fend for himself. He didn't give much for his chances out there in the city that still resembled the worst nightmare zombie movie ever made.

He felt deeply resentful that the people he had let into his home had turned against him. They should have been grateful that he was prepared to share the mall with them. He could have easily kept them out, like he'd done with Lex, Ryan and Zandra. There was enough stockpiled food to last him for a long time, while he searched the airwaves for adults to come to his aid. It wasn't possible that they had all died like Dal said, was it? He couldn't believe that.

He looked up at footsteps approaching. It was Lex, swaggering into the room. Jack was on his feet immediately, incensed.

'You promised you wouldn't let anything happen to me!'

'Nothing has happened to you yet,' Lex replied casually.

'So what am I doing in here?'

'Exactly, my friend. You're safe in there and not out in the street. You've got me to thank for that.'

Jack scoffed, sarcastically. 'Gee thanks!'

'How would it look if I let you get away with it? Don't worry I'll get you off with just a little more extra work.'

'No!' Jack punched his fist on the mesh of the cage and immediately wished he hadn't. It hurt. He sucked his knuckles then went on sulkily, 'This is my place and my food. If you don't stop them I'll tell about you ripping off the water!'

Lex came close to the cage and eyeballed him. 'Are you threatening me? 'Cos if you are I can arrange for you to leave right now.'

Jack glared back at him, fear of the outside outweighing his fear of Lex. 'Well I haven't got anything to lose, have I?'

'That's called blackmail.'

'Yeah, well now you know how it feels.'

Lex scowled. Jack was a nerd, but he seemed just about mad enough to bring down the whole pack of cards.

ONE HUNDRED AND SEVENTEEN

There was excitement in the air about the trial. Patsy, Paul and Cloe were noisily debating Jack's fate in the café and squabbling about food for breakfast at the same time. Trudy was lying on her bed in her room, while Bray gave the baby its bottle.

'Listen to them!' Trudy gasped, irritated. 'Fighting like animals over food! That's the future, isn't it? That's my daughter's future!'

Bray was trying to keep the atmosphere calm. 'It doesn't have to be like that.'

'Yeh?' said Trudy. 'Well how's it going to be then?' It wasn't really a question, more frustration turned to aggression

'People will learn to look out for each other. They have to.' Bray sincerely believed that. He couldn't function unless he thought things would really get better, but he knew it sounded pretty hollow right now.

'And who's gonna look out for me? Who's gonna want a single mother when there's all that talent flaunting itself!'

Bray sighed. He knew where this was going. Again. 'Trudy, I told you I'm not interested in Salene.'

'Well, she's interested in you! She can't keep away!'

His own level of irritation was rising. 'She wants to help with the baby. She does help. You couldn't manage without her.' He knew he'd said the wrong thing as soon as the words came out of his mouth.

Trudy sat upright. 'Oh! So I'm a lousy mother now am I?'

He tried one last time. 'Trudy, please don't do this.'

'I bet they're all thinking 'Look at her, the poor cow. She doesn't stand a chance'!'

Bray stood up to leave.

'Where are you going?'

'I'm going to the trial.'

'You said you weren't going.'

'Well, I've changed my mind.'

Trudy flung herself back onto the pillow. 'Suit yourself! You always do anyway.'

He looked at her, scrunched up with her back to him. Despite his irritation, he felt genuinely sorry for her. 'Maybe you should come too. You're spending too much time on your own.'

'Go! I'm sure Salene will be pleased! She's probably saved a seat for you right next to her!'

Bray grimace said he'd had enough. Slamming the bottle down he strode out.

Trudy sat up and called after him, in a pathetic voice. 'Bray! I'm sorry!'

He didn't turn back. Trudy lay back down close to tears. She knew she was driving him away, but no matter how she tried she couldn't control her emotions. She felt so vulnerable, so jealous. Salene had everything going for her. She was attractive, available, and not tied down with a baby. And she clearly adored Bray.

The tears, never far way, began to flow again. She curled herself up into a ball, feeling alone and helpless. She wished her mom and dad were here.

ONE HUNDRED AND EIGHTEEN

The chairs had been arranged in two rows facing the phoenix fountain. A table and two chairs stood beneath the soaring bird statue, which somehow seemed to give gravity and seriousness to the occasion. While they waited for Lex to bring Jack from the cage the argument flowed about punishment.

Dal was leading the discussion. 'If you throw somebody out for hoarding food, what do you do if they do something really bad?'

'What's worse than hoarding food?' Ryan asked seriously.

'Like hurting someone really bad.'

'Starve them,' Ryan said enthusiastically. 'No food for a week!'

'I think we should make up our own set of rules,' Amber suggested. 'Like a law. So everyone knows where they stand.'

'We don't want a law! We want to be able to do as we like!'

'And where would that get us, Zandra?' Amber countered. 'Precisely where we are now.'

Ryan got up animatedly. 'What about flogging! Didn't they used to do that? That'd make people think. If you had a public flogging!' He flailed his beefy arm viciously through the air. 'One! Two! Three! Four!'

Lex entered with Jack just in time to witness Ryan's spirited demonstration. Jack shot Lex a worried glance. The prospect of being flogged by an over-eager Ryan wasn't appealing at all.

'Ryan, sit down!' Lex barked. He pushed Jack into a chair behind the table, sat beside him and addressed Jack importantly.

'Now then, you know what you're accused of. How do you plead? Guilty or not guilty?'

'Not guilty!' Jack said determinedly.

There was general commotion among the others and cries of, 'Oh come on!' 'What?' 'Give us a break!'

Lex slammed his fist on the table. 'Quiet!'

The others fell silent.

'Now,' Lex continued, enjoying his new role as democratically elected leader. 'we'll hear the evidence against Jack and then hear what he has to say. Then I'll decide what happens.'

'You'll decide?' said Amber. 'I think we should all have a say.'

'I'm the leader, I'll decide.'

Bray was leaning back in his seat, with a skeptical expression. 'Why? Don't you trust us to make the right decision?'

Lex repeated assertively. 'I'm the leader. I'll decide!'

Amber was not going to be bullied. 'If someone's going to be punished it's too important just to be one person's decision. Just because you're leader doesn't give you the right to do what you like to us.'

Dal spoke up, 'Amber's right. It's not a proper trial without a jury.'

Jack got up out of his chair animatedly. 'I think Lex should decide!' Everyone stared at him curiously. Suddenly he realized he'd sounded much too keen. He stumbled on, 'I mean...he's the leader and...'

'Really, Jack?' Amber asked suspiciously, 'And why would that be?'

Bray joined in, echoing Amber's suspicion. 'Yes. Why do you want Lex to decide, Jack?'

Lex helped Jack out. 'Okay! You want a jury! We'll have a jury!'

'Who's gonna be the judge?' Ryan sounded keenly enthusiastic.

'You can,' Lex said offhand, disinterested. The trial was going to be a charade anyway, he thought. Why not make it amusing?

Ryan leapt up. 'I'll need my special hat for this!' he stopped beside Jack on his way out and bent over him. 'Cheer up, Jack, there's probably some vacancies with the Locos.'

As Ryan raced up the stairs, Lex continued. 'So, who wants to begin for the prosecution then?'

Amber put up her hand. 'I will.'

ONE HUNDRED AND NINETEEN

A grey drizzle was falling, making the ruined city look even more surreal, ghostly and unwelcoming. On such days very few of the tribes ventured out, which made it a perfect day for the move. There was not much luggage to carry. The Locos traveled light.

The construction of the Plaza Hotel had been completed only a few months before the virus struck. It was a garish monument to lavish living. Symbol of mankind's pre-eminence in the world. A vanity now brought to dust by a more powerful tiny, invisible force.

That morning, on Ebony's orders, the Locos had cleared out the few stragglers of a tribe that had made their home there. Now she was on her way to claim her bounty and put the Locos on the map, living in the most prestigious address in town.

Like all the other hotels in the city, the inside of the building had been looted and the top stories had been gutted by arson. But on the lower floors much of the opulence remained. Soaring marble columns, huge four-poster beds, voluminous chairs and sofas, expansive gardens and, Ebony's most coveted prize, a large sparkling-blue swimming pool.

All her young life Ebony had dreamed of living in a place like this. So very different to the places she had been brought up in as a child. As she strode through the vast entrance lobby, flanked by her hand-picked bodyguards, she smiled a beautiful smile that lit up her striking face. Her dream had come true.

ONE HUNDRED AND TWENTY

Beneath the glass dome of the atrium the mall looked as gloomy as the day outside. The daylight seeping in from above was feeble and grey. But no one in the little group far below noticed. All eyes were on Amber as she continued her prosecutor's speech.

'So if someone is selfish and they steal –'

Jack was on his feet. 'Objection! I didn't steal anything! It was my food!'

This was Jack's third interruption in less than a minute. Amber looked at Lex, lounging back in his chair. 'Are you gonna make him be quiet?'

Lex looked up at Jack. 'You wanna go back in your cage?'

'I'm not a thief!'

'You're as good as!' Amber retorted. 'Because you had food you knew we all needed.' She turned to address the others. 'If we allow this to go on, you can forget about staying alive for very long, because everyone will be too busy looking after themselves.'

Unseen by the group Trudy appeared on the balcony with the baby in her arms. She peered down, saw Bray sitting close beside Salene and walked silently away, distressed.

Amber was in full flow. 'So we have to cut it out now, or we'll end up like the Locusts.' She turned to face Jack, looking genuinely sorry. 'I'm sorry, Jack. There has to be a penalty for this. If we let one person get away with it, everyone else will think they can too. It has to be a real punishment, but not one we'll regret later.' She addressed the others. 'Let's remember that Jack is very intelligent and we need people like him in the tribe.'

As she sat down the incipient applause was drowned out by Ryan, who was standing at the head of the stairs, arms spread judicially on the balcony rail. He was wearing a white military helmet with the initials M.P. on the front 'Okay! All those in favour of slinging him out!' He raised his hand.

Lex sprang up. 'Hang on! We haven't found him guilty yet!'

Ryan frowned. 'Of course he's guilty!'

Amber stood up beside Lex. 'We have to hear what Jack has to say first.'

'Right.' Lex strode to Jack, pulled him roughly out his chair by his arm, and thrust him in front of the others. 'Now then. Do you deny hoarding the food?'

'No,' Jack replied sulkily, avoiding the eyes of the rest.

'There you are!' Ryan crowed.

'Well, why did you do it?' Lex continued.

Jack squirmed. He'd never been a good liar. 'I...I wanted to keep it to make it last longer.'

'Oh come on!' Zandra gasped.

Lex rounded on her. 'Let him talk! What else, Jack?'

'I knew if I told everyone it would all go in a couple of days. And I thought if the fighting stops we could trade it with the other tribes. I wanted to keep something to trade with.'

Bray's laughter rang round the mall.

Lex glared at him. 'You think this is funny?'

'I think it's a good story.'

'I can tell you there are people out there who want to trade!' Lex said adamantly. 'The tribes are making peace!'

Amber looked skeptical. 'How do you know?'

'I keep my ear to the ground.'

'I haven't heard anything about a truce.'

Lex rounded on Bray. 'Because you've been too busy playing 'daddy'! But it's a fact.'

'Tell me something, Lex,' said Amber. 'Why do you want to get Jack off so badly?'

'I'm interested in the truth, that's all. And here's another thing, if we find Jack guilty and punish him, it's only fair we look at all the other crimes.' He let his eyes roam past Ryan, Patsy and Paul meaningfully. 'Like people gambling for rations, and all the people who knew about the food stash and kept quiet.'

Under his icy stare the three exchanged guilty looks.

'Right,' Lex pressed on. All those of you who think Jack's guilty put up your hands.'

Amber, Bray, Dal and Zandra raised their hands.

Zandra noticed Lex's glare. 'What are you looking at me for?' she said defiantly.

Lex scowled. 'Not guilty?'

Lex, Ryan, Patsy and Paul put their hands up eagerly.

'Salene?'

'I'm not sure. It's difficult. I'll abstain.'

Patsy prodded Cloe's arm. 'Put your hand up, Cloe!'

Lex fixed Cloe with a look that she couldn't mistake. She raised her hand.

'Right, five to four!' Lex was triumphant. 'Jack's innocent!

ONE HUNDRED AND TWENTY ONE

Buoyed up by his triumph at the trial, Lex lost no time establishing himself as leader. He chose a vacant store overlooking the whole mall and instructed Ryan, Jack and Dal to find him a suitable desk and chair from among the other empty stores. The first desk they brought him he declared was too small. Taking the matter into his own hands, he roamed through the mall until he found what he was looking for in the antique shop, a large old mahogany desk. The heaviest item left in the building.

Lex watched at ease from his black leather swivel chair as the three youths struggled to carry the huge desk into his new 'office'.

'Why couldn't you have had one of the smaller ones?' Ryan complained.

'The boss always gets the biggest desk. That's obvious. A bit more this way,' he ordered.

After they had placed the desk as instructed, Lex put his boots up on it and leaned back. 'Very nice.'

'And I found this.' Ryan produced a desk sign that read 'Executive Director.'

Lex looked at the sign blankly, then at Ryan.

'Oh yes,' Ryan hurried on. 'It says 'Executive Director.'

'Very good,' Lex said.

Dal and Jack exchanged a look. Their new leader couldn't read?

Reading their look, Lex became businesslike. 'Right! First thing, work rota! Get some paper and a pen, Jack. We're going to put this place in proper order!'

ooo

Amber smiled as she read the new rota stuck to the café wall. It was written in Jack's bold hand and was exactly as she had expected. Lex was so predictable and was playing right into her hands. But there were a few steps to go yet.

The girls were all gathered round it in dismay. Salene was the first to break the silence. 'Look at this! Who does he think he is?'

'Our leader,' Amber replied.

'Well, I didn't vote for him. And I don't understand why you did either.'

'I thought he'd make a good leader,' Amber said disingenuously. 'Let's hope I wasn't wrong.'

'Washing up!' Zandra exclaimed. 'How am I gonna wash up without rubber gloves? I'll ruin my nails!'

Salene looked to Amber. 'What are we going to do?'

Amber shrugged. 'If you don't like it, go tell him.'

'Me?'

'Sure, why not?'

Salene looked uneasy. 'I'm no good at that sort of thing. Why don't you tell him, Amber?'

'Because if I complain he'll think I'm plotting against him.'

'Are you sure you aren't?' Salene gave her a look.

'Of course not,' Amber said lightly.

ooo

Lex was relaxing in his office, feet upon the desk, when the delegation arrived. It was led by Salene and Zandra, with Amber in the rear alongside Patsy, Cloe and Paul who were carrying broom heads with no handles.

Lex looked up from the gameboy he was playing. 'What's all this?'

Salene spoke up boldly. 'Why have you given all the work to the girls and none to the boys?'

'Because the boys couldn't possibly get their precious little hands wet!' Zandra said sarcastically.

Lex was unfazed, 'I think if you read the rota again, you'll see the men are doing weapon training. So if we're attacked we can protect you.'

'I thought all the tribes were about to kiss and make up?' Amber said innocently.

'They are, but a good commander has to keep his guard up.'

Zandra huffed. 'How is a little shrimp like Jack going to protect me!'

Lex smiled indulgently, in control. 'That's the point, Zandra. He has to learn.'

'Wouldn't it be better if we all learned?' Amber asked. 'Then we could all protect each other.'

Lex took his feet off the desk and put the gameboy down. 'Don't you understand? We're living in primitive times again! Like the stone-age. That means the men do the protecting and the women look after the home.'

'You're not doing much to protect my hands!' Zandra exclaimed. She held up her hands, showing her bright red, immaculate fingernails. 'What do you think these are going to look like after all that washing up?'

'So do them again.'

Zandra looked indignant. 'You think I've nothing better to do all day than paint my nails?'

Lex let that question go with an ironic look.

'So that's it?' Amber said. 'There's no way any of the boys are doing the cleaning or the cooking?'

'That's about right,' Lex replied complacently.

'Right. We'd better get on with it then,' Amber said and walked out.

Salene watched her go in surprise, feeling let down.

Lex clapped his hands. 'Well, go on! Get back to work!'

Patsy held up the handleless broom. 'We can't!' she complained. 'Someone's taken the broom handles!'

Zandra frowned. 'Who'd do a thing like that?'

'Someone very stupid,' Lex called, 'Ryan!'

Ryan popped his head round the door where he had been standing on guard. Lex took a broom head from Patsy and held it up to him questioningly.

'Know anything about this, Ryan?'

'You said to get some sticks for weapon training,' Ryan said.

'I didn't say broom handles, Ryan.'

'You didn't say not too.'

Lex sighed. It was beginning to dawn on him that the life of a leader could be a hassle.

ONE HUNDRED AND TWENTY TWO

By a curious twist of fate, in the wasteland that the once proud city had become, one tribe had gone its own way unmolested by any of the more powerful tribes. Its nucleus was a group of young circus performers, children of long-established circus families who had traveled the length and breadth of the country for generations. Maybe it was that sense of history, memories of happy childhood days spent in the big top, or maybe just because all the tribes wanted to let their hair down and have some fun, that Tribe Circus had been allowed to flourish among the decaying ruins.

Tribe Circus's Casino was the biggest draw in town. Housed in the original city casino, with the aid of a large diesel generator, it had retained most of its former glitz. The addition of circus acts performing spectacular and highly dangerous feats suspended high above the punters in the soaring reception area was an extra draw. People came especially to see the performers fall from the high-wire, or trapeze, onto the unforgiving marble floor beneath. It was rare, but it happened just often enough to keep the ghoul's interest.

Since money no longer had any value, punters at the roulette wheel or the blackjack tables paid for their gaming chips with whatever goods were acceptable; food, batteries, anything useful. The highly prized valuables of the past, like the jewelry that had once adorned rich ladies necks, dresses and fingers, were low down on the list.

Ebony had taken a long refreshing swim in her pool at the hotel before dressing carefully to visit the casino. She dressed like a pop-star warrior queen. Tight black leather trousers and tank top, adorned with real golden chains and sparkling multi-coloured baubles. Her long afro-braided hair was entwined with golden threads. She had taken a long time over her appearance, but she hadn't come to play.

When her entourage arrived at the reception she demanded to see the proprietor, Top Hat, in private. They were shown through the busy casino into Top Hat's comfortable office at the rear of the building.

He rose to greet her; a tall, gangly youth, wearing a ringmaster's red coat and trademark shiny black top hat.

'Ebony! Long time no see!' he beamed. 'I heard about Zoot. Tough.'

'What exactly did you hear, Top Hat?'

'Missing, presumed dead?'

'You better hope he doesn't hear that when he gets back.'

Top Hat frowned. 'He isn't dead?'

'When you need to know the Locos' business, Top Hat, I'll let you know. In the meantime, Zoot has left me strict instructions.'

Top Hat sat down. He didn't like the tone of that. 'Which are?'

'To take over the casino.'

He leapt up. 'No way!' he shouted.

Ebony went on calmly. 'We'll let you carry on running it for us, but as from now Tribe Circus Casino is ours.'

'You must be out of your tiny mind, Ebony! You and Zoot, if he is still alive!'

Ebony looked at him steadily, with the eyes of a predator. 'You have a choice, Top Hat. Keep running the casino and keep healthy. Or burn with it when we torch it.'

Top Hat wore a thin smile. 'This is some kind of joke, isn't it? No-one touches the casino. It's a rule.'

'Rules change.'

'But the other tribes –'

She didn't let him finish. 'You think any of the other tribes are going to take on the Locos over a lousy casino? Didn't you hear what we just did to the Demon Dogs?'

He had heard, very graphic descriptions from some of the survivors. The Locos had established themselves as the most feared tribe in the city, and Ebony was probably right. As long as the casino went on as normal, would any of the tribes care if it changed hands? He sat down again, crushed.

'You'll get a generous cut, naturally. All the food, booze and girls you want.' She smiled ironically. 'Sorry, in your case boys.'

At a gesture to her entourage one of the brutal-looking youths handed her a piece of paper. Ebony thrust it at Top Hat. 'Sign at the bottom.'

Top Hat glanced at the paper. It resembled a legal contract. Ebony was making a farce of it, but she wasn't laughing. His hands trembled as he picked up the pen, both from fear and anger. Fear was the most powerful. He scribbled his signature at the bottom, defeated.

Ebony snatched it up, delightedly. 'I'll just go and have this ratified at the Town Hall,' she quipped.

ONE HUNDRED AND TWENTY THREE

Trudy had been anxious ever since she saw Bray and Salene sitting close together at the trial. Despite Bray's claim that he had no interest in her, he always seemed to gravitate to Salene when she was around. Trudy couldn't blame him. Salene was developing into a statuesque, attractive young woman. By comparison, after the ordeal with the baby, Trudy felt washed out, dowdy and depressed. It was no contest and she was scared that she could lose him at any moment.

Salene was in the room, picking the crying baby out of the cot when Trudy came in. Trudy stared at her, with hatred in her eyes.

'Oh, there you are!' Salene said lightly. 'She was crying so I thought –'

Trudy's tone was murderous. 'Put her down!'

Salene took a step back at the tone and the fierce stare. 'What?'

'You heard me!' Trudy rushed at her and snatched the baby away.

'Trudy!'

'Keep your hands off her!'

Salene was confused and nervous. For a second she actually felt frightened. Trudy looked crazy. 'She was crying, all alone,' she tried to explain.

Trudy clutched the baby to her. Her voice was vitriolic. 'I know what you want! You want her for yourself!'

'No!'

'And Bray too! You've been after him up ever since we got here!'

'It's not true!' Salene lied, flustered. Trudy was right about that, and she felt guilty.

'Well, you're not getting him, so stay away from him!'

Drawn by the sound of Trudy's shrill voice, Bray had run up the stairs to the room. Trudy and Salene were standing confronting at each other as he entered. 'Trudy, what's going on?'

'Your tart's trying to take our baby, that's what!'

Salene felt her face flushing at the word. 'I'm not his tart!'

Bray was incensed. 'Trudy, stop!'

Tears were welling in Salene's eyes. 'How can you speak to me like this after everything I've done for you?'

'I don't want you to do anything for me! Just leave the baby alone and leave him alone too!'

Holding back her sobs, Salene rushed from the room brushing past Bray as she went. He watched her go, uncertain whether to follow the distressed young girl. Finally, he turned back to Trudy who was standing breathing heavily, looking self-righteous.

'Have you completely lost it? You need all the help you can get and you drive her away!'

Frightened by the raised voices, the baby was howling in her arms. Trudy stood rigidly. Everything felt like it was collapsing in on her. 'I hate this place,' she yelled. 'I hate it and I don't wanna be here anymore!'

Bray watched her, feeling helpless and oppressed. He felt a responsibility to Trudy, but the burden seemed to be getting heavier every day.

ONE HUNDRED AND TWENTY FOUR

Despite the chaos and disorder of the new world in which they forced to exist, people still seemed to gather around midday for lunch. It was a ritual, a moment of calm amid the confusion of everyday living. In the mall café Ryan was hungrily eyeing Lex's plate, piled high with food.

'How come you get more than anyone else?'

Lex stuffed a spoonful of baked beans into his mouth. 'Leaders get double ration. Have to keep up my strength.'

'You haven't done anything.'

'I've been using my brain, Ryan. Something you'll never experience.' He pulled a face. 'Oy, who cooked this?'

Zandra fluttered out of the kitchen. 'I did. Do you like it?'

'You're supposed to be doing the washing up, not cooking,' Lex said, irritated.

'The other girls helped me, so I'm helping them. I did yours especially.'

'Well, it's burnt.'

Zandra looked hurt. 'Only a tiny bit. Stop making such a fuss!'

Ryan looked up at her, his big brown eyes like a puppy dog. 'Mine's not burnt.'

Lex watched Bray coming along the balcony and into the café. His expression darkened. 'What are you doing here?' he said aggressively.

At the far end of the table, Amber looked up alerted by Lex's tone.

It looked like an effort for Bray to even speak to Lex. 'I've come to eat.'

Lex put his spoon down. 'I don't recall you doing any guard duty.'

'I had to stay with Trudy. She's not well.'

'If you don't work for the tribe, you can't expect the tribe to feed you.'

Bray looked at Lex's piled plate. 'Doesn't seem to be any shortages.'

Lex stared back at him. 'Sorry. No work, no food.'

With a frustrated sigh Bray replied, 'Alright, I'll take Trudy her share.'

Lex nodded to Ryan who got up and blocked Bray's path to the kitchen. The two youths faced each other. They were about the same size. The café could be wrecked if they started a fight.

'If she wants it she can come and get it,' Lex said stubbornly.

Bray was losing his patience. 'She won't come. I've tried.'

'Tough.' Lex sensed the rising temperature in the room. He felt his own blood getting hot, ready for action.

Bray rounded on him. 'Don't you understand? She's not well! If she doesn't eat she'll get worse!'

Salene had come out of the kitchen where she had been preparing lunch. 'Think about the baby, Lex!'

'I said 'No!'' Lex snapped.

Bray folded his arms. 'I'm not leaving here without her food.'

Everyone in the room was watching the confrontation anxiously, aware that Bray's ultimatum had raised the stakes several notches.

Dal was growing very concerned. As always the threat of violence unnerved him. 'Come on, Lex. She's gotta eat!'

'How can you be so mean!' Salene cried.

Bray looked at Ryan's plate and said calmly. 'Yours is getting cold, Ryan.'

Ryan didn't move. He remained grimly blocking Bray's path.

Amber put down her knife and fork. 'Lex, if Bray is willing to do guard duty tonight, maybe we could give him Trudy's share of the food?' She looked at Bray. 'Would you be willing to do that, Bray?'

'Double guard duty!' Lex said gruffly.

'Because if you were, Bray,' Amber continued with great emphasis, 'the rest of us could get on with our meal.'

Bray pulled a face and blew out his breath. 'Double guard duty it is then.'

The relief in the room was tangible. All except for Lex, who felt cheated. It could only be a matter of time before he and Bray would have to sort out their differences once and for all.

ONE HUNDRED AND TWENTY FIVE

Amber was concerned. Convinced that the burden of constantly having to make decisions would soon get to Lex, she had engineered for him to become leader. She hoped to try and teach him a lesson about leadership, but she didn't want the situation to get out of hand.

Even those who hadn't witnessed the lunchtime confrontation in the café had heard of it, and could feel the residual tension in the air. Everyone seemed tense and on edge. For the other girls it wasn't just the testosterone vibes that were a problem.

'If he thinks I'm doing this for the rest of my life he can forget it!' Zandra moaned, as she helped Amber and Salene clean up the lunchtime mess.

Salene looked at Amber. 'It wouldn't be like this if you were leader.'

'We have to give him time to learn,' Amber replied.

'For how long?' asked Salene. 'We could be washing and cooking and scrubbing 'til we're old women!'

'No way!' Zandra said emphatically.

'Well, maybe there's a way we could help Lex to learn faster?'

Salene and Zandra both looked at Amber. By the tone of her voice, she had something up her sleeve.

Amber smiled enigmatically and went on. 'Let's meet later when the guys are asleep and I'll tell you what I've got in mind for our Lex.'

ooo

In the afternoon, Lex got Ryan to put him through his paces in the mall storeroom. As a youngster Lex had become hooked on martial arts movies and had studied karate in a spasmodic way ever since. But as a sufferer of attention deficit disorder he found it hard to stick at anything for very long. He knew the theory of 'empty hand' combat, which is what the Japanese term karate meant, but he hadn't practiced for quite a while. Which, he knew, was crazy when you considered how dangerous everyday life had become.

After the altercation with Bray in the café, Lex felt he needed to brush up on his skills and his long-time mate Ryan was the perfect foil. Though his best friend had never studied martial arts, Lex didn't doubt that Ryan could beat him in a fight. Ryan was all brute force. Which made him the ideal practice opponent. You couldn't hurt Ryan, no matter how hard you chopped or kicked him. Or at least it seemed that way, and Ryan never complained.

That evening Lex climbed into bed, feeling revitalized, toned and ready. He was a match for Bray anytime. Let him step out of line one more time, and Bray was out of there. Him, his tart and the brat.

ONE HUNDRED AND TWENTY SIX

In the darkened mall, seated in a circle of candlelight, the girls waited excitedly to hear Amber's plan.

'Now we're doing this for the sake of the tribe, right?' she began.

The circle of young heads nodded solemnly.

Amber went on, 'The problem is we have a system that isn't working. When that happens sometimes you have to give the system a bit of a shock.'

Patsy was wide-eyed. 'An electric shock?'

Amber smiled. 'Sort of, but stronger.'

'What are we going to do?' Zandra asked expectantly.

'Nothing.'

Zandra frowned. 'Nothing?'

'Absolutely nothing. We don't cook, we don't clean, don't wash up. We don't lift a finger.' She looked round at the attentive, eager faces. 'You saw how much the boys liked how we cleaned up the café? Well we'll give them a choice. If they want it that way, they have to do their share of the chores. Or do it all themselves.'

The rest all looked at each other nervously. It sounded like a good plan, but it was scary, as Zandra pointed out. 'I love it. But Lex will go ballistic.'

Cloe looked concerned. 'What will he do to us?'

'What can he do?' Amber reassured them, 'The other boys won't let him hurt us.'

'Right,' Zandra said. 'Ryan won't let him hit girls, I'm certain.'

'How long do we do it for?'

'As long as it takes, Patsy.'

Zandra held out her hand. 'I'm in!'

Amber took her hand, happily. 'Anyone else?'

One by one they joined hands around the circle, and grinned at each other in the flickering light of the candle flames.

And then they heard it. A low unearthly wailing rising up from the sewers. They all looked at each other in alarm. The grins had gone, and were replaced by looks of terror.

ONE HUNDRED AND TWENTY SEVEN

The weird sound echoed throughout the darkened mall, bringing everyone out of their rooms, alarmed and frightened. The girls rushed out of their meeting place and gathered at the top of the wide staircase, all talking at once.

'What is it?'

'It's the Locusts!'

'It's Zoot's ghost!'

'Don't be silly, Cloe!' Amber said. 'There's no such thing.'

Patsy was terrified. 'Well, what is it then?'

The wailing seemed to grow louder, swirling around the darkness of the mall and fading way up into the atrium.

Amber looked grim. 'I don't know, but I think we're about to find out.'

By now the boys had joined the girls. Jack was rubbing sleep from his eyes, looking round confused. 'What's going on?'

'It's Zoot's ghost!' Patsy said, echoing Cloe.

'Rubbish, Patsy!' Amber snapped. 'Ghosts don't exist!'

Dal had come from his room grasping a cricket bat. 'Well, whatever it is, it exists alright!'

Trudy hurried from her room and found Bray standing a little aside. She clutched his arm. 'Bray!'

Bray bent close to her and whispered calmly, out of earshot of the rest. 'It's alright, Trudy. There's nothing to worry about.'

She looked at him, puzzled. 'What is it?'

He put a finger to his lips. 'It's nothing. Go back to bed.'

There was something so reassuring in Bray's voice that, despite the wailing and the sense of panic among the rest, Trudy calmly went back to her room, unnoticed by the others.

Ryan was listening keenly to the sound, trying to decipher it. 'Could be the wind. It's blowing hard outside.'

Jack wasn't that easily reassured. 'Nah, it's definitely something alive.'

Lex, bare-chested, hefting a heavy club and chain, took control. 'Well, it's not gonna be alive for long! Ryan, put the girls in the cage!'

Amber looked shocked. 'What?'

'You'll be safer there.'

'We'll be trapped!' Zandra cried. 'If it gets in, we'll be trapped in there!'

Lex waved his club in the direction of the café. 'Get in the café then, Grab anything you can as a weapon. Me and the troops are gonna investigate.'

'Troops?' Dal said faintly, turning to Jack.

Jack swallowed. 'I think he means us.'

'We've been training you for this,' Ryan said, 'Remember?'

Bray was standing to one side, aloof, observing the tense situation calmly.

Lex looked at him. 'You too, Bray!'

'What?'

'You're coming with us to investigate.'

Bray shook his head. 'No. I'm staying with Trudy and the baby.'

'I'm your leader and I gave you an order!' Lex barked.

Folding his arms, Bray leant nonchalantly against a pillar. 'And I'm refusing it.'

Lex tensed and tightened his grip on the club.

'Lex!' Ryan said. This wasn't the time for a confrontation.

Lex glared fiercely at Bray. 'I'll deal with you later!'

Patsy piped up. 'Lex! Sir!'

'What?' Lex snapped.

'Paul wants to come with you.'

'No way! He's a deafo! He'll be a liability.' He turned to the other boys. 'Come on!'

Grimly he led the little battle group down the stairs towards the sewers, where the wailing was still rising and falling eerily.

ONE HUNDRED AND TWENTY EIGHT

Gripping his club tightly in his fist and shining the torch ahead of him, Lex led the way cautiously along the main sewer tunnel. Ryan was close behind, with Jack and Dal bringing up the rear, nervously.

'It sounds like it's outside,' Jack whispered.

'Well, let's leave it there!' Dal replied.

Lex stopped and looked back at them, shining the torch in their eyes. 'And have it bring the Locos and the Demon Dogs?'

'Yeah,' Ryan said brightly. 'Let them deal with it!'

Lex was exasperated. 'And what if they get wind of us being holed up in here? So far they've no idea where we are. I want to keep it that way!'

'Perhaps it'll just go away?' Dal ventured.

'Or just lie out there and wait for the first person to go out food foraging!' Lex waved them on. 'Come on!'

They moved on a few paces, the wailing sound was becoming more distinct.

'It sounds kinda like an animal,' Ryan said.

'Not like one I've ever heard,' Jack responded.

'Could be a mutant or something. You know, from the virus.'

'Thanks, Dal,' Jack said sarcastically. 'I really needed to know that!'

ooo

The girls were building a barricade at the top of the stairs, with tables and chairs from the café.

'I can't get over Bray being a coward,' Zandra said.

Salene jumped in. 'I'm sure he's not! He must have his reasons.'

'Might have known you'd defend him.'

'Meaning?' Salene said defensively.

'Oh come on, Salene!'

Patsy came out of the café struggling with another chair. 'Where's Cloe! She's supposed to be helping!'

ooo

Bray and Trudy were seated on the bed in Trudy's room chuckling together as Amber walked in. She looked at Bray, puzzled and annoyed.

'What's going on, Bray?'

'What d'you mean?' he asked mildly.

'Why didn't you go with the others?'

'I'm looking after Trudy and the baby.'

'It's not just that. I mean you're not even worried. There's some kind of strange creature down there and you couldn't care less. You're actually laughing...' She looked at him accusingly. 'You know what it is, don't you? You know what that noise is!'

Bray shrugged in reply.

Amber was incensed at his cool, nonchalant manner. 'Bray!'

Salene rushed in, breathless. 'Amber! Cloe's missing!'

ONE HUNDRED AND TWENTY NINE

Even though after Zoot's death it was irrelevant, Bray had kept his side of the bargain with Cloe. He'd helped her tether the calf in a secluded place in the car park, and had watched with amusement how she contrived to slip away unnoticed every day, hiding a bottle of water under her coat. Unknown to Cloe and the rest, he had made a point of following her, unseen, just in case the little girl needed protection.

Despite the danger Cloe had taken the calf out to graze daily to the large grassy space that had once been the lunchtime spot for the city office workers. She was growing concerned that the grass there was nearly all gone, and she knew that she would have to go further from the mall to find fresh pasture for her pet. The thought scared her, but Bluebell was her only real friend. Someone she could confide all her thoughts and fears to. Something alive and warm that she could lose herself in for a brief moment every day, and forget the horrors of a world she didn't understand.

Now her friend was in danger of being discovered, and she knew what that meant. Bray had told her what Lex and the others would do to Bluebell if they ever found her.

She had managed to slip through the sewers ahead of Lex's group, but despite her pleas the calf continued to moan and resisted her trying to lead it away. 'Come on, Bluebell!' she urged. 'They can hear you! They're coming! Bluebell, please, they mustn't find you!'

ooo

Lex and the others emerged from the sewers into the surrounding darkness of the city night. Outside, undistorted by the sewer tunnels, the sound was much more obvious.

'Sounds like a cow,' Ryan said.

'Yeah, it does,' Dal sounded relieved. 'Just like a cow!'

The calf's cry was clear and nearby. 'It is a cow!' Lex said excitedly. 'You know what that means, Ryan?'

'Meat!'

'Exactly! Spread out! Hamburgers for breakfast!'

Jack stayed a pace behind. 'Careful! Cows can still be dangerous.'

Lex grinned, 'Not half as dangerous as Ryan when he wants a hamburger!'

He flashed his torch around the empty car park space. The roaming beam illuminated the calf and the little girl cowering in a corner.

Cloe put her hand up to shield her eyes from the sudden light. 'No!' she cried. 'Keep away! Run, Bluebell, run!'

The calf remained quiet and motionless as the youths approached. Cloe put her arms around the animal's neck protectively. 'Please don't hurt her! She's my friend!'

Lex stretched out the club and gently stroked the calf's forehead with it. 'Sorry. This little beauty will just about do us for a fortnight.'

'No!' Cloe's scream echoed through the empty space and out into the night. 'You can't eat her! You can't eat Bluebell!'

Ryan knelt beside the little animal and stroked its nose. 'Hello, Bluebell.'

'She'll give you milk!' Cloe cried desperately. 'Lots and lots of milk!'

'Yeah,' Jack said. 'That's an idea!'

'At last we'll have something to put on our cornflakes,' Dal said.

Cloe went on, encouraged. 'You will, won't you, Bluebell? Lots of milk!'

'It'll need to be taken out to graze,' Jack reminded them.

'There's plenty of grass in the park,' Dal replied. 'If we get up early enough, the tribes won't be around.'

Lex made a decision. 'Okay, we'll keep it!'

Cloe rushed to him and hugged him around his naked waist. 'Oh, thank you! Thank you!'

Lex shrugged her away. 'Gerroff!' he said gruffly.

ONE HUNDRED AND THIRTY

With the discovery of the calf relief flooded through the mall, but Amber was angry. She became even angrier when she found Bray and Trudy where she had left them, and saw their amused expressions.

'There you are! I suppose you think this is very funny?'

'Not especially,' Bray replied.

'Letting everybody get into a blind panic! The kids terrified! And all the time you knew! You knew what it was, didn't you!'

'Yes.'

His coolness brought her blood to the boil. Infuriated she raged on, 'Well, why didn't you say so? What are you playing at, Bray!'

'I promised Cloe I wouldn't tell her secret.'

Amber gasped out loud. 'Oh, that's absurd!'

'No, Amber, I don't break promises,' he said seriously.

'Oh, Mister High and Mighty! Mister Self-Righteous! You are a number one self-righteous jerk!'

The baby began to whimper, disturbed by Amber's raised voice. Trudy picked it up. 'You're upsetting the baby!'

Amber rounded on her. 'Well, why don't you take it away then? In fact why don't you all go! The three of you!'

Trudy was shocked. 'What?'

'You are both so selfish! You do nothing to help! You take and never give! You use Salene like a slave!'

Amber had hit a raw nerve.

'She pushed her way in!' Trudy snapped. 'She's after Bray!'

'Trudy,' Bray tried to calm her down.

Amber turned her attack back on Bray. 'You think you're so intelligent, so clever! Winding Lex up, trying to humiliate him! Well, at least he had the guts to stand for leader!'

'I don't believe in leaders.'

'Well, what precisely do you believe in, Bray? Anything? Nothing? Perhaps when you've figured it out you can come down off your pedestal and tell us poor little morons!' Amber could feel tears of frustration welling, but she wasn't going to give them that satisfaction.

Bray looked grim. 'If you feel that strongly, Amber, we can go.'

Trudy looked at him alarmed. 'Bray!'

'It's not gonna work with Lex as leader anyway,' he went on.

Amber looked at him, her expression hard. 'Don't you think I know that?'

Bray returned her look evenly, understanding.

'I figured.'

ONE HUNDRED AND THIRTY ONE

Ebony was awake as the dawn slowly woke the city. She stretched out luxuriously, naked, in the king-size hotel bed, feeling the cool cotton sheet caressing her skin. When the Locos moved into the Hotel Plaza, she had taken the bridal suite, with its sumptuous lounge, huge bedroom and ensuite. It was a pity she didn't have someone to share it with.

The hotel's state of the art power supply was fueled by a large generator which she could hear throbbing quietly several floors below in the basement. What they would do when the looted diesel ran out she didn't know, and at the moment didn't care. The future would look after itself. You could plan for it, but you could only live for today, in the moment.

Since the altercation with Spike she had posted a guard at her door, double-locked it, and slept with a weapon under her pillow. She still had nightmares. Some of Spike appearing at her bedside, a gleaming knife raised in his hand. Others were relics of the past, bad memories that she couldn't erase no matter how hard she tried. At times like these she felt very alone.

Things had moved fast since Zoot's disappearance. She had established dominance over the Demon Dogs, though she had no doubt they would be out for revenge. And taking over the casino from Tribe Circus was a master stroke. The braver, tougher members from all the city's tribes used the place. It was the hub of the city where information could be overheard or traded. And knowledge, as she knew, was power.

Any regime that stood still, Zoot had told her, ultimately perished. She believed that. She had to keep moving. One step ahead. While at the same time watching her back for the threat from within the Locos. She remembered a phrase from somewhere, maybe at school. Could have been that boring old guy Shakespeare. It was something like, 'Lonely is the head that wears the crown.' Well, he'd got that right.

ONE HUNDRED AND THIRTY TWO

Lex was feeling good. He'd bravely led his 'troops' to face the unknown creature, no matter that it had turned out to be a harmless calf. He felt more at home as leader now that he'd done something they all could admire and praise.

Even so Zandra still refused his advances.

'I don't care if it was only a cow,' she'd said. 'I thought you were very brave.'

'So what are you going to give me for protecting you?' he said expectantly.

She'd blown him a kiss from the balcony.

'Is that all?'

'Cheek. Some fellas would die for that,' she'd said as she flounced away.

He was seated in his office, with his boots on his desk. Ryan sat opposite taking notes.

'We need an extra amount of rations for the calf. And a rota to take it out to graze every day.'

Ryan looked dubious. 'That could be dangerous, Lex.'

'Well, unless you've got a spare haystack under your mattress, Ryan, what else can we do?'

'What are you going to do about Bray? Disobeying an order?'

'I'm gonna let him think he got away with it. Then when he drops his guard, get even.'

'How?'

Lex had thought about that. Bray was the one irritant in the mall. He was strong-willed and intelligent. Lex was wily, streetwise, but he often felt that Bray was one step ahead of him, and that made him uneasy. While Bray was there Lex would never feel totally secure.

'The trick to leadership, Ryan,' Lex said expansively, 'is never to be predictable. Keep 'em guessing. Oh, and I want you, Jack and Dal to fix up the pharmacy on the balcony.'

'What for?'

'For me. It's gonna be my penthouse.'

'What about the boutique?' Lex and Ryan had been sharing the same space since they arrived.

'I'm sick of it. Your feet stink and you keep it like a pigsty! I'm moving out. I need some privacy. And stick a double bed in there for when I'm ready to choose my First Lady.'

Ryan frowned. 'What, not Zandra, you mean?'

'Of course Zandra, you idiot! I'm just not going to rush it. Keep 'em guessing.'

Ryan suddenly lifted up his head and sniffed. 'What's that smell?' He stood up and sniffed again, amazed. 'Bread!'

At that moment Jack rushed in, agitated. 'Lex, the girls are refusing to cook our breakfast!'

ooo

After everyone had recovered from the scare over the ghostly noises, the girls rolled out Amber's plan for Lex. But the bread was Salene's idea. She'd discovered some dried yeast in the kitchen and the mall bakery had vacuum-packed flour that would last for a long time. At school domestic science had been Salene's favourite lesson and bread-making was her speciality.

'Have you ever known anyone who could resist the smell of fresh baked bread?' she said mischievously, as the other girls watched her kneading the dough.

By the time Lex stormed up the stairs and into the café, the girls were seated around the table enjoying slices of delicious warm bread smothered with jam.

He scowled. 'What's going on?'

'We're just sampling Salene's homemade bread, Lex,' Amber said matter of factly.

'It's delicious!' Zandra exclaimed.

Lex glared. 'Where's our breakfast? It's supposed to be ready.'

Salene smiled sweetly, 'Sorry, Lex, no can do.'

'What do you mean? Why? It's on the rota!'

Amber pretended to look puzzled. 'Rota? Have you girls seen any rota?'

They all shook their heads, mouths full.

Lex strode to the side wall of the café and pointed angrily to an empty space. 'It was there! Stuck up!' He slapped the wall in frustration. 'Write out another one, Jack!'

'Why bother,' said Salene. 'We're not doing it.'

'Oh, yes you are!' he said fiercely.

Zandra glared back at him, 'We're not going to be used as domestic slaves!'

'Shut up, Zan,' he snapped. 'You can't even spell 'domestic'!'

'We're not standing for this sexist division of chores,' Salene said determinedly.

'So we're looking after ourselves in future!' Zandra added.

Lex leaned over towards Zandra with a menacing look. 'Zandra, you are making me very angry!'

Amber stood up aggressively and confronted him. 'Don't even think about it, Lex!'

Lex rounded on Amber. 'You put them up to this, didn't you!'

Amber appeared as calm as he was angry, 'No, Lex, you drove them to it.' She smiled at Salene. 'Great bread, Salene! Zandra, weren't you gonna show me how to do my hair?'

Amber, Salene and Zandra got up to leave.

'We'll clean up our pots later,' Salene said as they went out of the café.

Lex called after them, 'You won't get away with this!' He stood fuming in the middle of the café impotent and frustrated.

'That bread smells good,' Ryan said wistfully.

'Gorgeous,' Jack agreed.

'Wonder if they left any?' Ryan wandered off into the kitchen with Jack following behind.

Lex kicked a chair across the room, narrowly missing Dal who came rushing into the café in an agitated state.

'Lex!'

'What?' Lex snapped.

'There's a leak!'

'Where?'

'Come here!' Dal waved his arms and rushed out again.

Exasperated Lex followed him down the stairs, with Jack and Ryan behind. In the centre of the floor a large puddle had formed.

'There! Dal pointed.

Ryan frowned. 'The floors all wet.'

'That'll be the water, Ryan,' Lex said sarcastically.

A single drop of water splashed into the puddle from a great height. They all looked up.

'Is it raining?'

'I don't think so,' Jack said. 'No, look, there's no rain drops on the glass.'

They stood for a moment, puzzling the situation.

'It's stopped,' Ryan said. 'Must have been the rain.'

Jack looked suddenly concerned. 'Or a leak...The water tank's right above there!'

'Yeh, but it's stopped,' Lex said. 'A leaking tank wouldn't just stop, would it?'

'Unless...' Jack didn't need to finish.

Dal gasped and put his hand to his head. 'Oh, no! We can't live without water..! Lex, what are we gonna do?'

Lex stood staring down at the puddle. An expression the adults used in the old days jumped into his mind. 'It never rains but it pours.' He knew the feeling.

ONE HUNDRED AND THIRTY THREE

Zandra was styling Amber's hair before the mirror in Amber's room. Salene was watching, seated, still buzzing from the confrontation with Lex. At first she had been afraid to take on what Amber had suggested, but now that they had done it, she felt elated.

'We did it,' she said, almost in disbelief. 'We did it and he couldn't stop us.'

'How long is it gonna take to work though?' Zandra asked.

'The longest journey starts with one step, Zandra,' said Amber. 'We've taken the step. And if we stick together...'

'There,' said Zandra proudly, standing away from Amber to look at her handiwork. 'The new you.'

Amber turned her head from side to side, looking at her image in the mirror. 'Brilliant! I like it.'

Zandra looked wistful, the past suddenly flooding back to her. 'I wanted to be a hairdresser. I was going to train and everything, after I left school.'

'You still can,' said Salene brightly, trying to lift the mood before Zandra took them all back to places they didn't want to go.

'How? There's nobody to train me.'

'There should be some books around,' Amber said. 'Or maybe even some DVDs.'

'There's no batteries for the laptop,' Salene reminded her.

'Well, I'm sure Jack and Dal will come up with something eventually.'

Zandra smiled, 'You're so positive, Amber. That's what I like about you. You always think things will get better.'

Amber shrugged, 'Well, I'm sure they will. It just takes time. After a while even people like Lex will realize violence doesn't work forever.'

'You should have been the leader, not stupid Lex.' Salene looked at Zandra. 'Sorry, Zandra.'

'Don't look at me, I'm not Lex's.'

'Yeah, but you're still lucky to have someone who fancies you so much.'

Zandra looked at her, mischievously. 'You could too.'

'Who?'

'Come on, Salene!' Zandra exclaimed.

Salene felt her face flush. 'What?'

'Amber, tell her!'

'Leave it, Zandra!' Amber said testily, wanting to avoid the subject of Bray. She was still very confused about her own feelings and Salene's crush on him didn't help the situation.

Zandra wouldn't be put off. 'Why? Everybody knows! You're after Bray!'

'I am not!' Salene protested loudly.

'Go on!' Zandra goaded. 'Don't say you don't fancy him!'

'It's not the same as being after him!' Salene said defensively.

'It is! You're in there all the time looking after the baby! Taking it for walks!'

Salene retaliated aggressively, feeling cornered by Zandra's accusations, which she knew in her heart were true. 'Only because Trudy doesn't care about it and I -!'

Zandra shouted her down. 'Only because it's Bray's niece!'

'No!'

'Hey come on, you two!' Amber raised her voice above the others. 'We're supposed to be sticking together, remember? Against Lex and the boys? We've got a real fight on our hands. We don't have to make up fights between ourselves!'

'Well -' Zandra began.

Amber's tone was firm and final. 'Zandra, if we fall out amongst ourselves we've had it!'

Salene and Zandra fell silent, feeling suddenly foolish. Amber was right. Outside in the city there were many dangerous enemies, but inside the mall their real enemy was Lex.

ONE HUNDRED AND THIRTY FOUR

The large water tank on top of the roof which supplied the mall was empty. Jack had climbed the ladder and tested the level with a stick. It had come out bone dry. The other boys stood below as he gave them the bad news.

'And water's the only thing we can't do without!' Dal said grimly.

Jack climbed down the ladder and looked at Lex. 'So what do we do now, boss?'

'Breakfast,' said Lex. 'Dal can cook.'

'No, I can't!' Dal protested.

'Well learn!' Lex strode away irritated. His day, which had started off so well, was going from bad to worse.

Jack hurried after Lex. 'Looks like we'll have to use your private water stash,' he said.

'Get lost! That's for an emergency!'

Jack looked surprised. 'Well, what do you call this! We'll die without water!'

'I'll think of something,' Lex replied grumpily. The truth was he hadn't a clue. Hungry and still smarting about the incident with the bread, he was getting a headache, and the water situation was the last straw.

ooo

Dal put the plate on the café table in front of Lex. Lex looked at it and screwed up his face. 'What's this'?

303

'It's beans on crackers,' Dal said defensively.

Picking up a blackened cracker, Lex thrust it in Dal's face. 'They're burnt!'

Dal shrugged. 'I tried toasting them.'

Lex hurled the plate away. It smashed against the floor, splattering the wall with beans. 'Why can't we have bread, like Salene's!'

'I never learnt!' Dal said crossly. 'I'm not a girl!'

'Well start now!' Lex ordered. 'You've got a brain, haven't you?'

'I thought we weren't doing girls' jobs?' Dal responded.

'That's right, Lex,' said Ryan.

Lex scowled for a moment, then a look of fierce determination came over his face. 'We're not! I'll fix 'em!'

ONE HUNDRED AND THIRTY FIVE

Amber was propped up in her bed, reading Machiavelli's 'The Prince.' It was relaxing losing herself in another time and place, in someone else's thoughts. Living in the present with its day to day problems was a strain.

The Renaissance philosopher's views about leadership were fascinating, though she didn't share his belief that evil was a necessary part of being a ruler. Lex would probably agree with that, she thought to herself with a smile. Though she had her doubts that Lex could actually read.

One sentence in particular caught her eye, about taking control of one's own future, rather than waiting to see what chance brings. That couldn't be more relevant in today's world. And if Bray was right about her being a natural leader, it was up to her to lead. It was time to finish the battle with Lex for control of the mall.

There was a knock on her door. She looked up, a little irritated at being disturbed. It was Trudy smiling nervously.

'Can I come in for a minute?'

Amber laid her book aside. 'Of course. Come in.'

Trudy looked around the room. 'This looks great, Amber. It's important to have a place of your own, isn't it?'

'Anything the matter, Trudy?' She didn't think Trudy had come just to discuss the décor.

Trudy sat on the bed, a pained expression on her face. 'It's Bray.'

Amber groaned inwardly. Of course, it would have to be. 'Yeah?'

'He's gone into a mood. He won't talk.'

'Seems to me Bray's always in some mood or other.' Amber realized she should try to keep her bitterness to herself. Trudy had feminine intuition in spades, and Amber didn't want the complication of Trudy being jealous of her as well as of Salene.

There was panic in the back of Trudy's voice. 'I think he's going to leave. After what you said this morning. You don't really want us to leave, do you? I don't want to go, Amber. I'm scared outside. Even with Bray. And now with the baby and everything.'

'Have you given her a name yet?'

Trudy looked shamefaced. 'No.'

'Don't you think you ought to, and start taking responsibility for her? She is your child, Trudy.'

'I know.'

'And it would give Salene less opportunity to always be around.'

Trudy's face changed from shame to anger in an instant. 'Huh! Her!'

'She's only trying to help, Trudy. She was brilliant when you were ill. She can't help it that she's fallen for Bray.'

'Well, she can keep her hands off him!'

'You're not listening, Trudy,' Amber said patiently, but feeling irritated inside. There was something about Trudy's pathetic little girl act that made Amber want to give her a good slap. 'I said she can't help the way she feels, but I don't honestly think she's trying to break you two up. You're doing that yourself.'

Trudy looked contrite. Her fingers picked at the bedspread. 'If...If I start to be a better mother, and stop getting at Salene..?'

Amber suddenly felt sorry for her. Her life must have been hell the last few months. 'I don't want you to go, Trudy,' she said honestly. 'I think you and Bray could be a great help to us. But that's up to you, and Bray.'

'Could you talk to him, Amber? I know he really respects you.'

Amber had mixed feelings about that, but she had decided to lead, hadn't she? 'I'll try. But Bray only does what he wants and if he's made up his mind...' She sat up, becoming practical. 'Now, what about the baby's name?'

At that moment Salene rushed in agitated. 'Amber!' There was an awkward moment when she saw Trudy sitting beside Amber on the bed.

'What is it, Salene?'

'Ryan's not giving us our water ration!'

Amber leapt up. Lex had made his move. It was time to retaliate.

ONE HUNDRED AND THIRTY SIX

Lex was in his office, calmly playing patience when Amber strode in followed by Salene, Zandra and Patsy. Ryan was behind them, looking a little sheepish.

Lex looked up. 'Hi, Amber. Been expecting you.'

Amber stood before the desk, arms folded. 'What's all this about water, Lex?'

'I told Ryan to tell you.'

'I did,' Ryan said uncomfortably.

Lex continued to lay down cards, irritatingly casual. 'There's no water left. Nix. You can go look for yourselves if you don't believe me.'

'There was a leak in the water tank,' Ryan explained again. 'It's empty.'

Zandra was alarmed. 'You're serious?'

'Yeah, but don't worry, Zan,' Lex said. 'I'm the leader and I've come up with a plan.'

'Which is?' Amber's expression showed she wasn't going to like the answer.

Lex stopped playing and laid down the pack of cards. He leant back expansively in his black leather chair. 'Jack said there's a stream not far from here. Comes straight from the mountains. Should be pure. You and the girls can go and collect some water from there and I'll send Ryan and the boys to protect you.'

Amber looked grim. 'Forget it, Lex!'

'What's the problem?' Lex was smiling. 'Women always used to fetch water, in Africa and that.'

'We said no sexist division of jobs!' Salene reminded him.

'Exactly,' Amber agreed.

'Be reasonable! You couldn't exactly protect us, could you?'

'We'll go together and all carry the water,' Amber said decisively.

'No way,' Lex countered. 'I'm not putting my men at risk. They need to be free to fight.'

Amber face was set. 'Then we'll go on our own.'

Lex rose and went round his desk, homing in on Zandra. 'Zandra out there with the Locos and the Demon Dogs around? Getting caught by that lot.' He stroked her cheek with the back of his hand. 'She'd be a real prize, wouldn't she? They'd really like her.'

Zandra shrank away, very frightened at the image.

'Then I'll go on my own, if I have to.'

'And I'll come with you, Amber!' said Salene resolutely.

Patsy chimed up. 'And me!'

Lex was getting annoyed. The girls were being more stubborn than he'd thought. 'I wouldn't let you go anyway. You'd get caught and give the rest of us away.'

'Then when the boys go, we'll come with you and fetch our own,' Amber said with an air of finality.

Lex rounded on her. 'This is your fault! You put 'em up to this!'

Amber was calm before his anger. 'No. It's a group rebellion, Lex.'

She turned and led the other girls out.

Lex yelled after them. 'We'll see who can go without water the longest!' He sat back in his chair, annoyed, but still feeling he had the whip hand in this situation.

Ryan was looking very unhappy. Lex guessed his thoughts. 'They're not gonna die of thirst, Ryan. They'll give in before that.'

'But how will we get water?'

'We use our own private stash.'

'But Dal doesn't know about that, Lex. And if we tell him, he's bound to tell Amber. They're mates.'

Ryan had hit on a good point for once. 'I'm sure you can persuade him to keep his trap shut, Ryan.'

Ryan persisted, like a dog with a bone. 'What if they get to know? They'll put you on trial like they did with Jack.'

'I'm the leader. They can't put me on trial.'

'Why not?'

The questions were beginning to irritate Lex. 'Because I won't let them, Ryan.'

'But those are the rules, Lex. We made them up about stealing and stuff.'

'They're not gonna know anyway. Not unless somebody tells them...' He looked at Ryan searchingly. 'You're not thinking of telling them, are you..?' Ryan looked away. 'Ryan!'

'What if they don't give in?' Ryan went on doggedly. He looked at his old friend, a serious look on his face. 'I'm not gonna let them die of thirst, Lex.'

Ryan walked out, leaving Lex looking thoughtful. It was annoying. For a leader, there seemed to be more questions than answers.

ONE HUNDRED AND THIRTY SEVEN

Ebony watched the Locos cavorting around the pool from her window. The city had gone quiet after the rout of the Demon Dogs and the takeover of the casino, and the youths were enjoying having time just to hang and fool around.

She looked at the naked bodies, both boys and girls, lying on sunbeds, splashing in the water, some even getting it on behind the bushes surrounding the sparkling blue pool. She felt envious. As leader she had allowed the downtime, but she couldn't join in. A leader had to keep their distance, be aloof. Being 'one of the boys' meant you could no longer keep your special aura. And without that, it was a short step to losing your power and control.

She sighed, missing the physical contact with Zoot. How she would love to have one of those naked youths in the bridal suite with her as compensation. There were several out there that she would have happily taken to her bed. But that was out of the question. In such a tightly-knit group as the Locos it could never be kept a secret. And to choose one over the others would create rivalries and jealousies she didn't need in her tribe. Those emotions were destructive.

Of course, if she chose, she could have any one of them. A different one each night. And sometimes, like now, watching those young toned, naked bodies outside, she almost gave in to her impulses. But she didn't want that kind of reputation. Despite the lack of decent role models in her childhood, somehow she had an instinct towards her own type of morality. Deep down inside something in her yearned to be respected.

She thought of him. The brother. And how she had lost his respect. For a moment she felt tears well in her eyes. She shook herself roughly out of her thoughts. Thinking too deeply was a weakness. A born leader worked on instinct. The instinct of a predator. Maybe one day there would come a time when she could truly enjoy the trappings of leadership, but for now it business as usual. Kill or be killed.

ONE HUNDRED AND THIRTY EIGHT

Amber had put her plan of action into operation. She had left the others to start it off while she went to see Bray, as she had promised Trudy she would. She approached his room hesitantly. That morning she had torn a strip off Bray. She had let her legitimate anger and her deep feelings for him get confused, and she had really let rip.

She felt embarrassed confronting him now. How much did he know about her real feelings about him? Did they show? Did he care? At times, even in their moments of confrontation, she felt there was something unspoken that passed between them. If she was right, that frightened her. She was resolved she was going to be leader again, and leaders had a duty to act responsibly. Taking Bray away from Trudy was not in the game-plan. Even if she could.

He was writing in a notebook when she knocked on his open door. He looked up, surprised.

'Amber?' He put down his pen and closed the book.

'I'm sorry, am I interrupting?'

'No, not at all. Come in.' He waved his hand towards an empty chair. 'Sit down.'

She sat down, a little surprised at his friendly welcome. 'What are you writing?' She went on hurriedly, 'Sorry, that's none of my business,'

He smiled. 'That's okay. Just a diary. My thoughts. One day, who knows, people may want to know what went on here. How we lived.'

'You believe in a future then? That we'll survive?'

He nodded. 'Yeh. But not necessarily with leaders. Leaders never got us anywhere. Look at the mess they got us into.'

'You encouraged me to stand for leader.'

'Because you don't really believe in them either, Amber.'

She frowned, puzzled.

'Don't you believe it should be everyone for each other?' he asked. 'Not everyone for themselves?'

Amber smiled. 'It's a nice dream.'

'Maybe for now. But if you don't have dreams, Amber, where are you..?' He smiled gently and looked deep into her eyes, holding his gaze. I know you have a dream.'

She felt fluttering in the pit of her stomach and alarm rising in her throat. She looked away. 'So when Lex cracks,' she said businesslike, 'How do you see it?'

'If he cracks.'

Amber smiled. 'Oh, he will. I know his type.'

'I bet you do.' He smiled enigmatically. 'Do you know mine?'

She could feel her breath getting short under his questioning gaze. Did he know? She returned his smile. 'Not yet. But I'm working on it.'

ONE HUNDRED AND THIRTY NINE

In the kitchen Zandra watched Salene skillfully rolling pastry on the table. Zandra was excited about Amber's plan. She wanted to be a part it, and was disappointed that she couldn't really contribute. Sometimes she wished she'd paid more attention at school, instead of spending all her time thinking about fashion, celebrities and boys. But that was the way she was made, she told herself in justification. She couldn't help it.

'Wish I could make pastry,' she said enviously.

'Didn't you ever learn at school?'

'Well yeah, I tried. But I kept getting flour in my hair and stuff.'

Ryan wandered in, drawn by the activity surrounding his favourite subject, food. 'What are you making?'

'It's a special treat,' Zandra said, teasing.

'What?' Ryan couldn't contain his interest.

'Meat pie.' Zandra announced.

'Pie?'

'Jack had some tinned meat in his secret stash.'

Ryan's eyes were wide with amazement. 'Really? Meat pie!'

Salene turned to him with a smile. 'With real stock gravy.'

'Gravy?' Ryan was salivating at the thought. He hadn't had proper home-made food since he could remember. And meat pie with gravy was one of his favorites.

'Well,' Salene went on, 'it would be if we had enough water.'

'It's a sort of celebration,' Zandra said in explanation.

'What for?'

'Trudy's going to give the baby a name,' said Zandra. She was excited about the whole occasion. Anything to do with babies was a dream.

'At last,' said Salene, not bothering to coneal the bitterness in her voice.

'What's she gonna call it?' Ryan could take or leave babies, but he was glad that 'it' was finally going to get a name. Everybody deserved a name.

'It's a secret,' Zandra said slyly.

'That's a funny name,' Ryan replied.

'No, it is a secret, dummy!' Zandra saw the pained expression in Ryan's eyes and immediately felt sorry. 'Sometimes, Ryan, I could kiss you.'

Ryan glanced at her, then looked down. 'Why don't you then?' he asked shyly.

Zandra gave him a look. She saw the embarrassment in the young man's gentle face. 'Alright, then, I will.'

She got up and planted a wet kiss on Ryan's cheek. She sat down again, leaving Ryan flushed and lost for words.

At last he started to speak. 'I love...' He saw Zandra glance up at him with a strange expression and stopped himself. 'I love pie...Haven't had one since...If I get some water for the gravy, can I have a piece?'

Salene and Zandra exchanged a secret smile.

ooo

Lex was in his office, playing cards alone. He looked up suddenly, some sixth sense alerting him. The mall seemed unusually quiet and empty. Now he thought of it he hadn't seen or heard anyone for quite a while. At that moment a peal of laughter rang out from the café, and a chatter of voices followed. He got up to investigate, with an uneasy feeling in his gut.

He bounded up the stairs two at a time and entered the café in time to see Salene placing a magnificent looking pie in the centre of the table. Everyone was seated around expectantly, including Ryan, Dal and Jack.

Lex glowered. 'What's going on?'

'Oh hi, Lex!' said Zandra brightly. 'We're having a banquet!'

Not to left out of the excitement, Patsy added excitedly, 'Trudy's giving the baby a name!'

'I thought you decided not to feed us men,' Lex said suspiciously.

'Well,' Amber said, 'Ryan did get us some water for the gravy.'

'And we're just showing Jack and Dal what they can get as a regular treat,' Salene said, very pleased with how her pie had turned out.

'As long as they agree to share the chores properly,' Zandra said, relishing the situation, and Lex's discomfort.

'Not that sexy rota!' Patsy said haughtily.

Bray grinned. 'Sexist, Patsy.'

Everyone around the table joined in his amusement.

Lex's face was set hard, 'Ryan, Dal, Jack, I wanna see you lot, now!'

Ryan looked pained. 'The pie'll get cold, Lex.'

'And the gravy,' added Jack bravely. 'Can't stand cold gravy.'

Dal was aware of Lex's thunderous expression. It looked like he could explode at any moment. He tried to deflect the explosion. 'We're just trying it out, Lex. We haven't decided on anything.'

'Why don't you come and join us, Lex?' Amber said pleasantly.

'In your dreams!' Lex snarled.

'Salene, it smells divine!' Zandra said, rubbing salt into Lex's wounds. 'Hurry up and cut it!'

Lex turned on his heels and stormed angrily out of the café. They listened to his boots banging down the stairs.

Ryan's eager voice broke the silence, 'Shall I cut the pie?'

'Hang on,' said Zandra, and looked at Trudy.

'Well, Trudy?' Amber prompted.

All eyes turned to Trudy, seated beside Bray.

'Oh yes...' Trudy began tentatively, with a quick glance at Bray. 'I've decided to call her Brady.'

Ryan frowned. 'Brady?'

At the head of the table Amber noticed Bray glance at Trudy. He didn't look thrilled.

Dal piped up, 'Oh yeah, I see it! It's a combination of Bray and Trudy!'

'That's pretty cool,' Jack said.

'Hurry up and cut the pie!' said Ryan. 'I'm starving!'

Amber and Bray's eyes met briefly from the opposite ends of the table. Bray looked away, a trapped expression on his face.

ONE HUNDRED AND FORTY

It was the morning after the banquet and the naming of Trudy's baby. Last evening, for the first time in a while there had been a sense of togetherness in the mall, except for Lex.

He had laid brooding in his bed, awake for hours, replaying the whole scenario with Amber over and over in his mind. He knew she was behind the rebellion that was threatening his control. And at the moment she seemed to be winning.

He heard Ryan waking up on his mattress on the floor. 'Ryan! You're out!' Lex barked.

Ryan was still half awake. 'Eh?'

'Get your own place!'

Ryan sat up, puzzled, rubbing the sleep from his eyes. 'I thought you were moving out? To your penthouse?'

'Nah. I'm gonna stay here!'

'What am I gonna do?'

'That's your problem,' Lex replied grumpily.

Ryan stood up and walked over the Lex's bed. 'You still mad about the pie thing?'

'Yeh, the pie thing, the rota thing!' Lex said bitterly. 'The fact that there's a traitor in my own camp!'

Ryan tried a smile, to make light of it. 'Lex, it was just a bit of gravy.'

'I'm sure the rota's pretty clear about who makes the gravy around here!'

'They didn't have any water!'

'They would have done if they'd have bothered to go and fetch it!' Lex snapped.

'It's hardly fair though, is it?' Ryan felt guilty about betraying his friend, but he thought Lex was out of line. He wished he could make him see. 'We all need water.'

'Fair! Where do you think we live, Ryan? Toytown? There's a bunch of crazies out there who'd tear this lot apart unless they have a strong leader!'

Zandra walked in, looking perky and bright. She walked up to Lex's bed and kicked it. 'Isn't it time you were up?'

'Get lost!'

'We've no water, we're all filthy and our wonderful leader lies in bed! Come on, Ryan! I think I can smell bread for breakfast.'

Zandra spun round and flounced out. Ryan looked at Lex, then he sniffed the air.

'It is bread!' He rushed excitedly out of the room.

Lex thumped the wall above his head, angrily. He had thought that after becoming leader everything would be plain-sailing. People would obey his orders and, as the most powerful man in the tribe, he would finally woo Zandra into his bed. But if his oldest friend, the loyal dogged Ryan, had turned against him he was in trouble. And the frustrating thing was that violence, the only thing he was really good at, wasn't the solution.

ONE HUNDRED AND FORTY ONE

There had been a death in the Loco camp. It was inevitable she supposed. Put dozens of youths together, armed to the teeth, primed for violence, and sooner or later it would happen. Now it had, and, as leader, she had to deal with it.

If it had been an accidental killing there would have been no problem. Give the victim a decent send-off, burn the body on a pyre, and come together in communal grief. Despite the violent world they all now lived in, it was still seen as the right thing to do to mourn the dead. But the facts were indisputable. It was murder.

Spike had taken it upon himself to arrest the culprit and bring him before Ebony. Ordinarily, as one of the Locos lieutenants, he might have dealt with it himself, but she knew that this was Spike's way of testing her out. Challenging her fitness to lead the tribe.

'He was jealous. He said he'd kill him if he went near his girl and he did,' Spike reported. 'Stabbed him in the back. Wasn't even a fair fight.' He looked Ebony squarely in the eye. 'What are you gonna do with him?'

Ebony glanced around at the gathered youths who had helped Spike bring the murderer to her office in the hotel. They were all looking at her expectantly. There were no rules anymore. She could do whatever she wanted with the guilty youth, but what she chose to do would be the mark of her leadership.

She had probably killed people before. She didn't know for sure, but some of the enemies she had hurt in the many street battles the Locos had fought may have died later from the injuries she had inflicted on them.   It was likely. There were no doctors, or hospitals with emergency units any more. If you were injured you just had to rely on whatever medicines your tribe had looted, your own strength of will to recover, and a big slice of luck. She may be a killer, but could she kill in cold blood? Because that was what the tribe would expect. An eye for an eye. It was what a lot of the adults did in their time. By hanging, lethal injection, the electric chair, or the gas chamber. Different methods, same result. Judicial murder. Did she have the stomach for that?

ONE HUNDRED AND FORTY TWO

After the standoff with Amber about getting water from the nearby stream, Lex refused to send the boys out to collect it, knowing that Amber would stubbornly stick to her promise to follow them and collect their own water at the same time.

Lex, Ryan and Jack could happily survive using the water stash that he had secretly created out of everyone else's ration, but it was getting close to desperate for the others. And there was the problem of Dal. He didn't know about the secret stash. How long before he got suspicious?

At the moment Dal was up on the roof, where Lex had sent him, repairing the leak in the water tank. He looked up at the cloudless sky. It hadn't rained for days. They had all heard about global warming, of course, before the adult world collapsed. The dire prediction had been for a long hot drought over the city. If that was the case they were in deep trouble, Dal knew. Some people believed that the adults were to blame for the whole thing. But blame wasn't any use to them right now.

ooo

Jack was cursing and fiddling with the plastic piping he had rigged up linking the water tank to the tap, when Dal returned looking grimy from working inside the tank.

'Fixed it?'

Dal nodded. 'Yeh'.

'Why are you so dirty?'

'I don't think the water tank's on the cleaning rota, Jack.'

'No, I suppose not.' He went on hesitantly. 'You gonna start, you know, doing a bit of the girls' stuff? Helping out?'

Dal looked equally embarrassed. 'Oh, I dunno...Maybe a little bit of this and that. Nothing too much.'

Jack grinned. 'Just so long as there's a pie in the oven, eh?'

'Or a bit of Salene's bread.' He suddenly looked concerned. 'Of course Lex is gonna murder us.'

'Yeh, but do you really think the girls are gonna keep it up?'

Dal grinned. 'He doesn't know Amber.'

They looked up as Ryan came in, looking businesslike. 'Lex sent me to find out how the water stuff's going.'

Dal looked at Jack. 'I've fixed the tank. How's the piping?'

Jack looked frustrated. 'Can't finish it.'

'What?'

He shrugged. 'Run out of wire.' He held up a small length of wire. 'That's all there is.'

Ryan beamed. 'I can get you some wire!' He rushed out.

'Great!' said Dal. 'Now all we need is rain.'

Jack looked thoughtful. Dal was right. They needed rain badly, or Dal would start putting two and two together about the water stash. And that could get very ugly.

ONE HUNDRED AND FORTY THREE

Trudy swept into Salene's room, holding the baby in her arms. Salene was packing small baby toys into a large plastic bag.

'Haven't you finished yet?' Trudy snapped.

'Just about,' Salene replied unhappily.

Trudy pasted on a plastic smile, 'She slept so well last night, didn't you? You like sleeping next to mommy.'

Salene was silent. She picked up the bag, walked around the bed and thrust it at Trudy. 'Here.'

The plastic smile continued. 'Thanks, Salene. You've been ever so...sweet.'

As she turned she met Amber on her way in.

'Hi, Amber! I'm just collecting Brady's toys. She likes having them around her, don't you pet?' With a last triumphant look at Salene, Trudy swept out.

Amber affected not to notice Salene's downcast look. 'Salene, have you seen the little ones?'

Salene punched a cushion angrily and slumped onto the sofa.

Amber sighed inwardly. Not again. She sat down beside her reluctantly. 'What's up?'

'That tramp!'

'What's she done now?'

'She just walks all over everyone!'

Amber didn't want to get into it. 'Yeah, well-'

But Salene was determined to get all her frustration out. 'And she doesn't care a bit about that baby!'

'Salene, she is her mom!'

'She wasn't her mom last week, was she? Just when she feels like it!'

Amber was growing irritated. There were more important things she had to deal with than teenage emotions. 'Salene, give her a break! She's had it rough.'

'Haven't we all!'

'Look, you'll still get to see Brady. She'll need plenty of help.'

Salene looked sulky. 'And Bray?'

Amber got up sharply. 'Salene, give them a chance.'

'Why should I?' Salene said defiantly, sounding like a petulant small child to Amber's ears.

'Bray will see who he wants to see. Just give him time. Let things work themselves out.' She looked at Salene pleadingly. 'Don't stir things, please. We've got enough problems.'

She was on her way out when she remembered what she had come to see Salene about. An idea to give Salene something to do other than sit around brooding about Bray.

'That piano. Why don't you try to teach the kids some songs?' She smiled encouragingly. 'They'd love that.'

There was no response. She left Salene sitting moodily on the sofa. On her own, Salene grabbed a cushion and hugged it to herself determinedly.

ONE HUNDRED AND FORTY FOUR

She had conducted a proper trial in front of the whole tribe. She had called witnesses, listened to the evidence and given her verdict at the end. The verdict was hers, and hers alone. There was no jury. The Locos weren't a democracy.

As she pronounced the guilty verdict, her brain was still racing. She had performed the first part of her duty as leader. Establishing that murder would not be tolerated in the tribe. Could she carry now out the final act?

The guilty youth was standing between two Loco guards, his head hanging down. She felt sorry for him. He was one of the naked ones around the pool that she would have been happy to invite to her bed. But to show any kind of leniency would be a sign of weakness, which Spike and his followers would pounce on hungrily. Giving the murderer a long sentence in prison wasn't an option. It was impractical to have the culprit guarded twenty-four seven, and she knew the Locos wouldn't stand for seeing their rations being fed to the guilty youth, who wasn't performing any useful function for the tribe.

She was seated on a raised dais in the ballroom with the tribe seated in rows before her. The chandeliers had long since been shattered and the furnishings looted or trashed, but the room still retained its spacious elegance. Part of her found the whole formality of the proceedings ludicrous, given the Locos creed of 'Power and Chaos'. But a leader had to look and act like a leader, even in the shambolic world that they lived in from day to day. She was sure that Zoot would have been amused.

'The sentence is death!' she announced in a powerful voice that echoed round the cavernous room.

In that instant the image of Zoot's amusement gave her the answer. Zoot would have played it as a game.

ONE HUNDRED AND FORTY FIVE

'Doing all the dirty work, Dal?' said Amber. She, Dal and Jack were lined up in the kitchen waiting to get their lunch from Zandra.

Dal grinned through the grime on his face. 'As ever.'

'How's the view from up there?'

'Clear skies, no smoke. Remember that?'

'Bad news for us,' Jack said gloomily. 'No rain.'

Zandra ladled soup into their bowls. 'It's nothing special, I'm afraid. Just canned. Salene didn't have any water to make real soup.'

As they sat down at the communal table to eat, Lex strode up the stairs looking grim. 'I thought I said no lunch til we have some water.'

'But we're famished!' Jack protested.

'Too bad!'

'Chill out, Lex.'

Lex grabbed Dal by the front of his tee-shirt and yanked him up. 'What do you mean 'chill out'!'

Amber intervened. 'We have to wait for rain, Lex!'

'Is that the best you can do?' He thrust Dal back in his seat.

Annoyed at being manhandled Dal snapped back. 'You promised us milk! Is that the best you can do?'

Lex looked down at him. 'You volunteering for cow duty?'

'Suits me.'

'Lex, you told Dal to fix the water,' Amber said reasonably. 'He can't do two things at once.'

'What's the rush if there's no rain? Cow duty!'

Bray walked in and went up to Zandra. 'Can I take Trudy's over to her? She's having a rest.'

'Of course,' Zandra said. 'How's little Brady?'

'We were just talking about getting little Brady-wady some milk,' Lex sneered.

Bray turned to him, fixing him with a look. 'And just how are you gonna do that, Lex?'

'We've got a cow now, haven't we?'

'The problem is, Lex, you've no bull.'

'Bulls don't make milk,' Lex said arrogantly.

Bray wandered over to him, an amused smile hovering on his lips. 'But no bull, no milk. Get it? End of story.'

Lex pondered this new information for a minute, then had an idea. 'That a fact? Well, looks like we're gonna have steaks for dinner after all.'

Dal stood up, protesting. 'You're not gonna kill it!'

Lex shoved him down again. 'Ryan, you'd fancy a quarter pounder, wouldn't you?'

Ryan looked perplexed. 'What, the calf?'

'We could use the fat for burning lamps!' Jack said enthusiastically.

Dal turned to him, shocked. 'What are you a caveman!'

Cloe had been drinking her soup quietly on her own. Generally she didn't listen to the conversation around the table, preferring to live in her own thoughts, but she was suddenly aware what they were talking about. She looked up alarmed. 'You can't kill Bluebell!'

'Lex, stop upsetting her!' Amber said sternly.

Zandra glared at Lex, 'You can't kill a sweet little calf, Lex!'

Lex folded his arms confidently. This time he held all the cards. 'What d'you wanna do? Keep it as a pet, eating all our food?'

'Let it go,' Bray suggested.

'What if it comes straight back?' Ryan said.

'With the Locos following it?' Jack added.

'You gonna give it your rations, Ryan?' Lex asked.

Cloe jumped up. 'I'll give it mine!'

Amber was unhappy. Concerned with the leadership struggle, she hadn't really given the calf any thought, but now the subject had come up she could see the problem. 'Cloe, we can't afford to feed it,' she said gently. 'Not if it's not going to give us anything back. See, Bob warns us about danger. He barks if he hears a strange noise. But Bluebell...'

'We're not feeding it,' Lex said determinedly. 'The calf dies.'

Cloe leapt up and rushed at Lex. 'You can't kill Bluebell! You can't!'

Lex fended her off roughly. 'Get off me!'

Bray intervened, taking hold of Cloe protectively. 'Pick on someone a bit bigger, eh, Lex!'

Lex didn't take up the challenge. He glared at them all. 'You're all weak! Soft in the head! Anyone who wants a decent meal follow me!'

He stormed away down the stairs with Ryan following. With an apologetic look Jack hurried after them.

Cloe flung herself away from Bray. 'You're as bad as him!'

'We're sorry, Cloe,' said Amber.

Cloe glared at them both, with tears in her eyes. 'I hate you! I hate you all!' She rushed away sobbing.

Bray watched her go feeling helpless and guilty. 'I should have kept my big mouth shut.'

Amber looked at him, understanding. She hated to admit it but Lex was making sense for once. But she dreaded what the killing of the calf would do to Cloe.

The little girl had made Bluebell her pet, and Amber was sure that Cloe had confided all her thoughts and fears to the animal. She was a withdrawn child at the best of times, seemingly to live constantly on the edge of sanity. Would this tip her over? That would be too much to cope with.

ONE HUNDRED AND FORTY SIX

Bray was seated on his bed deep in thought. He knew Amber was as concerned about Cloe's reaction as he was, but his concern was different. He felt deeply guilty. He had promised to keep Cloe's secret and he had, until the calf had given itself away. He knew how much the calf meant to the little girl. Now he was going to be responsible for the death of Cloe's pet. Perhaps her only real friend in the world. All because he wanted to make a cheap joke at Lex's expense.

He and Amber had talked about having to keep an eye on the little girl, to support her as much as they could, but he had to do more. Somehow he had to make amends. For Cloe and himself.

He looked up at a knock on his door, irritated at being disturbed.

It was Trudy, holding the baby. She smiled tentatively, adopting a bright tone. 'Hi. I've been fixing up the room.'

When Bray didn't respond, Trudy persisted with her cheerful demeanor. 'I put Brady's cot right beside my bed where she can see me. Babies like to look at their moms, don't they?'

'Yeah, yeah,' he nodded distracted.

Trudy frowned anxiously. For her being around Bray was like walking on eggshells. 'What's wrong?'

Bray sighed, he didn't want to get into it with Trudy, but he needed to say something to keep her happy. 'I'm just thinking about Cloe.'

She tried to look sympathetic, relieved that his mood had nothing to do with her. 'Yeah, it's sad. But I don't suppose there was much you could have done about it. I mean it couldn't stay, could it..?' She pressed on with the real reason for her visit. 'Anyway, the room looks great. There's heaps more room now. Room for your things.'

Bray looked up at her, puzzled. 'My things?'

She felt herself colouring up. 'Well, I thought that now I'm looking after the baby properly...And you're so good with her, and, I'd feel safer too. I don't trust that Lex.'

'He wouldn't touch you,' Bray said dismissively.

Trudy was stung. 'Why? I'm not attractive enough?' She went on before she could stop herself, 'I suppose if it was that Salene –'

Bray jumped up. 'Trudy!' He started to leave.

'Where are you going, Bray? What about the room?'

Bray stopped and looked at her wearily. 'I've let Cloe down. I've got to make it up to her.'

'She'll get over it.'

The selfish tone riled him. 'Trudy! It was her pet!'

He hurried from the room before the row could develop. Right now he had more important things to do.

ONE HUNDRED AND FORTY SEVEN

Lex led the way into the car park where the little calf was tethered. When it saw them it mooed as if happy to have some company. It had been used to having regular visits from Cloe, being brought water and taken to graze in the nearby city park. It was no longer afraid of humans. Humans were kind.

Lex stopped beside the calf, turned to Ryan and handed him the switchblade knife. 'There you go, Ryan.'

Ryan looked at him, uneasily. 'But I thought...You want me to kill it?'

'Yeah. Let's have some real juicy steaks.'

Ryan took the knife and tentatively flicked out the blade. He looked at Lex again. 'How? Do I just stab it?'

'Slash it across the neck, Ryan. There's a big vein there. It'll bleed to death.'

'We should have brought a bucket for the blood,' Jack said. 'You can make black pudding out of blood.'

'Yeah, well, we're not going back for that,' Lex said dismissively. 'Come on, Ryan! We haven't got all day.'

Kneeling down beside the calf Ryan put his arm around its neck and lifted up the head. The animal felt warm and soft. He could feel the steady beat of its pulse through his fingers.

'Hurry up, Ryan!' Lex urged.

As Ryan put the blade to the animal's throat the calf looked up at him with its big brown eyes. He took a deep breath, then lowered the knife and released the calf's head.

'What's wrong!'

'I can't do it, Lex.'

'I don't believe this!' Lex exclaimed.

Ryan stood up and handed Lex the knife with an embarassed shrug. Lex held out the knife to Jack.

'Here!'

Jack stared at the knife in horror. 'I can't! I can't kill anything!'

'But you'll eat it, won't you?' Lex snapped. 'You're pathetic, the pair of you!'

'It's the way it looks at you, Lex,' Ryan said, trying to justify himself.

Lex scowled and approached the calf. The other two were watching him intently. 'What are you looking at?' he snarled. 'This isn't a bullfight! Go on, get out of here!'

Ryan and Jack made their way out of the car park. Lex snorted to himself and knelt down beside the calf, the switchblade clutched tightly in his hand.

ONE HUNDRED AND FORTY EIGHT

The rules were simple. He had a head start, but he couldn't leave the hotel. There were guards at all the exits with orders to stop him escaping with 'extreme prejudice'. He could hide anywhere inside the twenty storey building. Then wait until the pursuing pack of Locos found him, and beat the defenseless youth to death. A deadly game of hide and seek.

This way was better than a cold-bloodied, judicial execution. As house to house fighting was a routine occurrence in their lives, it gave the Locos a chance to improve their hunting skills. What better way to practice than with a real live quarry?

It also took the burden from her shoulders. She would not be the one to land the fatal blow. Everyone in the tribe would have a hand in carrying out the sentence, which was how it should be, she thought. Nothing Spike could object to. Giving the others their fun.

She'd had a momentary pause before ordering the game. Would the Locos pursue one of their own to the death? The youth had been a popular and loyal tribe member, acquitting himself bravely in many street battles. It was a great shame to lose his skills, but he had left her no alternative. To allow murder within the tribe would be the death of it. Even in Zoot's world without rules, there had to be some, just to survive.

In the event the chase didn't last long. The youth fled from the lower floors of the hotel, which were more or less intact, into the upper floors badly damaged by arson. The pursuing pack, baying for blood like wolves, had to tread cautiously, picking their way through the debris, the collapsed walls, floors and ceilings.

On the twentieth and final floor, the youth ran out onto the roof and, without a pause, launched himself into the sky, arms outstretched, with a defiant cry.

Ebony heard the cry turn into a scream, and then the ugly, wet sound as the body hit the ground in front of the hotel. It was a fitting way to go. Screaming defiance. It was a death they could all be proud of. A Loco death.

ONE HUNDRED AND FORTY NINE

Zandra was shocked when she saw Lex staggering back into the mall holding his side and wincing with pain. She rushed to him, crying out.

'Lex! What happened?'

He leant against the wall, his clothes muddied, his face screwed up, both hands pressed to his ribs.

'Got jumped by the Locos!' he gasped out.

Zandra gave a little shriek and put her arms around him. It would be worth being beaten up just for that, he thought. He doubted he would have got a hug if he told her the truth. That he had bottled out of killing the calf.

It was as Ryan had said. The way those big brown eyes looked up at you. He had tried closing his own eyes, but still couldn't bring himself to slit the animal's throat. In the end he had resorted to tossing his 'lucky' coin.

'Heads you live, tails you die, Bluebell,' he'd said. The coin came down tails. 'Well, best of three, then.'

After the coin had landed tails twice in a row, he had untied the calf and driven it out of the car park towards the city park opposite.

He'd surprised himself. He'd always thought of himself as a ruthless killer, but it turned out he was as soft-hearted as Ryan where animals were involved. That wasn't something he wanted to brag about. He had an image to preserve.

ooo

They were in the café with Cloe and the others listening to Lex's story.

'It was all I could do to save myself,' Lex said, as Zandra tenderly bathed his muddied face with a damp cloth.

'What happened to Bluebell?' Cloe asked anxiously.

A malicious gleam came into Lex's eyes. 'Well, last I saw there were about twenty Locos hunting her down. Probably sacrifice it to some god or other. Slice open her throat. Eat her alive most likely.'

Cloe let out a loud cry and ran out of the café screaming. Salene rushed after her.

Amber glared angrily at him. 'That's very funny, Lex!'

Lex grinned in response. Infuriated Amber took a step towards him.

'He's just beaten off a horde of Locos!' Zandra said protectively.

Amber stopped. 'Yeah? Want my opinion? He had a fight with the calf and the calf won easy.'

Lex got up, stung. 'I've had enough of this! You don't believe me! I couldn't care less!'

Ryan entered the café as Lex strode past him and down the stairs. 'Hey, Lex, where's the meat?' he called after him, eagerly.

'Sorry, Ryan,' said Amber. 'It's off the menu!'

Ryan frowned. There was no way he could hide his disappointment. 'What happened?'

'The Locos attacked him and took the calf,' Zandra explained.

'Huh!' Amber scoffed.

'You've really got it in for him, haven't you?' Zandra said accusingly.

'It isn't him I care about, Zandra, it's us! He's doing a pretty good job of stuffing up everything we've got going for us!'

'You'd do better, I suppose?' Zandra said heatedly. Then in a softer tone she went on. 'Yeah, I suppose you would. But Lex isn't gonna give up being leader. No way.'

ooo

Salene flew down the stairs calling out after Cloe, 'He was just joking, Cloe! It's alright!'

Concerned about what the distressed young girl would do, she had visions of her rushing out of the sewers into the dangerous streets in search of her pet. At the bottom of the stairs she almost collided with Trudy who was walking Brady in the pram.

'Hey! Watch it!' Trudy gasped furiously.

'Sorry!' Salene said breathlessly. 'I was after Cloe. I didn't see you.'

'You wanna watch your kiddies' games! You could've hurt my baby!'

'It wasn't a game! She was upset!'

'She's always upset!' Trudy snapped.

'Look, I'm sorry, I didn't mean...' Salene began, but she was anxious to catch up with Cloe. 'Let's just forget it, okay?'

Trudy eyes narrowed suspiciously. 'Are you following us?'

Salene looked at her in surprise. 'What?'

'You're everywhere I go! Always creeping about!'

Salene shook her head. 'I don't believe this!'

'Just stay away from us!' Trudy warned.

'Us?' Salene looked at her questioningly.

'You think Bray's wrapped around your little finger, don't you? Well, he isn't, Salene! So forget it! He's family! He's with me now!'

'We'll see,' Salene replied stubbornly. Trudy had issued her a challenge she wasn't going to duck. The gloves were finally off.

Sensing Salene's resistance, Trudy thrust her face towards her threateningly, 'Come anywhere near Bray or Brady and I will scratch your eyes out!'

Salene raised herself up to her full height in face of the threat, and said in a composed voice, 'I think Bray will make up his own mind, don't you?'

She hurried off after Cloe, leaving Trudy planting imaginary daggers in her back.

ONE HUNDRED AND FIFTY

Throughout history all leaders had found that leadership brings its own rewards, and problems. That was becoming very clear to Lex. And at the moment there seemed to be few rewards and all problems. So when Amber arrived in his office he expected another one to land on his desk. He got ready to do battle, again.

Amber felt the situation was coming to a head. She had won the battle of the daily chores, but the crucial fight was over water. She had boldly threatened Lex that she would take the girls out to the stream to collect the water herself, but in reality that was a highly dangerous plan, and one she was only prepared to act on as a last resort.

Lex had his boots on the desk in his usual pose. Instead of standing as she normally did when confronting Lex, she took a seat, settled back and smiled at him. That made him even more uneasy.

'What do you want?' he growled.

'It's not easy getting folks to follow, is it?' she said casually.

Lex scowled. 'Thanks to your little rebellion!'

Her tone was mild, non-confrontational. 'It's not my rebellion, Lex.'

'No?'

'If you force people to do stuff they think is unfair, that's what happens.'

He took his boots off the desk and sat up, glaring at her. 'Helps to have a ring-leader like you though, doesn't it?'

'It just happened, Lex. The girls have been through a lot. They don't need a leader. And they don't want to be cooks, skivvies and cleaners anymore than you do.'

'Different people are better at doing different things,' he said stubbornly.

Amber jumped in. He had given her the cue. 'Exactly! I know that. Like you.'

He looked puzzled. 'What about me?'

'You're a fighter, Lex. You're tough and brave, we all know that. So you're the best person for defending the mall, protecting us. That's what you should be concentrating on.'

There was just a hint of self-pity in his reply. 'I would, if everyone else would stay out of my hair and do as they're told.'

Amber leaned forward, adopting a sympathetic pose. 'Why don't you leave all that hassle to me? I'll sort out the day to day stuff. The chores. I can take that off your hands.'

'You make it sound so easy.'

She knew she had got him. 'Let me try…What have you got to lose?'

Lex looked away at the wall, thoughtful. He turned back to her. 'Anything else?'

'Food, water and stuff. Bray would be good for that.'

'No way! He'd starve us!'

'I'm just trying to free you up so you can do what you do best. Head of Security.'

She let the title hang in the air. From his expression Lex clearly liked the sound of it.

ONE HUNDRED AND FIFTY ONE

After the lucrative takeover of Tribe Circus Casino and the successful murder trial of the Loco, Ebony was riding high, and beginning to feel more secure in her role as Loco leader. It was apparent in the way she strutted around the hotel. She wore a queenly air, and the Locos clearly deferred and looked up to her. Despite her deceptive, diminutive size they all knew how fierce and powerful she could be. She reveled in their adulation, but she knew deep down that she must never let it get out of control. The fine line between leadership and arrogance must never be crossed.

People needed leaders. Desired leaders. It was easier to have someone else to lead you, to tell you what to do. And most of the Locos wanted an easy life. As long as they could be left alone to terrorise other tribes, take slaves and supplies, eat and drink whatever they liked from the growing Loco stores, fool around in the hotel and make love whenever and with whoever they pleased, they were happy. For the young men in particular it was paradise.

But Ebony was very strict about any hint of sexism in the tribe. She was a girl and as far as she was concerned girls were as good as, and equal to, boys. Zoot hadn't allowed the Loco girls to be oppressed or put upon by the boys and she kept that regime firmly in place.

The murder had been over the affections of a girl. A late-night drunken squabble which turned deadly with tragic results. The girl was an innocent bystander, caught up in a male domination struggle. After the trial and the murderer's death some of the Locos had tried to take it out on the girl, but as leader Ebony had defended her. Banning any mistreatment of her. A good leader did not take sides between the sexes. Everyone was equal.

That was not the way she had been brought up. Far from it. As a girl she'd had to fight for her place in the world. And that fight had made her hard. Perhaps too hard she thought with a hint of regret. If she had ever needed a softer, gentler feminine side to her nature she couldn't remember when. Except for one time. A time she bitterly regretted. But what use was regret or a gentle feminine side in this new world?

ONE HUNDRED AND FIFTY TWO

Salene had taken Amber's advice and tried to relax about the situation with Bray by teaching Patsy and Paul to play the piano. They'd already had one lesson which didn't go so well because Salene couldn't concentrate for thinking about Bray, and the kids had gone off in a huff. But she had given herself a good talking to. She was determined to pull herself together and give it another go.

She was playing on the middle notes of the keyboard, with Patsy taking the lower keys. 'Just copy my fingers, Patsy,' she instructed.

'I can't!' Patsy whined.

'It's alright. Just try again.'

Patsy hammered on the keys. 'I can't do it!' She thumped hard on the silent keys, frustrated.

'Stop!' Salene cried. 'You'll break it!'

'It's not making any noise!'

Salene frowned. 'What's wrong with it?'

Paul pointed to the top of the piano. Salene lifted it up and immediately saw the problem.

ooo

Ryan was teaching Jack and Dal card tricks under the bird statue in the atrium when Salene arrived clutching a bunch of wires in her hand. She thrust them at the group, accusingly.

'Have fun did you?'

Dal looked up. What?'

Salene waved the wires in the air. 'Wrecking the piano!'

Jack stared at the wires concerned. 'Where did you get those?'

'From your contraption down there!'

Dal's face fell. 'Oh, Salene, you didn't!'

'What did you do to it?' Jack echoed Dal's concern.

Salene's anger and frustration boiled over. She had tried so very hard. 'You uncultured pigs!'

Dal turned to Ryan. 'Why didn't you tell us where you got the wires from?'

Ryan shrugged. 'You didn't ask.'

Jack was disbelieving. 'But, Ryan, the piano?'

Ryan grinned. 'Yeah, good idea, wasn't it?'

'You've ruined it!' said Patsy who had followed after Salene along with her brother.

'You can still play half of it,' Ryan replied reasonably.

'You're putting these back!' Salene demanded.

Jack got up. 'We're putting them straight back on the rain water pipes!'

'No, you're not!'

Jack snatched the wires from Salene and ran off. For a moment Salene stood looking helpless, then she flew at Ryan and started to hit him around the head.

'You great oaf!' she screamed.

Ryan fended her off easily and stood up. 'Hey, come on, we need water!'

Zandra arrived, drawn by the raised voices. 'He's right, Salene. It's much more important.'

'What about them?' She waved her hand at Patsy and Paul. 'Their education!'

'Never did me any good,' Ryan quipped.

Salene lashed out at him again. 'You stupid, stupid!'

Zandra tried to intervene. 'Calm down, Sal! I know you're upset about the baby, but don't take it out on Ryan!'

Salene was crying and beating Ryan on the chest, ineffectively, as Bray arrived carrying a large cardboard box.

346

He put down the box and took hold of Salene's arms. 'Whoa, steady there,' he said calmingly.

Salene relaxed. She felt embarassed in Bray's presence, knowing it was him she was really uptight about.

'What's in the box?' asked Patsy.

Bray opened the top of the box, reached inside and held up a live chicken.

Patsy looked inside the box and her face lit up. 'Chickens!'

Bray smiled. 'They're for Cloe to make up for the calf.' He handed the chicken to the delighted Paul.

At that moment Lex and Amber arrived, having heard the commotion from Lex's office.

'Bray's got some chickens!' Patsy announced excitedly.

Lex tried not to look impressed. 'Where'd they come from?'

'Around,' Bray said casually.

'Well, let's kill 'em before everyone gets too friendly,' Lex said, taking the chicken from Paul.

'No way!' Patsy cried.

'We can still get eggs, can't we?' said Amber.

'I mean we don't need a rooster for that?'

'No, just feed,' Bray answered. 'And I can get that.'

Patsy reached down and brought out an egg from the box.

Ryan beamed. 'Omlettes!'

Amber turned to Lex. 'Think we've found our provisions man?'

Lex shrugged and looked inside the box at the other two chickens. Secretly he had to admit they were an excellent find in a city starved of food.

Amber took Bray's arm and led him aside. 'Like the chickens.'

'I felt bad about Cloe.'

'Thanks. They'll cheer her up...Listen, Bray, I've been talking to Lex. He's had it with the leader business. So I cut him a deal. He can take care of defence. I'll look after the day to day stuff, and you can take care of provisions.'

Bray folded his arms across his chest. 'You don't give up, do you?'

'Where would that get us?' Amber answered brightly.

'Have I a choice?'

Amber grinned. 'Not really, no.'

Bray looked away, as if scanning the walls for a response.

'Is that a 'yes'?'

He sighed. 'I'll give it a try.'

'Good one.' Amber turned to the others, feeling happy for the first time in a long while. 'Lex, I think you have something to tell everyone?'

Lex put the chicken back in the box and jumped up onto the plinth surrounding the statue. 'Listen up everyone!' he said importantly. 'As leader I've been making a few routine appointments. Amber's now in charge of chores, and all the day to day stuff. And Bray is looking after food and water. So any problems go to them first, understood? Don't bother me. I'm Chief of Security.'

Amber smiled to herself and glanced at Bray. He was impassive. She wondered if she would ever get to know what went on inside his head. Probably not.

Ryan suddenly looked up, hearing a noise. 'Listen!'

They all looked up and heard the same unmistakable sound.

'It's raining!' Ryan cried.

ONE HUNDRED AND FIFTY THREE

Forked lightning lit up the mall with a stark white light. A rumble of thunder followed seconds after. Rain poured down from the dark clouds which shrouded the glass roof making the mall more gloomy than usual, but the mood inside was excited.

They were all gathered around Jack and Dal who were frantically working with pliers, securing the pipe-work with the rescued piano wires. Water was still dripping from the joint, but Dal picked up a glass and held it under a tap attached to the pipe.

'Give it a try!' he urged.

'Here goes!' Jack turned the tap. A spurt of muddy water filled the glass. A loud cheer and applause broke out from the others. As Jack held up the glass proudly the mood changed.

Salene pulled a face. 'Urgh! It's disgusting!'

'It's all mucky!' Zandra cried.

Bray was reassuring. 'It'll be alright.'

Lex sneered. 'You're kidding, aren't you?'

'We got you the water, didn't we?' Jack said defiantly.

'If you can call it that,' said Salene.

'Keep your hair on,' Dal said. 'We'll fix it somehow.'

'Well, I'll let you drink it first!' Zandra said haughtily.

Patsy was looking around the group. There was someone missing. 'Where's Cloe?'

They all looked at each other.

'Three guesses,' Jack said looking heavenwards. 'Like she's run away?'

'Oh, no,' Amber groaned. 'Not again.'

'I haven't seen her since that business with the calf,' said Salene. 'She was upset. I ran after her but I lost her.'

Another flash of lighting lit up the mall. The crack of thunder that followed was deafening. They looked at each other again. The mood in the mall was suddenly grim. Was Cloe outside in that storm?

ONE HUNDRED AND FIFTY FOUR

As Chief of Security Lex had divided the group into teams and sent each one off to scour the mall from top to bottom searching for Cloe. The storm was still raging outside when the teams began to come back from their search, looking unhappy.

'No sign of her?' asked Amber. She could see by their faces it was a redundant question.

Zandra shook her head. 'She's not in the mall.'

'Or in the car park,' Ryan said gloomily.

Amber was both worried and exasperated. 'She's got to stop this!'

'You're right,' Lex said. 'She's putting all of us in danger. If one of the other tribes follow her back here.'

Trudy perked up as Bray arrived back from searching the sewers. 'Aw, look who's back!' she cooed to Brady snuggled in her arms. 'It's your Uncle Bray!'

Ignoring her Bray approached Lex determinedly. 'We have to look outside for her.'

'We ain't,' Lex replied adamantly.

'You can't leave Cloe out there all night just to get back at me,' Bray protested. 'That's pathetic!'

'And you're pathetic if you think I'd do that,' Lex replied stubbornly. 'There's a storm out there. It'll be pitch black in half an hour. You got X-ray eyes, superman?'

'She's only little Lex,' Zandra said, 'out there on her own!'

Lex looked at Bray meaningfully. 'You don't have to be big to be an idiot.'

'Lex is right,' Amber chimed in. 'It's pointless to go out just now.'

'Thanks, Amber. At least somebody realizes I ain't Chief of Security for nothing. If she's not back we'll look first thing in the morning. Tonight she's on her own.'

'What am I gonna tell Patsy and Paul?' Salene asked. 'They're really upset about her.'

Trudy, standing beside Bray, addressed the baby in her arms. 'You'd never do anything as stupid as that, would you Brady? No, we'd look after you.'

Salene shot her a look. 'What are you trying to say, Trudy?'

Bray intervened to stop the incipient row. 'Tell them we'll find her, Salene.'

He was in two minds whether to defy Lex and go out looking for Cloe. But that would be a direct challenge to the system Amber had just managed to put in place. It would be churlish. And Lex and Amber were both right, he conceded. Finding her out there in the stormy night would be almost impossible. But he hated to think of the little girl outside in the dark and the storm alone. The only consolation was that at least neither the Locos nor any other of the tribes would be out that night. He still felt deeply guilty about his part in it. He doubted he would get much sleep.

ONE HUNDRED AND FIFTY FIVE

In the finger of woods that encroached into the city a mile or so from the mall, Cloe was trying to shelter beneath a large oak tree as the storm raged about her. But a fierce wind was lashing the rain in all directions and she was soaked to the skin.

After Lex had returned to the mall with his story about the Locos chasing Bluebell, she had rushed outside through the sewers to try to rescue her pet. When she got outside she'd expected to find the street full of Locos, but was surprised, and very relieved, to find them empty.

If the Locos had caught the calf, she had no idea where they would take her, so she wandered the deserted streets plaintively calling the calf's name.

She had walked a long way, far away from anywhere she knew. But she was determined to find Bluebell. She didn't know the city well, and was surprised to find a clump of trees leading towards a larger woodland area inside the city limits. If Bluebell had escaped, that would be the place she would run to.

The trees and undergrowth became thicker as she cautiously went further in. If the calf was there it would be hard to see it now. Despite the danger of being heard she had to call.

'Bluebell!' Her voice was lost among the dense foliage. 'Bluebell!'

Did she hear something? She called again as loudly as she could. 'Bluebell, I'm over here!'

Yes! She had heard it. There was a definite answering sound. It must be Bluebell! She rushed off in the direction of the noise, calling out the name, not noticing the scratches and stings she got from the briars and nettles in her path.

She was deep inside the wood when the sky went black. A flash of lightning heralded the storm sweeping in from the sea. Almost at once the deluge of rain began, as if someone had turned a gigantic tap on in the heavens. As the first peal of thunder echoed through the wood, she hugged the thick trunk of a tree for protection.

Cowering in the darkness she watched the flashes of lightning turning the waving branches into quivering ghosts. The thunder came on nearer, louder. A vivid, crackling fork of lightning struck the top of the tree above her head. Along with the tremendous peal of thunder she heard another violent crack. The tree she was sheltering under shuddered and split. Her scream echoed through the storm as the huge branches crashed down upon her, and the stricken tree burst into flames. As the flaming tree illuminated the woods above her, she struggled to escape, but it was no use, she was trapped.

ONE HUNDRED AND FIFTY SIX

Trudy had taken Brady to say 'goodnight' into the twins' room, where Salene still slept with Patsy and Paul. As she was leaving, for Salene's benefit, she remarked to the baby, 'We have to go now. Someone's coming to see us. Yes they are. Your Uncle Bray.' She left, giving Salene a spiteful look of triumph.

Bray made a point of putting the child to sleep each night. It had been his habit when Trudy was out of it, and he'd continued because it made him feel closer to his brother, Martin.

Trudy was standing beside him as he nestled the baby into the cot. He touched the baby's fingers gently. 'Aw, how sweet!' she cooed.

She reached in to repeat the gesture. The baby began to cry at the contact. Trudy recoiled and pulled a face. 'Not again!'

'She's tired. She needs her sleep.'

'She hardly ever sleeps,' Trudy said. 'Not unless you're around. She's really happy then. She really loves you, Bray, you can tell.'

As he smiled and made to move away, Trudy's tone changed to tetchiness. 'She'll be up again as soon as you go! I won't get a wink of sleep! I never do!'

'That's what baby's do,' Bray said gently. 'There's not much you can do about it.'

Trudy sat down on the bed pensively. 'Well...perhaps...if you stayed.'

'No, I don't think that's a good idea,' Bray replied, trying not to sound unkind.

She was suddenly close to tears. 'I do the best I can, you know! I do try!'

Bray knelt beside her and touched her arm. 'I know you do, Trudy.' It was true. He knew she was trying, even though motherhood didn't seem to come naturally to her. Unlike Salene.

Trudy pressed on, her voice breaking. 'It's so hard being on my own! Without a dad for her!'

He smiled sympathetically. 'You're tired. You should get some rest.'

She was close to tears. 'She won't let me! She'll start again as soon as you go!'

Bray looked at her tearful eyes, the desperate expression. He sighed. 'Okay, I'll stay.'

Trudy smiled up at him gratefully, the tears miraculously gone. 'Thank you.'

She slipped happily inside the duvet, leaving room beside her in the bed. Bray picked up a book and settled down in the armchair by the cot. Trudy looked disappointed. He looked up and saw her look.

'Sweet dreams,' he said.

Trudy forced a smile and settled down, not quite as happy as a moment ago, but she had made a start. She had got a big one over on Salene.

ONE HUNDRED AND FIFTY SEVEN

Bray had hardly slept for thinking about Cloe. The storm had stopped overnight, which was a blessing, but she was still out there somewhere. He just hoped she was safe.

As the first light of day crept into the mall, he got up from the armchair stiffly, and stretched. Trudy stirred.

'Bray?'

'Sshh, go back to sleep. I'm going out to look for Cloe.'

Trudy sat up, smoothed her hair and adjusted her silk nightgown. 'But it's hardly daylight. Do you have to go so soon?'

Bray hid his irritation at her selfishness. 'She's been out all night, Trudy. I want to find her as fast as I can. I'll see you later.'

As he emerged onto the balcony he saw Salene coming from her room. He was embarassed, knowing what it looked like, but there was no time to explain. 'Hi, Salene.'

There was no mistaking the disappointment on her face, or in her voice. 'Hi.'

'I'm going to look for Cloe.'

'I was going to come too.'

Trudy hurried out of her room, clutching a book. 'Bray, you forgot your book!' She stopped and looked at Salene, a triumphant smile flooded her face. 'Morning, Salene!'

Salene passed by without a word, and hurried down the stairs to where Lex and the rest were gathering.

ooo

'Right,' Lex said, 'all those volunteers for Operation Stupid Kid, put up your hands!'

Bray and Ryan raised their hands. The girls looked at Dal and Jack who were slumped on the stairs bleary-eyed.

'Dal and I can't go.'

'We've almost finished the water purification system,' Dal explained.

'Been up all night,' Jack added, yawning.

'Three of us will be enough,' Bray said, anxious to get started.

'I'll come!' Salene said.

Trudy had come down the stairs to watch. 'Don't be ridiculous!' she snapped.

'What's so ridiculous? Girls are as good as boys.'

'That's right, Salene,' Zandra chimed in.

Amber cut across. 'Patsy and Paul need you here, Salene. We don't want them worrying about you as well.'

'What about Bob?' Jack suggested. 'He could track her.'

'Leave it out,' Lex said. 'He's a mutt, not a tracker dog! He'll go chasing after some bunny rabbit and we'll all be stuffed!'

'I'll look after the kids, Salene,' Zandra offered. 'Cloe will be really happy to see you.'

Amber saw Trudy glaring daggers at Zandra. Sensing a situation she insisted, 'And what if they don't find Cloe? You're like a mother to the twins, Salene. You can't leave them here fretting on their own.'

'Alright, I'll stay,' Salene said reluctantly. 'You're right, I am the best mother here,' she added, with a glance at Trudy.

Trudy switched her furious glare on Salene, but stayed silent.

'Come on!' Bray said impatiently. 'Let's get going before the Locos get on the move.'

'Alright,' Lex said, eyeballing Bray, 'but remember I'm Chief of Security round here.'

Lex led the way towards the sewers with Bray and Ryan following behind.

Amber watched them go apprehensively. 'Let's hope they don't end up killing each other.'

ooo

As they emerged from the sewer entrance Bray made off in the direction of the woods.

'Oi!' Lex called. 'Where are you going?'

Bray stopped. 'To the woods.'

'On whose orders?'

'Cloe'll be looking for the calf, you said so yourself. Calves like grass not concrete.'

'But the Locos got it,' Lex turned to Ryan. 'Ain't that right?'

Ryan shrugged. 'So you said.'

'Right, I saw them.' Lex turned back to Bray. 'I mean, correct me if I'm wrong, you do know the Locos a lot better than I do. Green trees, pretty grass, not exactly their choice of hang-out.'

Bray stood looking at him resignedly.

'We're going to the city,' Lex went on. 'Concrete and decay. That's where they took it. That's where she'll be looking. Unless of course you want to make something of it.'

Lex squared his shoulders, confronting him. Bray sighed and changed direction. He walked past Lex towards the city. Lex watched him go, malevolently.

ONE HUNDRED AND FIFTY EIGHT

Cloe had spent a long, terrible night trapped between the fallen branches of the oak tree. When the tree caught fire from the lightning strike she thought she was going to be burnt to death, but luckily the lashing rain and fierce wind extinguished the fire before it really took hold.

But she couldn't move the heavy branches trapping her body and legs. She lay for a long time whimpering softly, wet, cold and frightened, not knowing whether she was badly hurt or not. Her legs felt numb, but that could be the cold and wet.

Finally she dropped off into a fitful doze, full of nightmarish images of scary creatures and Bluebell being sacrificed by the Locos. She was relieved when she woke up to see the first light of day touching the tree tops and find that the storm had passed.

She thought of the others back in the mall. Would they be worried that she was missing? Would they come looking for her? When she had gone missing before she knew that Amber had been angry. Maybe they would be annoyed this time too, and wouldn't bother to try to find her? It would serve her right they might say. Maybe it would. She couldn't rely on others. She had to help herself.

A large branch was lying across her body, pinning her into a hollow in the ground. It was the hollow that had saved her life, preventing the huge branch from crushing her to death. She heaved and heaved with all her might against the thick branch. It didn't move. She lay back out of breath. There was no way she could move the branch. There had to be another way.

She looked at her mud-covered hand. The ground beneath her was sodden from the storm. The mud was soft. Suddenly she saw her escape. It was difficult to move her arms properly, lying on her back and trapped by branches as she was. It would take a long time, but she could burrow her way out, like a little woodland animal. But she still couldn't feel her legs. She hoped that when she finally got out her legs would work.

ONE HUNDRED AND FIFTY NINE

In the mall the day dragged on as they waited for Lex's search party to return. To take their minds off Cloe, Salene was playing a board game with Patsy and Paul on the carpet. She picked up a tiny figure. 'Okay, I'll be Captain Dan!'

Patsy drew in her breath and glanced at Paul.

'What?' Salene asked.

'That's Cloe's piece,' Patsy said sadly.

'Oh, okay. I'll have the blue one then.'

Zandra arrived fussily with her nail polish, clearly halfway through colouring her nails. She plonked herself down on the sofa in a huff. 'You don't mind if I do this in here, do you? It's miserable on my own and Amber's no fun at all. All I said was 'Did you see where Bray slept last night' and she nearly bit my head off!'

Patsy was all ears. 'Where did he sleep?'

'Patsy, it's your turn,' Salene said hastily.

'Looks like Mother Superior's finally got her claws into him,' Zandra went on obliviously. 'I mean, he's never slept there before, has he?'

Salene was still trying to ignore Zandra. 'Patsy, that's five. You moved six.'

Zandra went on, unaware of Salene's discomfort. 'I suppose it had to happen eventually, the way she uses that baby to get his attention. Got more than his attention now, I expect.

Unable to stand it any longer, Salene scrambled to her feet.

'Where are you going?' Zandra asked, surprised at the suddenness.

'You take over!' Salene hurried away.

'But, Salene!' Zandra called. 'My nails..!' She looked at Patsy. 'What's got into her?'

Patsy was wide-eyed with excitement. 'Did Bray sleep with Trudy?'

Zandra closed her eyes and groaned. 'Oh, me and my big mouth!'

ooo

Amber was concerned to see Salene hurrying past her on the landing, clearly distressed.

'Hey, Salene, what's the rush? Is it Cloe? Are they back?'

Salene turned back momentarily. 'No. It's nothing.'

'Doesn't look like nothing.'

'Just leave it, Amber,' Salene snapped.

Amber was taken aback. 'Hey, come on. We're all in this together. You can talk to me.'

'Not about this,' Salene said emphatically.

'Try me.'

Salene was clearly irritated by the Amber's persistence. 'I don't want to.'

'Oh, I get it,' said Amber. 'It's about Trudy and the baby.'

'Congratulations!' Salene said sarcastically. 'You can add psychic to your long list of skills!'

'Hey, don't take it out on me! The baby belongs to Trudy, Salene, you always knew that.'

Salene was adamant. 'No. She may have had her and given her that stupid name, but it was me who fed her and got up with her in the middle of the night! She didn't want her until she suddenly saw her as a way of getting Bray into bed!'

'Oh, and you never thought of the baby in that way, did you?'

'Just keep your nose out of it, Amber! You're not as important in everyone's lives as you think. Some of us actually like to do things without checking with you first!'

Salene turned away and hurried off, leaving Amber stung and hurting. Amber sighed deeply. She had been upset by the news about Bray and Trudy too. But in her case, she had to keep it to herself, not broadcast it to the whole of the mall.

ONE HUNDRED AND SIXTY

The search party had drawn a blank among the ruins of the city. They had to take cover several times to avoid roaming gangs, making Bray more and more frustrated at the waste of time. He led the way back through the sewers still fuming about the fruitless search.

'We should have looked in the woods!'

'She ain't there,' Lex replied arrogantly.

'She could be, Lex.'

'Who asked you, Ryan? She could be in one of the Locos cooking pots too.'

Amber and Salene were waiting for them as they emerged from the sewer entrance.

'You didn't find her then.' Amber was saddened. 'Where did you look?'

'In the city,' Bray replied sullenly.

Trudy hurried down the stairs holding the baby. 'Look, Brady, Uncle Bray's back! The children are looking for you Salene,' she said waspishly.

Salene walked back up the stairs moodily. Trudy went to Bray holding out the baby.

'Not now, Trudy,' he said, irritated by the fussing in front of everyone else. 'I'm tired.'

Trudy brushed off the rebuff with a significant smile. 'So am I. See you later then. I'm going back to bed. I'm worn out.' She went back upstairs with another knowing smile.

Lex grinned at Bray. 'Oh, yeah?'

Brushing aside her uncomfortable feelings Amber pushed on. 'What are we going to do about Cloe?'

'We should look in the woods,' Bray replied.

'No way, man,'

Bray turned to Lex. 'You don't have to go.'

'I'm Chief of Security, remember? Nobody goes.'

'We can't leave her out there on her own, Lex,' Amber insisted.

'And we can't go wandering around out there either,' he responded. 'What if somebody sees us and follows us back? It's too risky. Better one of us gets caught than all of us. And if it's just her, just pray she doesn't blab.'

'All the more reason to find her, surely?' Bray said.

'What if she doesn't want to be found? She doesn't exactly stick around here much, does she?' With the subject closed as far as he was concerned, Lex turned and walked away.

ooo

Zandra found Salene hidden away in the dining room of the furniture store, a large gloomy room which no one ever went into. Bizarrely it still had a long wooden dining table set out for a formal dinner. Salene was seated at the end of the table out of sight from the doorway.

'Thought I might find you here. It's a good place to be on your own, isn't it?'

'I thought it was,' Salene said pointedly.

Zandra didn't get the point. 'Oh it is. No one ever thinks of looking in here.'

'Except you.'

Salene's tone was lost on Zandra. 'Yeh, well I'm a girl, aren't I? We're in tune you and me.'

'Look, Zandra –' Salene began.

'It's okay, you don't have to explain.' She took the seat next to Salene. 'That Trudy's a right cow! Don't worry, Salene. I'm sure Bray fancies you really.'

'I don't think so, Zandra.'

'He does!' Zandra insisted, 'I can read the signs. There's a real chemistry between you two.'

'And there's a baby between him and Trudy,' Salene replied moodily.

'That's just a responsibility. That's all it is with her. Duty. Hassle. He has a laugh with you.'

'And spends the night with her,' Salene looked close to tears.

'Yeah, well he's a guy, isn't he? They can't help themselves.' She noticed Salene's tearful expression. 'Don't give up, girl,' she encouraged. 'Just keep giving him those smouldering looks. He'll come round. Listen to your Auntie Zandra.'

'I do not give him smouldering looks.'

'No?'

'No!' Salene insisted.

'Well you should. I'll show you.'

'No thanks, Zandra. Bray isn't like Lex.'

'Sweetheart, they're all the same. And we girls have got to stick together, haven't we?'

Salene stood up.

'Where are you going?'

'I just want to be on my own.'

Zandra watched Salene leave. She shrugged to herself. Salene certainly didn't know anything about men.

ONE HUNDRED AND SIXTY ONE

She would use the search for Zoot as a pretext. For she was now certain he was dead, though she had not admitted that to the rest of the Locos. With her concern over Spike's leadership challenge and the threat of the Demon Dogs' retaliation, she'd had little time to think back over the events leading to his disappearance and come to the logical conclusion. The only conclusion possible.

Privately, she quizzed the Loco youth who had brought the note to Zoot. The note that had set the whole train of events moving. He had enlarged on his description. The messenger was tall, with long brown hair. That could fit many of the kids left in the city. Haircutting wasn't a priority nowadays.

He had used a skateboard, the Loco youth told her, and his clothes resembled the sort of backwoodsman that used to inhabit the surrounding hills until the virus wiped them all out. Buckskin and a poncho. The poncho was the final piece of the jigsaw. It was his favourite form of clothing.

It all fitted now. Zoot was intelligent, cunning and cautious. He would never let his guard down, not even to her. No one could ever have caught him unawares. But he was gone. She knew there was only one person he would trust with his life. Had he tragically misplaced that trust? Had he put his trust in his brother? She had to find out.

She led the search party herself, leaving the hotel early. She reasoned to herself that when the virus had ravaged the city and left it in ruins, the one place he would go was where he had always preferred to be. The place he felt at home and at one with. The woods surrounding the city where the place to look for Bray.

ONE HUNDRED AND SIXTY TWO

Thankfully the sun had been shining brightly all morning and Cloe now felt more or less dry. But the morning had turned to afternoon before she managed to dig a hollow beneath the branch large enough for her to squirm out of. And that was very hard. With no food, water and little sleep, she was exhausted from her ordeal. What was worse, she still couldn't feel her legs.

Using her shoulders and arms she at last wriggled free of the branch, and lay for a long while, relieved but close to tears. She couldn't walk. Her legs wouldn't move no matter how hard she tried to make them. She pinched the flesh on her thigh and felt nothing. Lying back on the warm earth she finally gave way to tears.

She must have cried herself to sleep and slept for hours, because when she woke the sun was casting long shadows among the trees. She sat up. There were voices far off in the woods. Her first instinct was to call out for help. But then she remembered that her world had changed. It was dangerous now. Full of very bad people. She lay back and kept silent.

After a while the voices seemed to fade away. She sat up again and felt a strange sensation. It was as if someone was pouring warm water all the way through her legs, right down to her toes. She dug her nails into her thigh and jumped. She could feel!

Holding the fallen branch to support herself she slowly stood up. Her legs felt weak but they supported her weight. She was standing again. Tentatively she put her right leg forward and then her left. She could walk! She smiled to herself. Now she could get back to the safety of the mall. But which direction was it? She looked about her at the thickly wooded trees. The joy of her escape and being able to walk again evaporated as quickly as it had come. She was lost. And the voices in the wood had returned.

ONE HUNDRED AND SIXTY THREE

The mood in the mall was sombre. Cloe was still missing and the day was drawing to a close. Bray had thought of defying Lex and going out to the woods to look for her, but there was some sense in what Lex said about the danger to the rest of the tribe.

Whatever he felt about it, Lex had been put in charge of the mall's security and you couldn't just pick and choose what order you obeyed. If they were going to start rebuilding their lives there had to be rules, and people to make them. Even people like Lex.

They were gathered in the mall for their evening meal. But very few of them had any appetite.

Patsy pushed her full plate away unhappily. 'I can't eat this! I want Cloe back!'

Lex reached over the table. 'I'll have it then.'

Amber stopped him with a look. 'Try to eat, Patsy,' she coaxed. 'What will Cloe say when she comes back and finds you've made yourself ill?'

They looked up expectantly at the sound of running feet. What it Cloe? Jack and Dal raced up excitedly waving two large plastic bottles.

'Da-dah! It's ready!' Jack shouted, waving the bottle in the air proudly. 'Clean water! Grab your glasses!'

Amber looked at the liquid in the bottles. It was crystal clear. 'Is that really the same stuff?'

'Yeah!' Dal was equally chuffed.

Zandra looked puzzled. 'How did you do it?'

'Sand and gravel filter,' Dal explained.

Ryan frowned. 'Can't see any sand and gravel in it.'

Jack pulled a face. 'There isn't any sand in it 'cos it's been filtered through it.'

Zandra wasn't convinced. 'Probably still some germs in it though. You can't see germs.'

'There isn't! It's purified,' Jack insisted.

'Who said,' Lex said skeptically. 'Taken it down to the lab, have you? Had it tested?'

'They've been doing this for years, Lex.'

'Centuries!' Dal added.

'Look, why don't we just try it?' Amber said.

'You first,' Lex replied.

Amber held out her glass to Jack. Jack filled it up and Amber held the glass up as a toast. 'To Jack and Dal, our technological wizards!'

As she drank Lex put his hands to his throat in mock strangulation.

'Lex!' Zandra admonished.

Amber beamed. 'This is great!'

'Give me some!' Ryan said.

Jack filled Ryan's glass and he took a hesitant sip. His face lit up in surprise. 'Tastes like real water!'

'It is real water, dummy!' Dal said.

Ryan glared at him stung. 'Hey, watch it!'

Amber was thrilled. 'It's amazing! Out of the clouds, onto our roof, to this!'

'It's like a miracle!' Zandra agreed.

'Perhaps it is!' said Patsy. She took the bottle from Dal, poured some water into a bowl and took it over to the dog, who was sitting patiently nearby.

'Oi, what're you playing at?' Lex snapped.

'It's for Bob.'

'No,' Lex corrected, 'it's for humans.'

Patsy pouted, put out.

Bray intervened. 'I'm in charge of food and water round here. Go on, Patsy.'

Lex gave Bray a hard stare but said nothing.

Jack looked around the table. He and Dal had been locked away working on the water purification all day. 'Where's Cloe? Isn't she back yet?'

The happy mood created by the news of the water changed instantly to gloom again.

ONE HUNDRED AND SIXTY FOUR

Cloe didn't know which direction the mall was, but she guessed if she kept walking she might come to somewhere she recognized, and could find her way back from there. She was walking very cautiously through the trees. The life was coming back into her legs with every step, but the strange voices were coming nearer now and she had no idea whether they were good or bad.

The sun was setting, casting its glow over the woods. Shafts of light shone through the trees turning the leaves to gold leaf, like in a palace. It was beautiful picture. But she couldn't appreciate it, concerned as she was about the strangers who were calling out to each other. They sounded like boys. Rough boys. And they seemed to be surrounding her.

Suddenly a cry rang out. 'Look! Over there!'

Cloe spun round and glimpsed a youth clad in body armour with wild hair and facepaint heading towards her. She took off through the undergrowth with the cries of the youths ringing out behind. 'Get her! Get her!'

Terrified Cloe flung herself through the briars and ferns, running for her life. Mercifully the undergrowth was dense and the pursuing youths could only catch glimpses of her as she raced through the light and shadows of the trees.

Breathless she stumbled on, crying now in terror. Rushing headlong over a steep bank she tripped over a log, lost her footing and plunged headlong down the slope, straight into a dense patch of undergrowth and briar that tore at her clothes and skin. She lay stunned, the breath knocked out of her body. And waited for the end.

ONE HUNDRED AND SIXTY FIVE

Salene had retreated to a gloomy corner of the furniture store. She kept turning the morning scene over and over in her head despondently. Bray coming out of Trudy's room. Trudy's malevolent look of victory.

She had been shocked and dismayed. She hadn't seen that coming. She was so sure she had felt something between herself and Bray, but he had made his choice. And it wasn't her.

Living in the mall now would be torture. Seeing them together every day. Knowing he was sharing her bed. But what alternative did she have? Where would she go? She heard footsteps approaching and huddled down in the armchair, not wanting to be seen.

'Hey, babe!' Lex had taken to doing a round of the mall each night, apparently taking his new security role seriously. 'You missed supper.'

'Very observant.'

Lex leant on the back of the chair, hovering over her. 'I feel for you, really. Zandra told me about Bray messing you about and he's no right. Not a classy babe like you.'

She turned round and looked up at him. 'What do you want, Lex?'

'I don't like seeing good people treated bad. After all you've done for Trudy and that.'

'What is this, Lex the agony aunt?' Salene said sarcastically.

'Look, I'm tough, okay. But it's a tough world out there. And I wanna survive. Doesn't mean I don't have feelings.'

He reached out, put his hand on her shoulder and began to stroke her gently.

Salene stiffened and turned to him. 'What exactly are you doing?'

Lex began massaging both her shoulders now, firmly, and with surprising dexterity. 'Best way to unwind. Massage. Feel good?'

Salene shifted under his hands, uncomfortable.

'Relax. Let Lexy take care of you.'

Despite herself, she began to enjoy the sensation and started to give in to it. 'Just remember I've got a great right hook,' she warned.

Lex slipped the wrap from her shoulders and put his hands on her bare shoulders.

'Lex!'

'Trust me, Sal.' His voice was soothing, his hands strong but gentle. 'You've got very soft skin.'

She sighed deeply, feeling the muscles in her neck and shoulders beginning to warm up and relax.

'Salene, Patsy wants –' Zandra stopped. She had come bustling in the other door and stumbled across the cosy scene. 'What the -!'

Salene jumped to her feet embarassed. 'It was nothing, Zandra! Lex was just –'

'I can see what Lex was 'just' thank you very much' she snapped viciously.

Salene rushed out of the room, leaving Zandra glaring at Lex in the gloom.

Lex spread his arms in a gesture of innocence. 'It was you who told me she was upset, Zan! I was just –'

'Save it, Lex!'

'Zan!' Lex pleaded, 'It was just a neck rub! Hey, Zan, you're my girl!'

'Yeh? Then stay away from Salene! Just because she can't have Bray doesn't mean she can have you, Lex! No way!'

'So you're having me instead?' Lex purred.

In reply, Zandra spun round and stormed out. Lex sighed, frustrated. The women in this new world seemed tougher than in the old one.

ONE HUNDRED AND SIXTY SIX

Salene lay on her bed, face to the wall, covers pulled up to her ears. She had gone to bed early, leaving Amber to put the twins to bed.

As she tucked them in, Paul signed something. Amber had been learning his language. 'You mustn't worry about Cloe now, Paul. Get some rest.'

Patsy noticed her concerned glance over to Salene.

'Salene's very upset, isn't she?'

Amber nodded. 'She misses Cloe as well.'

'I think it's about Bray and Trudy.'

'Sshh!' Amber put her finger to her lips. 'We all miss Cloe, Paul, but she's gonna be fine.'

Patsy wasn't easily convinced. 'Who's going to look after her if she's in the woods?'

Amber pondered for a moment. 'Remember Hansel and Gretel?'

Patsy nodded.

'They lived for ages in the forest, with all the little animals covering them with leaves and stuff.'

'That's Babes in the Wood,' Patsy said frowning.

'Oh, well never mind. Anyway the point is that Cloe's at least as clever as them. And she doesn't have a wicked witch to worry about.'

Paul signed again.

'The Locos won't be in the woods, Paul,' Amber said reassuringly. 'And first thing tomorrow we'll look for her again, okay?'

'Bob would have found her by now,' Patsy said sulkily.

'We don't know that.'

'Lex is horrible!' Pasty said.

Amber smiled. 'Yeah, well we do know that. Sweet dreams...' She got up and looked over to Salene. 'Night, Salene.'

There was no response. Amber sighed and left the room.

ooo

Trudy was feeling calmer and more in control. Over the past twentyfour hours she has pushed Salene's nose out by getting Bray to stay in her room overnight. At last she felt she was making progress. That evening she made a special effort with her makeup and, while Zandra was out of the way, had borrowed some of her special perfume, which she put behind her ears and at the base of her throat.

Bray had come to put Brady to bed as usual. The baby was asleep in Trudy's arms. 'She's settled now,' she said to Bray. She handed the sleeping child over to him, feeling the warm closeness of their bodies as he took the baby from her arms. She watched smiling as he gently placed the baby in the cot. 'It's lovely, isn't it?'

'All babies are lovely,' he replied.

'Not just her. I'm so glad you decided to be wth us, Bray.'

He looked up at her tone, alerted. 'She's family.'

'We're family. Almost. You, me and Brady.'

Bray straightened up, about to leave.

'It's all been so horrible,' Trudy changed her tone. 'Zoot dying. And my illness.'

A momentary sadness clouded his face. 'That's all over now.'

'I've been so scared!' she went on. 'She's only a tiny baby but she needs so much!'

'I know,' he said soothingly, sitting beside her on the bed. 'I know it's been hard.'

She looked into his eyes longingly, 'But it's going to be alright now, isn't it? I don't know what I'd do without you, Bray.'

He shrugged it off. 'You'd cope.'

'I don't think so.' She took hold of both his hands.

He pulled back. 'Don't, Trudy.'

'It's okay, I want this!' she said intensely.

Bray tried to pull away gently. 'No, you've had a long day. You're tired.'

'No! I want you! I want us!' she pleaded.

He held her back as she tried to put her arms around him. 'No,' he said firmly.

'Why?' She was beginning to whine. 'You know you want to!' She reached up and ran her fingers through his hair, desperately.

He took hold of her hands firmly. 'Trudy!'

'You know I never loved Zoot!'

Bray broke from her and stood up abruptly. 'This isn't the time!'

There was confusion in her voice now. 'What's the matter?'

'Cloe's out there on her own, Trudy!' he snapped. 'Aren't you just a little concerned for her?'

Disturbed by the raised voices the baby began to cry. Bray glanced at it momentarily then left the room.

Trudy sank back against the bedhead miserably. The baby began to howl.

'Oh shut up, Brady!' she cried.

ONE HUNDRED AND SIXTY SEVEN

She had spent another night in the woods, lying buried in the thicket where she had fallen. Her fall had plunged her so far into the tangle of bush and briar that, miraculously, the two youths chasing her had failed to spot her lying in the deep shadow. They had scouted the area, puzzled, as she lay panting and in pain. It felt like the fall had injured her ankle.

Finally they had given up the search but had made camp close by, building a little fire to sleep around. Cloe was cold and her body ached. She longed to be able to cuddle up beside a fire, like her two pursuers. She was close enough to hear them talking, and listened as they talked about how much they could get for her as a slave, after they had finished with her.

'We could get ten credits for her at the casino.'

'Then lose it all on the tables! They're rigged! Anyway, Ebony would have us killed if she found out.'

They had argued about the honesty of the Tribe Circus Casino, and the dangers of going against Ebony, until they drifted off to sleep. She lay awake most of the night, listening to their snoring, mingled with the sounds of the nocturnal creatures foraging for food.

Last evening she had been saved by the shadows made by the setting sun, but when the morning came she knew they would be able to easily spot her in her hiding place. She had to move at first light before they woke up. But her ankle was aching and swollen now. She wouldn't be able to run.

ONE HUNDRED AND SIXTY EIGHT

Jack was admiring the water filter, a large glass container filled with layers of sand and gravel which filtered out harmful bacteria from the rainwater collected in the tank. It was such a simple method, but so effective. Miraculous almost.

He had read up about the process in a science book left in the looted boostore, but it was Dal who had found the all parts they needed to build the system, and it was his practical expertise that made it work.

Jack stroked the side of the container proudly. 'It's amazing! I'm a genius,' he announced to himself. 'I am a genius!'

Dal caught the last sentence as he bustled into the room. 'What are you on about?'

'Pure rainwater, collected, filtered and fit for drinking. Just looking at it make me feel kind of –'

'Humble?' Dal said ironically.

'Yeah, that's it,' Jack said seriously. 'That's the word.'

Dal scooped up a bundle of empty plastic water bottles which Jack had gathered waiting to be filled.

'Hey, what are you doing with those?'

'They're going to the stream to collect some water.'

'But we've got water here from the roof,' Jack patted the container.

'Sorry to break it to you, Jack, but we need a lot more water than that thing can supply. Unless you can find a way to make it rain three times a day. Shouldn't be too hard for a genius!'

Jack stopped Dal on his way out. 'Dal, wait. I didn't mean it like that. Obviously you played your part too.'

'Thanks for noticing.'

'I was in the driving seat, but you were the best assistant I could ever wish for.'

Dal did a mock bow. 'Always a pleasure to serve, Jack!'

ooo

Zandra had been angry and concerned finding Lex with Salene last night. She may be holding out herself until she felt secure in their relationship, but she didn't want Lex going off finding what he wanted somewhere else in the mall before she was ready.

Salene was clearly hurting over Bray. It seemed like she had given up. And if she had, then feeling depressed and abandoned, she would be easy prey for a predator like Lex. It certainly seemed like she was enjoying the massage last night. Zandra decided to steer her in the right direction as they were washing up after breakfast.

'You think Bray's different just 'cos he's always rushing about playing the superhero? All men are the same. He's just a two-timing rat.'

'No,' Salene protested. 'He is different! He has principles.'

'What principles? Leading you on like that. He's no better than the rest of them.'

'Leave it, Zandra.'

'Tell me I'm wrong,' Zandra persisted.

Salene put down the dishcloth firmly and turned to Zandra. 'First of all he isn't two-timing anyone. He had a choice and he chose Trudy. That's the end of it.'

'I know it might seem that way, Sal, but, if you really feel that way about him, let's not be hasty...'

Salene frowned. 'What d'you mean?'

'Have it out with him at least, Salene. If he's got principles like you say he has, he must be feeling guilty about the way he's treated you. Talk to him! Don't give up without a fight!'

'You've just been telling me he's not worth it.'

Zandra grinned. 'True. But at least he's good-looking. All I'm saying is if you really want him, Salene, do something about it!'

ooo

Amber was in the atrium with the twins, watching Bray and Ryan prepare for water-gathering trip to the stream. Paul was signing something rapidly, agitated, which Amber couldn't understand.

'What's he saying?' she asked Patsy.

'He says we can't just give up on Cloe.'

'I know.' She leant down to Paul. 'Look finding Cloe is more important than getting water I agree, Paul, but we're not giving up. When we've stocked up on our supplies we'll be able to go out and search for Cloe, okay?'

Paul nodded reluctantly. Amber smiled. 'Now go off and play with Bob. He needs his exercise.'

Lex watched the twins run off with the dog. 'Poor kid,'

Amber looked at him. 'Paul?'

'Aren't you ashamed leading him on like that? We're never gonna see Cloe again and you know it. My guess is she's probably left the sector, maybe even the city, that's if she hasn't been captured.'

'How can you be so sure?'

'We looked everywhere. All the places she used to sneak off to. She's gone.'

'Listen, Lex,' Amber said firmly, 'you stick to your job, security. Leave missing persons to me.'

'You just don't want to face it. She never wanted to be part of this outfit in the first place.'

Amber gave him a look. 'I wonder why?'

Bray came up loaded with canisters and water bottles. 'We're leaving.'

Amber gave him an encouraging smile. 'Good luck. Take care.'

Salene hurried down the stairs, dressed for the outside. 'Bray! I'm coming with you!'

'Hang on, Salene!' Amber said.

'What? Those water bottles will be heavy!'

'I'm sure they can manage.'

Salene set her face. 'I can't believe this!' she said angrily. 'Do I have to get written permission everytime I want to do something!'

Amber tried to calm her down. 'Let's talk about this.'

'Nothing to talk about,' Salene replied stubbornly. 'I volunteer to help get water.'

Amber looked at Bray. 'Bray?'

Bray shrugged. 'I guess...another pair of hands.'

'Thank you,' said Salene

With a defiant look at Amber she walked off determinedly towards the sewers. Bray and Ryan followed behind.

Lex watched them go, a smile playing over his face. 'It'll all end in tears.'

Amber looked at him unhappily. He was probably right.

ONE HUNDRED AND SIXTY NINE

At the first light of dawn Cloe had crawled warily out from the thicket. It wasn't easy. Her clothes had become caught on the briar thorns and she had to carefully release each one before she could finally scramble free. As she suspected her swollen ankle couldn't support her weight, so she crawled away holding her breath, expecting the two youths to wake up at any moment.

She was thirty yards away in the undergrowth when her knee snapped a dry branch. The loud crack resonated in the still morning air. The two Locos sat up, looking about them. Their voices carried to her in the quiet of the woods.

'Did you hear that?'

'Could be her!'

Peering fearfully through the undergrowth Cloe saw the youths get up and begin searching the woods with their eyes. She daren't move for fear of making another sound. But if she stayed where she was they would be bound to find her. It was all over. She closed her eyes and prayed.

As she prayed she could hear the youths searching nearby. They were getting closer. She kept her eyes tight shut. And heard a footfall right behind her ear. She looked up and reacted in surprise. Standing above her was a strange looking girl, a teenager, but not like one she had ever seen before.

She was a tall, slim Oriental girl, with long black hair tied flat to her head, and two decorated plaits hanging down. She wore a multicoloured kimono tied with a broad sash and instead of tribal makeup she had a fan of coloured beads attached to her forehead. But it was the glasses that made the girl look so strange. There were black, horn-rimmed spectacles with thick tinted lenses like the ones that Cloe's headteacher had worn. They gave the girl an owlish, ethereal look, a cross between a Buddist monk and a gheisha.

The girl put her finger to her lips and crouched down beside Cloe. As one of the youths grew near, the girl reached out calmly, picked up a stick and hurled it effortlessly far away through the trees. Both Locos looked up. One pointed.

'Over there!'

As they hurried off in the direction of the noise, Cloe heaved a sigh of relief. The girl looked at her and smiled.

'Who are you?' Cloe asked, still a little awed by her rescuers calm demeanor.

'My name is Tai San,' the girl replied. 'Now no more questions, please. We're not out of danger yet.'

ONE HUNDRED AND SEVENTY

Zandra was seated with Lex in the café. He had told her about Salene going off with Bray to collect water and seemed mischievously pleased. Zandra was secretly delighted to hear that Salene had taken her advice so quickly. Though she generally made a point of not waiting on him, she had made Lex a coffee to celebrate.

Lex gazed at her admiringly, as she picked the baby up from its pram and began to gently rock it in her arms. 'It's all genetics. That's what they say.'

Zandra frowned. 'What who says? The grown-ups?'

'They used to say. From the moment you're born you either take the lead or follow it. I mean look at Ryan carrying those water bottles for Bray like a pack mule. Sad part is he enjoys it.'

'So?'

'Well one day,' he went on, 'and pretty soon by the looks of things, you're gonna want a baby of your own. And I'm just saying that's where you should start looking.' He grinned lasciviously. 'In my jeans.'

Before Zandra could respond Trudy wandered into the café. 'Have either of you seen Bray?' she asked.

Lex leaned back, sensing an opportunity for fun. 'No, not for a while. He took Salene and went off into the woods for some reason.'

Trudy was momentarily shocked, then her face turned black with anger. 'He what!'

Lex grinned as Trudy rushed out in a panic.

Zandra was glaring daggers at him.

'What?' he said innocently.

ooo

Amber was folding bedclothes in her room. In the past, like many girls of her age she had always been a little careless about keeping her own room tidy at home, but having everything neat and tidy now was part of the new life. Discipline was part of surviving.

She saw Trudy striding towards her room and knew by her expression what was coming.

'Is it true?' Trudy blurted out as soon as she entered the room.

'Is what true?' Amber replied casually.

'Bray's gone off with Salene!'

Amber looked at her calmly. 'Trudy, they're collecting water.'

'Sure!' she snapped, disbelievingly. She glared at Amber. 'You're in on it! You planned this, didn't you? You and Salene!'

Amber was affronted. 'I did what?'

'Don't deny it!' Trudy's face was flushed with anger. 'You're all against me! You didn't want me when I first arrived and you still don't want me now!'

'This is crazy!' Amber said impatiently.

'Bray was mine before we ended up in this dump! But you couldn't leave us alone, could you! You had to break us up!'

Amber was angry now. 'Me? I'm the one who tried to stop her going!'

'Oh, so you admit she's after him?'

'Well that's not exactly hard to spot. You'd have to be Ryan to miss that! Why come to me anyway? I'm admin, not marriage guidance!'

'You're on her side! You always have been!'

Amber threw a pillow onto her bed. 'Look, just believe whatever you want, Trudy. Just get out of my hair!'

Tears welled up in Trudy's eyes. Angry and hurting at the same time, she turned and rushed away. Amber heard her sobs begin as Trudy ran along the balcony. She sat down on the bed and sighed. It was very hard keeping things neat and tidy in this world.

ONE HUNDRED AND SEVENTY ONE

After the Locos who had rushed off in the direction where she had thrown the stick, the Oriental girl, Tai San had carried Cloe away in her arms. Now they were nestled in a secluded spot by a stream while Tai San expertly bound Cloe's ankle. Despite her ordeal, Cloe was beginning to feel much better. Tai San had given her some water and nuts and berries, which she'd devoured ravenously. It was two days since she'd had her last meal.

'There!' said Tai San. 'Try it.'

Cloe stood up testing her ankle. 'It feels better already. What did you put on it?'

'Wild herbs, arnica and comfrey.'

Cloe looked around her. 'Where to now?'

Tai San smiled. 'I was hoping you'd tell me. What are you doing out in the woods all alone, Cloe?'

'It's a long story. I had this pet calf, Bluebell. They wanted to eat her, but she ran off and I followed her here. But I couldn't find her.' She looked sad. 'I didn't have a chance to say 'goodbye'... What about you? Why are you here?'

'My story's not important, except that it brought me to you.'

'Thank you for saving me.'

'It was written,' the girl replied mysteriously. 'Just as it is written that I must follow you.'

Cloe looked puzzled. 'Follow me? But I'm lost.'

Tai San smiled. 'Often when people say they are lost they are just not listening hard enough,' she said enigmatically.

'Listening to what?' Cloe said frowning. Her rescuer talked in a strange way.

'Their heart,' Tai San replied. 'If you had to choose a path which way would you go?'

Cloe looked around at the trees surrounding them. They all looked the same and she had no idea which way she had come.

'No, don't look, just listen,' Tai San instructed. 'You remember the way. You've just forgotten that you remember it.'

That sounded very odd to Cloe, but the girl seemed very certain of what she said. Cloe closed her eyes and listened. She could hear the birds singing and the breeze rustling the leaves. It all seemed so peaceful, standing in the sun-kissed woods. As she listened it suddenly seemed to come to her. She pointed.

Tai San smiled.

ONE HUNDRED AND SEVENTY TWO

They had made their way to the stream without incident. The stream wound its way from the woods into the heart of the city, where it became contaminated by the filth and detritus left by weeks of looting and ransacking. But here the water looked crystal clear and pure.

Keeping an eye out for roaming gangs they quickly filled the water containers they had brought with them. Ryan was further down the stream looking along the path that led from a wooden bridge crossing the stream.

Bray stood up and turned to Salene. 'That's it. That's all we can carry. Thanks, Salene, it was a good idea for you to come along.'

'Don't mention it.' She felt her cheeks flush. She had been very quiet on their way to the stream, but she had to say something before they set off back with Ryan tagging along.

Bray looked at her quizzically. 'Are you okay?'

'I didn't really come here to help out,' she began. 'At least that wasn't the only reason.'

Bray frowned. 'Oh?'

'I needed to talk to you about some things. But I guess I can never be like Zandra.'

'Zandra?' He looked even more puzzled.

'I could never be angry with you if I tried.'

'That's nice to know,' he said uncomfortably.

Salene suddenly burst out, unable to keep it in any longer. 'Bray, why are you doing this? I thought we had something special between us! Why do you want to hurt me?' she cried.

He looked a little annoyed. 'Well, if it's not too much to ask, what exactly are you talking about?'

'You and Trudy, what else? Don't lie to me! That's what's so hurtful! Don't lie about it! You could have let me down gently.'

Bray's face was set, looking grim. 'Let's start over with this. If you must know I'm not getting on with Trudy. She's driving me nuts. Though why it's any of your business-'

'Well that's even worse!' she blurted out.

'What?'

'Sleeping with her when you don't even care about her!'

Before Bray could reply Salene turned away, snatched up a water container and walked off. At that moment Ryan came racing up. 'Bray there's a gang coming along the path. Could be Locos.'

'Okay, let's go,' Bray said. Picking up his containers, he set off after Salene, grim-faced.

ONE HUNDRED AND SEVENTY THREE

Amber was deep in thought. What a strange new situation she found herself in. She tried not to think about her life before the virus. It was still very painful to recall her parents, family and friends that she had loved and spent so many happy times with. Maybe there would be a time when she could do that, to give the departed the respect those memories deserved, but that time wasn't now.

She had to live in the present now, and to plan for the future. If there was going to be one, she couldn't just let it happen. She had to take control of her life and, it seemed, of others too. But that was the hard part.

When she and Dal had set off from the neighbourhood they had grown up in, and were so fond of, her intention was to escape into the countryside beyond the city. There they had planned to live off the land, foraging whatever food and water they could, until they found a place, maybe far away, where they could put down roots and start a new life. A life quite different to the sophisticated, hi-tech world they had grown up in.

It was very clear that life in cities would be difficult and dangerous for a long time to come. She knew from her history lessons that primitive societies gradually became civilized and learned to live together, if not in total peace, at least with enough tolerance to make everyday life possible. But there had never been a time quite like this. When a civilized society had collapsed back into primitive, savage times. Except in wartime, and that was where they were now. At war.

She had not set out to be a leader. At school she was happy to be part of a crowd, a popular member of a lively group of friends. But circumstances had changed. Without even knowing that she possessed them her leadership qualities had come to the surface in the troubled times they all found themselves in, and the others had instinctively responded to that.

She hadn't wanted to, but she knew that someone must take on that role in the mall. There had to be structure in their lives. The young ones needed to continue their education. They had to start building a new life, whatever that may be. There were so many things to do and someone had to take the lead.

Though she had urged him to, Bray had refused to stand as leader. Maybe he was right to? Perhaps he knew more about himself than he showed? He was intelligent and self-aware. He must have his reasons. Whatever they were they had left her with a dilemma.

Lex was a natural bully, but bullies weren't leaders, not in her eyes. Leaders led the way along paths that, deep down, people wanted to go themselves but were too timid, or idle, to tread. Bullies whipped people down tracks that were narrow and fearful, where only the bullies wanted to go. She had taken Lex on and defeated him with cunning and guile.

But, delighted as she was by that, it had set her apart. People now came to her with their problems, and often blamed her if she couldn't solve them. Everyone's lives had been turned upside down and somehow they expected their leader to be able to make them right side up again. Never in her young life had she felt so isolated. How she longed for a shoulder to lean on. One particular shoulder that she wouldn't, and daren't, go near.

ONE HUNDRED AND SEVENTY FOUR

Jack had been pondering the problem of security ever since he'd found the mall, deserted and ransacked, and decided to make it his home. The grills at the main entrance weren't a problem. The mall was only recently completed when the virus struck and they had been made of a state-of-the-art material that could withstand the impact of a tank. It was the sewers that were his concern.

It was vital to have a safe and secure escape route just in case the unexpected happened. The sewers provided that. But, though they were easy to escape along, they also had to be difficult to get into the mall from, as Amber had said. He had stayed up late into the night thinking through various solutions and rejecting them all. But he had finally found what he was looking for, and, he thought, it was another of his strokes of genius.

He had gone with Dal to see Lex in his Chief of Security office and began to outline his idea.

'Hang on,' Lex said before Jack had got very far. 'I thought you said all the batteries were dead?'

'Nearly all,' Jack admitted. 'I saved a couple in case of a real emergency.'

Lex looked a little miffed about Jack keeping this from him, but waved him on. 'So, this great idea?'

'Okay,' Jack went on excitedly, 'suppose you're a Loco armed to the teeth, creeping along the sewers trying to break in. It's dark, it's quiet –'

'Get on with it, nerd!' Lex growled. 'I'm not in the mood for bedtime stories!'

Jack was thrown a little, but gathered himself and persisted with his story. 'Like I said, it's dark and quiet, but you're not scared 'cos you're a Loco.'

'And you're armed to the teeth,' Dal reiterated, helpfully.

Jack gave him a withering look. 'Thanks, Dal, whose idea is this?'

'Sorry.'

Lex folded his arms impatiently. 'When you two girls have finished your playtime fight, can we get on!'

'I don't know where I was now,' Jack complained.

'You're not scared 'cos you're a Loco,' Lex said snappily.

'Right. But your pulse rate is up just a little bit, and your palms are beginning to get a bit sweaty-'

'Get on with it!' Lex barked.

Flustered Jack stumbled on, 'Well, the next thing you know...' He pressed a key on his laptop. The terrifying cry of a pack of wolves filled the room. 'You're surrounded by wolves!' Jack shouted above the din. He let the cry go on for a moment then turned it off and looked at Lex with a cocky grin.

Lex got up, stonyfaced. 'Let me know when you get it working.'

Jack watched, deflated as Lex strode out of the office. 'Doesn't that guy ever praise anyone?' he said sulkily.

'True men of vision are never recognized in their own time, Jack.'

Jack gave Dal a grumpy look.

Dal relented. 'Come on, Jack. It's a great idea. Let's get it rigged up.'

ONE HUNDRED AND SEVENTY FIVE

Trudy was sitting motionless on her bed. She had been staring into space for over an hour, waiting for Bray to return. Ever since Lex had told her about Bray going off with Salene, her mind had been in a turmoil of anger, jealousy and paranoia.

That cow had gone behind her back and taken her chance to move in on Bray. She would be left on her own to cope with Brady in this crazy, dangerous and ugly world. She would get no help from anyone else. She had alienated them all, she knew. They all hated her. But tears wouldn't come. She felt numb.

She prepared herself as she heard his footsteps approaching the room. Bray entered looking tired and unhappy. He tossed a full bottle of water onto the bed and sat down wearily.

'What's that?' she said stonily.

Bray noted the tone and groaned inwardly. 'Water. What d'you think?'

She spun round on him, her eyes flashing angrily. 'Exactly what am I supposed to think? You've been off collecting water, you and your 'friend'!'

Bray sighed, put his hand to his forehead and closed his eyes. 'No,' he said, not in denial, he just didn't want to get into this again.

But Trudy was determined to have her say. 'Well I hope you're satisfied! Everyone's laughing at me! Stuck here holding the baby while you're off partying! How do you think that makes me feel..? So was she good?' she said viciously. 'Was it worth it?'

Bray stood up to leave.

She was suddenly anxious. 'Where are you going?'

'I'm not even going to bother to explain,' he said in a cold flat voice. 'You wouldn't understand anyway.'

Her voice was suddenly tiny and pathetic, pleading. 'Bray..! Don't go!'

He tried to placate her, just wanting to get away. 'Trudy, I just want five minutes peace. We'll talk later.'

As he made to go Paul rushed up to him excitedly gabbling a word over and over.

Trudy frowned, irritated. 'What's he saying?'

Bray looked at Paul. 'Cloe?'

ONE HUNDRED AND SEVENTY SIX

Amber raced down the main staircase as she saw Cloe enter the mall from the sewers. The little girl looked tired and her clothes were torn and muddy, but she was wearing a broad smile.

'Cloe!' Amber exclaimed delighted. 'You're back! We were so worried!'

As she hugged Cloe, the others began to gather from all over the mall.

'What happened?' Salene asked.

'You alright?' Jack asked, seeing the state of her clothes.

Amber noticed the bandage. 'What happened to your foot?'

'I got chased by the Locos. I fell over and broke it.'

Tai San emerged from behind a pillar where she had been waiting to assess Cloe's reception. 'It's not broken,' she explained calmly. 'Only sprained. She'll be fine.'

Everyone stared silently at the apparition in front of them. They had all grown used to weird and wonderful sights since the virus, but the newcomer's look was unique.

Cloe smiled. 'She rescued me. If it wasn't for her I'd have been a Loco prisoner by now.'

Amber smiled at the girl. 'Thank you.'

Lex arrived, glaring suspiciously at the strange figure. 'What's going on here? Who's she?'

Tai San gave Lex a calm, measured look.

'She brought Cloe back to us,' Amber explained happily.

Lex didn't look at all happy at the news. 'How did she get in here? Jack, didn't you get that alarm fixed yet?'

Jack was silent.

Lex turned his attention to Cloe. 'What are you trying to do, get us all killed?

'You must be starving, both of you.' Amber said, breezily taking charge. She smiled at the girl. 'Welcome to the mall.'

'Tai San, this is everyone, 'Cloe announced. 'Everyone, this is Tai San.'

Tai San looked around at the smiling group. The only one not smiling was Lex.

ooo

They had all gathered in the café, keen to hear Cloe's story and learn about the strange newcomer, Tai San. As Amber brought them bowls of soup the rest fired questions at Cloe.

'Were they really Locos?' Dal asked. 'The woods aren't generally their patch.'

'Well, they were bad people, whoever they were,' Cloe replied. 'I heard them talking about selling me as a slave.'

'If you were that close why didn't they see you?' Jack asked.

'It was night-time. I could hide in the bushes. But if I'd known the secret I could have found my way home anytime.'

'Secret?' Salene was intrigued.

'Listening. Tai San showed me how,' Cloe replied, proud of her secret and her new friend.

'But why did you run away, Cloe?' Amber asked kindly. 'Were you upset about Bluebell?'

Before Cloe could reply Lex cut in sharply. 'Yeah, well that's all ancient history. Forget it.'

'I heard her outside in the woods,' Cloe answered. 'But then she ran off.'

Amber looked puzzled. 'You heard her?'

'Yes! It was Bluebell. She was in the woods, but she ran off and I couldn't find her.'

Amber looked up at Lex who was standing a little apart, sullenly. 'Lex, I thought you said the Locos had taken Bluebell?'

Lex shifted on his feet. 'That's right. They must have let her go again.'

'Oh, that'll be it,' Amber's expression was amused. 'They must have all turned vegetarian,' she said sarcastically.

Lex changed the subject abruptly. 'Am I the only one that's noticed? We're faced with a total breach of security here! A complete stranger wanders into the mall and no one bats an eyelid. Nobody questions it. Well, I've got a couple of questions for you Tai San, or whatever you call yourself!' he said agressively. 'Who are you, where'd you come from and what do you want?'

Ryan frowned. 'That's three questions.'

'Shut up!' Lex snapped.

'If you're quite finished Lex,' said Amber calmly but forcefully. 'Tai San is our guest. Are you gonna show some manners?'

Lex gave her his surly look. 'Have it your own way, Amber. You usually do. I'm gonna go and see about making this place secure. Jack, Dal, with me!'

He strode away down the stairs with Ryan, Jack and Dal following behind.

'I didn't mean to cause so much trouble,' Cloe said apologetically.

Amber smiled and touched her arm. 'You haven't. Don't be silly. We're just delighted to have you back safe and sound.'

Patsy leapt up excitedly. 'We should have a party! To celebrate getting Cloe back!'

Tai San looked around at the others and smiled to herself.

ONE HUNDRED AND SEVENTY SEVEN

Holding the torch for them to work by, Lex watched Jack and Dal as they fixed up the tripwire system in the sewers. He smiled. They seemed to know what they were doing. Ever since he could remember he had always thought of the brainy kids as nerds, and made it his business to make their lives hell, in school or on the street. Now he was beginning to admit they had their uses. He didn't regret the years of bullying he'd subjected the nerds to. They'd been fun, and made him feel like top dog. But in this new world, the nerds were starting to earn his grudging respect. Not that he would ever let them know that.

'So how does the tripwire set off the laptop?' he asked.

'That's Dal's area,' Jack replied, with the end of a wire clenched between his teeth.

'Since when?' Dal said. 'Don't tell me. Since you realized you don't know how to do it.'

'I'm the ideas man. You're the chief engineer.'

'You're giving yourselves titles now?' Lex mocked.

Jack looked at him. 'Oh, is there something wrong with that, Mr Chief of Security?'

They looked up as Amber appeared behind them. 'How's it going?'

'Too early to tell,' Dal replied.

'I'm sure it'll be fine,' Amber said. 'Can I drag one of you away for a minute?'

'Why, what's up?' Lex asked.

'We think it'd be a good idea to have a little party for Cloe. To celebrate her getting home safe. She's been through a lot. She's been very brave.'

'Very stupid!' Lex retorted.

'Whatever. Could one of you two techno wizards organize some music, please?'

Jack jumped up. 'Sure! Dal you can finish this off.'

Dal pulled a face.

'A party?' Lex wasn't asking a question.

'Oh, don't start, Lex!' Amber said without any malice.

Lex wasn't going to be put off. 'With music? Don't you think this could be what she planned? This could be the signal for the rest of her tribe! Before we know it we could be overrun!'

'Better fix that alarm then,' Amber said with a grin.

Lex stood up and confronted Amber. 'You don't know anything about her! She got Cloe to lead her straight to us!'

'She rescued Cloe, Lex!'

'That could have been part of the plan!'

'You're right, Lex. We have to be careful.' Amber conceded. 'But I'm pretty sure about one thing, she's not a Locust or a Demon Dog. Anyway, we could do a lot worse than being overrun by a tribe of spaced-out hippies.'

Amber turned away, with Jack following behind.

'I don't see how,' Lex said grumpily to himself. As Chief of Security he could stop this. He'd been given the authority. But a party? A great way to let his hair down with Zandra. And who knew what else?

ONE HUNDRED AND SEVENTY EIGHT

Salene had been surprised and shocked by her conversation with Bray at the stream. She didn't know what she thought she would gain by confronting him about Trudy, but she had taken Zandra's advice and had it out with him. At least she had let Bray know how she felt about him and that was all she could do.

What she didn't expect was his admission that he didn't feel anything for Trudy. She found that so hard to believe. Bray had always seemed to her to be the perfect man. Honest, principled, gentle and sincere. A man she had always hoped to find. One she could love and be loved by him in return. But he had openly admitted that he was sleeping with a girl he didn't care for. A girl he even seemed to despise. That seemed incredible to her.

Zandra had told her that all boys were the same. She hadn't wanted to believe that, but what did she know? She'd never really had a boyfriend. She'd always been a little afraid of boys. And Zandra seemed to be very worldly-wise. She had never asked her about it, but from Zandra's obsession with her appearance, and her confident air around boys, she assumed that Zandra must be experienced in a way that she wasn't. But she still found it hard to believe about Bray.

She felt sorry for Trudy. The poor girl had put up with so much in her young life. How she got mixed up with Zoot, close enough to have a baby by him, she couldn't imagine. She was obviously crazy about his brother, Bray. But she was being used by him. There was no way she could tell Trudy that.

Trudy would think she was just being jealous and trying to break them up.

But she still felt guilty and had to make amends.

ooo

Trudy was alone in her room, lying miserably on the bed, when Salene arrived.

'Trudy?' she said tentatively.

Trudy sprang up furiously. 'Get out! Leave me alone!'

For moment Salene thought the angry young girl might fly at her and hit her. 'Listen! I did go with Bray to fetch the water!' she confessed. 'Well, to talk to him...I thought...I don't know what I thought.'

'You thought you'd take him off me!' Trudy spat out the words bitterly.

Poor girl, Salene thought, he's not really with you. 'Yes, maybe I did...Well, I was wrong. And I just wanted to say I'm sorry. And I won't try and interfere between you anymore, okay? I promise.'

Trudy was silent. She sat down with her back to Salene.

'I promise,' Salene repeated.

There was still no response. Salene prepared to go. She had done what she came for. To put Trudy's mind at rest about her. As a girl she longed to tell the other girl the truth. What Bray had said about her. To save her more pain. But that was impossible. One day Trudy would find out for herself, and that day would be terrible. She pitied her.

ONE HUNDRED AND SEVENTY NINE

Jack was sorting through CDs from the music store, preparing for the party, as Dal came up to him. At a distance Tai San was seated beneath the phoenix statue calmly talking to the others, as if she was holding court.

Jack shook his head. 'There's something not right with that girl. Every time you look around she's staring at you. Spooky.'

'More spiritual, I'd say, Jack,' Dal replied.

Jack looked at him askance. 'Do you believe all that stuff?'

'What stuff?'

'Spirits and,' Jack shrugged, 'I dunno...'

'There's a lot of things we don't know,' Dal said.

'Yeah, like who started the virus.'

'And what will happen to us,' Dal added.

Jack nodded and looked back towards Tai San who was till talking. She was definitely weird.

'Jack, you remember what you were saying about you being in charge and me being the assistant?' Dal asked.

'Well, I wasn't really being serious about that, Dal.'

'No, but I was. I think you should be the boss. Take responsibility for everything.'

Jack looked pleased. 'Really? Oh, okay!' he said readily.

'Good,' Dal grinned. 'First thing you can do is go tell Lex we're not sure whether the alarm's working.'

Jack scowled.

ooo

'It's a time of great loneliness,' Tai San was saying to the others. 'We all feel the need to belong. That's why it's good to be part of a tribe.'

'If you'd met the Locos you wouldn't think so,' Zandra said cynically.

'But all this will pass in time. Even the Locos must grow older and wiser.'

Ryan sniffed. 'If the virus doesn't get them first.'

'What about you, Tai San?' Amber asked. 'Do you belong to a tribe?'

'Of sorts,' Tai San replied. 'But my path is different. I've elected to follow my heart, wherever it may lead me. I cannot stop until I find what I am seeking.'

Amber was curious. 'And what's that?'

'The truth.'

Lex was standing behind Amber. He leant forward and whispered in her ear. 'I think I'm gonna throw up.'

'So what are you called?' asked Tai San, looking around at the gathered group.

Zandra frowned. 'Called?'

'Your tribe?'

'We don't have a name,' Cloe answered.

'We just sort of came together accidently,' Amber explained.

Tai San looked at her, smiled, and said sincerely. 'There are no accidents in this world.'

'I've got a name for us!' Lex declared. 'The Rats!'

There were murmurs of dissent around the group. No one liked that name.

'Why not?' Lex went on. 'We live like 'em! The rats in the sewers, hidden away, scrabbling for food.'

'I know!' Pasty chimed in. 'How about the Dolphins!'

Her suggestion was met with groans.

'Nah! I can't even swim!' Ryan said.

'Come on, let's be the Rats!' Lex urged, suddenly enthused by his own idea. 'I can be King Rat! I've got a battle cry that'll strike fear into the hearts of all our enemies!'

He stood forward, cupped his hands to his mouth and let out a wolf-like howl that echoed throughout the mall. The rest grinned, amused, as he repeated the cry more loudly. Their grins turned to fear, when his cry was mirrored by the sound of the wolfpack alarm baying in the sewers.

ONE HUNDRED AND EIGHTY

The search of the woods had drawn a blank. She had made the Locos go through them with a fine tooth comb, and if Bray had been living there they would have found traces of him at least. There was nothing in the woods except trees and animals.

But there had been rumours for days. Reports of sightings, glimpses of a mystery figure roaming the city. A figure who seemed fearless and confident, as he skateboarded along the deserted streets. When the rumours had eventually got back to her, she quizzed people for a description. It matched. It was the same youth. The one who had sent the mysterious note to Zoot. The note that had caused Zoot to disappear. It could only be one person.

So Bray was alive and living in the city. That thought made her pulse race. She needed to take control of herself and gather her thoughts when the truth came to her. Zoot was dead, she was now certain. For whatever reason, however it had happened, Bray had led Zoot to his death. It seemed unbelievable. She couldn't think of a reason why he had killed his younger brother, the kid brother she knew he adored. But she had to find the answer.

The city was huge. Despite the Locos fearsome reputation it was still a dangerous place to go looking for clues. For answers to the mystery. But go looking she would. She would search every sector, every building, every alley, every sewer. She would not stop looking until she had found him, and learnt the truth from Bray's own lips. No matter what it took.

The Locos had been robbed of their charismatic leader. A leader who, she was sure, would have taken over the city. Sometimes she thought, maybe even the world. If he was responsible, no matter what her feelings, Bray would have to pay.

ONE HUNDRED AND EIGHTY ONE

The girls waited anxiously in the mall as the boys went to investigate the cause of the alarm. With the sound of the wolves howling in their ears, Lex led the others into the sewers, each carrying a weapon in their hands.

'Go on,' said Bray. 'I'm right behind you.'

Shining his torch along the tunnel ahead Lex called out, 'You out there! We're not afraid! Come out and face us!'

There was no sound but the baying of the wolves coming from the laptop alarm.

'Jack! Can you stop that thing!' Lex ordered.

By the light of his torch, Jack found the laptop and punched a key. The sound of howling wolves stopped abruptly. In the gloomy sewers the sudden silence was a shock. The sound of trickling water came to their ears, and then another sound. It was a dog, barking.

'Bob?' Bray cried out. 'Is that you?'

There was an answering bark.

'It is Bob!' Dal cried.

Bray led the way along the tunnel and found the dog at the far end, entangled in the tripwire. Bray burst out laughing, followed by the rest. Grinning, Bray knelt to free the animal. 'You had us all fooled there,' he said.

'At least we know the alarm works,' said Jack with double relief.

ooo

Moments later, back in the mall Amber patted Bob, who barked excitedly at being the sudden centre of attention. 'What were you doing, Bob, frightening us all like that?'

Patsy grinned and stroked the dog's head. 'We thought you were the Locos!'

Tai San looked at all the others gathered around smiling and relieved. 'You see?' she said.

Amber looked up. 'What?'

'The happy spirit of the tribe spelling hope for the future.'

Lex grimaced. 'What's she on about now?'

Amber shushed him. 'Go on, Tai San.'

Looking around at the gathered children Tai San continued. 'We've come together for a purpose. We are a tribe, but we are still lacking something. An identity. An identity to give us pride in who we are.'

'What's this 'we' are a tribe business?' Lex said aggressively. 'Nobody's invited you to join us.'

Tai San met his aggression with a quiet calmness. 'And yet I am here. Perhaps that's why I have been brought here. To restore your pride and faith in one another by giving you a name.'

Lex raised his eyes skywards and blew out his breath.

Unphazed by his cynicism, Tai San stood up and said quietly, but with great authority. 'Please, let's form a circle. Everyone join hands.'

The rest glanced at each other with uncomfortable and skeptical expressions. Each waiting for the other. It was Cloe who stood up first and put her hand in Tai Sans. Paul was next, linking hands with Cloe.

Amber shrugged. 'What harm can it do?' She stood up and took Tai San's hand.

Standing apart Lex scoffed, 'All this for a name?'

Tai San looked at him steadily. 'It's more than a name. It's the future.'

Bray stood up and joined the growing circle. Impulsively, Salene was quick to take his hand. She smiled at Bray, embarassed at herself.

Lex watched in amazement as Ryan went to take Zandra's hand. 'Ryan? Not you too!'

'Lex,' Amber said, 'just grab someone's hand.'

The others were all now in the circle. Lex sighed. 'I'll join on one condition. We're called the Mall Rats. Any objections?'

'Actually,' Jack said brightly, 'rats are very intelligent creatures! Highly developed family units.'

'Yeah, I read that,' Dal agreed.

'So we could do worse,' Amber said with an air of finality.

Lex shook his head. 'I can't believe I'm doing this!' He pushed his way into the circle and took Zandra's hand.

Tai San smiled, gratified. 'Let's all close our eyes and focus for a moment.'

'Wait!' a voice cried. It was Trudy standing above them on the balcony. They watched as she came down the stairs and self-consciously pushed herself between Bray and Salene. Zandra smiled to herself.

Amber looked around at the others in the circle. They were standing below the phoenix statue, the symbol of life rising from the ashes. Though it had only been a short time since they had been thrown together, she sensed that there was something unique about them. Something to build on. But so many problems lay ahead.

The world outside the mall was still a crazy and dangerous place. One that wouldn't go away very soon. They would have to find a way of surviving the Locos and the Demon Dogs if they were to survive at all.

And inside the mall? There were problems too. Lex would always be unpredictable, threatening violence. And he wasn't going to wait forever for Zandra. He wasn't the waiting type. She could see trouble when he finally made his move. Jack and Dal had talents that could maybe save them all eventually, if the two young boys could keep from falling out. The children and the baby? They were the future. They had to be taught the right values in a world that seemed to have lost them all. And Bray? Poor Bray pulled between Trudy and Salene. She smiled sadly. He was his own person, with his own values. In time he would make his choice. And hearts would be broken. Hers, for sure.

And the newcomer, Tai San? Who knew what fresh hope and problems her strange philosophy would bring?

Amber turned to her and smiled. 'That's it, Tai San. We're all here.'

Tai San looked at each one in turn, then began. 'As of this day all who join hands here are bound together as brothers and sisters. Supporting, caring and protecting one another as one tribe. The Mall Rats!'

'The Mall Rats!' they all solemnly repeated. They looked at each other, self-consciously. But they all felt it. In that moment there was a fleeting sense of pride and optimism. No matter what lay ahead, whatever trials and dangers they may have to face, they had joined themselves to each other and to the future. The Mall Rats had been born.

The Tribe: A New World

by A.J. Penn

The official story continues in this novel, set immediately after the conclusion of season 5 of The Tribe.

Forced to flee the city in their homeland - along with abandoning their dream of building a better world from the ashes of the old - the Mall Rats embark upon a perilous journey of discovery into the unknown.

Cast adrift, few could have foreseen the dangers that lay in store. What is the secret surrounding the Jzhao Li? Will they unravel the mysteries of The Collective? Let alone overcome the many challenges and obstacles they encounter as they battle the forces of mother nature, unexpected adversaries, and at times, even themselves? Above all, can they build a new world in their own images - by keeping their dream alive?

Keeping The Dream Alive

by Raymond Thompson.

The fascinating inside story about the making of the cult television series, The Tribe.

An intriguing memoir charting the life and times of how someone growing up on the wrong side of the tracks in a very poor working class environment in post-War Britain was able to journey to the glittering arena of Hollywood, providing an inspirational insight into how the one most likely to fail at school due to a special need battled and succeeded against all the odds to travel the world, founding and overseeing a prolific international independant television production company.

With humorous insight into the fertile imagination of a writer's mind, the book explores life away from the red carpet in the global world of motion pictures and television - and reveals the unique story of how the cult series 'The Tribe' came into being. Along with a personal quest to exist and survive amidst the ups and downs and pressures of a long and successful career as a writer/producer, culminating in being appointed an Adjunct Professor and featuring in the New Years Honours List, recognised by Her Majesty Queen Elizabeth II for services to television.

Jail Tales: Memoirs of a 'Lady' Prison Governor

by Chris Duffin

(aided and abetted by Harry Duffin)

As the first woman governor into HMP Strangeways and the notorious Dartmoor Prison, Governor Chris Duffin was a ground-breaker.

In 'Jail Tales' she recounts some of the many stories and incidents from her twenty-year career both as a lowly 'screw' and as a prison governor.

Whether it's flying out of the UK with a briefcase full of class A drugs, talking to the BBC News in her nightie, displaying a naked hunk's willy on her office wall, or having Myra Hindley as her tea-lady, these tales will amuse, entertain and definitely change your view of life behind bars.

Lightning Source UK Ltd.
Milton Keynes UK
UKHW040837211119
353845UK00014B/10/P